UNDISCOVERED

AMOVEO  RISING

SARA
HUMPHREYS

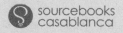

sourcebooks
casablanca

Published by Sourcebooks Casablanca, an imprint of Sourcebooks, Inc.
P.O. Box 4410, Naperville, Illinois 60567-4410
(630) 961-3900
Fax: (630) 961-2168
www.sourcebooks.com

Printed and bound in Canada.
MBP 10 9 8 7 6 5 4 3 2 1

Praise for the Amoveo Legend series

"Spellbinding… This fast-paced, jam-packed thrill ride will delight paranormal romance fans."

—*Publishers Weekly*

"Humphreys' skillful storytelling is so intriguing, you'll have a hard time putting this book down."

—*RT Book Reviews*, 4.5 Stars,
Top Pick of the Month

"Compelling… Searing lovemaking, interesting world-building—lions and tigers and bears, oh my!"

—*Booklist*

"Plenty of action, paranormal influences, and romance to satisfy your appetite. Being sated but greedy, I am waiting patiently right now for the next Amoveo adventure."

—*Night Owl Reviews*, 5 Stars, Reviewer Top Pick

"A fast-paced, gripping story that starts out with a bang and continues straight to the explosive ending."

—*Fresh Fiction*

"Sexy and unique… a must read for any paranormal fan!"

—*Booked and Loaded*

"Sara Humphreys knows how to keep a reader turning the pages."

—*Book Lovin' Mamas*

Also by Sara Humphreys

For my husband, Will...

"Once in a while, right in the middle of an ordinary life, love gives us a fairy tale."

—Author unknown

Chapter 1

MINE. THE DEEP, GRAVELLY VOICE OF THE BEAST reverberated through the air and ripped into Rena's mind with terrifying force. *Mine. Mine. Mine.*

The ferocious, ear-splitting roars of the winged monsters rumbled through the forest, and the earth trembled as the vicious battle raged on. The nightmare had persisted for months, and even though she was all too familiar with how it would play out, it continued to horrify her.

Frightened and exhausted, Rena McHale crouched behind the trunk of the towering pine tree and prayed they wouldn't see her this time. Her heart thundered in her chest, and she pressed her hands against her ears, attempting to drown out the stomach-churning bellows of the monsters. Sweat trickled down her back, and she kept her eyes squeezed shut, trying to slow her breathing. She had been here countless times before, and though the nightmare was always the same, Rena prayed this time would be different.

It wouldn't be. They would find her, and they would kill her. She would wake up, terrified and drowning in pain, seconds after being swallowed by a sea of agonizing flames.

Wicked heat flashed behind her and seared her shoulder. She bit her lip and swallowed the scream, but she didn't move from her hiding spot. The snarls and sharp sounds of gnashing teeth had gotten closer. Dirt, leaves, and bits of rock rained over her as an enormous clawed foot skidded past as one beast slammed into the other. Shrieks of fury filled the forest, and the sound was more than she could bear, because Rena knew what would come next. There would be nothing except excruciating pain while she burned alive.

"Not again," she whimpered. "Shit, not again."

The monster scrambled to its feet, and Rena opened her eyes in time to see its long, spiked tail whip past. She yelped as the weapon-like appendage slammed into the tree above her head, and bits of bark showered down, stinging her skin.

"No more! Stop it!" The words ripped from her lungs in scream after scream, and she shut her eyes, not wanting to see the fire this time. "Go away and leave me alone! I want to wake up. Help! Someone, please help me! I can't take it anymore."

Rena didn't know how long she sat there, screaming the words over and over again. She fully expected the fire to claim her as it had every time before. But this time, the flames didn't come.

Exquisite silence filled the air, and other than the sound of her own breathing, Rena heard nothing. The earth no longer trembled, there was no more snarling or growling, and instead of fire, a cool mist drifted over her bare arms like a soothing blanket. Though her heart still beat wildly against her rib cage, Rena finally found the courage to open her eyes. The woods were now bathed in golden rays of sunlight, and a white fog rolled low along the ground, covering any evidence *of the destructive battle that had been raging only moments ago.*

With trembling hands, Rena pushed her stiff body off the ground and stood on shaky legs. She brushed leaves and dirt off the back of her pajama pants and her tank top, the outfit she had gone to sleep in that night. She gripped the tree trunk, the bark rough beneath her palms, and looked around warily, half expecting the beasts to spring out at her from between the trees, but she was alone.

"That's it?" Her voice shook and sounded odd as it broke the silence. "All I had to do was have a crybaby fit to make those two assholes vanish?"

The words were barely out of her mouth when the earth shook with the familiar thunderous footsteps of the monsters.

"Oh great," Rena whispered. She pressed her back against the tree before peering around the trunk in search of the threat. Another tremor rattled the ground, and the tree branches wavered above as her heartbeat picked up. "Wake up, girl. Come on. Wake the hell up."

Run. *The man's voice, a deep, gritty baritone, whispered around Rena out of nowhere, making her go completely still. This was new.* Right now. You can't let him find you. Not like this. He won't understand.

Her eyes flicked open, and she scanned the misty woods for the source of the voice. "Who won't understand what?"

As far as she could see, there was no one there but her. Rena gasped as another tremor rocked the earth so hard she almost lost her footing. It was getting closer.

Now! *His voice, filled with urgency and a hint of*

impatience, seemed to come from nowhere, and yet, he was everywhere. Run, woman. Move!

Another tremor. Stronger now. Dangerously close.

"Where the hell am I supposed to run?" Rena asked in a shaky whisper. "This is a nightmare, and there's no place to run to, unless I wake up. Which I would love to do, by the way."

A brilliant crimson light flashed past the trees to her left, like a mirror glinting in the sun, and that's when she felt it.

The spirit stream.

The warm, soothing strand pulsed and wiggled through the air before sliding beneath her skin like ribbons of silk. Rena sighed at the pleasurable sensation as it seeped into her chest.

Moments later, she detected the source. It was coming from the red light flashing in the distance, calling her to safety like a siren.

Spirit streams, a term she had come up with years ago to describe the unusual phenomenon, were like an invisible trail of bread crumbs only Rena could see and feel. She had no idea why or how she was able to sense them, but she had never been more grateful for the gift than right that second.

Ever since Rena could remember, she had been able to detect the invisible trail left behind by all living creatures. She could find any person on the planet by simply connecting with their spirit streams. She had never found one in a dream before because she had to touch an object the other person had held in order to connect.

But then again, this was no regular dream. More like a recurring nightmare.

Move your ass! *The man's voice was louder this time and rife with impatience.* Unless you enjoy getting fried like a chicken?

"Bossy and sarcastic?" *Rena glanced over her shoulder as another tremor hit.* "What a charming combination."

Rena ran as fast as she could toward the otherworldly red light, her arms pumping with the effort. She ducked beneath a low-hanging branch but stumbled when the ground shuddered again beneath her feet. She regained her footing when an earsplitting roar filled the air, but Rena didn't look back. Fear gripped her by the throat, and her heart threatened to beat right out of her chest, but she kept running toward the light.

If she followed the spirit stream, it would lead her to safety. She didn't know how she knew that; she simply did. Deep in her gut, she was confident whoever was talking to her was inherently good. Spirit streams didn't lie, because they possessed the essence of the person they belonged to.

Good or evil, the truth was revealed every time.

A wave of heat flashed over her back as the deafening sound of the beast's footsteps grew nearer still. Leaves crunched and branches cracked loudly as the monster tore through the woods, giving chase. With one final push, Rena broke through the tangle of branches and found what looked like a dead end. A rocky wall blocked her path, but the spirit stream drifted to the right, and Rena followed it, even though it seemed to be going nowhere.

When she rounded the side of the mountain, she discovered a small opening in the rocks, and the crimson light flashed from within. With the beast bearing down, there was no time to ask questions. She dropped to her knees and crawled into the narrow space, inching along on her belly. Rocks and dirt scraped at her, but she kept moving toward the light, which glowed brighter and larger.

With sweat dripping into her eyes and panic creeping in, Rena finally came to the other end of the narrow tunnel, and what she found left her speechless. It emptied into an enormous cave with a glittering pool of bright-blue water lit from beneath. She climbed down the sloped, rocky wall carefully, and when she finally reached the bottom, she looked around in awe. The sheer size of the underground chamber and the serenity of the space was enough to leave her humbled, but it was what was buried inside the wall that left her speechless.

Curled up in a fetal position, behind layers of translucent quartz and stone, was one of the beasts that had been haunting her nightmares. Rena let out a shuddering breath and moved closer to the crystalline surface. The creature was as beautiful as it was terrifying. A prism of crimson and gold glinted behind the frosted wall in a breathtaking kaleidoscope pattern.

"Whoa. That is so cool. I've never seen one when it wasn't trying to kill me. What is it? It looks kind of like a—"

She reached out to touch it.

Don't! *The man's voice echoed through the cavernous space.* Not in the dreamrealm.

Rena dropped her arm to her side and spun around, scanning the mammoth cave for any sign of her new friend.

You must go to him and find the others like yourself. The Amoveo can help you…and him. He must be awakened in the earthly plane by his mate. It's the only way to break the curse, and we are almost out of time. If you don't reach him by All Hallows' Eve, he will be trapped here forever.

"Okay, first of all, what curse, and who are the Amoveo?" Rena said slowly. "Second, there are no others like me. Trust me. I'm a total freak. Just ask any of the foster families I lived with, and they'll confirm it."

Silence.

"Hello?" Rena settled her hands on her hips and looked around. "Yo! Mister? You still here? And what's this business about a mate?"

You don't know about the Amoveo? His voice was thick with surprise and a fair amount of confusion. How is that possible?

"Please." Rena scoffed and swept her arms in a big circle. "This fits right in with the rest of my weird-ass life. Listen, I appreciate you saving my ass back there and everything, even though this is only a dream. Albeit a really weird dream, but what's with the monster in the rocks? Why have those two assholes been killing me night after night, and who must I go to?" She settled her hands on her hips again and arched one eyebrow. "And while we're at it, who the hell are you?"

Silence, heavy and thick, filled the cave once again, and Rena practically choked on it.

I've never encountered one like you before.

His voice and spirit stream bounced off the nooks and crannies of the rocks, effectively masking his location. Another first.

"Yeah? Well, I've never been interrogated in my own dream before. I call us even."

What's your name?

*She answered the ludicrous question. "Rena McHale."
This dream was her subconscious. Why would she ask
herself her own name? "Why? What's yours?"*

Pick up the stone.

"That's a weird name," she deadpanned.

Pick it up! We don't have time to waste. Not anymore.

*His voice boomed louder, from behind her this time.
Rena spun around and spotted a jagged piece of red
quartz perched precariously on a rocky outcropping
along the wall. About the size of a large egg, it glowed
from within, like the water in the pool. Rena let out a
slow breath and ran both hands through her short
brown hair before lacing her fingers behind her head.*

*"Does this have to do with that curse you men-
tioned?" she shouted to the empty cave. "I'm not buying
what you're selling, dude. I have enough problems without getting involved with some weird curse."*

Pick it up. Now! It's the only way.

*"It's a good thing you're a disembodied voice and
not a real live guy." Rena dropped her hands to her side
and cautiously approached the stone. "I'd have to deck
you for being so damn bossy."*

Please. *He dragged out the word as though it was
painful for him to ask her nicely.* Pick up the stone.

*"Jeez." Rena rolled her eyes before scooping it
up. "Fine."*

*The instant the quartz touched her fingers, the cave
erupted in an explosion of light. Another spirit stream
that was almost identical to the other but far weaker in
strength whispered beneath her flesh. Rena sucked in
a shuddering breath and wanted to open her eyes but
couldn't. They were heavy with sleep.*

As darkness closed in, the man whispered, You are his only hope.

—⁓—

Zander Lorens rubbed the sleep from his eyes as he reached around blindly for the cell phone that was somewhere next to his sleeping bag. Early morning sunlight streamed in through the vents of his tent, and he squinted against it while swearing under his breath. The dream was still fresh and the woman's face securely imprinted on his mind, to say nothing of her energy signature.

For the first time in five centuries, Zander had hope that the curse could be broken.

When his fingers curled around the smooth, familiar device, he snatched it and sat up. Bleary-eyed, he scrolled through the screen, looking for the old witch's phone number. It was one of the only non-business-related contacts he had in there. Referring to Isadora as a friend was probably a stretch, especially since it was one of her sisters who had cursed him and his brother all those years ago.

Over the years, in spite of the history between their families, she had become a trusted acquaintance. Hell, she was a powerful old broad, and if she wanted to hurt Zander, she could have done it a hundred times over. Complicated past aside, Isadora was his only surviving connection to the supernatural world.

Zander had no other options.

The early morning chill of the surrounding mountains crept in, but Zander barely felt it. Excitement and a healthy dose of nerves had his blood humming. He pressed the phone to his ear and unzipped his tent.

Sucking in a deep breath of crisp morning air, he stepped out, uncaring of his nakedness. There was nobody there to see it other than the forest creatures, and since he wasn't exactly Snow White, they wouldn't be paying him any mind.

After six or seven rings, Isadora finally picked up.

"You better have a damned good reason for calling an old woman at this hour," she croaked. "The sun is barely up."

"I found her." Zander tried to keep his voice even and his eagerness at bay, but it was no use. "Last night. In the dreamrealm. Arianna was gone, and a woman I have never seen before had taken her place. She was—"

"Hold on a damn minute," she rasped. "Slow down."

"Zed spoke, Isadora. He actually spoke." He let out a short laugh of disbelief and pushed his shaggy, dark hair off his face while staring at the rising sun. "The voice was more beast than man, but he uttered the same word over and over again as soon as he saw her: *mine*. Don't you see? The woman in the dreamrealm, whoever she is, *has* to be Zed's mate."

When the old witch didn't respond, Zander thought the connection had been lost. He pulled the phone away and checked, but he had plenty of bars. He growled with frustration and put it back to his ear, but two seconds later, a crackling sound erupted behind him.

Zander spun around to see the old woman standing there, a cloud of purple smoke disappearing around her in the early morning light. Her long, straight, salt-and-pepper hair hung to her waist, and her tanned, wrinkled face was covered with a mischievous smile. Those dark eyes of her twinkled wickedly as they flicked over his naked body, lingering longer than he'd like on his dick.

"I thought we should talk in person," she said with a wink. Isadora pointed one crooked finger at his crotch before leaning both hands on her tall walking stick. "You better cover up, or I'm going to get the wrong idea."

"I'm too old to go diving behind a tree."

Zander hit End on the phone and strode toward the tent as her cackling laughter filled the air. Nudity wasn't a big deal for the members of his race. Shit. After five hundred years on earth, trapped in his human form, *nothing* was a big deal anymore.

"And I'm too old to take advantage of the situation," she snickered. "In this body, anyhow. Now, if I had used my younger-self potion before my travelin' potion, we wouldn't be doing very much talking, if you know what I'm gettin' at."

"I have an idea." Zander threw his cell phone in the tent and grabbed his jeans, trying not to imagine what the old woman looked like under her long robe-like dress. "You know, we could have continued this conversation on the phone."

"Where's the fun in that?" She leaned on her cane and gave him a sly smile as he pulled his pants up. "'Sides, given everythin' you were goin' on about, we need to be real clear about what comes next. Best to have this talk in person."

Zander nodded his agreement and settled both hands on his hips as he studied the ancient witch woman closely. Her energy signature, like most supernatural creatures, was far stronger than a human's. It was the spiritual fingerprint each individual possessed. After

Zander had been cursed, being able to detect those powerful streams of energy was the only gift he had left.

Well, that and being immortal. But as far as he was concerned, immortality wasn't any damn gift he'd ever wanted. At least, not like this.

"Now, let's get back to business." Isadora thumped her walking stick into the ground with her gnarled hands. "You think you may have found a way to break my sister's curse? I thought the only way to get rid of it was for one of you boys to commit an act of pure, unselfish love?"

"Since Zed has been trapped in hibernation in his dragon form for the past five centuries, it cut our odds in half."

"Fair point." She let out a groan as she settled her round backside on a tree stump next to Zander's makeshift fire pit. "But you're still here. Why ain't you been able to get rid of the curse? Ain't you done any good deeds in the last half a millennium?"

"What a load of crap that turned out to be," Zander scoffed under his breath. "I've spent the last five centuries doing good deeds and random acts of kindness all over the globe, and not a damn one worked. Do you have any idea how many cats and drowning kids I've saved?"

"Nope."

"Well, it's a lot. Shit," he huffed. "I've lost count. I've fought in wars for the greater good, built homes for the downtrodden, and bought groceries for strangers. I've tossed countless coins into paper cups that were clutched in the hands of homeless men, women, and children. Nothing has made a difference. The curse has remained in place. Zed is stuck in the dreamrealm, and I'm...here."

"Yeah." She sighed. "You and your twin brother got screwed."

"He got it worse than me," Zander said quietly. "Zed has been languishing in the dreamrealm. Night after night, we relive that fight—the one that changed everything. I've tried to reason with him, but he stopped hearing me long ago. He's...tortured."

"Grief and regret will do that."

"He's been reduced to his most savage state. The man is gone, and only the beast remains."

"Right, I know all that," she said with waning patience. "So what makes you think this woman is the key to breaking the curse?"

"He saw her, Isadora," Zander said with a smile. "And he *spoke*. I can't tell you the last time he did that. It was only one word, but it was a damn good one."

"Mine," Isadora said quietly. Worry edged the wrinkles around her eyes. "So you're tellin' me that you think this woman in the dreamrealm is Zed's mate?"

"Zed sure as hell thought she was. Besides, why else would some random woman land in there with us?"

"Why do you think—"

"She's Amoveo," Zander said quietly.

Isadora's eyes widened, and she nodded slowly as an expression of understanding washed over her. The Amoveo, an ancient race of shapeshifters similar to the Dragon Clan in many ways, found their mates in the dreamrealm. Once they connected there, they could find each other in the physical plane.

"She's a shifter. Like you were."

"No." Zander's jaw clenched. "The dragons were cousins of the Amoveo. We aren't the same."

"Pfft." She rolled her eyes. "That's what you call semantics. The Dragon Clan was considered the eleventh clan of the Amoveo by most everyone—except the dragons. Which of the ten Amoveo clans is she descended from?"

"From the Fox Clan, I think."

"Like someone else we knew." Isadora sniffed. "Seems a little too coincidental for me."

Zander pretended to ignore that last comment.

"Her *name* is Rena McHale, but I don't think she's a pureblood. If she was, she would know what she is, because she would have gone through her first shapeshifting episode during puberty, like all of the Amoveo do. There's *no way* she knows there's Amoveo blood in her veins, which is going to make this a hell of a lot more difficult. I had no idea the Amoveo could even breed with humans."

"Most of 'em don't know what they are," Isadora said flatly. "Comes as quite a shock to 'em."

Zander stilled.

"You mean there are more like her? Part human and part Amoveo?"

"Yes, sir. Prince Richard has had his men out looking for 'em and bringin' 'em back to his ranch, over in Montana."

An image of Zed in his hibernation cocoon flashed into his mind. His twin brother was deep beneath the earth, where no one would find him. Humans rarely ventured that far under the ground, and other than Zander and Isadora, nobody even knew Zed was there.

"They still occupy that land? I thought for sure they would have sold it off over the years."

"You didn't sell yours," she said, referring to his property in West Yellowstone.

"It's all I have left of my clan."

"Maybe they feel the same. You aren't so different after all." She shrugged her narrow shoulders and waved one hand. "Richard and Salinda's place is more of a compound, really. They had themselves some trouble over the past few years. Purist Amoveo caused a ruckus. Guess they were none too pleased about these hybrids popping up. The Council has been dissolved and—"

"You're not serious."

The Council was the Amoveo's governing body and was comprised of two members from each of the ten clans. Eons ago, long before Zander and Zed were born, the Dragons had even been a part of it. He couldn't imagine the kind of chaos that must have ensued with the dissolution of the Council.

"Deadly so, I'm afraid. There were assassination attempts. Nasty business. I ain't seen the ten Amoveo clans fight among themselves like that since...well... since that business with you and your brother and that Fox Clan girl."

"That was a long time ago, and this woman, whoever she is, isn't Arianna but she *is* Zed's mate."

"Or yours," Isadora whispered.

"No," he said adamantly. "I'm not letting that happen again. She's meant for Zed."

"Who she's meant for ain't up to you, now is it?"

"This woman is his only hope."

Zander grabbed two large, thick branches and

snapped them in half, using his pent-up frustration to do it. Silence settled between them as Zander squatted down and arranged some sticks in the fire pit. He stuffed some newspaper underneath before lighting it up.

"'Bout time," she groused. "It's colder than a witch's tit out here."

Zander let out a huff of laughter at her silly comment and shook his head before sitting beside the fire. Isadora always did have a way of diffusing tense situations. He pulled his knees up and settled his arms over them as the heat washed over the bare flesh of his chest. The crackle of the wood as it was consumed by the flames filled the air, instantly putting him at ease.

For most people, the power of fire was frightening, but it made Zander feel at home.

"You miss it, don't you?" she asked, her voice pulling him from his memories. "The dragon."

"Embracing my dragon again is all I've wanted, and ironically, it's the very thing that's tormenting Zed." He tossed another branch on the fire, sending sparks into the air. "If I can get this woman to the cave where Zed is hibernating *and* give her a spirit stone from our tribal land, she might be able to use it to wake him up."

"That's a big might," Isadora said firmly. "Boy, you got nothin' but *maybes* and *could bes*."

"Yeah. That's about all I've got, *and* we're running out of time. This Saturday is—"

"Oh hell." She tapped her cane on the ground and pursed her lips. "It's All Hallows' Eve, ain't it?"

"Yes."

"Damn," she said with a sigh. "Those five hundred years surely did fly right on by."

Zed let out a bitter laugh.

The past several centuries had felt more like millennia as far as he was concerned. However, he clamped down on his moment of self-pity and reminded himself that nothing he went through could compare to Zed's painful existence.

"That's why I need your help. If we don't break the curse before sunset on Saturday, then it will never be over, and Zed will be trapped there. Forever. Tormented. Alone. I can't live with that, and thanks to your sister's curse, I can't even put myself out of my own misery." He sighed wearily. "Living forever sucks...at least living like this."

He turned his gaze to hers and threw a prayer to the universe that she would take pity on him. The old woman, her long white-and-brown robe draped over her thin form, stared into the fire but said nothing. He sensed she was weighing her options.

"Please, Isadora. Put me in touch with the prince or one of his people. I've *got* to get on that property. You and I both know that I can't just walk up to the gates. And I can't try and sneak on, because they'll sense my presence. You know I'm right."

"Can't say you're wrong." A look of understanding flickered over her weathered face, and she nodded. "But if you had an Amoveo hybrid with you...one looking for sanctuary..."

"We kill two birds with one stone: Rena can connect with her people, and I have a chance to free my brother."

"Seems more complicated than you're makin' it."

Zander let out a beleaguered sigh.

"Can you help me or not?"

"Yes."

She pushed herself to her feet, using her cane for support. Zander hopped up before going around the fire and scooping the tiny old witch up in a big hug. Her frail, five-foot-tall frame was easily engulfed by his far larger one.

"My sister was a troublemaker and always sellin' her magic to the highest bidder. It ain't right, and if she weren't already dead, I'd have a mind to kill her myself. It's witches like her that gave all of us a bad rap. I swear. The fairies are a bunch of troublemakers and *we're* the ones who look bad in the human stories. Ain't right, I tell ya."

"Thank you, Isadora."

He set her down and planted a kiss on her soft cheek as his gratitude swelled.

"All right, now." Her wrinkled cheeks pinkened, and she patted him on the arm. "Better be careful with all that kissin' on me. We may be about the same age, but my body ain't weathered the years as well as yours."

Her brow furrowed, and her smile faltered as her gaze skittered over his bare chest. She tapped one of several scars on his torso with a gnarled fingertip and made a tsking sound.

"I guess you aren't exactly unscathed, are you?"

"No, ma'am." Zander pressed both hands to his chest and stepped back before extending his arms wide. "But thanks to your sister, I *am* indestructible."

"And handsome as ever." She pulled a small glass bottle from one of the folds in her robe and flipped the cork out with her thumb. "Better stand back, boy."

Zander did as she said and put a healthy distance between them.

"I'll get a message to the Amoveo. If I had to venture

a guess, you'll be gettin' a call from a Dante Coltari. He's the one been wranglin' the hybrids to the ranch, but that's all I can do for you. After that, you're on your own. I don't like to meddle where I don't have to."

Zander arched one dark eyebrow at her, and she shrugged.

"Yeah, that ain't true. I love messin' with people. Keeps my mind and magic sharp."

She was about to swallow her potion, but Zander held up one hand, stopping her.

"Don't give them my real name. Tell them—"

"Won't matter. Trust me."

"Isadora," he began, "I hardly think they'll welcome a dragon to their property. Even before my people were extinct, we were the outcasts. Some of the Amoveo even helped the human dragon slayers hunt us into oblivion, Arianna's father for one."

Anger surged at the painful memories, but he stuffed it back down. Better to save it for another day. If he was going to have to deal with a ranch full of Amoveo, he would need all of his strength. In his experience, rage was one hell of a weapon.

"Yeah," she snorted. "But you ain't a dragon no more. The dragons are all gone and only exist in human fairy tales and folklore...for the most part."

Before he could protest further, Isadora swallowed her potion and vanished in a cloud of purple smoke. As the haze of her departure dissipated, Zander's thoughts went to the woman from the dreamrealm.

If she didn't know who and what she really was, how the hell was Zander going to tell her about him and his brother? Or that she was Zed's intended mate?

What a shit show.

Yep. He was fucked. Again.

All he knew was her name and where she was located. Though the curse had stripped him of virtually all of his Dragon Clan abilities, he was still able to identify her unique energy pattern—and it showed him exactly where she was.

He wasted no time. Zander packed up his tent and backpack and pointed his Harley in the right direction.

Chapter 2

"BUT YOU HAVE TO COME OUT TONIGHT," PAT SAID WITH A dramatic whine. "It's my annual birthday boozefest, and it wouldn't be the same without you. Come on, girl."

"Pat, you know you're my best friend," Rena said, while stifling a large yawn.

"Bitch, please, I'm your *only* friend."

Pat settled her leather-clad backside on the edge of Rena's desk and checked her bleach-blond reflection in the wall mirror. She pulled a lipstick from the pocket of her pink satin jacket and quickly touched up her lips. She had been a showgirl in Vegas for years and dressed the part on- and offstage.

"Yeah? Well, you aren't exactly swimming in a girl squad are you, Pat?"

"Whatevs." Pat sighed. "You're smart and tough. You'd be surprised how many broads out here can't stand on their own two feet. And if there's anything I can't abide, it's a weak chick."

"Says the woman whose last serious boyfriend drained her bank account of ten grand and split in the dead of night."

"Hey! Can I help it if he was a thief?"

"I still can't *believe* you got bamboozled by that guy."

"What can I say? He was superhot and off-the-charts awesome in bed. I must've had sex-brain. That's my only excuse."

"What on earth is sex-brain?" Rena asked, while keeping one eye on her computer screen. The topic of sex made her uncomfortable and not only because she hadn't had much of it. Intimacy of any kind made Rena feel off-kilter or on guard. In her experience, allowing herself to be vulnerable, physically or emotionally, only ended up causing her pain.

"You'd know if you ever got laid."

"Please." Rena rolled her eyes. "Sex is overrated."

"Says the woman who hasn't done it in three years." Pat smirked. "Or is it four? Girl, you need some good old-fashioned nookie."

It was four but who's counting? Rena squared her shoulders and typed two more figures into the spread-sheet. The last guy she had slept with was only inter-ested in his own pleasure, and even though he'd tried to fake it, Rena knew he didn't even remember her name afterward. She hadn't been looking for the dude to pro-claim his love to her or anything, but he could at least have gotten her name right.

After that humiliating experience, she decided sex wasn't worth the trouble.

"Look at the mess your libido got you into. I'll stick with running my business and my ongoing love affair with Netflix."

"That's depressing." Pat hopped off the desk and smoothed the back of her pants. "Tank may have been a thief and a liar, but we should thank him. If I hadn't hired you to track that shithead down, *we* would never have met."

"That's true." Rena winked and smiled at her one and only friend. "It was my best case ever. Well, the one with the best fringe benefits, anyway."

It had been a win for both women. The only person

who didn't benefit from it was Tank. The big brute had coughed up the money once Rena got her hands on him. Actually, it was more like her mind. A smile curved her lips as she recalled the look on his face when she was able to tell him all the deep, dark secrets she saw in his head. He'd spazzed out and called her the devil but not before giving back the cash he'd stolen.

Maybe, Rena thought with a sigh, she was a devil of some kind, but at least she wasn't the thief.

Freak? Sure. Thief? Nope.

She didn't even know *what* she was exactly. Only that she was *different*.

Rena let out a short laugh and shook her head as she typed another piece of information into the Excel spreadsheet. She kept her gaze on the screen because she hated to admit Pat was right. Rena had never been good at making friends, or keeping them, anyway. It had always been easier to hold most people at arm's length. If they couldn't get close to her, then they couldn't hurt her. It was a survival skill she'd picked up long ago, after the first foster family sent her away. There was no point in getting attached to anyone, because once they realized Rena was different, they couldn't get away from her fast enough.

She had always been something of a loner, at least until a few years ago.

"Sad but true." Pat giggled.

"It is sad." Rena yawned yet again. "Jeez. I am totally wiped out. I didn't get any damn sleep *again* last night, and I've been tied to my desk all day getting my quarterly taxes done for my accountant. Vito always took care of this stuff but…well…now it's on me."

"Sorry, babe." Pat's voice softened. "How's the old guy doing, anyway?"

"He's...the same." Rena stilled and forced herself not to cry. Vito was the first person Rena had allowed herself to care about in years. "The assisted-living place he's in is great, but it costs a damn fortune. Thank God business has been good, but you know what they say: there's *never* enough money. I have no idea how long he'll be staying there, so bring on the cases and the cash. Besides, you know me. I thrive on work."

"What are they gonna do if you don't pay 'em?" Pat scoffed. "Kick him out? The guy is, like, almost a hundred, and he's got full-on dementia. Is there anywhere else he can go that's not so expensive?"

"There are state-run places, but I wouldn't put a dog in one of those, let alone the only semblance of a family I've ever had. Vito took me in when I had *nobody*. Hell, he taught me this business, and he's the *only* person who has ever given a damn about me." Anger shimmied up her back at the notion of taking her beloved friend out of the Sunnyfarm Retirement Community. "Besides, they have the best program in the country for Alzheimer's and dementia patients. He has to stay there...even if he doesn't know where the hell he is from one minute to the next."

Rena's heart squeezed in her chest when she recalled the vacant, lost expression on Vito's face. It was the same one she saw every time she visited him now. No matter how many times he looked at her that way, she would never get used to it. The irony of her situation wasn't lost on her. She had pushed people away her entire life, and the first person she opened her heart to no longer remembered her.

Tears stung the back of Rena's eyes, but she willed them away and cursed herself for her foolishness. The ache in her heart wasn't Vito's fault; it was hers. She was the dummy who had allowed herself to care about him. He wasn't hurting her on purpose, but that didn't make her feel any better.

"He still sayin' wacky stuff?"

"Yeah," Rena said on a sigh. "When I saw him yesterday, he thought I was his daughter, and since she's been dead for decades, he's obviously confused. Sometimes nothing he says makes sense, and then other times, he's totally normal. Every time I go visit him, I'm not sure which version of Vito I'm going to see. Usually it's the one who looks at me like he's never seen me before, like the last few years never happened, and I'm just some stranger."

"Jeez," Pat whispered. "It's like a roller coaster, huh?"

"Yup." Rena rubbed at her bleary eyes before forcing herself to refocus on the computer screen. "An expensive, heartbreaking, cruddy carnival ride that nobody should have to get on. I'm only twenty-five, but lately I feel like I'm a hundred and five. My body and brain are on the fritz. I think it's all his crazy talk about monsters that has been giving me nightmares."

"All the more reason you should come out with me tonight and party a little. Come on! You need a break, girl, and Dino's Place is always fun."

"I don't know…"

"Pleeeeeease." Pat put her hands together as if in prayer and batted her big blue eyes at Rena. "Come on, Rena. It's my birthday, and my cat doesn't like going to the bars. So you're my only hope."

"What if I hadn't solved the case and gotten your money back for you?" Rena flicked her narrowed gaze to Pat. "Would we still be friends?"

"Hell no," she snorted. "Because then I'd be out my ten grand *plus* your fee. Besides, I knew you'd be able to do it."

"Oh yeah?" Rena laughed. "How's that?"

"My sixth sense." Pat tapped her temple with one long red fingernail. "I get hunches, and they're never wrong."

"Really?" Rena's eyebrows raised and a smile curved her lips. "Then why didn't those *hunches* lead you to the deadbeat with all your cash?"

"They led me to you, so him taking my money was actually a good thing in the end. Shit, not all of us get the crazy, weird vibes like you do."

Rena stilled for a second. She'd never told Pat about the way she was able to find people. She didn't mention the fact that when she held Tank's old T-shirt in her hands, she had been able to see everything. All of his dirty secrets—and the guy had a few. Including a wife and three kids. Once Rena called him out on the secret family, he had been more than willing to give back the money.

In fact, she'd never told anyone about her gift. Hell, Rena rarely got close enough to anybody to tell them the way she liked her coffee, let alone her deepest secret. And hers was a whopper. The people who sensed that Rena was different or got weirded out by her hunches always gave her that *look*. The one that made her feel like a Martian, and she sure as hell didn't want to see an expression like that on Pat's face.

"Anyway, are you coming tonight or what?"

"What do your hunches tell you?"

"Screw you." Pat laughed.

"Well, since you asked so nicely…"

"Excellent." Pat leaned across the desk and planted a lipstick-laden kiss on Rena's cheek. Rena wasn't great with the huggy and kissy stuff, but she'd learned a long time ago that Pat was an expert hugger and kisser. "I'll meet you at Dino's Place at eight, and don't be late!"

"Yes, ma'am!" Rena saluted dramatically.

"Bye, baby." Pat waved before disappearing through the door and walking out into the hot Vegas sun.

An ear-piercing squeak filled the small office as the door closed, and finally, Rena was left in blissful silence. She had always enjoyed being alone, and even though she adored Pat, Rena could only handle her friend's energy in small doses. The woman's vibe was something akin to a Tasmanian devil and tended to put Rena's unusually heightened senses on overload. Her hearing had always been phenomenal, but today it seemed to be on hyperdrive.

Rena could even hear the people in the travel agency downstairs. Not just muffled voices but actual words. She stilled and tilted her head, instinctively sharpening her focus, trying harder to hear every word. However, she swiftly pulled back and shifted her attention to the sound of the ticking clock. Just because she had weirdly awesome hearing didn't mean she should use it.

Eavesdropping was rude.

Letting out a slow sigh, she glanced at the clock above the door. Two more hours. She'd call it quits at six, which would give her time to shower and change. It would be a short trip home, since her studio apartment was right behind her office, though the entrance was separate. Business was booming, and she could have afforded one of those huge McMansions that had popped up outside the city, but that wasn't her style. She preferred her cozy, neat little apartment to a sprawling, vacant house.

Besides, having such a quick trip home would even give her time to grab a nap before going out.

Rena *shouldn't* go out tonight. What she should do was go to bed and try to get some more sleep, because the nightmares were kicking her butt and interrupting her sleep patterns. Not only did it make her physically exhausted, but it also seemed to weaken her special abilities. If she didn't get enough sleep, her radar could get fuzzy. Rena saved the file on her computer and opened her email. She hadn't gotten a good night's sleep for the past several months, and last night was the worst ever thanks to yet another freaky-ass monster dream.

What was the deal with these weird nightmares, anyway?

The sudden roar of a motorcycle rumbled outside, and Rena winced as the shock of it pulled her from her memories. A shudder whispered up her spine as she recalled the energy signature from the man in the dream. The dreams typically lingered, but this one was practically alive around her in the air. She easily recalled the man's voice; it was deep and gravelly and seemed as though it had imprinted on her brain or something. She couldn't shake him, or the memory of him at least.

Powerful. Dark. Seductive.

This was nuts. A disembodied voice in a dream—a voice that belonged to nobody other than her own subconscious—got her more hot and bothered than any living, breathing guy. Maybe Pat was right and Rena needed some nookie. Would some no-strings-attached sex with a hot stranger help her snap out of—

No. She answered her own question before she even finished the thought.

Rena closed her eyes and sucked in a deep, cleansing breath in an attempt to clear her head. Weird dreams aside, she had work to finish, but with no new cases on the horizon, she would likely have plenty of time to analyze her crazy subconscious later.

"I'm being ridiculous," she muttered under her breath. "Sex with a stranger is the last complication I need...and *now* I'm talking to myself."

Rena grabbed the glass of water on her desk and was about to take a sip when she spotted a layer of dust floating on top. She grimaced. How long had it been sitting there? Gross.

Letting out a sigh, she rose to her feet with glass in hand, but as she rounded the desk, a hauntingly familiar spirit stream curled around her. Dark and erotic, the ghostlike tendril made her stop short, and all the breath rushed from her lungs. Rena's body tensed, and a shiver of lust mixed with surprise and excitement sizzled beneath her skin. Warmth seeped through her chest, and her eyes tingled—an odd pins-and-needles sensation—and her breath came in quick, jagged gasps.

Rena's entire body went into some kind of haywire overdrive that she had zero control over.

The spirit stream grew stronger, and sweat broke out over her skin. Rena's fingers curled tighter around the glass. Her mind raced, fighting to break through the myriad sensations and identify the source of the spirit stream. Who could possibly be having this kind of effect on her?

Mine.

The gruff, gravelly voice rumbled through her mind as the glass shattered between her fingers and sliced her flesh. She barely felt the pain or the blood, hot and wet, as it dripped from her hand, because at the same instant, the door of her office flew open and a towering man filled the space. Light from the setting sun glared behind him, blocking out everything but the massive size of him, and in that moment, Rena realized the voice in her dream, the man she had heard—he wasn't her subconscious at all.

He was real...and he was here.

———※———

Zander Lorens had traveled the entire globe over the past five centuries, and Las Vegas was one of his least favorite places. The city was saturated with greed and layered with the worst aspects of humanity, traits he had gotten to know all too well during his time on earth. He never thought anyone or anything would get him to come back here, but then again, he hadn't expected to find his brother's mate living in Sin City.

Shit. He hadn't expected to find her anywhere. Ever. He had all but given up hope. Zander had resigned himself to their cursed fates long ago, and with the five-hundred-year anniversary fast approaching, he thought they were both done for.

Six hours after waking from his dream, he arrived at his destination, but he still didn't have a damn clue about how to approach her.

Zander slowed his Harley and pulled up to the curb of the small office building, the rumble of the engine echoing around him in the narrow side street. He kicked the stand down and shut off the bike with a hint of apprehension glimmering in his chest. Slipping his hands into his pockets, he curled his fingers around the piece of red quartz. The familiar feel of his family's spirit stone tumbled against his palm, instantly putting him at ease.

The lumpy rock from his clan's land was all he had left of his former life and his people. It had always been his most prized possession but now more than ever. A knot of apprehension curled in his gut as he stared at the small, brick building. She was in there. Her energy signature pulsed and throbbed from the second-story office. Thick and humming with a soft musical lilt, it curled around him like smoke.

A sudden rush of lust shot through him, making his blood hum.

"Shit," he hissed under his breath.

Mating for the dragons, as with the Amoveo, had always been predestined, and his father had said it was the universe's way of helping their people avoid base emotions like jealousy. Dragons had naturally fiery dispositions, and jealousy did not serve them well.

That was probably why identical twins were practically unheard of among their kind. As Zander and Zed discovered, being identical twins messed up the natural order of things.

Zander released the stone and tore his hand from his pocket. He would not allow history to repeat itself. It had simply been far too long since he'd felt the touch

of a woman, and it was obviously beginning to grate
on him.

"Hey, handsome."

An older blond woman winked at him as she slipped
on a pair of oversized black sunglasses and sashayed
off the steps of Rena's building. She pulled a pack of
Virginia Slim cigarettes from her pocket and waved.

"Got a light?"

Zander nodded and snagged the Zippo lighter from
his back pocket. Still seated on his bike, he flicked the
flame on as she leaned in and puffed away, quickly
lighting her cancer stick. The blond peered at him seductively over her sunglasses before taking a long drag.

"Thanks, kitten." She stuffed the pack into the pocket
of her satin jacket and smiled broadly. "I've never seen
you around here."

"Passing through."

"That's too bad." She jutted her blond head toward
the building behind her. "It's my birthday, and my girlfriend and I are going out for drinks tonight. Sure would
be fun to have a handsome fella like you join us."

She looked like Las Vegas come to life. Satin and
leather covered most of her limbs, and she wore a heavy
layer of makeup. Many men found that attractive, but
not him. He preferred a natural beauty to the overglam-
orized type. Zander turned his gaze to the door at the top
of the staircase.

The name emblazoned on the window in large, white
letters immediately captured his attention.

Fox Investigations

Interesting name choice for her business.

"Your friend works for that investigation place?"

"Works for it? No way, baby. Rena owns it. Well, she took it over when old Vito lost his marbles." Her high-pitched voice bounced around him in the air. "The girl is better at it than the old man ever was. She found my deadbeat ex and got me back the ten grand he split with. Rena has an uncanny sense and can find almost anybody. Never seen nothin' like it. Vito said she was a natural."

Bingo.

Zander dragged off his Ray-Bans and hooked them in the collar of his T-shirt before giving the woman a smile. Her cheeks pinked and, for an instant, the older, worn-out woman looked like a young girl, flirty and full of life. He sensed excitement from her, but there was no attraction for him. Truthfully, he couldn't remember the last time a woman had turned him on. He was so damn bored and tired of living, not much got him excited anymore.

"Your birthday, huh?" He stuck out his hand, and she shook it delicately. "I'm Zander. And you are?"

"Patricia," she simpered. "So whaddya say, Zander? You wanna join me and my friend, Rena, for a drink or two tonight? We're meeting up at Dino's Place around eight. It's not far, just about two blocks from here."

"I'm sure I can find it."

"Yeah." She laughed. "You can Google it."

"Right." Zander nodded.

He had a phone but barely used it. He wasn't a fan of technology.

"Great." She took another drag and smiled. "Catch you later, kitten."

Maybe the universe was giving him a break after all.

He had found Rena and even got an invite for drinks. He let out a low grunt of appreciation as Pat disappeared around the corner. His gaze skittered back to the second-story window of Fox Investigations.

If Rena was a finder of the lost, then this woman could not have been more perfect, because nobody needed to be found more than Zed. A plan began to come together. He wouldn't have to tell her who she really was, because once she found Zed, like he was going to hire her to do, she'd figure it out for herself. Zander ran both hands through his windblown, shaggy brown hair before climbing off his bike. After ensuring his bike and bag were secure, he trotted up the steps toward what he assumed was Rena's office.

Inside this building was the answer to his long-unanswered prayers. He stopped, his hand hovering above the doorknob, as a flicker of uncertainty filled him. It had been centuries since he'd encountered an Amoveo face-to-face. He'd bumped into a vampire or two and even crossed paths with a few of the fae, but not an Amoveo, the dragon's closest relative. Probably because there were so few of them left.

Would she know what he really was, or would the curse keep him camouflaged the way it had with the other supernaturals? Zander shook his head and shoved the concern aside. It would be what it would be. She was his brother's mate and the answer they had been looing for. He curled his hand around the cool steel knob, and the memory of Zed's haunted voice flickered through his mind.

Mine.

A moment later, the sound of glass breaking and a

woman's cry filled the air. Panic fired through him. Without bothering with the formality of knocking, Zander tore the door open and stormed into the office, but he stopped short when he found himself staring into a pair of glowing amber eyes.

It had been so many years since Zander had seen the clan eyes of an Amoveo, he was rendered speechless. However, within seconds, the woman's eyes flickered and shifted back to their human state—a lovely shade of brown.

"I guess you don't believe in knocking?"

Chapter 3

RENA McHALE STOOD AT THE CENTER OF THE SMALL office with broken glass littering the wooden floor around her feet, seemingly unaware that her eyes had shifted. An Amoveo would never allow their clan eyes to be seen by a stranger who was *presumably* a human.

"You're bleeding," he blurted out.

"Damn it," she hissed.

She had blood dripping from her right hand, and the other was balled into a fist, ready to fight. Rena McHale was every bit as beautiful in person as she had been in the dreamrealm.

Scratch that. More so. The woman was breathtaking.

Chestnut-colored hair cut in a chin-length bob and highlighted with bright-red streaks framed the determined expression on her oval-shaped face. Irritation and a hint of surprise danced in her brown eyes, which were flecked with gold. She was dressed in a simple blue suit with a crisp, white shirt unbuttoned just enough so he could see the curve of her cleavage.

"Staring at my boobs after you barge into my office is a ballsy move, my friend."

Zander flicked his gaze back to hers, and the moment their eyes locked, it sent a shock straight to his dick. *Son of a bitch*. That'll wake a man up. He bit back the urge to swear out loud. The woman was bleeding, and he was ogling her like a creep. He made a mental note to keep his eyes on her face.

That wouldn't be a problem.

"Sorry," Zander murmured. He took a step back and raised both hands as if in surrender but pointed at the blood dripping onto the floor. "You want some help with that, or do you just wanna bleed to death?"

She sighed. "That seems a little dramatic."

She arched one dark eyebrow and stepped over the broken remnants of what looked like a glass of water before grabbing a roll of paper towels off a file cabinet. She tore off a large wad and immediately pressed it to her wound while eyeing him warily.

"How can I help you?"

"You might need stitches," he said quietly. "There's a lot of blood."

"It looks worse than it is. I'll throw a couple of butterfly bandages on it." She gave him a quick once-over but didn't make a move toward him. "I heal like a champ, but thanks for your concern."

He bet she did. Amoveo were known for their ability to heal swiftly. Even a hybrid like Rena would enjoy that particular gift. A *hybrid*. He still couldn't wrap his brain around this piece of the puzzle. His brows knit together as she pulled a first aid kit from the bottom file cabinet drawer and swiftly tended to the cut on her hand while keeping one eye on him.

When had the Amoveo started breeding with humans, and why the hell doesn't she know what she is? Where were her people? He glanced around the office. There were no personal pictures anywhere. It was sparse and strictly business.

This was going to be more difficult than he thought.

"Do you always barge into people's offices, sir?"

"Only when I hear a woman scream." He dropped his hands to his side and kept his voice low. "Breaking glass and screaming don't usually bring good news."

"True," she said with a small smile. "Now that you know I'm not a damsel in distress and only a little clumsy, tell me who you are and why you're here."

"It's my brother."

"Hold on." Rena tossed the bloodied paper towels and bandage wrappers into the garbage can next to the desk. "Let's start with your name."

"Zander."

She smirked and gingerly smoothed the bandage over the side of her palm. "Last name?"

"Lorens." He stuck out his left hand and slowly closed the space between them. The light, sweet scent of pears wafted over him, and he couldn't help but breathe a little deeper as he got closer. It was a stark contrast to the city she lived in. "Zander Lorens."

Rena shook her head and laughed while waving her injured right hand. He stilled as the light, musical sound of her amusement hit him in seductive waves. His gut tightened with need, which was disarming and disconcerting.

"Right." He cleared his throat, quickly dropping his arm. "Sorry."

Just as well. What was he thinking? Touching her would not be a smart move. Zander's body was sending signals that were confusing the hell out of his brain. He would keep his distance. Nature had messed up once before, and it was up to him to make it right.

Once she connected with Zed, everything would be as it should be.

"No problem." Rena went behind her desk and gestured to the chair in front of it. "Have a seat, Mr. Lorens. Sorry about the bloody debris field."

"Zander."

"Zander." Rena's eyes narrowed slightly, and her intense gaze skittered over him from head to toe. "I'm betting the bike I heard pulling up outside belongs to you."

Zander nodded and stepped around the broken glass before sitting across from the increasingly intriguing woman. In his experience, most women who cut themselves and bled the way she did would be crying or freaking out. Not Rena. She seemed more annoyed by it than anything else. The lady didn't flinch from the pain or grimace when she put on the butterfly stitches.

Rena McHale was tough as nails and, of course, that only made her more attractive. Damn it all. Why couldn't she be a mousy, waif-type girl or maybe a glamor puss like that blond? After five hundred years, the universe could have thrown him a bone and given Zed a mate that Zander wasn't drawn too.

No such luck.

"Okay," Rena said slowly. She leaned back in her chair and settled her hands in her lap as she gave him a once-over. "Then let's get right to it. What has brought you to Fox Investigations? Something about your brother?"

"Yes. He's lost. I want you to find him."

She studied him silently, as though deciding what to say next. Zander had the distinct impression she was holding something back, but he hadn't a damn clue what it could be.

"My fee is ten thousand dollars. Half up front and half when I find your brother. I have a money-back guarantee. If I don't locate the lost within a week, then you get your deposit fully refunded. No harm, no foul."

Zander didn't flinch when she mentioned the fee, though he sensed she was expecting him to. Based on the modest office space, he also suspected this wasn't her usual fee. Amusement, a feeling he'd practically forgotten, bubbled up. The vixen was trying to play him. He didn't look like a guy with a fat portfolio, and he liked it that way. Between his long hair, the Harley, and his road-weary outfit, most people mistakenly assumed that he was broke.

"My case is *unusual*, and I'm going to need more personal attention than most of your clients."

"Really?" Her eyebrows lifted, and a hint of curiosity flickered in her eyes. "What kind of attention?"

"I want to be involved in the search. My brother was last seen near a ranch in Montana and I—"

"Hang on." Rena held up her injured hand, and a stony look settled in her eyes. "That goes against my policy. I have a *unique* investigation style, and I work alone."

"I'll pay you thirty grand."

Rena stared at him with silent disbelief, the only sound in the office that of a car driving by. Zander held her stare and suppressed a smile. He could tell she wasn't used to being surprised. Add that to her list of attractive qualities.

"Let me make sure I heard you correctly." Rena leaned both elbows on her desk and peered at him intently. "You want to pay me thirty thousand dollars to go *with* you to Montana, and who knows where else, to find your brother?"

"Yes." Zander kept his tone and his expression neutral. "You heard me right."

"No offense, but you don't look like a guy who can throw around that kind of cash."

"I get that a lot." He smirked. "I'd like to get started as soon as possible. We can leave—"

"Sir, I don't know you well enough to tell you how I like my coffee, let alone go on a road trip with you."

"Zed's situation, like your investigative technique, is unique. My presence is required. You're going to have questions, and it'll be easier for everyone involved if I'm there with you to answer them."

"If you have all the answers, why do you need me?" She was smart too.

"I'd like to leave first thing in the morning," he said quietly.

"What makes you think I can, or will, drop everything and leave town tomorrow?" A wicked smirk curved her lips and her eyes crinkled at the corners. "Maybe my husband wouldn't like that."

Zander stilled. Holy shit. The possibility had never even crossed his mind.

"You're married?"

A dark, dangerous surge of jealousy boiled up, and the muscles in his neck and shoulders tensed. Something deadly curled and stretched inside his chest, reminiscent of a time long ago. It was as if his dragon, buried deep within his soul and long dormant, had suddenly awakened.

But that was impossible.

"Are you?" he asked in a barely audible voice. "Married? Do you have a family?"

The amusement that had edged those brown eyes seconds ago faded, and she shifted in her chair as though suddenly uncomfortable. Her energy signature skittered around him, reflecting her uneasiness and confirming his suspicions.

"No." She moved a small green paperweight in the shape of a frog and briefly avoided his gaze. "Not that it's any of your business, but I'm single. No kids. "

"I see." Tension seeped from his shoulders and the tingling in his chest dissipated. "Then you should have no trouble taking this job."

"You are a piece of work." She laughed. "Just because I'm not married doesn't mean I don't have other responsibilities. Are you one of those eccentric millionaires who never hears the word no? You're used to getting whatever you want?"

Any humor Zander felt vanished. If she only knew how long it had been since he truly had what he desired. More years than he could count.

"No." Zander rose to his feet slowly. Rena mirrored his position. "This isn't a matter of what I want but what my brother needs. This is a case of life and death, to put it bluntly. I'll meet you here at nine tomorrow morning."

He heard her unamused huff as he turned and strode to the door.

"I never said I would take your case, and besides, how do you know I don't have other cases to tend to?"

"Do you?" he asked, turning to face her.

"I have two others on the docket but—"

"They can wait. My brother can't."

Her intelligent gaze bored into his, and her lips lifted at the corners.

"Given the extra money you're paying," she murmured, "I can put off the next two cases for a little while. I'll still only give you a week though."

"Good. You're hired."

"Wait. You haven't told me—"

"We'll have plenty of time to talk on the road."

"You really are something else, aren't you?" She laughed softly and folded her arms over her breasts. "First of all, there's paperwork you need to fill out *if* you really want to hire me. And if you're telling me we need to go to Montana, that would require travel arrangements. The travel agency downstairs books all my flights and so forth but—"

"I don't fly," Zander said flatly.

"What?" A look of disbelief washed over her. "Who doesn't fly in this day and age?"

"Me."

"Why not?" she asked incredulously.

"Men don't belong in the sky." He suppressed the whisper of irritation he felt every time he thought of the way humans had taken over the skies—skies he and his people used to dominate. "It goes against the natural order of the universe."

"So does a parent abandoning their kid, but that didn't stop mine."

A pang of empathy tugged at Zander. He had been alone for centuries, and long ago had mourned the loss of his family, but at least he had known the love of his parents. This woman had no one. Her Amoveo relatives and her human parent had obviously shunned her.

It made sense, then, that she would be a seeker of the lost. She herself was among them.

"I'm sorry," he said quietly.

"Oh well. I'm over it." The tone of her voice was light, and she waved it off as though she didn't care, but he sensed sorrow beneath it. "I got a raw deal in the family department, but life goes on."

"You seem to have done all right for yourself in spite of it."

"Thanks."

She stared at him wordlessly for a few seconds.

"Your offer is for real? Thirty grand to find your brother—*if* I go with you."

"Yes."

Zander pulled the Ray-Bans from the collar of his T-shirt and slipped them on before tugging the door open. The amber light from the late-afternoon sun spilled into the room and lit up the red highlights in Rena's hair as she stood studying him from behind her desk.

"Coffee?"

"What?" She blinked.

"How do you take it?"

"Uh." A look of confusion flickered over her face. "Black."

Made sense. A woman like her wouldn't want or need to sweeten her coffee.

"See you tomorrow. Nine sharp."

"I'll be here." Rena waved at him with her injured hand. "See you then."

He sensed that she didn't believe him or his offer, but that was fine, because he had a hunch convincing her was going to be half the fun. Maybe he could do a little more persuading over drinks tonight.

The smug smile on his lips faltered as he straddled his Harley. What the hell was he doing? He wasn't here to flirt with this woman over drinks. She wasn't *his*, and boozing it up with her at a bar would only confuse matters.

Besides, there were only six more days until the anniversary. He didn't have time to dick around. If she didn't connect with Zed and awaken him by the time the sun set on All Hallows' Eve, his brother would remain trapped forever.

Zander started the bike and revved the engine. A whisper of awareness tripped up his spine as he became mindful of someone watching him. Sure enough, Rena stood in the window of her office, her steely gaze pinned to him. Her energy signature pulsed faster and swirled around him like a tornado. Looked like he wasn't the only one affected by their encounter.

A slow grin slid across his face, and he tipped his head to her before pulling away from the curb. Well, maybe one drink wouldn't hurt.

Chapter 4

RENA WAS LATE, AND SHE HATED BEING LATE TO ANYTHING, but after the bizarre visit from her dream man who turned out to be a *real* man, she was way behind schedule. She tugged open the front door of Dino's Place, and her eyes quickly adjusted to the dim light inside the fifties-themed bar. She'd always had great eyesight, even in the dark. Tonight, however, it seemed particularly sharp, because it only took about two seconds to spot Patricia's annoyed expression.

"I'm sorry!" Rena hurried over, trying not to trip on her heels, and gathered Pat in a huge bear hug. "I know, I know. I'm late, and it's your birthday, and I suck. Drinks on me all night."

"You're lucky I love you." Pat kissed her cheek before swiping at what was surely a red lipstick streak. "You're gonna have to catch up with me. Dino already bought me a couple of birthday rounds."

"Thanks, Dino," Rena shouted. She waved at the owner who was, as usual, dressed like a member of the Rat Pack and working behind the bar.

A Frank Sinatra tune filled the small club, and Rena noted they were the only two customers in the place. It was still early, as it was a Tuesday night in September, but she couldn't help but feel sorry for Dino. Business was slower than usual.

"Come on." Pat grabbed her hand and tugged her

over to the small table in the corner. "I already have a drink ready and waiting for you."

She could have kissed her again. If she ever needed a drink, it was tonight. Rena had been off-kilter ever since meeting Mr. Sexy Pants, Zander Lorens. It was rare that a man could capture her attention the way he had, but then again, a guy in her dreams had never turned up in person before. If she were being honest with herself, she hadn't been able to get the hunky, mysterious stranger out of her head since he'd left her office a few hours ago.

There was something about him that Rena couldn't shake, and it wasn't just his lopsided grin or that sexy swagger. There was far more to Zander than met the eye. His energy signature, for one thing. It was as if the residue of it, thick and musky, clung to her like smoke.

Maybe a good stiff drink would help get the man out of her head.

"Thanks."

Rena draped the strap of her small black purse over the back of her chair and sat down. The leather leggings she wore squeaked on the seat as she scooped up her shot glass with shaking fingers. Her body was still humming after the visit from the mysterious Zander Lorens, and she suspected it would be for a while. A shiver rushed up her back when she recalled the way he looked at her. It was like the guy saw right through her. As if he knew her. But that was crazy, because she had never set eyes on him before today.

"Here's to another twirl around the sun and many, many more. Happy birthday, girl."

The two friends tossed back the shots, which were quickly followed by sucking on a sour slice of lemon.

Patricia giggled and turned her shot glass over on the small, round table, placing it next to the two others she'd had before Rena got there. Patricia loved to party, and if she kept going, Rena was going to be babysitting her later that night.

"You okay, doll? You look weird. Like freaked out or something."

"Yeah." Rena laughed shakily. "I'm sorry I kept you waiting but—"

"Come on." Patricia giggled and playfully slapped Rena's arm. "I'm not pissed at you for being late if that's what you're worried about. Dino kept me company. So what gives? Why do you look like you seen a ghost or something?"

Rena fiddled with the lemon rind and bit her lower lip, debating just how much to tell her friend. She knew it was better to keep her gift a secret, but every now and then, Rena longed to be able to share it with someone, to have *somebody* tell her she wasn't a total freak. Patricia didn't know about her gift or whatever you called it, so how could Rena tell her about the supersexy dream guy?

Easy—she couldn't.

There were moments, like this one, when the burden of keeping her power a secret weighed on her more than the gift itself.

"Some guy came into the office and said he wanted to pay me thirty grand to go with him to Montana to find his brother. Can you believe that? Sure. Pull the other leg. I mean, the guy looked like he didn't have two cents to rub together, let alone a small fortune."

"Thirty grand!" Patricia pulled out a cigarette and lit it. "Honey, for that kind of money, I'd go almost anywhere."

"Tell me about it. That would pay for Vito to stay at Sunnyfarm for the next year and then some! It's not like I'm hurting for cases, far from it, but it would be nice to have some extra financial wiggle room."

"You gonna take it? That's a lot of dough."

"There's *no way* his offer was for real. I'm telling you, there is no chance this man has that kind of money." Rena waved her hand in a dismissive gesture. "I'll believe it if he shows up with the cash. Until then, I'm not counting on anything."

"Are you sure? I mean, like, why would some random guy come to your office and make something like that up?"

"Who knows? Maybe he was casing the place to see if there was anything worth stealing. Maybe he's plain old crazy. I'm leaning toward the crazy option. This is Vegas, and we've got plenty of whackos lurking in the shadows."

Rena wasn't sure if she was referring to him or herself.

"I guess you didn't get one of your infamous hunches about him, huh?"

Rena shook her head.

She could have found out more about him the same way she saw the truth about her other clients. If she'd given him a pen and the clipboard with the client sheet to fill out, all Rena would have had to do was take those items back. Two seconds later, she'd have gotten a bird's-eye view into the guy's mind.

But she hadn't done that.

She had been so freaked out by his arrival, she hadn't even wanted to shake the guy's hand. In hindsight, it had been a stupid choice, but her head had been spinning, and the cut on her hand had hurt like hell. It was all she could do to keep her game face on and maintain some kind of composure.

"No," she whispered. "No hunches."

"Hey." Patricia pointed at Rena's bandage. "What the hell did you do to yourself?"

"I broke a glass. Right before Mr. Fake Client barged into my office."

"No way. He just, like, stormed in?"

"He said he heard glass breaking and, well, *supposedly* he thought there was trouble and wanted to help. If you want to know the truth, *he's* the one who looked like trouble."

There had been darkness layered within his distinctly unusual spirit stream that was unlike any she had encountered before. It was fuzzy. Unclear and muddled somehow but, at the same time, stronger, thicker, and more powerful than any other person she had ever met. Of course, that only intrigued her more. The truth was, everything about her mystery visitor piqued her curiosity.

Maybe it was because she couldn't figure him out. After all, with her power, nobody on earth could hide from her. But this man could and did. That was it—it was her inability to read him like an open book that turned her on. He challenged her, and when was the last time anyone had done that?

Rena's body warmed as she recalled the fierce expression stamped onto his ruggedly handsome face. The shaggy dark hair had drifted over his eyes, partially obscuring her view of his piercing, green stare. There was something savage about him and dangerous that lurked beneath his calm exterior. She sensed it in his spirit stream, but she could also see it in his eyes.

She told herself the shimmery heat whispering under her skin was from the tequila. But that would only have been partially true. Her cheeks heated as she recalled his unwavering stare and the way he had studied her with unsettling, quiet intensity. Had anyone ever looked at her so thoroughly before?

Nope.

Zander had turned the tables on Rena, and she had been the one under the microscope. For once, she was intrigued by the idea of letting someone see past her facade. It was terrifying and exhilarating all at the same time. What would it be like, to allow another person to see everything and expose the most intimate aspects of her soul?

A rush of excitement fired through her at the thought of it.

"He was a hottie, huh?" Patricia gave her a sly smile. "I mean, he musta been. You're blushing."

"No. I mean, yes. I mean. Gah!" She was stumbling over her words, trying to explain it to Pat without blurting out the whole story. "He was totally strange. Add the encounter with him to the weird-ass dreams I've been having lately, and I can chalk today up to a big bag of crazy. Never mind. I'm exhausted, and my lack of sleep is starting to show."

"I dunno, girl. Maybe you need a little crazy. All work and no play is no way to go through life. *In fact*, I met a hottie today myself. *And* I invited him to join us for a drink."

"You didn't." Rena groaned. "I thought you were going to try the single life for a while?"

"I didn't ask him here for me." She arched her back and stretched her long arms over her head and winked at Dino. "Unlike you, I have no trouble getting laid."

Rena glanced over her shoulder and caught the bartender staring at them before he turned his attention back to drying the glass in his hand.

"No way," Rena whispered. "You and Dino?"

"Yeah." Patricia's eyes twinkled with childlike giddiness. "He's sweet."

"When and how?" Rena shook her head and leaned over the table toward her friend. "Let's go. Start talking."

"A couple of weeks ago, I ran into him at the grocery store by the butcher counter, and we started chatting about which cut of beef we liked best and, well, you know. Things just kinda went on from there. He's not like the guys I usually go for, but he's nice, and I could use a little nice in my life, you know? He treats me like a princess, and a girl could get used to that."

Rena's heart squeezed in her chest as Pat quickly swiped at her teary eyes. Pat's track record with men was less than stellar, and if anyone deserved a man to be good to her, it was Patricia Langan, Vegas showgirl with a heart of gold.

"Yeah," Rena whispered. "She sure could."

"*Any*way." Patricia sniffled and adjusted her boobs, which looked like they were about to pop out of her top. "You shoulda seen this guy I met today. Holy cow. I seriously think my ovaries almost exploded when I saw him. We're talking melt-your-panties hot. The fact he was riding a big-ass Harley didn't hurt either. Sexy as all get-out."

"A motorcycle?" Rena grabbed Pat's hand, and panic

shimmered in her chest. "Honey, where did you meet this guy?"

"Outside your office. Why?"

Rena licked her suddenly dry lips and fought to find her voice. She would say this was a coincidence, but Rena didn't believe in accidents. In her experience, everything happened for a reason.

"Sh-shaggy, dark hair, Ray-Bans, and a leather jacket?" A knot of nerves curled in her gut along with a whisper of lust. "And really beautiful, light-green eyes?"

"Yes!" Patricia's face brightened, and a huge, red-lipped smile bloomed on her face. "His name is—"

"Zander," Rena said quietly. "Zander Lorens."

All the hairs raised along the nape of her neck when a now-familiar spirit stream wafted into the bar as his name slid from her lips like silk.

Rena turned toward the source just as the door of the bar swung open and a hulking, broad-shouldered silhouette filled the space. He stepped inside, and the door swung shut behind him. Even in the dim light, she couldn't miss those strikingly pale-green eyes, which were pinned directly to hers. Rena's heart raced, sweat broke out on her brow, and she was unable to move beneath the weight of his gaze.

Wearing the same outfit from earlier today but with the sunglasses notably absent, Zander Lorens strode into the club, which suddenly felt much more crowded. How could one man fill a room simply by stepping into it?

"And he's here."

"Oh my God!" Patricia shrieked. Tossing both hands in the air, she hopped off the chair and scurried over to Zander. "I'm so happy you showed up."

Zander accepted Patricia's bouncy hug. His glittering eyes peered at Rena between strands of dark hair, and her stomach somersaulted in response.

"Dino!" Pat grabbed Zander's hand and brought him over to the table. "This is the guy I was tellin' you about, baby. The one I wanted Rena to meet."

Zander nodded at the bartender, and Rena quickly smoothed her long black-and-blue silk tank top. She crossed her legs and tried to look casual but was pretty sure she failed miserably. It was rare for her to be surprised once, let alone twice in a day, but this man sure as shit had done it.

"As fate would have it," Patricia purred, "it turns out you two already met."

"Hello again," Zander murmured.

Rena gave him a tight smile but said nothing. She wasn't used to being caught off guard, and it was beginning to feel like Zander was born to make her feel that way.

"Hang on a sec." Patricia grabbed another chair and pulled it over. "Have a seat, Zander. What do you want from the bar? First round is on Dino. Right, baby?"

"Whatever you say." Dino waved. "It's your birthday, kitten."

"You're the best, babe." Patricia sidled in behind Zander and patted his wide shoulders with both hands while making an oh-my-God face at Rena. "What'll it be, my friend?"

"I'll take whatever beer you have on tap." His lips tilted up at the corners, and his voice was low and gruff. Rena could swear she practically felt it skitter over her flesh. "Thank you."

An Elvis Presley song came on over the speakers. Rena wasn't sure which one, because she was too busy trying to figure out what the hell was up with this guy.

He was different from anyone she'd ever met before. For starters, nobody else had ever appeared in her dreams *before* being in her *actual* life. And very few people surprised her or intrigued her. This guy did both.

"Nice to see you again, Ms. McHale."

"Unexpected." She narrowed her eyes and folded her arms over her breasts, hoping to quell her quivering body. "But you don't seem all that surprised."

He leaned back in the chair and his legs splayed out, taking up space the way only a cocky man could. His long fingers laced together in his lap as he studied her boldly. Rena had been hit on plenty of times, but there was usually some sly game that came with it. Not this man. He oozed confidence and something else she couldn't quite put her finger on. Zander looked like he was maybe in his midtwenties, but he had a worldly air about him, as though he had lived several lifetimes instead of only one.

"I'm not."

His voice was quiet and deep; most people wouldn't even have heard him over the music, but Rena's hearing was unusually acute. Even the steady sound of his breathing rose above the din of the club. It was more than that though. He was inescapable. Everything about him surged over and around her, like some kind of spiritual tsunami.

"Are you stalking me or something?"

"No. Your friend invited me here, and since I'm trying to hire you, I figured it couldn't hurt to come by.

You didn't seem all that convinced by my offer earlier, and time is of the essence."

"Right. It's not every day someone walks into Fox Investigations and offers to pay me that kind of money."

"Why Fox?"

"Excuse me?" She blinked at the sudden shift in the conversation. Everything about Zander Lorens was throwing her off her game, and she didn't like it one bit. She was the one who threw people off, making them uncomfortable. It had never been the other way around.

Until now.

"The name of your company. Why is it called Fox Investigations?"

"It was my friend Vito Fox's business, and after I took it over, I never bothered changing the name. He trained me. It felt wrong to mess with it. He's the closest thing to family that I've got. Besides, I've always had a thing for foxes. They're cute."

Rena crossed her legs and didn't miss the way his gaze flicked over her with appreciation. He was studying her as closely as she was him, and it gave her the distinct impression she was being hunted. In the game of cat and mouse, Rena was used to being the cat, but Zander Lorens was no mouse.

He wasn't prey. He was a hunter, just like her, and she hated to admit it, but it turned her on.

"You're loyal," he said quietly. "Good. I like that."

"Yes, I am." She draped her elbow over the back of her chair and leveled a challenging gaze at him. "Especially to Vito."

"Why?"

"That's an awfully personal question." Rena let out a

curt, incredulous laugh and shook her head. "You want to do business, so let's do business. You have thirty grand you want to pay me, and if you have the cash, then we have a deal."

"Actually," he began slowly. "I think my initial offer was off the mark."

"I knew it," Rena said with a smile. "Let me guess. You are no longer offering thirty thousand dollars?"

"No." He shook his head slowly. "I'm not."

Rena glanced over to the bar to call Patricia over for a get-a-load-of-this-guy moment, but Patricia was taking her sweet time getting the beer and canoodling with Dino. Rena was on her own. She turned back, ready to lambaste him for being full of it, but her mind went blank when Zander slapped a huge brick of cash onto the table.

She blinked. *Where the hell did that come from?*

"Thirty now and thirty *after* we find my brother."

His long, strong-looking fingers slid from the huge, crisp stack of hundreds, and Rena licked her suddenly dry lips. *Focus, Rena.* She kept her sights on the money while she sharpened her connection with his spirit stream. It pulsed slowly and steadily around her with the same cool confidence he exhibited on the surface. If he was a liar, then he was one of the best she had ever met. There wasn't a hint of nervousness or uneasiness.

The man was as smooth as a razor's edge.

She flicked her eyes to his, and her heart skipped a beat.

And twice as sharp.

Rena glanced back at the cash but didn't make a move to touch it.

"Sixty thousand dollars?" she whispered. "Are you serious?"

"After our meeting earlier today, I realized that asking you to go with me on a road trip to find my brother was a bigger deal than I'd originally thought it was." He lifted one shoulder in an oddly casual gesture. "You know how it is. Sometimes we get an idea in our heads that seems normal, but then when we say it out loud, well, it's not."

"Do you always walk around with a brick of hundreds?"

"No." He smirked. "This is Las Vegas. Getting your hands on some cash is pretty easy."

"*Some* cash?" She pointed at the stack of bills. "Did you hit the jackpot on the slots or something?"

"I earned it. Every penny." All humor left his face. "Let's just say I've invested well over the years."

"Over the years? What are you? Twenty-five? Twenty-eight? Did you start investing when you were four?"

His spirit stream flickered, and his eyes narrowed almost imperceptibly. The change was subtle, and if Rena hadn't been looking for it, she may not even have noticed it. Like a record skipping or a hiccup, and gone as quickly as it came, but there was no mistaking the change when she challenged him.

She had obviously touched a nerve of some kind, and it didn't escape her attention that he hadn't answered her question regarding his age. *Interesting.* A slow smile curved her lips. It was something of a comfort to know this guy wasn't infallible and that she'd rattled *his* cage for a change.

"Aren't you going to count it and make sure I didn't fill it with blank paper?"

"Did you?"

"Only one way to find out." His eyes crinkled at the corners. "Go on. Count it. I won't be insulted."

Rena slid her hand slowly across the slightly damp surface of the wood table, but her eyes remained locked with his. He was challenging her, daring her to call him on his bluff or merely gloating because he came through with money she'd never thought he really had. Excitement swirled in her belly as he threw down the proverbial gauntlet.

Rena loved a challenge, probably because she was so rarely faced with one.

"Fine." Her hand hovered over the chunk of bills, still not touching them. "While I do this, why don't you head over to the bar and find out why Patricia is taking so long with your beer?"

"Happy to." Zander rose slowly to his feet. He leaned both hands on the table and moved in so his face was scant inches from hers. "I trust you won't run off with all my money."

Rena sucked in a deep breath, and her head was filled the scent of leather and a musky cologne of some kind. Or was that simply *him*? Sex. He smelled like great sex—at least that's what her passion-starved brain told her. Rena swallowed the sudden lump in her throat and forced herself to form a coherent sentence.

"It's a little early in our relationship to be talking about trust," she murmured. "Don't you think?"

"No, I don't." Zander's pale-green eyes shimmered between strands of dark hair. "And we don't have a *relationship*. It's business, Ms. McHale. Like you said. Not personal. I am hiring you to find my brother. That's it."

Her jaw fell open. *What the hell?*

Before she could come up with any kind of retort, he pushed himself off the table and strode to the bar, where Patricia and Dino were waiting. Rena couldn't help but allow her eyes to wander over the full length of him. He looked as good from the back as he did from the front. The black leather jacket and dark-gray T-shirt, emblazoned with some punk rock band logo, concealed what looked like a well-sculpted torso. His well-worn Levi's fit him exactly the way a pair of jeans should fit a man— hugged his ass and covered his long legs with perfection.

Zander glanced over his shoulder just in time to catch her staring at his ass. Her cheeks flamed, and she quickly looked back at the money. He was right. If she was going to take this job, then the only thing between them could be business. It was unethical to get involved with a client.

Even if he was the sexiest and most desirable man she had ever set eyes on.

Rena let out a long, slow breath. It was now or never. She'd been holding out long enough, and even if she didn't take the gig, at the very least, she was going to find out what Zander Lorens's story was. She let out a curt laugh because, in about two seconds, she was going to know way more about him than he likely wanted her to.

Bracing herself for the change in her environment she knew was inevitable, Rena curled her fingers around the paper-banded stacks of hundreds, and in a split second, the bar and all the people in it vanished.

A buzzing sound, one only Rena could hear, grew louder, and then she was blinded. Rena fought for a sense of calm as she waited for the world around her to become clear again. She hated this part. It was like being thrown in a murky, foggy limbo land. Nothing and no one was real. Not even her. This place, amorphous and intangible, made her feel like she was dissolving into nothingness.

A tiny part of her, one she rarely entertained, feared that if she stayed there too long, she would never find her way back and end up lost in the fog forever.

Rena pushed harder, needing to immerse herself in Zander's memories so she could see it all. A bright light flashed, and pain blazed through her chest—it was like having a red-hot poker jammed into her breastbone. She fought the urge to cry out, but the glimmer of fear abated when the ground was solid once again beneath her feet.

No longer sitting in the dark, moody bar, she was now inside one of Zander's memories. Rena laughed softly, feeling a strong sense of accomplishment, and glanced around, but the smile faded when she realized she was standing in an all-too-familiar space.

This was the forest from her dream. The one with the monsters.

A rumbling sound, one she could feel deep inside her chest, filled the woods, and a blast of hot air puffed over her from behind. Zander's spirit stream swirled around her, and she knew he was there.

Rena mustered up the courage to turn around. She was as terrified as she was curious about what she would find.

With her gaze pinned to the leaf-covered ground, Rena spun around slowly, and a gasp escaped her lips when an enormous pair of clawed feet came into view. They looked like they belonged to a mammoth bird, but the scaly skin, a blackish brown with flashes of iridescent reds and golds, didn't look like any she'd seen before. Her heart skipped several beats as her gaze moved slowly upward, taking in the massive beast before her.

It was larger than life, right out of the pages of a fairy tale—a dragon.

Sitting on its hind legs, it had to be almost thirty feet tall. The animal's thick, muscular body was covered in the same scaly skin as its feet, but a lighter shade of red bathed its chest and belly. A huge pair of wings were tucked in above its back. Curved, razor-sharp-looking talons on the feet were almost identical to the ones on its hands.

The beast was a magnificent combination of breath-taking beauty and otherworldly power.

Instinctively needing to put space between her and the mythical creature, Rena backed up and fought to find her breath, which seemed to have stopped all together. When her butt hit the rough bark of a tree, she let out a yelp. A split second later, the beast dropped its clawed hands to the ground. The force of the impact shook the earth, and Rena felt it in her bones.

Standing on all fours, the dragon lowered its massive head so it was almost face-to-face with Rena. Glowing, crimson-colored eyes peered at her beneath two long, curved horns, which seemed to be extensions of the creature's eyebrows. The horns gleamed like satin. About the same shade of red as its eyes, they were matched by a series of spikes that littered the spine and stretched all the way down the tail, which the beast had curled around its body like a cat.

All that I am is yours. I give you my heart and my life. I would never harm you, my love.

There was no mistaking it. That was Zander's voice coming from the creature and tumbling in Rena's mind like ribbons of velvet. Smooth and rich. The dragon's mouth didn't move, but the voice definitely came from the beast. The beast with Zander's spirit stream was speaking telepathically.

Zander was the dragon?

It rested its snout on its clawed hands, and its eyes fluttered closed. With no thought to the consequences, driven totally by instinct and moving through the memories of another, Rena reached out to touch it.

MINE!

Another dragon, identical in color and size, flew down from the sky as its rage-filled cry shattered the night. Its winged body blocked out the light of the moon, darkening the forest that had been serene and silent only moments ago. Rena tumbled to the ground, and the intruding beast's burning, hateful gaze was the last image that filled her mind.

"Rena!" A strong hand curled around her shoulder and shook her gently. "Hey, are you all right?"

Rena blinked rapidly as the fog of the vision lifted and the world around her came back into sharp focus. Zander's worried gaze was the first thing she saw. Pat and Dino stood right behind him with equally concerned expressions.

The dragon was gone, but the voice was the same. Zander was definitely the dragon, but that was crazy, wasn't it?

People couldn't turn into dragons.

Hell, the damn things weren't even real.

Rena's gift allowed her to slip into the past and visit the memories of other people, but how the hell could *that* scenario have been one of Zander's *memories*?

There was no such thing as dragons.

Yeah right. And there was no such thing as getting visions either.

"You okay, sweetie?" Dino had his arm around Patricia's waist, and he wiped his sweaty, balding head with his free hand. "It's like you were sleeping with your eyes open or something."

Rena sucked in a shuddering breath and tried to appear more confident than she felt. Coming out of her visions was never a problem, but she rarely took the chance in front of other people. She scolded herself for the foolhardy move and forced a smile.

"Musta been getting her hands on all that dough." Patricia let out a weak laugh. "Right?"

"Dough?"

Rena blinked and then looked down at her lap. The brick of cash was clenched tightly between her fingers. Her face heated with embarrassment, and she promptly put it back on the table.

"Musta been," Zander murmured.

His palm, warm and rough, slipped from her bare arm as he slowly rose to his feet with an expression on his face that hovered between concerned and curious.

Damn it. This was mortifying. At least she hadn't fainted or fallen out of her chair or anything.

"Jeez, doll," Patricia snorted. "You were, like, totally spaced-out. *Again*."

"Again?" Zander asked. "This sort of things happens a lot?"

"Pfft, yeah it does. She usually gets one of her crazy hunches after she spaces out like that. Don't ya?"

"Patricia," Rena said in a warning tone. "I'm fine. I-I was just thinking about something."

"Uh-huh." Pat gave her a skeptical look. "I thought you were gonna go see the doctor about that spacing-out stuff. I told you it could be seizures or something. I saw a documentary all about it."

Rena let out a small laugh, and some of the tension in the room eased back. Patricia loved documentaries about weird medical problems. Maybe Rena should ask her if she ever watched one about dragons and psychics.

"I'm fine." Rena pushed the hair off her forehead and adjusted her position in the chair. "Really."

"Are you sure?" Zander asked quietly. He sat in the chair across from her. "You were definitely…elsewhere."

"Yes. I'm sure." She waved her hand dismissively. "I'm just tired. I haven't been sleeping well lately."

"Bad dreams?"

Rena stilled, and her eyes locked with his.

Son of a bitch.

He *knew*.

Somehow, this man knew about her gift or her dreams or *something*.

Then again, after what she saw in his memories, why would that surprise her? Not only had she dreamed of him, but she was also seeing him as a dragon in his memories. This was too damn weird. She had absolutely no idea what was happening, but she was sure as hell going to find out.

"Maybe you should go home," Patricia said, "and get some sleep."

"You're right, Pat. I've got a big week ahead." She grabbed the brick of cash and quickly put it in her purse. "As of tomorrow, Mr. Lorens and I will be on our way to Montana."

"What made you change your mind?" His voice was quiet and gruff. "Was it the money or…something else?"

His eyes searched hers, and a spark of awareness flickered in the air between them. A connection. A sputtering moment where one soul recognized the other. But like a flame in the wind, it vanished as swiftly as it appeared, making her wonder if it had been there at all.

"Like you said earlier." Rena lifted one shoulder, attempting to be matter of fact about it all. "I'm going to have questions, and you're the only one with the answers. Right?"

Silence hung between them for three beats of her heart, and for a nanosecond, Rena thought she had made a horrible mistake. Maybe her sleep-starved brain was making more out of this situation than was really there. Was her mind creating images of dragons when there were only clouds in the sky?

Or was Zander Lorens the answer to her lifelong questions?

"Right." Zander rose to his feet. "I'll meet you at your office in the morning. Nine sharp."

"O-okay. But let's make it eight. There's still paperwork to fill out and our travel arrangements."

"I'll cover all of the travel."

"You said you that you don't fly, so—"

"We'll be taking my Harley. It's about a sixteen-hour trip, give or take, and I've already mapped the route, including the stops along the way. I figure we can do it in three days if the weather holds up."

"You expect me to ride on the back of your motorcycle all the way to Montana?"

"Doll, for sixty grand, you're lucky he ain't makin' you walk," Patricia said through a snort of laughter.

"Honey," Dino interjected, "why don't we let them finish this in private? It's business. Right?"

"Right," Rena and Zander said in unison.

A small smile curved Zander's firm-looking lips, and Rena couldn't help but smile back as Dino and Pat made themselves scarce. An awkward silence swelled between them, and Rena quickly tore her gaze from his.

"Have you ever ridden a motorcycle before?"

"Nope."

"A virgin, huh?"

"What?" Rena's heart lurched in her chest, and her eyes flew to his. "No. I mean, I've had a few boyfriends but—"

Zander's pale-green eyes crinkled at the corners, and her stomach fluttered as wildly as her heart. He wasn't talking about sex. Rena's cheeks flamed, and she gaped at him while trying to figure out how to take her foot out of her mouth.

"It's okay, Rena." Zander winked. "All you have to do is hold on tight and let me drive."

Desire surged, and Rena couldn't have suppressed the smile if she'd tried. She had no idea what Zander's deal was, but she knew it was going to be fun as hell trying to figure it out.

"That won't be a problem, Mr. Lorens, at least when we're on your motorcycle." Rena rose slowly from her

seat and extended her hand. "You have yourself a private investigator."

Zander flicked his gaze to her fingers briefly before
gathering them in his far larger hand. When his flesh,
rough and manly, connected with hers, a shiver of
awareness tripped along her skin and made her catch her
breath. His eyes widened, and the hint of smile lingered
there, as though he knew exactly the kind of effect he
had on her. He squeezed her hand lightly and ran his
thumb over the sensitive flesh before letting her go.

"And you have yourself a client, Ms. McHale."

Without another word, Zander strode out the door.
Rena kept her eyes on the entrance to the club, half wishing he would come back and at the same time praying he
wouldn't. She settled back into her seat with far more
questions than she should have when taking on a case.

Rena was treading in uncharted territory on every
single level.

When she'd touched the money Zander had given
her, she had fully expected to find all the answers she
was looking for but instead ended up with a ton more
questions. Why the hell was he in her dreams, and *why*
would she see him as a dragon in *his* memories? Why
had she agreed to take this case and run off to Montana
with a total stranger when she didn't know a damn thing
about him?

It came to one major leap of faith *and* her insatiable
need to know the truth.

Rena knew, deep in her gut, that helping Zander
Lorens find his brother would also help her discover
more about herself. He was the first person she had ever
met who was as full of oddities as she was.

For the first time in her life, Rena believed she would get the answers she had been looking for. The blank spaces, the ones that haunted her, would finally be filled.

"Are you sure about this, Rena?" Patricia hurried over to the table and looked at Rena with genuine concern. "I mean, what if he's a crazy psycho serial killer or somethin'? I saw a documentary about guys like that, but I'll admit none of 'em were as hot as Zander."

"I can take care of myself, and I'll be taking my gun with me. I'll be fine."

"I dunno. I know you're tough, but maybe you should find out more about this guy before you just take off with him?"

"That's exactly why I'm going. I need more answers," Rena said quietly. "His brother isn't the only one who's lost."

Chapter 5

FOR THE FIRST TIME IN AGES, ZANDER DIDN'T BATTLE WITH Zed in the dreamrealm while he slept. There was only one other phase during his five hundred years when he hadn't relived that fateful battle in his dreams.

At the turn of the last millennium, Zander had an epiphany that basically added up to *Screw it*. None of his attempts to break the curse had worked. He was pissed off, tired, and had finally resigned himself to his fate. He drank himself into oblivion for more nights than he could count, because that was the only thing that would keep the dreams at bay.

Until it wouldn't.

Zed eventually came to him again in the dreamrealm, tortured and confused, and after hearing his brother's tormented soul, Zander knew he couldn't give up. He had to find a way to break this damned curse and free Zed from his brutal existence. His brother was still reliving the horrible moment that had sealed both their fates and destroyed the only woman he had ever loved, Arianna.

The only woman *they both* had loved.

Until last night.

No dreams. No Zed. No Arianna. No Rena. Nothing.

It had been the single most restful night of his unusually long existence. When he awoke in his hotel room, it took him a minute to realize he had slept at all. He wasn't sure how or why his sleep had been dreamless, but the early-morning sun streaming through the cracks of the drapes of his hotel room confirmed his suspicions.

Zander should have been grateful, but instead, he was left feeling out of sorts, off his game. He suspected the absence of dreams had something to do with Rena's presence. Maybe Zed had recognized her, and they made a mate connection in the dreamrealm last night? If they had, then it made sense Zander would be shut out. After all, the first place that mates connected was in their dreams, and only then could they make contact in the physical realm.

An odd feeling of emptiness swelled in his chest. His hunch about the woman had to be correct. Rena *must* be Zed's mate. That was the only explanation that made any sense.

His brother's mate. Not *his*. Good. It was as it should be.

If she had connected with Zed in the dreamrealm, then it would make the rest of the journey even easier. Things were going better than he could have hoped.

So why didn't he *feel* any better?

He paid the old man at the deli before picking up the coffee tray and small, brown bag. Zander's gaze skittered over the street, scanning the area for any danger. It was a habit he'd picked up soon after being cursed. Without the keen senses of his dragon, or any of the other powers that came with it, Zander had learned how to navigate the world as a man for all intents and purposes.

Albeit an immortal man.

Coffee tray in hand, Zander trotted up the steps of Rena's building. He had to keep his focus on getting Rena to Zed and lifting the curse. Nothing else mattered except freeing his brother and, if there was any kind of justice in the universe, maybe himself too.

When he reached Rena's office door, he paused for a moment to steel his resolve. There was no denying he was attracted to her, but she wasn't for him, and it was a fact he had to keep mind; otherwise, history would surely repeat itself.

"I know you're out there! I heard you coming up the stairs." Her voice was muffled but welcoming. "Come on in. We have paperwork to deal with."

Zander balanced the coffee tray carefully and opened the door before quickly stepping inside. His secret hope that she would somehow be less attractive than yesterday was swiftly squelched when he got an eyeful of her. Wearing a well-fitted brown leather jacket, a clingy black blouse, jeans that seemed to be painted onto her rounded derriere, and a pair of tall, black boots, she looked even more desirable than the day before.

He must have stood there staring for longer than was socially acceptable, because the look on her face quickly shifted to one of concern.

"What?" She brushed at her blouse and closed the file cabinet drawer. "Did I get something on my shirt?"

"No." He looked away quickly and adjusted the tray of coffee in his hands. "You look fine."

"Gee, thanks," Rena said with a sigh. "Just the level of awesome I was going for."

He had insulted her. Perfect. Sure. This was *exactly* how he wanted to start their journey. Could he be a bigger asshat? Rena must have been asking herself the same question, because she gave him the side eye before opening the folder in her hands.

"Please, sit down." She slipped into the chair behind her desk and gestured to the seat across from her. "I have the forms you need to fill out a—"

"Black, right?" Zander placed the cardboard cup on the desk along with the bag and sat in the chair across from her. "I wasn't sure what you wanted for breakfast, so I got a couple of options. There's a chocolate doughnut, a bagel, and in case you're one of those noncarb eaters, I threw in some beef jerky and a cheese stick."

"Thank you," Rena said slowly.

She stared at the coffee for a few seconds before finally picking it up. Her energy signature rippled as her fingers curled around the cup, and those big, brown eyes widened slightly. He had obviously surprised her. Good. He liked knowing he could ruffle her tough exterior. This was a woman who tried to act like she had it all together, and for the most part, she probably did.

Zander blew on the steaming cup in his hands and tried to hide a satisfied smirk. Rena studied him warily and opened the lid, peeking at the liquid inside before closing it up again.

"You did say you take your coffee black, didn't you?"

"Yes." The word fell from her lips slowly. "Thank you."

She glanced in the bag and, to his great delight, pulled out the chocolate doughnut and proceeded to take a big bite.

"That's really flipping delicious," she said around a mouthful of the pastry.

"I'm glad you're enjoying it. It's refreshing to meet a woman who isn't afraid to indulge in something sweet or worried about getting fat."

He liked women with curves. It gave a man something

to hold on to, and Rena McHale certainly had a body he would—

What the hell was he thinking?

Zander cleared his throat and sat up straighter in the chair. Rena was about to take another bite, but the doughnut hovered in midair, and she gave him yet another look that told him he was an idiot.

"I'm not saying you need to watch your weight. I just meant that—"

"Don't worry about it," she said, rolling her eyes.

"I'm sorry if I offended you. I'm not great with people, and I put my foot in my mouth a lot."

Why was he bringing her coffee and breakfast, anyway? He should stick to business and keep the pleasantries to a minimum. Trying to be nice was only making it awkward between them.

"Then you and I should get along great," she said with a laugh. "I'm not one to beat around the bush. I prefer being direct."

"Yeah, I noticed."

Rena's intelligent eyes peered at him above the rim of her cup, and she took another sip. Zander stilled as she studied him wordlessly. A surge of heat flashed in his chest as he held her gaze, and even though he wanted to blame it on the hot coffee, he knew that would have been a lie. There was no denying that she stirred something inside him, a deep, primal urge to claim her and mark her as his, but he also knew it was not to be.

Not if he wanted to free his brother. Keeping her all to himself would have been selfish, and it was that kind of bullshit that had gotten them into trouble in the first place.

"You mentioned paperwork," he said quietly.

"Yes." Rena blinked and shook her head. "Sorry, I spaced out there for a second."

"Do you do that a lot?"

Her energy signature skittered around him nervously. She looked away and put some papers and a pen in front of him on the desk. When her body language matched the shift in her energy pattern, he realized what it was. She was hiding something, and it had to be connected to the way she spaced out here in the office and last night at the bar.

And he was damn sure going to find out what it was.

"I haven't been sleeping well lately."

"I have," he said flatly.

"Yeah, well, if you don't, I highly recommend some of that Nite-Aid stuff. I took one of those babies last night and I was out for the count. Actually, last night was the first good night's sleep I've had in months. I don't know why I didn't think to try some of that stuff sooner."

Son of a bitch.

Rena hadn't connected with Zed last night, or with him, because she'd taken a sleeping pill. Zander's brow furrowed, and a nagging sense of unease shimmied beneath his skin. That explained why Zander wouldn't have seen her in the dreamrealm, but where was Zed? Why wouldn't they have battled again, just as they had every night for the past five centuries?

Rena waved a folder at him. "Are you awake? Looks like I'm not the only one who's tired. Anyway, you need to—"

"I'm not filling out those papers."

"What?" Her brow furrowed. "Why not?"

"I handed you thirty thousand dollars in cash last night, and after we find my brother, I'm going to give you another thirty grand." He lifted one shoulder. "I like my privacy, and unlike most of modern society, I'm not comfortable having my business floating around online or in anyone's filing cabinet. I want absolute discretion. That's part of what I'm paying you for."

A slow grin curved her lips as she scooped up the papers and slipped them back in the folder.

"I figured as much."

"How so?"

"I ran a background check on you." Rena rose to her feet and placed both hands on the desk, leaning toward him. "You don't exist, Mr. Lorens, and in this day and age, that's one hell of an accomplishment. I've never had a client who hadn't left some kind of electronic footprint in the world. No pictures. No social media. I couldn't even find a birth certificate that matched. No businesses or marriages or divorces. Not so much as a parking ticket. Nada. Nothing. Zip."

"Your point?"

"My point is that you are lying about something, Zander Lorens, and I'd have to bet it starts with your name and goes from there." She shoved herself off the desk and settled her hands on her hips. "I don't like being lied to."

"I'm not lying to you." He kept his voice calm and even. "My name is Zander Lorens, and my brother needs your help."

The air was thick with silence and her obvious frustration, but Zander refused to budge. He wasn't lying to her. He wasn't exactly telling her the whole truth either, but how was he supposed to do that?

"I can't work with you if you're not going to be straight with me."

"I need your help finding my brother." He stood up and tossed his empty coffee cup into the small garbage can next to her desk. "His life depends on it, and he's running out of time."

"If you want me to help you, then you have to be honest with me. Who are you?" Her voice wavered. "I know you're not who you're pretending to be, but there's more. For starters, why is there such a time issue? Is he going to turn into a pumpkin at midnight?"

She folded her arms over her breasts, and her energy signature fluttered wildly around him with an unmistakable whisper of fear threaded through it. Damn it. He was cocking this up at every turn. First he insulted her, and now he was scaring her. What the hell could he say or do to put her fears at ease? If he told her the truth, she would call him crazy.

There was no way to prove who and what he really was. Hell, she didn't even know who *she* was.

"What are you hiding, Zander?"

Her energy signature, thick with frustration, rolled around him, and a split second later, Rena's eyes shifted into the glowing amber eyes of her clan. There was no doubt in his mind which clan she was descended from. Only the Fox Clan had those shimmery, amber eyes flecked with gold. His heart squeezed in his chest because hers were so much like Arianna's had been centuries ago.

Rena's body had an instinctive, involuntary reaction to her intense emotions, and it was exactly what he needed to help his cause. It was also a sign that her connection with Zed in the dreamrealm was moving things forward. Her eyes had shifted twice in the past twenty-four hours. That could only mean the connection with Zed was deepening and her Amoveo powers would continue to emerge.

They were running out of time on all counts.

"Stupid mascara keeps getting in my eyes." Rena swiped at them quickly and let out a hiss of irritation. "I must be allergic to it or something."

"It's not your makeup."

"Oh really?" She smirked. "Wear a lot of mascara, do you?"

"Rena," he whispered. "Turn around."

"Why do you want—"

"Just turn around and look in the mirror." He pointed to the wall behind her desk and slipped his hands in the pockets of his jeans "You'll see."

"Great," she huffed. "What? Do I have it all down my—"

Full of fire, she spun around and was likely ready to give him a piece of her mind, but when Rena caught sight of her reflection, she fell silent. Her mouth opened slowly as a look of utter disbelief washed over her lovely face, and her energy signature whipped around the office like a tornado.

"What on earth?" Her voice shook as she brought her quivering fingers to her cheeks and moved closer to the mirror. "My eyes… They're…"

"Beautiful," Zander murmured.

He meant it too. It had been so many years since he'd seen the clan eyes of an Amoveo, Zander had forgotten how utterly exquisite they could be. A longing swelled in his chest, and a rush of loneliness fired through him. Time had soldiered on, and so had Zander. He'd become accustomed to his solitary existence and rarely lingered on how isolated he had been, but seeing Rena like this made it all painfully real.

Even though his instinct was to move closer, to gather her in his arms and comfort her, he stayed where he was, with the desk between them. He could be her friend and guide her on this journey, but he knew, for his own sanity, there had to be a line in the sand. If he allowed himself to explore the physical attraction—the one he knew was only a product of being Zed's identical twin—it would lead to disaster.

"Why aren't you freaked out by this?" She captured his gaze in the mirror. "D-did you do this to me?"

"No." He kept his voice calm and even. "And you aren't all that freaked out by it either, are you? You're different, Rena. You've always known that."

"I—I know, but...what's happening to me?"

Her voice, a shaky whisper, tugged at Zander's heart, and when one tear rolled down her cheek, he thought it would break him. Sucking in a deep breath, he moved slowly around the desk but still kept some distance between them.

"Your true self, the part of you that has been dormant, has woken up and is beginning to emerge. You are Amoveo, Rena, or at least part Amoveo."

"Amoveo?" Her brow furrowed. "I—I've heard that before...in a dream...but..."

"They are an ancient race of shapeshifters with ten animal clans among them. You are descended from the Fox Clan. Though, I have to admit, you are the first

Amoveo I've met who isn't from a pure bloodline. I didn't even realize they could mate with humans."

"What the hell are you talking about?" She spun to face him, and her surprise was replaced with anger. "*I'm* human. I'm not a shapeshifter. There's no such thing."

"Yes, there is. You are human, *and* you are Amoveo." His mouth set in a grim line. "Had any interesting dreams lately?"

"Oh my God," she said in a breathy rush. "Are the nightmares because of you or something?"

"Not exactly. Dreams play a pivotal role in a shifter's…evolution." He paused, debating whether or not he should mention the part about Zed being her mate. "When you walked in the dreamrealm, it was the first step toward embracing who you really are and your future. The rest of your abilities will manifest over the next few days, and they'll come to full power when you connect with your mate. The dreams come first, then telepathy, and finally the mate tattoo, but—"

"*Mate* tattoo?"

He was pretty sure she had only heard about a quarter of what he had just blurted out. Zander could practically see the wheels turning in her head as she tried to wrap her brain around everything he was dumping on her.

Could he be a bigger moron?

"The man in the dream… He said something about… It *was* you! You were really there," she whispered. Her brows knit together, and an expression of understanding slowly covered her face. "I'm *not* crazy. The voice in my dream… It *was* you in the cave. You saved me from that *thing* that was chasing me and then you told me to pick up…"

Zander removed the lump of quartz from his jacket pocket and held it up between his thumb and forefinger.

"The stone," she whispered. "That's it. It's the same as the one I picked up in the dream. What the hell is going on?"

"It's how I was able to find you, Rena. When you touched this in the dreamrealm, I imprinted on your energy signature, and it led me to you."

"How the hell is all of this possible?"

"This is the spirit stone of my cl—my family," he said, quickly correcting himself. "It's connected to me, and everyone else in my family, spiritually and physically. We are all given one the day we are born. It comes from the caves deep in the earth on our family land."

"S-so you're an Amoveo too? One of these shape-shifters?" She studied him warily. "Then why aren't your eyes glowing?"

Zander's jaw clenched as he wrestled with exactly how much he should share with her right now. Too much too fast, and she could totally freak out. Who was he kidding? She was already freaking out. Not that he could blame her.

"No," he said. "I am not Amoveo."

It wasn't a lie exactly. The Dragons were cousins of the Amoveo, and he hadn't been a true dragon for centuries. It was a generous stretching of the truth perhaps, but definitely not a lie.

"I'm only a man, a man whose job it is to reunite you with your people, including the man who will be your mate."

"My *mate*?" She scoffed. "You do know how

ridiculous that sounds, don't you? How every inch of this sounds?"

"Yes, I do, but all of the Amoveo have one predestined life mate and—"

"Do me a favor," she said quickly. "Stop with the mate stuff, okay? This is weird enough without adding that little tidbit."

"Sorry." He briefly held up both hands, as if in surrender. "I know this is a lot to digest."

"Yeah, and please, keep telling me you're *only a man*. A regular guy wouldn't know about shapeshifters and act like it's no big deal that my eyes are glowing," she said through a shuddering breath while looking him up and down. "Why now? I'm twenty-five years old. Why is all of this happening *now*? Where the hell were you when I was living on the streets as a kid or running from one foster home to the next, fighting for my life?"

Her energy signature undulated with frustration, but sadness and confusion were woven between, creating a heartbreaking tapestry of emotion. He sucked at handling tender emotions and had done his best to avoid them, but standing in the midst of Rena's swirly energy pattern, there was no escaping it.

No escaping *her*.

"I'm not entirely sure." Zander rolled the stone between his fingers. "The universe isn't fond of explaining itself. But you *are* Amoveo, Rena. I came here to bring you to your people. They can teach you everything you'll need to know and show you how to make the most of your abilities. Their leader has a ranch in Montana."

"That's why you're here?" she asked warily. "To cart me away to a shapeshifter ranch?"

Her wary, glowing gaze flicked over him, and she took a step backward. Did she think he was going to kidnap her and drag her off like some caveman?

"You don't have to go. I'm not going to force you, but don't you want to know where you came from?"

She let out a slow breath and took one more step away, clearly wanting him to keep his distance. Her energy pattern was slowing down, which gave him hope. She was out of full-on panic mode and, hopefully, making her way toward problem-solving.

"Let's say I agree to go with you to Montana. Why didn't one of those Amoveo dudes come and get me? Why you?"

Zander held his breath for a moment. He didn't want to lie to her, but at the same time, he wasn't sure how much more she could handle at the moment. Moving closer, he took her hand in his and turned her palm up, the whole time trying not to notice how soft and warm her flesh felt beneath his. Rena licked her lower lip, and her energy signature picked up in pace, skittering around him rapidly. He bit back the surge of attraction and gently placed the stone in her palm.

"Fate, Rena." An ache of longing swelled in his chest. "All of us are at its mercy. The time has come for you to meet yours."

The instant Rena curled her fingers around the stone, her eyes glowed brighter than any Zander had ever seen—right before they rolled back in her head. Her body went rigid as she cried out in pain. Zander cursed loudly and caught her before she fell onto the ground.

He dropped to his knees with Rena's convulsing body cradled against him, and pure unadulterated panic fired through him.

What the hell had he done? Damn the fates and damn the curse.

"Rena!"

He shouted her name again, but the spasms continued as the stone remained clutched in her hand. Zander held her tightly against his chest with one arm as he pried her fingers off the piece of quartz and quickly took it away.

As soon as he removed the stone, the seizure stopped and her body became soft and pliant, immediately relaxing against him. Zander let out the breath he hadn't even realized he'd been holding and pushed the hair off her face. Her fair skin was flushed and damp with sweat, but the crisis seemed to have passed.

A powerful wave of relief surged in Zander's chest, and he held her a little tighter. Her body shivered against his, or maybe he was the one shaking? He could not let anything like that happen to her again. She may be the key to saving Zed, but he never believed it would mean harming her in the process.

Damn it all to hell. Fear was not an emotion Zander was familiar with. In fact, the last time he'd felt anything close to that was the day Zed had caught him with Arianna in the woods. His heartbeat thundered against his rib cage, and he fought to keep his emotions in check.

Losing his cool now, so close to his goal, wouldn't help Rena or Zed.

"Rena," he whispered. Zander cradled her face and gently ran his thumb over the velvety-soft skin of her cheek. "Rena. Can you hear me?"

She stirred. Her eyes flickered behind her closed lids, and she moaned softly. After what felt like forever, her lashes fluttered open, and he found himself staring into her warm, brown eyes. Zander stilled as she lifted her hand and pressed her quivering fingers against his cheek. Her touch was tender, and he flinched from the unexpected contact.

"Your eyes…" A smile curved her lips, and through a weak laugh, she murmured, "They're glowing…like the dragon."

Rena's hand fell limply from his cheek as she passed out again. Zander cursed under his breath. She must have been talking about the dreamrealm. He glanced over his shoulder at the small love seat along the right side of the office. He had to get her off the floor. Zander rose to his feet with Rena cradled in his arms, but he stopped short when he caught a glimpse of himself in the mirror.

For the first time in five hundred years, Zander saw a reflection he never thought he'd see again—the burning scarlet eyes of his dragon.

Chapter 6

RENA WAS BACK IN THE FOREST. IT WAS NIGHT, AND SOFT moonlight bathed the large clearing surrounded by towering trees. She stepped out from behind the thick trunk of a tree and looked around warily. At first, she thought she was alone, but the sound of leaves rustling to her left caught her attention and made her duck quickly behind the trunk once again.

A young woman wearing a medieval-style dress with waist-length auburn hair emerged from the tree line and stood in the clearing while staring expectantly at the night sky. A thick whooshing sound filled the air, and Rena immediately recognized it as the wings of a dragon—just like the one in her dreams. She was about to shout a warning to the girl, but a smile bloomed on the stranger's face as a massive shadow passed overhead—accompanied by Zander's thick, unmistakable spirit stream.

Rena gasped but covered her mouth to stifle the sound as his enormous form came into sight. The beast landed on his hind legs with a muffled thud that shook the forest floor, and he quickly tucked his massive wings behind his back. Rena was riveted to her spot and couldn't look away. This was the memory she had stepped into yesterday, but this time, instead of being a participant, she was an observer.

Apologies for keeping you waiting. *He dipped his huge head in a regal gesture of deference as his voice rumbled through Rena's mind.* You should not be out here alone at night.

"*I wanted to see you in all your ferocious glory, and I never tire of watching you fly.*" *The girl's light, melodic voice was in stark contrast to Zander's massive size and formidable presence.* "*My father says the Dragon Clan is only capable of destruction, but you've shown me that is a lie. You dragons are quite beautiful.*"

Our clan is not known for a delicate nature. *Zander's glowing eyes flickered brightly in the night.* You would be wise to heed your father's warnings. Neither I nor my brother are meant for you. We are not to be, my love. None of us bear the mate tattoo.

"*Nonsense. Why, my heart beats faster when I think of how powerful you are. More so than any of the Amoveo clans. Even the tiger warriors could not best you in battle.*" *The girl giggled and waved him toward her.* "*The fates can be damned, for I shall choose who wins my heart. Come closer, my love. I can only see you like this in the evening, and I wish to waste no more time.*"

Nor I.

Zander let out a snort and shook his huge head before dropping to all fours and resting his head on his hands. His long, spiked tail curled around him in a catlike motion, and he remained in an almost submissive position. The girl moved closer and pressed her delicate-looking fair-skinned hand to his snout. The contrast between the two was even more pronounced with the tender gesture.

"You would fight for me, wouldn't you?" she simpered. "You would do anything to prove your love to me?"

I pledge my love to you and shall be your servant… if not your lover.

Uh-oh. Rena knew a brush off when she heard it. Zander was trying to let the girl down gently, but sister friend didn't seem to be getting the message. There was no way this situation was going to end well. Then again, did they ever?

"Would you die for me, Zander?" She pressed a kiss to the tip of his snout and acted as if she hadn't even heard what he had just said. "Would you kill for me?"

Rena's heart beat faster, and a feeling of foreboding tripped up her spine. Who the hell was this chick? Asking a guy to die for her was more than a little dramatic. Even if he was a dragon. Jeez. Why would she want to know if he'd kill for her? Rena had always heard that the medieval era was a rough one, and this whole situation made modern dating look like a piece of cake. Most guys nowadays got squeamish about committing to dinner, let alone vowing murder.

"Tell me, Zander," the young woman whispered, a wicked smile curving her lips, "what would you do to prove your devotion to me?"

The dragon's gleaming scarlet eyes fluttered closed as she gently stroked his scaled flesh, and Zander's deep, gravelly voice drifted in the air.

All that I am is yours. I give you my heart and my life. I would never hurt you, but we can never be… The fates have other plans for both of us.

An odd twinge of jealousy flashed as Rena observed the intense display between beauty and beast. It was silly to be envious of the love and obvious loyalty Zander felt for the girl. The dragon was being noble and throwing himself on his proverbial sword, but the girl simply wasn't hearing him.

Rena couldn't linger on the situation for long. Moments later, another shadow passed over the forest, blotting out the luminous moonlight. A knot of dread curled in Rena's gut, because she knew what was coming.

Her fears were confirmed when another dragon, identical to Zander in color and size, swept down from the sky. Glowing red eyes, these filled with rage, zipped through the night with the girl in their sights. The young woman shrieked and stumbled backward as Zander reared up on his back legs and spun around to face their attacker. He stood on his hind feet and opened his wings in a defensive posture, with the young woman sheltered safely in back of him. He curled his tail around her protectively as she peeked out from behind his massive body.

MINE! *The intruder's voice, not quite as deep as Zander's but filled with fury, thundered through the air as he landed on the forest floor with an earth-shaking crash.* You have no business with her! Betrayer!

The intruder dropped to all fours, and his red eyes glowed brighter, matching his increasing anger. He snorted and shook his head, shifting his weight from one massive foot to the other. Leaves and other debris scattered into the air with each huffing breath, and Rena pressed her body deeper against the rough bark of the tree. She was terrified of what might come next but also found herself unable to look away.

Please, Brother. *Zander's voice was steady and reso-lute*. Zed, I do not wish to fight you.

Brother? Rena gripped the stone in her hand tighter. This was the brother Zander needed to find? They were the two monsters fighting in her nightmare, Zander and Zed?

Yes, and she has chosen me! *Zed roared and opened his wings as he reared up onto his hind legs*. You do not bear the mate tattoo.

Nor do you, Zed. She is not for you or me to claim.

But I did claim her. *Zed snorted, and smoke blew from his nostrils as his eyes gleamed brighter*. She's mine!

The fates have toyed with us, my brother, *Zander growled*. With all of us.

The beautiful object of their affection stepped out from behind Zander and stood between the two towering drag-ons. Her tiny, delicate form, clad in a pale-yellow dress, stood out amid the tense scene and reminded Rena of fairy tales from her childhood. The girl brushed her long auburn locks off her shoulders and clasped her hands in front of her as she looked from one dragon to the other.

"You're both so angry." The young woman's voice was smooth as silk, and though she sounded sweet, there was something dark that lurked beneath it. "Are you going to battle over me?"

I will fight to the death, *Zed growled*. I have told you many times, no sacrifice is too great to prove my love for you.

Zed's eyes gleamed brighter, and his long, spiked tail swayed behind him in a slow, pulsing motion, like a snake poised and ready to strike. His wings spread wide, and he opened his mouth, revealing rows of razor-sharp teeth. Rena shuddered with dread as a sickening, growling groan rumbled through the air.

Please, Zed. Don't do this.

The time for talking is done…Brother. *Zed opened his mouth wider and let out a roar that shook Rena's bones.*

Run! *Zander tossed his head toward the girl, and moonlight flashed over his iridescent hide.* You must go back to the village. Now!

Rena thought the girl would hightail it out of there, but she didn't. Instead of being frightened or begging them to stop, a wicked grin of satisfaction spread slowly across her face as she backed up, making way for the impending battle.

Holly hell. This crazy little bitch wanted these two guys to fight over her.

As Zed launched his huge body at Zander and the dragons tumbled together, the earth shaking with the ferocity of their battle, Rena's attention was focused on the woman who had intentionally caused the chaos. With dust and debris clouding the air, snarls and gnashing teeth rising to a deafening level, Rena couldn't take her gaze off the girl.

Her eyes had shifted into glowing amber orbs—just like Rena's—but something else had shifted as well. The young woman was no longer there. In her place, along the edge of the clearing, was a small, red fox with eyes that lit up the night.

Just like the ones Rena had seen in her own reflection.

Shock and disbelief rushed through Rena, and her fingers unfurled from around the stone. Her visions never lied.

Everything Zander had told her was true.

As Rena emerged from the vivid memory-vision, she heard Zander calling her name. His voice sounded far away at first, but as the darkness began to give way to the light, she forced herself to tune in to his deep, soothing baritone, wooing her back to reality. When she finally opened her eyes, she found herself staring into his worried face. Tension had settled in his square, stubble-covered jaw as he loomed over her and strands of his dark hair drifted over his eyes.

In that moment, it struck her how much he resembled the dragon in the vision and her dreams. It wasn't one particular feature but rather the intensity of his gaze. There was darkness in him and danger, but there was also restraint, because beneath it all was undeniable power.

It was an odd experience to look at a man but see the spirit of a beast shine through. Maybe it had been there all along, but she didn't recognize it for what it was.

Until now.

"Rena, are you all right?"

Zander was seated next to her on the edge of the little red love seat in her office. He must have put her here after she fainted. How embarrassing. Rena wasn't used to accepting help from anyone, let alone a client. Her cheeks flamed as she pushed herself up to a more seated position, but Zander didn't move. His body caged hers with one hand braced on the back of the sofa and the other brushing her hair off her forehead. Rena tried not to notice the delicious friction of his fingertips along her flesh, but it was impossible. His hip pressed against her leg, firm and unyielding, a stark contrast to the soft cushions of the couch and far more enticing.

Every single aspect of Rena's being was *awake*.

It was as if a switch inside her had been flipped. The world around her was sharper. Clearer. It felt like she had been hooked up to some kind of spiritual electric current. Rena stilled as the sounds outside the building seemed far louder than they ever had before. Cars. Horns honking. The sound of footsteps and chatter from people on the street.

Until that moment, she had been drifting through life half-asleep, only seeing or hearing a fraction of the world.

Not anymore.

Colors were brighter. Sounds sharper. Each of her senses had been heightened somehow by the vision she had when holding the stone. While all of her senses were enhanced, the one that was leaving her incapable of speech was her sense of touch.

She was acutely aware of each spot where Zander's body met hers. Warmth shimmied beneath her flesh where his hip settled along her thigh. The breath-stealing sensation radiated out in delicious ripples, going all the way down to her toes. A low pulse of desire thrummed in her blood and had her aching for more of him and his touch.

What the hell was happening?

Having Zander this close, surrounding her and caging her in, was making the synapses of her brain misfire. For all intents and purposes, she had devolved into a moon-eyed, horny-as-hell animal. Lust seeped from every pore. Rena stifled a moan and curled her fingers around the cushions on either side of her. She hoped concentrating on the feel of the fabric beneath her hands would take her mind off the way Zander's body heat washed over her in seductive, skittering waves.

It didn't.

She flicked her tongue over her lower lip and sucked in a slow, deep breath. A move which was meant to steady her increasing heartbeat, but it had the converse effect when Zander's musky, male scent filled her head.

The myriad of sensations swamping her were muddling her brain and making it difficult for her to form a coherent sentence. If she didn't say something soon, the man might think she had completely lost her marbles.

Maybe she had.

"I fainted, didn't I?" Rena asked in a low, raspy voice, one she barely recognized as her own. "And you had to carry me over here like some kind of child. That's not exactly a normal day at the office for me."

"Nothing about you or me or this situation is *normal*."

"Right." The word came out on a shaky breath. "I—I'm sorry."

"I'm the one who's sorry." Zander's voice was as gentle as his touch. He ran his thumb over her cheek, leaving a trail of fire in its wake. "I didn't know the spirit stone would hurt you. That wasn't my intention."

His brow furrowed, and a fierce look settled in his eyes as he stroked her cheek again. Rena swallowed the thick surge of lust and closed her eyes, needing to regain her focus and get some kind of control on her overheated body. But closing her eyes only heightened her other senses, and when Zander's thumb brushed her lower lip lightly, Rena's eyes tingled sharply, and she sucked in a quick breath. She knew now what that sensation meant. The knowledge that her eyes had shifted should probably have frightened her, but it didn't.

Instead, Rena was empowered and energized by it.

"I've never fainted before," she whispered. Her eyes fluttered open and latched on to his. "Thanks for catching me."

Zander groaned, and his body tensed against her when their gazes locked.

"God, you're beautiful," he murmured.

As the words slipped from his lips, Zander's eyes shifted into the glowing, scarlet eyes of the dragon. Rena's breath quickened as his spirit stream raced around her in the air, dancing with hers. Everything spun wildly, a hurricane of sensations in body and mind. A whirling dervish of lust and power. Erotic and enticing, his desire for her was as unmistakable as her own ferocious need. Rena's pulse thrummed wildly as Zander curled his hand around the nape of her neck and pulled her closer.

"So are you…"

In a blur of speed, his mouth crashed over hers, and Rena opened to him with a throaty groan of strangled, desperate need. It wasn't a matter of choice but more like instinct. Her body had developed a mind of its own, and all it wanted was more of Zander Lorens. He tasted hot and sweet and fleetingly reminded her of licorice. Rena moaned as his firm lips melded against hers with perfection, each pass of his tongue growing more demanding than the last.

Rena threaded her fingers through his shaggy hair and rose to meet him, the simmering heat of their desire erupting in a flurry of teeth and tongues. She tilted her head, angling to deepen their kiss. God. She wanted him to touch her everywhere. To feel the full weight of his body over hers.

Without breaking the kiss, she lay back on the sofa, pulling him with her. Rena opened her legs, needing and wanting him to settle there, to blanket her with his hard masculinity. She arched her back, her breasts pressing against his chest, urging him to take what she offered.

Instead of moving closer, he moved away.

Confusion slid into Rena's clouded, lust-fogged brain as Zander curled his fingers around her wrists. She whimpered when he broke the kiss and gently pulled her hands away before settling them on her chest. He pressed them there firmly, like an exclamation point on a humiliating sentence.

His broad chest rose and fell in time with his heavy breaths. His eyes still glowing brightly, Zander shook his head adamantly and rose from the sofa. Rena struggled to catch her own breath, mourning the loss of his touch as he stepped backward, increasing the distance between them. Confusion washed over her as she slowly sat up and straightened out her shirt. Embarrassment wasn't far behind.

"We shouldn't have done that," he said gruffly between heavy breaths. His eyes shifted back to their human state and peered at her coldly between dark strands of hair. "I'm sorry. It was a mistake."

Her mouth fell open, and she pushed her bangs off her forehead, struggling for some kind of dignified retort. What could she say? She couldn't act like she didn't want him, since she'd been mauling him about ten seconds ago.

"*You* kissed *me*, buddy," she said with an indignant huff. "Let's keep it straight, hot lips."

Oh yeah. *That* was dignified. It was official. She was a babbling, horny idiot.

"I know." His jaw clenched, the muscle flickering beneath the dark stubble. "I lost my head for a minute. You reminded me of someone and—"

"Are you for real?" Rena shot to her feet. "So not only are you telling me that kissing me was a mistake but you weren't actually kissing *me*?"

Zander lifted one shoulder in an annoying, typically male, noncommittal gesture. Rena fought the urge to punch him in the face. She should. She should haul off and give him a knuckle sandwich. But that would only make her look like she gave a shit, and she didn't.

Liar.

Whatever. It was only a kiss. No big deal. Right?

Her gaze skittered over his tall, masculine form, one that was seemingly devoid of anything other than muscle and bone, and the dull ache between her legs throbbed. She was in big, fat, stupid trouble. She wanted him—she couldn't deny it—but he was obviously mooning over the crazy broad from the vision.

That realization stung more than anything else, but Rena shoved the growing humiliation aside. Zander held the answers to her increasingly long list of questions, and telling him to piss off would only hurt her in the long run.

She hated to admit it, but she needed his help, and Rena wasn't used to needing anyone. It made her uncomfortable to have to rely on another person because, in her experience, most people weren't reliable.

Once she got her answers, *then* she could punch him in the nose.

Or kiss him.

Crap.

"Like I said, it won't happen again," Zander murmured. "When your eyes shifted, I got caught up in the moment and—"

"Let me guess." Rena folded her arms over her breasts and closed the distance between them. "I remind you of that crazy girl that you and your brother fought over? Right? The one who turned into a fox? Yellow dress, long reddish hair, and an I-like-to-mess-with-a-man's-head grin?"

Zander's expression faltered, and Rena couldn't help but let a smug smile curve her lips. It was nice to shock him for once, and it made her feel a bit more like herself. Because, so far, being around Zander had her feeling like a stranger in her own body.

Anger flickered briefly over his sharp features but was swiftly shoved behind his calm, cool facade. Rena's lips tilted. She had hit a nerve. Good. She wasn't the only one feeling off her game. At least she was starting to learn which buttons to push if she had to.

Zander loomed over her, intentionally crowding her space. Rena looked him up and down, a sense of empowerment flooding her. If she was going to head out on a road trip to some ranch full of shapeshifters, then she damn well had to keep a balance of power.

Kiss or no kiss.

"How do you know about her?"

Rena sucked in a deep, cleansing breath and focused on shifting her eyes back to normal. With a tingling snap, she willed them to their human state. She lifted her eyebrows triumphantly, daring him to question her abilities. Zander's eyes widened slightly when she exerted control over her newfound abilities.

"Good." He nodded curtly. "You're a quick study. Now, tell me how you knew about—"

"You're not the only one with a few surprises up their sleeve."

"Go on."

Rena shrugged and walked around Zander to the other side of the office. It was time for Zander to get thrown a curveball or two. She could feel him staring at her, but she didn't give him the satisfaction of looking at him. If there was one thing Rena couldn't abide, it was feeling out of control, and it was about time she took control back.

"I get visions when I touch stuff sometimes. Always have."

A feeling of pride filled Rena, along with a sense of relief, as she finally shared her secret. She had waited her entire life to be able to talk openly about her abilities with someone. She always thought she would be terrified to utter it out loud, but the opposite was true. Rena was empowered by the freedom of unloading her secret, and it was mostly because of Zander's reaction.

He didn't even flinch. Zander didn't look at her like she was a freak. On the contrary, he seemed impressed.

"Interesting." He folded his arms over his broad chest and remained completely tuned in. The guy was hanging on every word she said. "Go on. What else?"

"The visions aren't enough?" she said with a nervous laugh.

"No." His eyes crinkled at the corners, and humor laced his voice. "That's not what I meant. I want to know how it affected you. It can't have been easy to keep that secret."

"Oh…that. Yeah, I wasn't great at making or keeping friends. Or a family." Rena tucked her hair behind her ear and looked away, suddenly feeling exposed. "It toughened me up, I guess."

"I'm sorry," he said quietly.

She could feel him staring at her. Studying her. Maybe this whole sharing her secret business wasn't all it was cracked up to be. Rena had always been an expert at hiding the truest part of herself from the world, but now, here she was, with nowhere to hide.

"It's fine," Rena said quickly. "It freaked me out when I was a kid, but once I learned how to control it, it was all good. If I want to, I can slip into the memories of the person by touching something they touched. I tune in to their spirit stream and—"

"Spirit stream? You're talking about an energy signature," he said with a hint of awe. "That's what we call it, the spiritual fingerprint all living creatures have. The Amoveo's energy patterns are particularly strong, but so are most supernaturals."

"Okay," Rena said slowly. "I guess it's the same thing. Sounds like it. Anyway, if I touch something that *you* touched, and you're hiding something…I'm gonna find out what it is. And I'm gonna find you. Nobody can hide from me. I'm like a living divining rod. Once I connect with their spirit—energy signature," she quickly corrected, "I can find them anywhere."

"The money." His voice was quiet but steady. "When you spaced out at the bar, you were having a vision, and you were in one of *my* memories?"

"Yep. Part of one, anyway, and I saw even more when I touched the stone."

"Patricia mentioned you had a sixth sense." His eyes flicked over her quickly. "You're psychic."

"Give the man a prize," Rena said with a sweeping gesture. "Ding, ding, ding. You win."

"Visions like yours are rare among humans, Rena. The Amoveo have several gifts, but I've never heard of one who could see into the past."

"Yeah." She rolled her eyes. "Well, it felt more like a *curse* until I met Vito and he taught me the business. My visions or whatever you want to call them gave me a unique advantage when looking for people. Especially those who don't want to be found."

"Then this Vito person knows about your ability?"

"No," Rena said abruptly. A glimmer of fear flared in her chest at the idea of Vito knowing exactly how weird she was. "And it's going to stay that way. Vito and Patricia are the only real family I've ever had, and they *never* treated me like a freak. Anyway, I owe him everything. It's because of him that I found a way to turn my freakishness to my advantage. The more I used it, the more I was able to control it."

"You didn't look very controlled when you fainted."

"I never held an ancient spirit stone before either." She arched one eyebrow at him. "And definitely not one given to me by a guy who can turn into a dragon."

Zander stilled but didn't confirm or deny the part about the dragon.

Interesting. Rena studied him closely as silence hung between them, the sound of the ticking clock and the cars outside filling the void. She had just called him out as a dragon shapeshifter. Why not admit or deny it? His choice to gloss over it gave her more pause than anything else.

She wasn't the only one who was used to hiding the truth.

"I didn't know the spirit stone was going to hurt you."

"Be serious," she replied. "You must've thought it would do something, or you wouldn't have given it to me."

"I had hoped… Shit." He ran both hands over his face and let out a growl of frustration. "I'm sorry."

"Don't be." Rena lifted one shoulder in a nonchalant gesture. "I think it woke up more of my powers or whatever."

"How so?" His eyes narrowed, and a hint of concern edged his voice.

"My hearing and sense of smell have always been sharp but now…" She trailed off, her mind instantly going to Zander's musky, male scent and the sweet licorice taste of his kiss still lingering on her tongue.

"That's not surprising. Members of the Fox Clan have excellent hearing and a strong sense of smell, even in their human form."

"Hmmm. Well, let's just say that it feels like they've been supercharged. Even the vision I had was different than the others."

"Why? What did you see?"

She grabbed her brown leather duffel bag off the floor and tossed it on her desk before unzipping it. Keeping her back to him, she put the brick of cash into the bag and closed it back up.

"When you put the stone in my palm, I saw that whole drama in the forest play out like some kind of medieval soap opera. Usually, I'm *in* the memory or kind of a participant. But this time, I was just an observer and, boy, oh boy, did I get an eyeful. The fox-girl, she totally goaded you and your brother into fighting over her," Rena said.

"It wasn't like that," Zander bit out. "At least, it wasn't supposed to be."

"How long ago did all that happen, anyway?"

"Does it matter?" he asked flatly.

"Yes, it does. I need the whole story."

His jaw clenched, and he sucked in a deep breath, as if deciding whether to answer her question.

"You won't believe me."

"Dude, are you serious? I get visions when I touch stuff, and now my eyes have started glowing like I'm a human Lite-Brite. Come on, Zander," she said playfully. "I showed you mine…"

"Fine." His lips set in a tight line. "It was five hundred years ago."

Rena looked him up and down, her gaze lingering on his strong, stubble-covered jaw before locking eyes with him once again. Her gut instinct told her there was no way that could be true, but then again…why not?

"You look pretty good for a guy who's five centuries old," she teased. "What kind of weird, supernatural creature are you? Are you an alien or something?"

"No," he said with mild amusement. "Just a man who's been cursed."

"A man, huh? Well, I guess you're sort of right." She slung the bag over her shoulder and moved around the desk toward him. "You and your brother weren't exactly *men* in the vision I saw. More like a couple of *dragons*."

He paused, and his square jaw clenched as though he was searching for the correct response.

"Not anymore," he rasped. "Not for more years than I care to recall."

"I thought you said you weren't one of those shape-shifter Amoveo guys."

"I'm not Amoveo," he said through a clenched jaw. "I *was* born into the Dragon Clan, but *now* I am only a man."

Rena adjusted the strap of the bag on her shoulder and let her gaze wander up and down the length of him slowly. Her eyes narrowed. He was wound tight, every inch of him looked ready to bolt, and that was the body language of a man who was hiding something.

He wasn't telling her the whole truth.

"Right, a *cursed* man who's five hundred years old but doesn't look a day over twenty-eight, and his eyes glow bright red like a siren," she said through a laugh. "There's more to your story, and you'll tell me eventually, one way or the other. Even if you don't tell me, I'm going to figure it out. Like I said…nobody can hide from me."

Without waiting for him to respond, Rena strode around him and went to the front door. She hit the light switch, leaving the office lit only by daylight, and tugged the door open.

"Let's go." She nodded toward the street. "I need to make a stop before we hit the road, but it's on the way to the interstate."

"That's it?" Zander asked warily. "You don't have any other questions?"

"Are you kidding?" Rena slipped on her aviator sunglasses. "Questions are all I've got."

"I'm impressed." Zander moved toward her slowly, until he stood beside her in the open doorway, once again crowding her personal space like it was his job. "After everything I told you and what you saw…you're still willing to go with me? You aren't afraid?"

Hell yes, she was scared, but she surely wasn't going to tell *him* that. If ever there was a time to bluff her ass off, it was now.

"First of all, dragon boy, I don't scare easily. I've been on my own since I was fourteen years old. You should see some of the stuff I've gotten a peek at over the years."

"I can imagine," he said solemnly. "I've seen what humans are capable of."

"I'm going with you for two reasons." Rena inched closer, so their bodies were a breath apart, and she kept her voice low. "One, I'm going because what I've learned about so far is only the tip of the iceberg, and I want to know more. I've wondered where I came from for my entire life, and it looks like you and these *Amoveo* are the only ones with the answers. Number two, you're paying me a ton of cash, and you know what they say—cash is king. But I do have one condition."

Rena stilled as the smell of leather swirled around her with a gust of wind. Jeez. She resisted the urge to lean closer and breathe him in, because with the sure shot of lust came the pulsating instinct for her eyes to shift. By some miracle, she was able to keep them from going all glowy and weird.

"What is it?" Zander asked, his deep, gravelly voice sliding over her seductively. "I'll keep my hands to myself if that's what you're worried about."

Yup. She was worried that he *would* keep his hands to himself. Why did he have to smell so damn delicious? A hint of licorice bathed her tongue, a remnant of the kiss they had shared, and she fought the urge to moan. It was just the shapeshifter stuff, right? Her senses were on overdrive because of her heightened powers and not because of Zander.

That was her story and she was sticking to it.

"It's not your hands I'm worried about." Rena tilted her chin and adjusted the strap of the bag, praying he wouldn't see right through her. "You be straight with me from now on. You obviously made up that story about finding your brother so you could get me to Montana to meet the rest of these Amoveo people or shifters or whatever they are."

He opened his mouth to respond, but she held up one hand, stopping any bogus excuses. She knew, deep in her gut, there was more to this thing with his brother, and she'd bet the thirty grand in her bag it had to do with their big, bad fight in the woods—and the woman at the center of it.

"A simple yes or no will suffice." Rena dropped her hand to her side. "I ask you honest questions, and you give me honest answers. No more phony stories. Do we have a deal?"

"Yes."

Zander moved past her and headed down the steps toward his Harley, which was parked at the curb in front of the building. Rena locked the door of her office as the roar of his motorcycle filled the air, and the sound sent a shiver up her spine. When she turned around, Zander was staring at her and revved the engine again, as though taunting her.

There were about fourteen hundred miles between them and their Montana destination. Plenty of time for her to get the answers she was looking for and to find out what else Zander was hiding.

Chapter 7

RIDING ALL THE WAY TO MONTANA WITH RENA SNUGGLED up against his back was going to be torture. Hell, the ten-minute trip to the old man's nursing home made Zander break out in a sweat. He opted to wait outside while she went in to visit Vito. He hoped some distance would help him regain control over his body's reaction to the nearness of hers.

The cruel irony of the universe and the fates was never lost on him, but being around Rena sure as hell brought it to the forefront. His body might not be cooperating, but Zander's brain sure as shit had to. He would not let history repeat itself and screw up the one last chance to free his brother.

Mind over matter. He kept repeating the mantra to himself over and over. His body was reacting on an animalistic level, but his brain, the one with five centuries worth of experience, was in control.

It had to be.

Zander refused to allow his starved libido to run the show. All he had to do was get Rena to the Amoveo ranch and then let nature take its course. Rena would awaken Zed and lift the curse. Then Zander would high-tail it out of there, so she and his brother could complete their mating bond and live happily ever after.

If he stuck around the two of them, he would only be a distraction.

Rena's warm, curvy form had fit against his with torturous perfection, and when she settled her hands over his stomach, holding on for the ride, it took significant willpower to keep his eyes from shifting. The primal urge of the beast surged as Rena's body and sweet scent surrounded him, but Zander managed to keep the eyes of his dragon at bay.

It may have been five centuries since he had experienced any of his clan abilities, but his instincts were still there and surprisingly sharp. He suspected it was because Rena had made direct contact with his memories and was well on her way to mating with Zed.

Some effects of the curse were beginning to fade, but it wasn't enough.

To top it all off, Zander's body and mind were at war. He was completely conflicted, and it was his own damn fault. *Stupid, stupid move*. If he hadn't kissed her, then maybe he wouldn't be feeling so confused.

He swore under his breath and tugged the strap of his duffel tighter against the back of the bike. Kissing her had been careless and foolish—a dangerous mistake he would not be repeating. He had allowed his animal instincts to take over, but he couldn't afford to let it happen again. Zed sure as hell couldn't afford it either.

Only Rena could lift the curse entirely and bring his brother out of the dreamrealm, and Zander *refused* to get in the way of that.

No matter how alluring she was.

Shit.

Frustration tinged with anger and resentment fired through him, but he stuffed it back down. Being pissed

off and horny wouldn't help him or his brother. Zander
shoved his hands through his hair in an almost violent
gesture before looking at his watch. The woman had
been inside for almost half an hour.

They didn't have time to waste.

The clock was ticking, and his patience was waning.
Feeling restless and tired of wallowing in his private
pity party, Zander headed up the walkway of Sunnyfarm
Retirement Community. When he stepped inside the
cool, air-conditioned lobby, his senses were assaulted by
a heady combination of too much perfume and whatever
the dining room had served up for breakfast. None of
which helped his grouchy mood.

"Can I help you?"

Zander snapped his head toward the female voice,
and he must have been glowering. The young woman
behind the counter was peering at him warily over her
wire-rim glasses. Not that he could blame the girl. He
was a stranger and wasn't exactly looking his best. He
ran one hand through his shaggy hair as he walked over
to the desk and forced a smile.

"You okay, mister?" She pushed her glasses up the
rim of her nose. "You lost or something?"

"No. My friend is here visiting someone, and I just
wanted to see how much longer she was going to be."
Zander glanced around the bright reception area with
the simple but welcoming decor with a homey feel to it.
"Her name is Rena McHale."

"Oh! Of course." A big smile bloomed on the young
woman's face, and her entire demeanor changed at the
mention of Rena's name. "She's here all the time visiting Vito. He's lucky, you know. Some of the folks in

here never get visitors. It's kind of ironic too, because he never even remembers that she was here."

"I see." Zander nodded his understanding. "Can you tell me where to find her?"

"You just missed her," the girl said brightly. "Rena went upstairs about five minutes ago."

"She's been in here for over half an hour," he grumbled. "She just went up there now?"

"Oh, she was in the business office for a while, but now she's up on the third floor with Vito."

The business office? He immediately thought of the money she had taken from the desk. Zander glanced around the lobby and noted the expensive lighting fixtures and lush furnishings. This place wasn't cheap, and he could only imagine what the medical expenses were like.

Was Rena supporting the old man?

The girl pushed a clipboard toward him. "I'll just need to see your ID and have you sign in."

Zander flashed her his driver's license, one of many forged IDs he had had over the years, and signed in as she requested.

"Thanks. Take the elevator to the third floor, then go to the left, and they'll buzz you in." She lowered her voice in an almost conspiratorial whisper. "It's the Alzheimer's and dementia wing. They have to buzz you in and out so the residents who live up there don't have a mishap."

"Right. Thanks."

Zander strode to the elevator bank and passed a stately looking elderly couple who were on their way out of the building. Hand in hand, they moved slowly to the glass doors, smiling at him as they passed. How many years had they been together? Likely more than most. What was that like? To experience life, day in and day out, with another person? To share each other's hopes and dreams?

He had no idea and likely never would. A solitary existence was all he knew, and if this damned curse wasn't lifted, it was all he would ever know.

Zander stepped into the elevator and hit the button for the third floor. Rena's sweet, fruity scent lingered, and the instant it filled his head, a surge of lust swelled. Damn it. He slipped his hand into his jacket pocket and curled his fingers around the spirit stone. Having the weight of the lumpy piece of quartz against his palm helped calm his body's instinctive response to her energy signature, the one infused with a hint of pears and vanilla. The memory of their kiss flickered through his mind, the sugary taste of her haunting him too, but he shoved it aside.

There was no point wasting time with thoughts about what could never be.

As soon as the elevator doors slid open on the third floor, Rena's energy signature floated around Zander seductively. It permeated the hallway in enticing pulses. He pushed the button on the wall and waved at a nurse through the glass windows in the door. The older woman with lovely ebony skin smiled broadly and waved him in as the door swung open.

"Well, now," she said jovially. The nurse gave him a look of appreciation. "Who might you be?"

Zander was never a fan of being in the spotlight, and his instinct was to shrink from the attention. He had spent countless years flying under the radar and doing his best not to be noticed. When you didn't age like a regular man, it was best to keep your head down before eventually moving on.

He rarely stayed in one place for more than a few years.

Zander scanned the area, and his energy signature immediately connected with Rena's again, putting him at ease. He sensed a peaceful contentedness within it that was distinctly different from what he'd noticed before. Ever since he had found Rena, the woman's energy had been swollen with tension, like she was waiting for the other shoe to drop.

Even in the dreamrealm. But not now.

A sense of serenity and happiness soaked her energy pattern. A smile tugged at Zander's lips, and he absently rubbed at the warmth that began to seep through his chest. What the hell was he doing, getting all sappy and mushy over a woman's feelings?

"Hello?" The nurse snapped her fingers. "You awake, handsome?"

"Yes. Sorry about that." He blinked and let out a short laugh, doing his best to be friendly. Which wasn't exactly his comfort zone. "I'm a friend of Rena's."

"Are ya now?" Her accent, one that conjured images of blue oceans and sandy beaches, brightened the reception area like the sun. "I been hoping our girl Rena had herself a nice boyfriend. She's always tellin' me she don't have no time for a man, but now I know that she just wants to keep ya all t' herself."

"Just a friend," Zander said with a wink. He flicked his gaze to the white name badge on her scrubs. "I'm Zander. It's nice to meet you, Maude."

"Pleasure's all mine, darlin'." She laughed, flashing him her pearly-white teeth. "You can go on down to the sittin' room. Straight down the hall. On the left-hand side. Ya can't miss it. Vito likes to sit by the window, and I believe Miss Rena is in there with him now."

Zander nodded politely and followed Rena's energy signature down the long hall with the pale-blue carpet. He passed a few rooms, each occupied by one or more elderly residents. Their energy signatures were even weaker than typical humans, which was common when someone suffered from a mental or physical ailment. A twinge of sadness tugged at his pathetic excuse of a heart, and Zander rolled his shoulders, trying to shake off the uncomfortable feeling.

Most emotions made him uneasy, and he had always viewed them as a form of weakness. Except rage and frustration. He practically wore those like a damn suit of armor. They were familiar and comfortable and had been his travel companions for centuries. Zander was a pro at wielding them like weapons and using them to fuel his mission.

Anger simmered in his blood, and in some ways, it had become as much a part of him as a physical body part. Rage lingered beneath the surface, ready and waiting at all times to serve him if and when he needed it. And over the course of five centuries, he'd sure as hell needed it plenty of times.

Besides, being pissed off kept most people at bay. Love was what had gotten him in trouble in the first place, and all the acts of kindness he had committed over the centuries had done nothing to help him free Zed.

Lost in his thoughts and a fair amount of self-pity,

Zander turned the corner into the large common room. The sun-filled space was enormous, with a series of couches, armchairs, and coffee tables arranged in clusters throughout. There were two gas fireplaces, one at either end, and a bank of windows covered the wall across from the entrance. He scanned the room quickly, and though he could feel Rena's energy signature, it was suddenly muddled, like a song filled with static.

She wasn't in there.

Anxiety flickered up Zander's back as he stood in the doorway and shifted his steady gaze around the room. There were two older women chatting on a sofa with a nurse seated next to them. Three elderly men, all in wheelchairs, were parked in front of a television that was airing an episode of *Bonanza*, but all of them were asleep.

There was one other man in the room.

Sitting alone, he was slightly hunched over in a wheelchair with his back to Zander. A shock of white hair was coiffed neatly on his head, but it was his energy signature that captured Zander's attention. It was a low, pulsing stream far thicker than a typical human's, especially one with dementia.

And it was filled with static.

Humans didn't have static in their energy patterns.

"What the hell?" Zander whispered.

He took a step closer, but Rena's voice stopped him in his tracks.

"Hey! What are you doing up here?"

Her energy signature, once again strong and clear, swirled around him like a tornado. The easygoing feelings he had sensed from her earlier were gone.

Thanks to him.

Zander turned around to find her looking as irritated as she sounded. Her dark eyes were stormy, and she had two bottles of water clutched in her hands, which were clenched into fists. For a split second, he thought she was going to punch him right in the jaw.

"Where have you been?" he asked tightly. "We need to get going."

"I was solving world peace," she said sarcastically. "What does it look like? I was getting Vito some water. His medication makes him thirsty. You'll just have to hold your horses while I visit with him for a few minutes. I usually see him every day, and I want to let him know I'm going to be away for a while."

"Does it matter?" Zander glanced at the old man. "I thought he didn't remember anything."

"It matters to me," she said quietly. "You need to work on your sensitivity. You know, for a guy who's been around as long as you have, I would think you'd have better people skills."

Rena went to walk past him, but Zander stepped to the left, blocking her path.

"We don't have time for this."

"He's the most important person in my life, so I *always* have time for him. Maybe if you cared about someone other than yourself and what you want, you'd understand that."

Zander blanched but held his ground. Maybe he was being insensitive, but after getting so close to an answer after five hundred years, waiting longer was torture. He sucked in a slow breath but was greeted with the scent, vanilla and pears, which only muddled his brain.

Why did she have to smell so damn inviting?

Focus, he thought. *Jesus. Get your head on straight.*

"What have you been doing in here all this time?" He swallowed a groan when her body heat flickered over him in wicked, little waves and bit out, "It's been close to an hour."

"Not that it's any of your business, but I had to take care of Vito's bill." She tilted her chin defiantly and held up the two bottles of water. "This stuff ain't cheap, and I'm not talking about the water. I told you I had more than one reason for taking this job. The money you paid me is going to cover the next year of his care, and when you pay me the rest, it'll cover another."

"You're telling me that you support him?"

"Yes."

"What about his family?" Zander asked, tuning into the man's unusual, static-filled energy signature again. "Where are they? Why aren't they handling this?"

"Like me, he doesn't have any. His wife is dead, and so is his kid. I'm all he's got." Rena poked him in the chest with one of the water bottles and gently pushed him back. "Now, please move your big, brooding self out of my way. We'll take off in fifteen. Okay?"

Undeterred, her warm, brown eyes held his gaze. The woman was unyielding, stubborn, and tough as nails. She was also loyal, and that was a quality lacking in many. Shit. It was lacking in him.

"Fine." He flicked his eyes to her mouth, and his gut tightened before he quickly looked away. "Fifteen minutes."

Zander stepped aside but kept his sights on her. He leaned against the doorjamb and folded his hands in

front of him as she settled into a chair beside the old
man. It didn't escape Zander that the moment she smiled
at Vito, her energy signature lightened.

All the tension eased away.

The ache in Zander's chest, the one that had ebbed
and flowed ever since finding Rena, began to throb as
she flashed a gorgeous smile at the old man. Her entire
face lit up and matched the luminous swell of her energy.
He almost didn't recognize the sensation at first. It was
both foreign and hauntingly familiar. Like a tsunami,
the realization washed over Zander with such force, he
could have drowned in it.

Love.

Pure love, like that of a father and daughter, flowed
between Rena and Vito. It was authentic. Untainted
by greed, jealousy, or pride or any of the other ugly
human emotions that could swiftly and completely cor-
rupt something genuine. Any doubts he might have had
about Rena being the answer to his prayers were swept
away in the tide. If her devotion and commitment to
Vito were any indication, then this woman would be a
good mate.

For his brother.

Not him.

Damn it.

"Hey." Rena waved him over and pulled him from
his self-pitying thoughts. "Come here. I want you to
meet Vito."

She wanted to introduce him? Great. Zander sighed
and pushed himself away from the wall. He didn't want
to get involved with Rena any more than he had to. After
all, she was going to be Zed's mate, not his. But he

also had to play nice, because there were a lot of miles between them and Zed.

"Vito?" Rena settled her hand on his forearm and rubbed gently, her demeanor tender and sweet. A far cry from the tough girl she pretended to be. "This is the man I was telling you about. It's thanks to him that you're gonna be able to stay here *and* in your private room."

As he got closer to Rena and the old man, the buzzing and static in the guy's energy signature grew louder. Zander's brows knit together, and his mouth set in a tight line. With each step closer, his anxiety ratcheted up a notch. The guy's hands curled over the armrests of his wheelchair, and a flash of gold caught Zander's gaze. He shut his eyes for a moment, not entirely believing what he had seen was real.

It couldn't be. Could it?

His heart thundered in his chest as he inched closer and kept his sights on the large, gold ring on the man's gnarled, arthritic right hand. The emblem of a dragon, wings extended, head reared back, as though roaring at the world, looked exactly as it had five hundred years ago. The two pieces of red quartz for the dragon's eyes glinted in the sunlight and jostled memories from his previous life.

The static in the energy pattern now made sense.

Son of a bitch.

Zander knew that ring, and the emblem on it, as well as he knew his own face. He had seen it every single day of his life until the spell had been cast. The heirloom had been passed from generation to generation in their clan's family line, from father to eldest son, and it should have gone to Zander, who was one minute older than Zed.

The ring, like so many other things, should have been his.

His fate could have been so different.

If Arianna hadn't been killed.

If he and Zed hadn't been cursed.

If Zander's father hadn't been murdered.

The list of unfulfilled possibilities and broken dreams could have gone on forever. Much like his rootless existence over the past five centuries.

His life that could have been…but wasn't.

All of it destroyed because of hatred, greed, and jealousy.

And love.

Misery was all that love had ever gotten him. What it had gotten *all* of them.

Anger shimmied up his back hotly, and his hands curled into fists as he moved slowly around the man's chair. He had to see his face. Confirm what he already knew in his gut. Rena was saying Zander's name. Her voice and energy signature were soaked with concern and uncertainty, but he could barely hear her. Every single fiber of his mind and body was wound tight, zeroing in on the slouched, decrepit form of the old man in the chair.

Zander stood between the foot of the man's wheelchair and the windows, wanting to be sure the bastard would see him. His gaze drifted slowly over the scuffed brown shoes, the tan slacks, and untucked, striped shirt over a round belly. The man before him was trapped in a wrinkled, weathered body that had once been full of vitality and life. Anyone else, including Rena, looked at him and saw an elderly man who resembled many of the other residents in the rest home.

But Zander knew differently.

His fierce gaze latched on to Vito's face, and all of his suspicions were confirmed. Years may have ravaged his body, but no amount of time would erase those eyes from Zander's memory.

They were the last ones he had looked into before being cursed.

A pair of watery, pale-brown eyes lurched up, locking on to Zander's with a vacant stare. At first, there was nothing. No recognition. Not a hint of memory. But then, a flicker of awareness sparked in the old man's eyes. His mouth twitched at the corners, and his gnarled hands tightened their grip on the arms of his wheelchair as a gurgling groan rumbled in his chest. His lips pursed, and spittle clung to them while he struggled to speak.

Zander wasn't sure if it was age or fury that muddled the old bastard's speech. Like all Amoveo who were widowed, Victor had aged and lost his powers. Essentially, he had become human. Zander crouched down so he was face-to-face with the man, a shell of a creature from days gone by. Folding his hands in front of him, Zander allowed his gaze to drift over the enemy from his past. A cruel smile tugged at his lips. How many nights had he lain awake thinking about what he would do if he ever crossed paths with him again?

"Hey!" Rena swatted his arm. He'd practically forgotten where he was. "What the hell is going on? You're upsetting Vito. You're obviously freaking him out. He doesn't know you."

Oh yes, he does, Zander thought.

The old man gurgled some more, his white eyebrows furrowed, and anger was carved into the deep lines that marred his face. Zander flicked his gaze to the ring and then back at Vito's furious glare.

He knew those eyes.

They belonged to Arianna's father.

The eyes of *his* father's killer and the man who'd had him cursed.

—◊◊◊—

Rena grabbed Zander's arm and pulled him to his feet as she glanced over her shoulder at the other residents. Luckily, none of them seemed to have noticed what was going on over there. That was fine, because Rena didn't know what the hell was happening either.

"Hey," she said in a harsh whisper that wasn't really a whisper at all. "Cut it out. You're upsetting him."

Zander's expression was stone-cold, and the glint in his eyes bordered on murderous, but she let out a slow breath when he took a step back, increasing the distance between him and Vito. She sensed Vito's anxiety ease back, and a few seconds later, the vacant look on his face returned. It was as if Zander had never even been there. She looked back and forth between the two men, not needing her psychic abilities to see that this wasn't the first time they had met.

Add that item to the long list of weirdness that had become her life.

"Okay," she said with a rush of air. She put her hands out to the side and placed herself between the two men. "I don't know what the deal is with you two, but you both better cool it."

"We'll talk about it later," Zander said coldly. His words were clipped and short. "We have to leave, and since he obviously isn't going anywhere, I can deal with him later."

"You are not doing *anything* to him. Now *or* later."

"He has something that belongs to me." Zander inched closer to her, his voice barely audible. "But then again, you probably already knew that, didn't you?"

His energy swam around her at a furious pace, and even with Vito's buzzing one nearby, Zander's was still far stronger. It almost drowned out the older man's entirely, but it didn't diminish the sting of Zander's accusation. She had shared her deepest secret with this guy about an hour ago, and now he was accusing her of keeping information from him.

What. The. Hell.

"Dude, the longer I hang around with you, the *less* I know. Okay? All you've done is give me even more questions than I already had."

"You asked me to answer your questions honestly, and I will, but I expect the same from you."

"Fine."

"Good."

"What do you want to know?" She folded her arms over her breasts, attempting to still her shaking limbs. "Shoot."

"Not here." Zander's brow furrowed, and he shot a glance at Vito. "We have to go. Right now."

"I don't think—"

"Hello again!" Maude's bright, cheerful voice cut into the room, halting further conversation. "It's time for Mr. Fox's physical therapy session, Miss Rena. I came to take him down to the PT suite."

"Okay, Maude." She forced a smile, not wanting to raise any red flags with the nurse. "Thank you."

Rena sliced a side eye at Zander before squatting next to Vito. Her anger and irritation melted away as soon as she took his hands; weathered and battered from the life he had lived, it always made her feel better to gather them in hers. It was as if his years of experience could soothe her ever-present feelings of uncertainty.

When she gently laced her fingers with his arthritic ones, life flickered in his eyes, and he turned his watery gaze to Rena's. Recognition lit up his timeworn face, and the relief tugged at Rena's heart.

It was a gift any time he remembered her. Even if it was only for a moment.

"There's my girl."

His voice was brittle and cracked, but it was music to her ears. He wasn't her father, but as far as she was concerned, that was semantics. She couldn't imagine loving her biological parents more than she loved him. Sorrow swelled with the tide of tender emotions and reminded Rena why she never let people in.

It hurts too damn much.

"Hey, Vito," she said, her voice strangled by the threat of tears. "I'm going out of town for a little while, but I'll see you when I get back. Okay?"

"You watch out for those devils," he said through a cough. "They only come out at night though. After the sun goes down. You remember what I told you. Those beasts only bring death and destruction."

"Okay, Vito. You got it." He was doing it again. "I'll be sure to keep my eyes peeled."

Rena learned a long time ago to never attempt to correct someone with dementia. It only made them more confused or scared. So she would simply smile and nod and reassure him, no matter what crazy stuff he came out with. What else could she do, really?

"All right, Mr. Vito." Maude took the wheelchair handles and released the brake. "She'll be fine now. Look at that big man she's travelin' with. Ain't nobody gonna mess with her."

Vito's eyes widened, and panic glimmered there, but he didn't take his gaze off Rena's. Seeing fear and confusion in his face was like a stab in the heart. Rena leaned over and pressed a kiss to his cheek, paying no mind to the remnants of beard stubble.

"Maude's right. It's gonna be okay. I promise. And when I get home, you and I are gonna get outside." She rose to her feet and squeezed his hand one last time before releasing it. "We'll take a spin around the grounds. How does that sound?"

As Maude backed up the chair, Vito's pale-brown eyes flicked past Rena, and she knew he was looking at Zander. The panic that had been there only moments ago immediately shifted to anger.

"He's going to be the death of you," he murmured.

"Come on now, Mr. Vito. Time to go."

Maude gave Rena a look that said *don't worry about it* and pushed Vito's chair toward the doorway.

"Listen to me," he rasped. "Please!"

Rena hugged her arms around herself and fought the shiver that whispered over her flesh as Vito's voice faded down the hall. He had often made incoherent references to monsters and demons, but Rena had always dismissed them. Yet, given all she had learned in the past twenty-four hours, she couldn't help but feel a sense of foreboding. Were his words merely the ramblings of a confused old man, or was this one of his moments of clarity?

The last thing she heard him say before his voice faded was, "I love you, Arianna."

"Rena…not Arianna," she whispered. Her shoulders sagged, and she let out a weak laugh. "So much for remembering me."

Rena swiped at her eyes, wishing she wasn't getting all girly and emotional in front of Zander. The truth was that part of her wanted to turn around and seek comfort. Bury her face against his broad chest and just cry it out. Weep for Vito, all the time and memories he had lost. For all the memories they never had a chance to make together.

But she didn't have to worry about Zander noticing her emotional moment or offering her comfort. He had already walked past her and was waiting impatiently in the doorway.

"Time to go."

No emotion. Not a drop of empathy. The man was like ice. As he disappeared around the corner, Rena told herself that it was for the best. It was better for both of them. No emotional involvement. Fine. If that's the way he wanted to play it, then two could play at that game. If he wanted to be a cold bastard and keep their relationship strictly business, then Rena would be more than happy to oblige.

Her eyes narrowed as she followed him down the hallway. This guy had no idea who he was dealing with. If anyone could keep their distance emotionally and shut people out, it was Rena. She had done that her entire life. She was good at being on her own. Hell, it was her comfort zone.

Zander Lorens may possess the long sought-after answers to her questions, be drop-dead sexy and filthy rich, but there was one thing he didn't have.

Rena's trust.

No man, regardless of how mind-blowing his kisses were, would gain access to her heart or her body without earning her trust first.

After the exchange with Vito, Zander had none of it.

Chapter 8

THEY HAD TRAVELED IN SILENCE FOR ALMOST SIX HOURS, and if it weren't for Rena's earbuds and streaming music on the highest volume, she might have lost her patience with the whole damn situation. Existing in conflict, her body and mind totally at war, was testing her limits. Sitting tucked up against Zander on the back of the Harley with her arms curled around his waist did little to cool her physical reaction to him.

On the contrary, all it managed to do was get her more turned-on than ever.

Zander's legs were hot and hard, and she had no choice but to settle hers alongside them. His back, a broad expanse of muscle and bone beneath well-worn leather, pressed against her breasts with tantalizing perfection. Not even the strong smell of exhaust could drown out his manly scent of leather and musk, which seemed to have settled firmly inside Rena's head.

There was no escaping him or the way he made her feel.

It was maddening. Especially given his ability to go from hot to cold in a split second, kissing her one minute and interrogating her the next.

At first, she'd had her arms around his waist, with her palms settled over his rock-hard abs, but once she'd gotten the hang of it and felt balanced on the back of the bike, she held on to the metal support behind her back.

She had tried talking to him before they hit the road, but Zander would barely look at her, let alone speak to her. This, of course, only wounded her further. And that was a hell of a pill to swallow for a woman who prided herself on her ability to remain detached. They had stopped once at a gas station to use the bathroom and grab a protein bar. Zander had dazzled her with a couple of grunts, which she supposed meant no when she asked if he wanted anything.

Big, handsome jerk.

The sun had gone down, and the temperature had dropped right along with it. The crisp fall air had felt okay when the sun was out, but now, with the darkness of the evening and only the moon lighting the empty highway, Rena had started to shiver. She didn't want to wrap her arms around him again, but the need for warmth overtook her pride.

Grumbling under her breath about how annoyed she was with herself, Rena caved in and curled her arms around him. She let out a sigh of relief as his body heat quickly seeped into her skin, even through the layers of blue jean and leather. Shivering so hard her teeth were chattering, she turned her face and rested her helmet-clad head between his shoulder blades, pressing her body firmly against his.

Zander's muscles stiffened as she tightened her grip.

He was probably annoyed that she was hanging on to him like a baby spider monkey, but that was too damn bad. *He* was the one who had insisted on riding this loud, rumbling contraption all the way from Las Vegas to Montana. His heart was beating hard against his rib cage and reverberated through her body along with the ass-numbing vibrations of the motorcycle. She licked her lips and clutched the leather of his jacket between her fingers. The combination of his heartbeat and having her body wrapped around his was beginning to drive her wild.

And not in an I-want-to-punch-you kind of way. More like a I-want-to-strip-you-naked-and-climb-you-like-Mount-Kilimanjaro kind of way.

Rena squeezed her eyes shut and struggled to get her uncooperative hormones under control. Why was she so insanely attracted to a man she was annoyed with? It was infuriating and made no sense.

Focus on something else, she thought. *Anything other than the feel of him. Jeez.* Patricia was right. Maybe if she hadn't been so sex starved, she wouldn't be as affected by Zander's...everything.

She needed to get off this bike and obtain some distance between his body and hers. However, his brooding, monosyllabic routine was wearing on her patience, and when they finally stopped for the night, he was going to have to start talking.

As though reading her mind, Zander hit the blinker, the yellow light throbbing eerily along the dark highway. Rena lifted her head and peered over his broad shoulder. They were approaching an exit ramp, and not too far beyond, there was a blazing red-and-blue neon sign for the Eat, Drink, and Be Sleepy Motel.

Rena almost wept with relief.

She was exhausted in body, mind, and spirit.

Zander gestured with his right hand, pointing to the exit as he veered the bike toward the little motel. With a light at the end of the proverbial tunnel, Rena let out a slow breath and kept her sights on the land of salvation. The beds were probably musty and the sheets scratchy, but it would do.

He brought the bike to a stop in one of the only empty spaces in the lot, and Rena hopped off before he even cut the engine. She stretched her arms over her head and arched her back in an attempt to work out the kinks. Among other sensations.

Zander flipped up the visor on his helmet and seemed to be surveying the quiet, dark parking lot of the diner and motel. Rena tugged off her helmet before propping it on her hip and quickly fluffing her hair with her free hand. She probably had major helmet hair. Not a good look. Not that she cared what he thought or anything.

Rena rolled her eyes at her foolishness. Yeah right. She did care, and that was more disturbing than anything else. Twenty-four hours ago, all Rena cared about was her work, Vito, and Pat. The rest of the world could be damned. Now, here she was, at a no-tell motel with the one person in the world who knew her secrets.

And he wanted nothing to do with her.

She was his job or assignment or pet project. He didn't care about her, and the sooner she accepted that fact, the better off she would be. Zander may have cracked the safe cocoon Rena had constructed around herself, but that didn't mean she had to let him tear the whole damn thing down.

She fleetingly recalled a paper cut she got the other day. It stung like crazy. One of the cruel ironies of the universe was that sometimes the smallest wounds carried the biggest wallop.

"We'll get our rooms, and if you're hungry, we can

grab a bite at their diner." He swung one long leg over the bike as he dismounted and then nodded toward the little eatery. "Sign says it's open twenty-four hours."

She didn't want to sit at a table with him or anywhere else. She needed space in order to regain her bearings and get her control back. All she wanted was a shower and a warm bed, so she could get her head on straight. He clearly wasn't in the mood for talking, and she wasn't in the mood to try and wrestle answers out of him. In the morning, after she'd had a good night's sleep, she would be prepared to deal with Zander and tackle the first few items on her unending list of questions.

"I'm not really hungry. Where are we, anyway?"

"Utah. We still have about ten or twelve hours of road between us and the ranch."

"Utah, huh?" She looked around and tried not to look as unimpressed as she felt. "For the past three hours, it's all looked the same."

"We'll be passing through more mountainous terrain tomorrow."

He continued avoiding her gaze, and her stomach flip-flopped as disappointment welled. Zander was doing his damnedest to keep his distance from her. It was for the best. She knew that. Then why was she feeling let down?

"Great." Rena gave him a thumbs-up. "Listen, I'm exhausted, and I have a hunch you're going to want to hit the road right after the sun comes up. Let's just get our rooms and then to each his own. Okay?"

Zander didn't look at her but gave her one of his guttural grunts as he removed his helmet. Any attraction she felt for him withered amid his clear disinterest in her. Typical. She had finally met a guy she was hot for and he was acting like she had the plague. She had put plenty of men in the friend zone in her day, but this was the first time someone was doing it to her.

It sucked.

He handed Rena her bag off the back of the bike and, without another word, headed for the motel office. She went with him, matching his silence with her own but all the while trying to pinpoint when everything went to shit, and the answer was obvious.

Zander's chilly demeanor toward her had everything to do with Vito. She knew it. They had obviously known each other before, and based off their combined reactions, it wasn't exactly a happy reunion. Whatever went down between the two men must have been a bad scene.

Okay. Fine. She could get her head around the weirdness of the fact that they knew each other. But seriously? What were the odds?

What bothered her more than the rest of it, though, was that Zander was acting like Rena had betrayed him somehow, or was in cahoots with Vito.

What a tangled mess. She knew they had to sort it all out, but she was too exhausted to even attempt it at the moment. Rena needed sleep and some alone time to get her bearings back.

She adjusted the shoulder strap of her bag as they stepped inside the small motel office. An older man, maybe in his late sixties, was watching *Jeopardy!* on a small black-and-white television while smoking a fat, stubby cigar. He hoisted his rotund body off the chair with a grunt and waved them over to the counter.

"You folks looking to check in?" He puffed a cloud of cigar smoke before placing the burning stub in a well-used crystal ashtray. "I only got one more room left, so you're in luck."

Zander's energy signature whisked faster around her at the same instant her own heartbeat ratcheted up a notch. Or twelve.

"Great," she said under her breath. "More cozy togetherness."

"You're welcome to go somewhere else, but the next closest place is about seventy-five miles up the road, and ain't no guarantees they'll have two rooms neither."

She fought the urge to comment again and sliced a glance at Zander, who didn't seem to be bothered by the situation at all. Jeez. Did anything get under this guy's skin?

"Oh man," Rena sighed. "I can't do another hour on that damned bike tonight. I need sleep. So please tell me it's a room with two double beds."

"Sorry, sweetie." The man laughed, a raspy, phlegmy sound, and winked at Zander. "Just the one. But it's a king-size bed, so there's plenty of room, if that's what you're lookin' for."

Rena was about to tell the old pervert to shove his cigar up his nose, but Zander interrupted.

"We'll take it." He pulled a wad of cash from his pocket. "How much for one night?"

"Don't I get a say in the matter?" she asked incredulously.

"You're the one who said she didn't want to ride for another hour. We could camp, but I only have one tent, and you don't seem like the outdoorsy type."

"But..." Rena let out a sound of disgust, because

he was right. She hated the notion of camping, and the motel was all the roughing it she wanted to deal with. "Oh, for goodness' sake. Fine. We'll take the room."

"Right then. That'll be eighty-five for the one night, and I'll need a credit card for a security deposit."

"Never use 'em." Zander peeled off three crisp one-hundred-dollar bills and placed them on the red counter. "How about three hundred and we call it even?"

"Fine by me, son." He scooped up the cash with his pudgy fingers before handing Zander a room key with a red-and-blue, diamond-shaped plastic tag. "Unit twenty-five. All the way down at the end. The diner's open all night, and we have the best pecan pie this side of the Mississippi. My wife, Myrtle, she bakes 'em fresh every day."

"Thanks." Zander nodded and went to the door. "You coming?"

Was a hint of a smile playing at his lips, or was she imagining it?

Rena let out a huff of frustration and brushed past him and out to the sidewalk. When they reached the room, it was as uninspired and boring as she had expected it to be, but the bed was enormous. It took up most of the space in the red, white, and blue motel room.

The bed was big, but the room was small, and when Zander stepped inside and closed the door, it got even smaller. Rena swallowed the lump in her throat and did her best to ignore him. Without waiting for him to say a word, Rena tossed her duffel on the bed and poked her head in the bathroom. It was simple and sterile-looking, with a tub and shower.

"At least it's clean," she said with a weak smile.

She lingered in the bathroom doorway for a moment, uncertain of what to do next. Before stepping into this room with Zander, the idea of getting in the shower had sounded awesome. Now, with him right there, in such close proximity, it seemed like a rather frightening prospect. Not because she thought he would hurt her or take advantage of her. Quite the opposite. He seemed annoyed by her presence.

For the first time in many years, Rena was unsure of herself.

"Uh...do you mind if I shower first?"

"Do whatever you want."

Rena winced and folded her arms over her chest, instinctively wanting to shield herself from Zander's frosty attitude. He was angry with her, but she didn't have a damn clue as to why. Even worse, she cared that he was upset with her, and she found that more unsettling than anything else.

Rena bit her lower lip and finally forced herself to ask the question, even though she was afraid of the answer.

"Why are you angry with me?"

Zander remained silent and tossed his leather jacket on the bed. He turned his back to her and stared out the window with his hands settled on his narrow hips. His tense energy signature bounced around the room like a ricocheting bullet, and she fought the instinct to duck.

"I get visions, but I'm not a mind reader," she whispered.

The conversation, the one she had been avoiding since leaving Vito at Sunnyfarm, was about to go down, and it scared the shit out of her. Not Zander. She wasn't afraid of him. Her gaze skimmed over his broad-shouldered form, and the tension in his body was matched by the agitation in his energy signature. There were secrets buried beneath the surface, and she knew, deep in her gut, that they had something to do with Vito and with her.

And *that* was what scared her.

What did Zander know about Vito? More to the point, did she really want to know? Not really, but she was sick and tired of the blank spaces that riddled the past, and she sure as hell didn't want any more of them in her present. And definitely *not* in her future. She squared her shoulders and struggled to keep her voice calm.

"Okay," Rena said quietly. "You're obviously pissed at Vito *and* at me, but I have no idea why. You wouldn't talk to me back at Sunnyfarm, and you've given me the silent treatment for the past several hundred miles. The only reason I've put up with it is because *technically,* you're my client, so how about we stop playing games and you fill me in on how you know Vito?"

"Bullshit," he said gruffly.

Zander grabbed the edges of the red-and-white-striped drapes and tugged them closed before spinning around to face her. The feral look in his glowing, crimson eyes made her take a step backward, but Zander didn't move. He stayed where he was but continued to glower at her.

"Excuse me?" Rena let out an incredulous laugh.

"Nobody can hide from you, Rena. That's what you said. Right?"

"Yes, but—"

"You can touch an item, *anything*, that he's held, and you could have seen right past his facade to who he *really* is." Zander moved toward her, slowly closing

the distance between them. "So don't stand there and
tell me you don't know what he did or what he is
capable of."

He was close now, his body so near to hers, his
musky cologne with the hint of leather swamped her
senses, making her dizzy. But Rena held her ground.
She never backed down from a challenge, and she sure
as hell wasn't going to start now. Especially not from
this accusation. Rena was many things, but a liar wasn't
one of them.

"How dare you presume to know what I can or
can't see?" Her eyes tingled with the surge of emotion,
and she let them shift. "You don't know a damn thing
about me."

"And *you* don't know a damn thing about Vito or
what he's done! Given your psychic ability, I can't for
the life of me figure out how that's possible."

"I only use my powers when I want to or need to,"
she shouted. "I told you, I learned how to control it when
I was a kid, because if I hadn't, I probably would've
gone bonkers by now. And I don't get any say in *what* I
see, only if I want to see it."

"I think you're lying to protect the old son of a bitch."

"Don't talk about him like that, and don't call me
a liar."

He took a step closer. "Then tell me what you know."

"I know he loved his wife and daughter more than
life itself."

"Is that what he told you?" Zander scoffed, a low,
gruff sound filled with contempt. "Love is a lie, Rena.
It's fleeting and a futile emotion that brings nothing but
pain and misery."

"Well, I'm sorry to burst your cynical, unfeeling bubble, dragon boy, but it's what I saw." Rena leaned in and took two steps toward him, so only inches separated their bodies. "And don't lecture me about the dangers of loving people or caring about them, okay? I know all about the pain it can inflict. I have a lifetime of proof. Do you have any idea what it's like for a six-year-old to be shoved aside like she's defective merchandise?"

Rena's voice wavered, and all the pent-up emotions, the feelings of rejection and loss, the ones she had stuffed down deep inside, began to boil over.

"Do you have any idea how many foster homes I've lived in?"

"Rena—"

"Twelve." The word was clipped and strangled, and her throat was thick with impending tears. "Twelve, Zander. It got to the point where I didn't even bother to unpack my bags. Not one family—not a single one— wanted me. No matter how much I begged or pleaded. Nobody would let me stay. I was a freak, a little weirdo who knew stuff she couldn't possibly know and made the bigger mistake of talking about it. Even the social workers looked at me like I was a mini mental patient. After being tossed from one place to the next, I finally split. I ran away and lived on the streets in Vegas."

"I didn't know that," he said with something that sounded a lot like regret.

"Vito does, or he did before he lost his marbles. I was picking pockets and, eventually, using my gift to get money out of tourists with a fortune-teller bit. Vito came around from time to time and tossed money in my hat. Never asked me for anything or tried to hit on me.

He was just a nice old man. Until one day, he offered to teach me his business, and *that's* when I looked in his memories. All I saw was a lonely old guy weeping and grieving for his wife and daughter. He *loved* them, and that was all I needed to know."

"You should've looked further, Rena." His voice was deadly quiet but carried a wallop. "Then you would have seen the truth. He isn't the man you think he is."

"I'll tell you *my* truth," she seethed. "Vito took me off the street when I was seventeen. He clothed me, fed me, and treated me like I was his family. He is the *only* person on this planet who ever gave a crap about me or my well-being." Rena poked him in the chest with one finger, punctuating her last word—all of it fueled by her love for Vito and her fierce desire to protect him.

Zander grabbed her wrists and tugged her up against his firm, unyielding body. His eyes glowed brightly at her between the long strands of hair that always drifted over his forehead.

"He's a liar and a murderer," Zander said. "He doesn't care about you any more than those other people. He's been using you, Rena. Plain and simple."

"From where I stand, *you're* the guy who's been shady from minute one."

"His name isn't even Vito Fox."

Rena stilled but said nothing as Zander's gaze flickered over her face as though seeking her reaction, but she gave him none. His thumbs rasped along the inside of her wrists, and his chest expanded and contracted against hers. It was remarkably unsettling to be attracted to someone who was also pissing her off.

"So what?" she huffed, trying to focus on how annoyed she was instead of the shimmer of lust. "People change their names all the time."

"His real name, the one I knew him by, was Victor Pamchenko, and I can promise you that he's done *nothing* but lie and manipulate you from the moment he found you."

"Let me go." Rena tried to pull herself free from his ironclad grip, but it was no use.

"Do you really think he found you by accident, Rena?"

He walked her backward as he spoke, and she gasped when her butt met the wall. Zander pressed her hands there, along either side of her head, and held her in place. She arched her back in an effort to make him move, but all it did was press her breasts against his chest.

He didn't give an inch. The man was an immovable force of nature.

"You said he treated you like family?" Zander's voice was quiet and gruff, barely above a whisper. "That's because *you are* his family—his clan."

"What are you talking about?" Rena said in a shaky whisper.

A feeling of dread curled through her like smoke, because somewhere, deep down, Rena knew what Zander was going to say.

"Victo—Vito is Amoveo, from the Fox Clan." Zander's jaw clenched. "Just like you."

"He can't be." Her throat tightened, thick with emotion as she fought to comprehend what Zander was saying. "That's ridiculous... He's not a shapeshifter. I would've seen that."

But even as the words tumbled from her lips, Rena

knew she wasn't being honest with him or with herself.
She had no control over what she saw in her visions. If
what Zander said was true, then the one person in the
world she believed loved her…never did.

"Oh, not anymore," Zander bit out. "But he was a
shifter from the Fox Clan… He's Amoveo…like you…
and her."

Her gaze swept up his throat and over the hard lines
and sharp angles of his square jaw, as a few more pieces
began to fall into place. Fox Clan? Memories of the
vision and the young woman in the yellow dress came
flooding back, and Rena's blood ran cold.

"The girl in the woods," she murmured. Her eyes
locked with his as the truth began to come into focus. "The
one you and your brother fought over…I-I saw her…she
changed into a fox. You mean *she* was Vito's daughter?"

"Arianna." Zander nodded.

"Oh my God."

Rena knew it was true. That was the name Vito called
her in his dementia-filled moments. A chill whispered
over her flesh, like the kiss of death, as the name, the
one Vito had called her countless times, hung in the air
like a dead weight. Her stomach churned as the horrible,
ugly truth settled over her with brutal force.

Arianna.

All this time, the one person she thought had truly
loved her didn't love her at all. Not really. Instead, he
had been using her to replace his dead daughter. A deep
ache welled in Rena's chest, and tears stung the backs
of her eyes, but she refused to let them fall in front
of Zander.

"But you aren't her," Zander murmured.

"No, I'm not," she whispered. "I'm just a freak of nature. Not human. Not Amoveo. But something unwanted and in-between."

"You are *not* unwanted, Rena." Her name dragged from his lips gruffly as the weight of his body pressed harder against her. "And no one has the right to make you feel less than the beautiful, remarkable creature that you are."

His glittering gaze skittered over her face before lingering on her mouth. His hips tilted. Rena sighed as she slipped her leg between his and was met with hard heat. It was erotic and enticing to have his body pressed along hers. To be pinned between Zander and the wall with nothing separating them but the thin fabric of their clothing. His chest rose and fell in time with his heavy breathing, contracting and expanding, and making her acutely aware of every spot where their bodies met. She opened her clenched fists and immediately tangled her fingers with his.

"What am I?" she asked through trembling lips.

"Exquisite," Zander murmured.

Rena wasn't sure if he leaned down or she reached up, but when his mouth crashed over hers, everything was blotted out other than the feel of him. A strangled groan of lust rumbled in his throat as he pressed her harder against the wall as he devoured her. Rena arched her back, her breasts melding deliciously against the hard planes of his torso as his tongue swept along hers.

Heat flared between her legs, and the dull, aching throb swelled when Zander pressed the firm plane of his thigh against the heat of her sex. Rena slowed the kiss and rotated her hips, riding his leg in time with each deep, sweeping pass of his tongue. Desire coiled deep in her belly, and she reveled in the decadent swell of lust, floating in the sensation, wanting and needing to get swept away by it.

She didn't want to think anymore, to dwell on questions or Amoveo or betrayals. All she wanted to do was drown in the erotic feel and taste of *him*.

Zander kept her hands pinned high above her head and trailed his lips down her throat. Rena gasped when he tilted his hips, putting more pressure on her most sensitive spot, which sent wicked licks of need flickering beneath her skin. But she wanted more. Rena wanted to lose herself in the feel of him, to run her lips and hands over his body, giving him the same pleasure he was giving her.

"Wait." She curled her fingers around his, and her lips grazed his ear as he nuzzled her neck. "I want to touch you, Zander."

Her body was tight and primed, ready for more, but on a dime, everything changed.

Zander cursed quietly, his hot breath fanning over the flesh of her throat as his entire body stilled against hers. He lifted his head slowly, and when those shimmering crimson eyes bored into hers before flickering back to their human state, Rena's stomach roiled. She had expected to see lust or need, but instead, all she saw stamped into his features was regret. Confusion, abrupt and heart-wrenching, washed over her as Zander slowly released her hands and stepped away. His cold expression and sudden change of demeanor stole the breath from her lungs.

As the space between them increased, her heart

sank and her body cooled with sickening speed. Rena dropped her arms and folded them over her chest, feeling self-conscious and exposed. She pushed her body harder against the wall, wanting nothing more than to disappear. The pitying look in his eyes was like a kick in the gut.

"I'm sorry."

His voice was as gruff and coarse as the change in direction.

"Don't apologize," she said in a voice that sounded stronger than she felt. "Just tell me what's wrong."

"All of it," he ground out. The line between his eyes deepened, and grief edged his words. "Everything. Don't you see? Vic—Vito chose *you* because of *her*. Because of Arianna. This is all fucked up because of her. He used you, Rena."

"Right." Her voice trembled. "Well, I guess he's not the only one. Is he?"

Rena's heart sank as the truth set in. The heated, primal look in Zander's eyes and the intimacy of his touch hadn't been meant for her at all. Every time this guy looked at Rena, and especially when he had kissed her, he was seeing his dead girlfriend.

Rena tilted her chin defiantly and arched one eyebrow, stuffing the pain and regret deep down under the surface. She was good at that. Rena was an expert at acting like she didn't give a shit about anything or anyone.

"What's your point?"

"You aren't her," he murmured.

"No, I'm not, *Mr. Lorens*. Which is something you would do well to remember. I'm not some lame, reincarnated version of your girlfriend, okay?" Rena dropped her arms to her sides and her hands curled into fists, but it didn't stop her body from shaking. Adrenaline pumped through her veins at a furious pace as she struggled to make sense of her increasingly insane world.

"Agreed." He gave her a curt nod, his breathing heavy. "However, there is one way you are alike."

"Oh yeah. How's that?"

"You aren't for me."

Rena blanched but held her ground. She didn't think a physical blow would have hurt half as much as the force of his words had. It wasn't the first time she'd been wounded by what someone said, but somehow, the sting seemed far greater. She could have blamed it on her enhanced Amoveo senses, but deep down, Rena knew that would be a lie.

There was nothing supernatural about getting your feelings stomped on. Suffering a broken heart was part of the human experience.

"Well, thanks for the tip." She settled her hands on her hips. "And one more thing: I may not know every tidbit about Vito's past, but I do know that he loved his daughter. But *she* is dead. He knows it too, even if he gets confused sometimes. Which, by the way, isn't his fault. You know what else, Zander? I *am* here. Living and breathing and taking care of him. His daughter is dead and buried. Arianna died a long time ago."

"I know." Zander strode to the door and yanked it open. He stood in the doorway in silence for what felt like forever. Before he stepped out into the night, he murmured over his shoulder, "I'm the one who killed her."

—∾∾—

The all-consuming desire to shift into his dragon hadn't been this strong in centuries, and the futility of it was maddening. Zander stormed along the sidewalk, the motel room doors a blur in his peripheral vision. Every inch of his body was taut with anger, shame, and frustration. His hands were clenched in tight fists, and he kept his furious burning gaze on the dark silhouette of the mountain in the distance.

He had to get out of that room and away from Rena.

If he had stayed in there one more second, there would have been no stopping him from repeating his sins of the past. The woman had no idea who she had been dealing with when it came to Vito. The son of a bitch didn't give a shit about her or her well-being. He was only using her to replace the daughter he had lost.

The old bastard didn't deserve her love or tenderness.

Then again, neither did Zander, but that hadn't stopped him from wanting her. Damn the universe and the fates for their twisted plans, and damn him for being a fool for allowing himself to feel *anything* for her.

A group of leather-clad bikers, rowdy and most likely high on something, came stumbling out of the diner, but he kept moving. If he paused, even for a moment, he would find a reason to release his rage on them, and that wouldn't end well for anyone.

He needed space for his mind and his body.

Zander slipped past the building and broke into a jog. He pumped his arms faster. His boots hitting the dirt rang through the moonlit night, the only sound in the deserted field. Like much of the scenery in this part of Utah, dusty fields dotted with brush and cactus stretched for miles.

He closed his eyes, his breath coming quickly, wishing now more than ever he could shift into his dragon and take to the sky. An image of his brother, Zed, in his dragon form flickered through Zander's mind, and with it came a wave of regret. The one thing he longed for was all that his brother had, and he was being tormented by it.

Slowing his pace, Zander finally came to a stop. Self-pity wouldn't free Zed or him, and it definitely wouldn't do anything to help Rena. He had to keep the ultimate goal in mind—breaking the curse and freeing Zed. Getting distracted by Vito or his own misplaced attraction to Rena would achieve nothing. Vito obviously wasn't going anywhere, and Zander could deal with him after Zed was freed.

And being focused on his goal did *not* mean screwing around with his brother's intended mate. No matter how beautiful or maddeningly stubborn she was. He rolled his shoulders, attempting to rid himself of the need to crawl out of his skin. If only he could fly. That had always been one remedy that never failed him, but, of course, it was also the one he had learned to do without.

Breathing heavily, with sweat covering his skin, he turned his face to the starry, moonlit sky and stretched his arms wide. He squeezed his eyes shut and fought to recall what it had felt like to shift into his dragon. To break free of his far smaller and weaker human body and embrace the power of his clan. A smile curved his lips, and he reached wider still.

If he united Zed and Rena and the curse was lifted, then he would no longer have to rely on memories of days long ago. His eyes tingled and shifted as the ghostly reminder flickered over his skin. Like a kiss from a long-forgotten lover, it whispered through him with haunting clarity.

If he concentrated hard enough, he could almost feel the heat of the beast as it fought to break free. Images of Rena, her fiery-amber eyes flashing with gritty determination, whisked into his head, and with them came a searing flash of pain down his left thigh. The sudden onset of agony took him by surprise and sent him to one knee. Gasping for air, his left quad throbbed as the burning sensation seared deeper. Zander's right knee dug into the bits of rock in the dirt, and he pressed his left hand over his thigh, as though it might ease the sting.

He had many scars on his body from various mishaps over the years, but they rarely gave him pain. The one that marred his left thigh was a bullet wound from a run-in with a pissed-off card player outside a saloon in what is now called New Mexico. The bullet wound was alongside a six-inch gash from a motorcycle accident back in the fifties, but like his numerous other scars, it had never bothered him.

Until now.

"What the hell?" he whispered through hitching breath.

The light of the moon, along with his newly returned clan vision, allowed him to see his jean-clad leg clearly, and he smiled in spite of the pain. His night vision, a gift he hadn't used in centuries, was sharper than ever. Zander let out a slow breath and brushed at his jeans with his fingers, but there was nothing except dust.

There was still one gift other than his dragon he desperately missed.

Communicating with the earth.

Zander closed his eyes as he lay both hands on the dusty, rocky ground. He sharpened his focus but, as he suspected, was met only with darkness and silence, as he had been since the spell had been cast. No images came. Even with five centuries behind him, Zander could recall the rush of power that surged when he could channel the knowledge of the earth. It was how his people could see all that they had missed when emerging from a long hibernation.

"Still nothing," he whispered into the darkness.

He sighed and rose to his feet, but before he could wallow in self-pity, something completely unexpected occurred.

Out of nowhere, Rena's voice whisked around him in the night and into his mind. *No more lies. I want the truth.*

Every single muscle clenched, and his breath caught in his throat. Zander shook his head, believing he must have been imagining it. No one had spoken with him telepathically since the day he had been cursed.

He looked around, turning slowly, scanning every single inch in his vicinity. Though he could see every detail, each blade of grass and the edge of every crag and rock, there was no sign of Rena. Other than a few creatures scurrying along the brush, Zander was alone.

He swallowed hard as his heart rate picked up and his mind raced. Then he heard her again. Rena's voice, soft and gentle, whispered into his mind like a caress and soothed his tortured soul like a balm on a wound.

You can't hide from me.

Desire flared brightly as her mind touched his with the most intimate form of communication. Eyes blazing,

Zander spun around, and a growl rumbled in his chest as he took off toward the motel. His worst fear was being realized in the form of exquisite torture.

The universe had definitely screwed it up again.

Chapter 9

RENA STARED AT THE CLOSED DOOR OF THE MOTEL ROOM for a good five minutes while trying to process what Zander had said before storming out. *He* had killed Arianna? That made no sense. He loved her, and while Zander might be stubborn, he wasn't a murderer. He was a good man, if not a tortured one, but at least now she knew why he was all messed up.

Sort of.

Arianna had done one hell of a number on Zander and his brother. Not only that, but whatever she did or however she had behaved had gotten her killed, and *that* had been torturing Vito and Zander.

Nibbling her thumbnail, Rena paced the room a couple of times, debating whether or not she should go after him, before flopping back onto the bed with a huff. In the process, she knocked Zander's leather jacket onto the floor. With a groan, she pushed herself up and leaned over the edge of the bed before grabbing his jacket and tossing it over to the chair in the corner. As the coat hit the arm of the chair, the spirit stone came tumbling out and onto the busy red, white, and blue carpet.

It rolled to a stop in front of Rena's boot-clad feet. She bit her lower lip and stared at the stone for a second. If she wanted to get some answers, that damn piece of lumpy quartz would give them up sooner than Zander would.

No more lies, she thought. *I want the truth.*

Rena dropped to her knees beside the stone and rubbed her sweaty palms over her jeans. Letting out a slow, steadying breath, she reached out with shaking fingers and hovered her right hand above the stone. Last time she'd touched this thing, she had been taken by surprise, but now that she knew what to expect, Rena hoped she'd be able to control the slide into Zander's unusually powerful memories.

"Here we go," she whispered.

You can't hide from me.

Rena closed her eyes and focused on her breathing, keeping it slow and steady and in time with the beat of her heart. With her mind and body focused, she lowered her hand and curled her fingers around the cool, bumpy stone. A current of electricity shimmied up her arm and slithered beneath her flesh, like an eel sliding through the water, but Rena remained calm as the world around her shifted from solid to ethereal.

She floated in spiritual limbo as the foggy darkness enveloped her, but this time there was no pain. The throbbing in her chest, which usually accompanied the transition, was gone and replaced by a tingling of static electricity. Tied to neither her body nor the earthly plane, Rena focused on the stone and the spirit streams that were embedded in it to guide her.

Zander's was clear and familiar, strong and steady.

There was another one there as well. Though similar, it was frenetic and muddled. A riot of confusion.

That one had to belong to Zed, so similar to Zander's and yet different at the same time. Almost like two sides of a coin. Back to back. Bound but separate.

As the fog lifted and the world came into view, Rena recognized the now-familiar scenario of brother against brother. She stood behind the tree and winced as Zed's enormous body crashed into Zander's. The identical dragons slammed into the tree line along the clearing, sending branches and debris flying through the air.

With the battle raging on, Rena scanned the forest for Arianna. It only took a minute to find her. She was in her fox form and sitting by the base of a tree, watching the entire battle like she was sitting ringside at some medieval ultimate fighting match.

Rena was about to try and make her way around and get closer to Arianna when a huge stream of fire shot across the clearing. She shrieked and ducked behind a tree for cover as Zander's voice thundered through her mind.

Stop, Zed!

Zander and Zed faced off, their wings spread wide as they shifted their weight from side to side. The moonlight glinted off their hides in flashes of iridescent red and gold as their muscular bodies moved, each carefully eyeing the other. Rena's gaze flicked over the flattened patches of trees, and the sight of them made her heart race. She'd never seen such destruction before. No wonder these creatures hadn't survived. There would be no way for them to exist in the modern world.

How could they?

Rena swallowed hard and focused on the spirit streams of the brothers, instead of the immense power they possessed. Their strength and size fascinated and terrified her, as did their potential for absolute destruction. Zander and Zed breathed deeply, and their bodies *heaved with effort. Neither was letting down their guard, but Zander was the first to break the silence. He shook his enormous head and snorted loudly, which sent puffs of smoke into the night.*

I came to tell her good-bye!

Then, in a blinding eruption of fire and smoke, Zander shifted from dragon to man before Rena's eyes. The transformation was swift and effortless. He looked much like he did today except for the old-fashioned clothing. Like Arianna, he was dressed in an outfit from another time.

Rena bit her lower lip and glanced from man to beast.

"Arianna is not my mate, Brother." Zander took a step toward Zed but stopped when the dragon growled. "We cannot fight fate, and I will die before continuing this battle with you."

Fire flickered brightly as it licked up the tree beside Rena, the remnant of their fight lighting up the night with a macabre orange glow. She held her breath and clutched the tree trunk, the heat of the neighboring flames washing over her flesh almost to the point of pain. The tension in the air was thick with fury, and for a split second, Rena thought Zed was going to roast Zander like a marshmallow.

But he didn't.

Zed spread his wings wide, and in a flash of flickering fire and smoke, he vanished, and when the cloud dissipated, the dragon was gone, and a man stood in his place.

Holy crap. They're identical twins.

Zed looked exactly like Zander but was dressed in an outfit that she had only seen men wear in the movies. A light-colored, long-sleeved shirt was belted at the waist, and his brown pants were tucked into well-worn knee-high boots. He had the same tall, broad-shouldered, manly build, and his eyes glowed red, like Zander's. The only difference, other than his energy signature, was his hair, which was far shorter.

Physically, Zed and Zander were identical, but that was where the similarities ended, at least as far as Rena was concerned. Zed's face was carved in a mask of contempt and anger, and his energy pattern was as tumultuous as ever.

Zed's riotous nature was a far cry from Zander's calm, strong presence.

"You lie!"

The girl piped up, and the two men looked equally surprised by her outburst. Rena had practically forgotten Arianna was even there. She had shifted back to her human form, and the woman was pissed. She stormed over to the brothers and pointed at Zander accusingly as she sidled in next to Zed, snuggling up to him like a snake.

"He is speaking untruths, Zed. Zander begged me to run away with him tonight." She turned to Zed and batted her big eyes at him in a disgustingly coquettish move. "I told him that I loved you, not him. He spoke of killing you, my love. I couldn't bear it."

"Traitor," Zed seethed. He pulled Arianna tighter against him as his furious gaze glowed brightly at his brother. "You shame our clan with your lies and deceit."

The horrified expression on Zander's face was nothing short of heartbreaking, and it made Rena want to punch that Arianna broad right in the nose. Chicks like her gave the rest of the women in the world a bad rap.

"Arianna!"

The booming and familiar male voice ricocheted through the woods, and Rena was stunned to see Vito, far younger and full of life, step out of the burned forest. This wasn't the old, fragile man she had known over the past seven years but a vibrant, virile figure brimming with energy and youth. He didn't look much older than Arianna and could have passed for her brother. The white hair Rena knew was instead a dark blond, and his barrel-chested build was leaps and bounds away from the frail form back at Sunnyfarm.

Vito brandished a massive sword in one hand and grabbed his daughter by the arm before yanking her away from Zed.

"I warned you to stay away from these creatures, Arianna." He waved the tip of the sword toward the devastation and then aimed it at Zed. "Look upon the havoc they wreak. These beasts do nothing but burn and destroy. 'Tis why their clan is all but extinct. They fight among themselves like the simpleminded monsters they are. The Amoveo Council has forbidden them from mixing with our clans, a law you are all too familiar with, Arianna. The slayers shall wipe them all out before long, and I, for one, would be happy to help."

With no warning and in a flash of fire, Zed erupted into his dragon and let out a roar that shook the earth. The fear and surprise on Vito's face as he stumbled backward was rivaled by the expression of satisfaction covering Arianna's.

"NO!" Zander shouted. "Zed, stop!"

Arianna's father increased his distance from the brothers, pulling her with him as Zander shifted into his dragon and tackled Zed with the full force of his massive body.

The dragons clashed and tumbled into the trees as Vito and Arianna shifted into their fox forms and scurried into the woods. Rena cried out when a blazing stream of fire shot through the air and engulfed the forest in flames. The intense heat made Rena step back, and her arm flew in front of her face in an attempt to shield herself. Even though it was only a memory, it felt as real and raw as though she had been there.

The strangled, anguished cry of a man cut through the night, the sound of it bringing the battle to a halt. Rena swiped at her eyes, the smell of burned wood and something far worse filling her nostrils. Smoke clung to her, smothering her. She coughed and stumbled to the left, gripping the trunk of the tree to keep from falling.

The clearing was charred and black, leaving the moonlit forest a smoldering mess of scarred trees. Amid the ashes and destruction, there was the unmistakable form of a woman, frozen in time, like the images Rena had seen of Pompeii, people who had died where they stood, consumed by ash and lava.

The brothers had done exactly what Vito had said they would do. They destroyed and burned everything in their path.

Including Arianna.

———

Zander burst into the motel room and found Rena kneeling on the carpet. Her eyes were closed, and based on the radiant reddish light emanating from her hand, she was holding the spirit stone. Sweaty and still catching his breath, Zander closed the door quietly and moved cautiously toward Rena.

Unlike the first time she had taken hold of the stone, Rena was completely calm and oozed serenity. He didn't want to do anything to disturb her, but he also didn't want to take his eyes off her in case the situation changed. Her powers were emerging with surprising speed, and given that she was a hybrid, Zander didn't know what to expect next.

Whether or not she was aware of it, Rena had spoken to him telepathically. How far behind were the rest of her Amoveo gifts? For all he knew, she could shift into her fox at an inopportune moment. Like on the back of his motorcycle, for example.

Shit. He hated flying blind, and after five hundred years, there was little that surprised him. Meeting Rena had changed all of that.

He knelt down beside her, and right when he was about to call her name, her eyes flicked open, and the spirit stone tumbled from her hand, onto the rug. Zander studied her carefully, waiting for her to say or do something, but she continued to stare straight ahead. Finally, after a dramatic pause, she turned her gaze to his and, without any warning, slapped him across the face.

Hard.

The stinging on his cheek was nothing compared to his bruised ego. It wasn't the first time he'd been slapped by a woman, but somehow, being smacked by *this* woman was worse.

"What the hell did you do that for?" Rubbing the side of his face, Zander stood up and stepped back, giving her the space she clearly wanted.

"*That's* for jerking me around and turning my life upside down."

Rena rose to her feet and pointed at him accusingly. Her eyes shifted to glowing amber with flecks of gold, and her hands curled into fists at her side.

"How about if you cut the crap and tell me what's going on? Stop doling it out to me a little bit at a time, like you're giving me some kind of awesome surprise at the end of it all."

Rena inched nearer, her oval-shaped face carved into a mask of determination. Her cheeks were flushed, and strands of chestnut-colored hair tinged with red framed her determined chin. Indignant outrage only made her more beautiful. *Damn it*.

"Not a little bit at a time. Not *some* of it. I want to know *everything*. About you, your brother, Arianna, Vito…and me."

Zander met her fierce gaze with his but remained motionless as she continued to advance. Rena stopped about a foot away from him, and the heat of her body flickered over him in wickedly enticing waves. He swallowed the surge of lust and the finger-twitching urge to stroke her soft, satiny skin, to soothe the swirl of anger and indignation.

"Right now," she said through clenched teeth. "Or I'm getting out of here. You and your brother can go straight to hell, and I'll go back to pretending I'm not a complete freak of nature."

Zander's jaw clenched while debating exactly what to say, but an old adage ran through his head: it's not what you say but how you say it. Though it had been years since he had tried to initiate telepathy with anyone, his instincts kicked in as his energy signature tangled with hers in an invisible dance.

His lips quirked. It was like riding a bike.

For starters, your ability to telepath has kicked in.

The expression of surprise on her face would have been comical if it weren't so sad. Her eyes shifted back to their lovely shade of brown, and her lips quivered as her mouth fell open in disbelief. She shook her head and slowly backed away.

"What the hell was that?"

"Telepathy," he said calmly. "Most supernaturals can do it. The Amoveo and Dragons among them."

All Amoveo can communicate this way. I heard you in my mind before you picked up the spirit stone. Your powers are emerging more quickly than I expected.

"Hang on." Rena held out both her hands as she continued backing up. When her legs bumped the edge of the bed, she sat down abruptly. "Wh-what else? And just tell me the regular way, please. No more weird mind talking."

Zander nodded curtly and squared his shoulders. Her confusion was heartbreaking, but he knew there was no going back. He could no longer take her transition as slowly as he had originally hoped or wait until they reached the Amoveo's ranch.

Their time was running out in more ways than one.

As he spoke, he moved closer but kept his voice calm and even, hoping it would soothe her. The woman's energy signature was racing around the room like the Tasmanian devil and tangling with his calmer one in the process.

The sensation was as enticing as it was distracting.

His heartbeat ticked up, and desire stirred in his blood, but Zander forced himself to focus on Rena. Zander could handle discomfort—he had gotten used to it—but he wanted to minimize Rena's if he could.

"Pureblooded Amoveo begin to gain their powers during puberty. It starts with dream walking, then telepathy, then shifting into their clan animal, and at full strength, most can use the power of visualization. They can use it to travel with the speed of thought and make almost anything materialize purely with the power of the mind. Dragons, my people, have these gifts as well. Though we have other gifts the Amoveo do not have."

"You mean aside from me *supposedly* being able to turn into an animal—"

"A fox."

"Right," she laughed, but it held little humor. "I will also be able to simply think about something and make it appear. Like, think about a book I want to read, and boom, there it is? Or I blink like Jeannie, and wham, I'm in New York City?"

"Yes." A smile tugged at his lips, and he bent at the knees in front of her. "There's a bit more to it, but that's the idea. Your mind is your most powerful tool. But since you are a hybrid, I'm not sure how many of the Amoveo gifts you'll have."

"This is insane," she whispered shakily. "Like, there isn't one single bit of this situation that isn't completely outrageous."

Rena was looking down at her hands, which were clutched in her lap. He could see she was trying to hold it together but worried that she was reaching her limit.

Unable to stop himself, Zander covered her fingers with his and gave them a gentle, reassuring squeeze.

"Your hand seems to be feeling better." He brushed the edge of the gauze with his thumb. "If you pull back that bandage, I bet you'll find that the wound is completely healed."

Wordlessly, Rena peeled off the bandage, and her eyes grew wide as she studied the scar that had already replaced the bloody wound.

"I-I hadn't even realized…" Her voice trailed off as she lowered her hands back into her lap, running one fingertip over the pale red mark. "Everything's happening so fast," she whispered.

"Richard and the other Amoveo at the ranch will be able to explain things to you better than I can."

"Because you aren't Amoveo, you're a dragon?" She shook her head as though trying to rid herself of something unpleasant. "I cannot *believe* I just said that out loud. It sounds even crazier than it does in my head."

"The Dragons are related to the Amoveo. We— they—are all shifters, but some of our powers are different. Or in my case…*were*."

She lifted her face, and when her teary eyes met his, it was like a kick in the gut. He tangled his fingers with hers and stroked his thumb over the top of her hand, which was far smoother and softer than his own. A knot of need curled in his stomach. Touching Rena, even if it had only been meant to comfort her, had been a mistake.

"Were?" Her brow furrowed. "What happened to them?"

"My people are all gone, Rena. Zed and I are the last, but—"

"You and your brother are dragons," she whispered.

Her brow furrowed as her warm, brown eyes searched his. "You fought over Arianna, and she was killed during the battle. That much I got, and now I understand why Vito was so upset by seeing you."

Zander nodded and swallowed the bitter swell of guilt as he tore his gaze from hers and stared at their intertwined fingers. Her smooth, fair skin stood out against his more weathered hands, the contrast only highlighting their differences. In spite of knowing what the right choice was, all Zander wanted to do was drop to his knees, wrap his arms around her, and bury his face against her soft, warm body, seeking shelter though he deserved none.

"It was an accident, Zander."

The gentleness in her voice called to him. Zander tightened his grip on her, mesmerized by the slow stroke of her thumb over his. With each sweep of flesh against flesh, more of his resolve crumbled. She was like the tide rippling over the sands, wearing away layer after layer, leaving him bare.

"Perhaps," he whispered, "but there hasn't been a single day in all the years since that I haven't wished I could go back and change it."

"When *did* all of that happen?" She let out a nervous laugh. "You guys looked like you stepped out of an episode of *Game of Thrones*. And why do *you* look exactly the same, but *Vito* is an old man now?"

"After Arianna was killed, Vito enlisted a local witch to curse us because he believed death would have been too kind. We were stripped of our powers. I was trapped in my human form, and Zed was banished to hibernation. He's walked the dreamrealm in his dragon form, and it's driven him to madness. If the curse isn't broken by the five-hundred-year anniversary, then Zed will be trapped there forever, lost and confused with no way out."

"Let me guess…the deadline is…"

"All Hallows' Eve."

"Halloween. That's this Saturday."

"Yes." His voice was gruff and strained. He should let her hands go, but her womanly skin felt like satin against his. "For five hundred years, I've tried everything else, but nothing has worked."

"I still can't believe you're five centuries old, but you are, aren't you?"

He nodded curtly but said nothing, studying Rena closely for her reaction. Her eyes drifted over him, and her energy signature began to smooth out, some of the tension easing back. The hard knot of unease in his chest began to unfurl bit by bit when she didn't freak out, like he thought she might.

"I'd say you and Vito both fared pretty well," she said with a nervous laugh. "Although you don't look like you've aged at all."

"I haven't, and believe me, living forever isn't all it's cracked up to be." He closed his eyes and reveled in the gentle weight of her hands in his. "It's lonely and, at times, hopeless."

"Zander?" Her voice was soft and hesitant. Rena cupped his cheek with one hand and gently lifted his face, so he would look her in the eyes, which were filled with determination. "What *exactly* does all of this have to do with me?"

"There is only way I know of to free my brother."

"Okay," she said slowly. "Why do I feel like I'm not gonna be psyched with what you're about to say?"

"Zed's mate, the one woman who is destined to bind her life with his, should be able to release him."

His heart clenched in his chest as he forced himself to speak the words for the first time. He didn't think it could sound worse if he said it out loud. However, as the truth tumbled from his lips and he stared into her large brown eyes, filled with a desperate need to understand, to comprehend the enormity of what he was telling her, something in Zander's chest crumbled.

The loss of everything he had wished for in the secret, unspoken corners of his heart was swift, immediate, and crushing.

"You are Zed's mate, Rena. Only you can free him from the curse. Free both of us."

As her brow furrowed, she opened her mouth to argue with him, but Zander shook his head, forcing himself to release her hands before rising to his feet. He went to the door and yanked it open, his frustration increasing by the second. All the muscles in his back bunched as the image of his dragon flickered through his head.

"No way." She shook her head furiously. "You're telling me that I'm supposed to go find some cursed dragon and be his *mate*? Some guy I've never even met? This is the twenty-first century, Zander. Stuff like this doesn't happen. Hello? Ever heard of feminism? I get to choose who I want to be with. It's not supposed to be dictated to me."

"There's no fighting fate, Rena. You belong to him— to Zed." Zander couldn't look at her any longer, because if he did, it would shatter the last of his resolve. "I'll go get us something to eat. You should get a shower. I'll sleep on the floor. The bed is yours."

Without waiting for her to respond, he shut the door and strode toward the diner. It was all out in the open now. She was meant for his brother, not for him. There were no more surprises waiting for either of them, and the path ahead was clear. By Saturday, Zed would be free, and so would Zander. This was what he had been wishing for, for the past five centuries. He should be elated. Jumping for joy. Instead, he wanted to beat the piss out of someone.

Zander tugged open the door to the diner with another familiar saying drifting through his mind.

Careful what you wish for…you shall surely receive it.

Chapter 10

EVEN WITH THE SLEEPING PILL SHE HAD TAKEN, RENA HAD barely gotten any rest last night. Between the latest revelations from Zander and the physical exhaustion from the road trip, to say nothing of the draining visions, Rena had tossed and turned for hours. She hadn't dreamed either, but since she hardly slept, that was no big shocker.

Her emotions were all over the map.

Excitement mixed with fear about her newly discovered heritage, but curiosity dominated, which was why she hadn't hightailed it out of there. She had spent most of her life wondering where she came from, and while the answer wasn't anything she had ever expected, it sure as hell was interesting.

The part that *wasn't* so interesting and the piece of this little adventure that really pissed her off? Being somebody's mate. What the hell kind of crap was that? Zander said she "belonged" to his brother? This was the twenty-first century, and women didn't *belong* to anyone other than themselves.

Not to mention that she had the hots for Zander, her supposed mate's brother. This situation was a class A clusterfuck.

The one question she would likely never get a truthful answer to was in regard to Vito. Had he only used Rena as a replacement for his dead daughter, or did he really, truly care for her? She tried to convince herself that the not knowing was worse than anything else, but it was futile to agonize over it. Vito was lost in the topsy-turvy world of dementia and would never be able to give Rena the answers she wanted.

Maybe it was better that way.

Rena was in such turmoil, she had opted to retreat to bed. By the time Zander had gotten back with the food, she was already showered and under the covers. She had pretended to be asleep and kept the blanket over her head. He had been true to his word and slept on the floor, and she wasn't sure if she was relieved he didn't try anything or insulted.

Or disappointed.

When she woke up from a fitful snooze, the sun was streaming in the room, and she was alone. Zander's pillow was on the chair, with the blanket folded neatly on top. Who knew the guy who looked like a bad-boy biker was a folder of blankets? There was a cup of coffee on the nightstand and a chocolate doughnut sitting on top of it. Next to it was a note scrawled on a piece of scrap paper that simply said:

I'm outside. Ready when you are.

At least the guy had left her breakfast.

That was more than she could say for men she had actually slept with, let alone one who had voluntarily spent the night on a questionable-looking rug with a lame blanket and even lamer pillow.

She showered and dressed quickly. When she got outside, Zander was standing by his motorcycle. Clad in an outfit almost identical to the one the day before, he had his back to her and was looking toward the mountain in the distance. Rena adjusted the strap of the bag over her shoulder while she tried to figure out what to say.

"Give me your bag." He stuck out his hand but didn't turn around. "I'll strap it on the bike."

Well, so much for making conversation.

"I'm not an invalid, thank you." Rena's cheeks flamed, and she let out a sigh of frustration. "I can do it myself."

She made quick work of unhooking the bungee cords already strapped over his bag. She could feel his eyes on her and sensed he was right behind her. Watching her every move. In about three minutes, and with a bit more struggle than she would have liked, Rena had her bag securely tied down with his.

"There." She pushed the hair off her face and smiled with satisfaction. "We're ready. Let's go."

Without so much as an okay, Zander shoved the shiny black-and-silver motorcycle helmet in front of her. Rena grabbed it with both hands and put it on her head with more force than necessary.

"So, what's the plan for today?" she asked, not sure if she really wanted the answer. "Ride until my butt is numb all the way to the shapeshifter ranch?"

"We still have at least nine or ten hours to go."

Zander straddled the bike with the ease of experience. There was something about the way he carried himself—pure confidence and total command of his body that sent a shiver of desire up Rena's neck. She brushed at it absently and forced herself to focus on his words instead of his long sexy bod.

Why did he have to be damned good-looking?

"Okay." She clapped her hands together. "Are we doing it all in one shot?"

Please say no. That's a long damn time on a motorcycle.

"No. We have to make one more stop, anyway. There's something we'll need to bring with us. It should help you free Zed."

"Right."

Rena didn't want to think about that at the moment, but it seemed it was the only thing on Zander's mind. She had to do something to make him realize that she didn't belong with some guy she'd never even met.

"Besides, a storm is coming in from the west. Heavy winds and rain." He grabbed his helmet, avoiding her gaze. His rough, gravelly voice was barely above a whisper, but she had no trouble hearing him, even with the unseasonably warm winds rushing in her ears. "We'll stop about halfway. I own a place in Yellowstone, Montana. That's a little over four hours from the Amoveo ranch, and we can ride out the storm there. We should get there before it hits."

"I didn't find any properties listed for you when I did a background check."

"That's because it's not under Zander Lorens."

"How many names do you have?"

"A few."

"Is Zander Lorens your real name?"

"Yes," he replied gruffly. He stilled for a moment before putting on his helmet. "I haven't lied to you, Rena."

"Not exactly, but you haven't been entirely honest either." She arched her eyebrows and took a step nearer. "Like when you kissed me, for example."

Zander stilled, and heat flashed in his eyes. "That was a mistake," he growled, "a momentary lapse of judgment."

"So you don't want me?"

"No." His husky voice was barely audible, and he tore his gaze from hers. "Get on the bike."

"You're lying."

"What I want doesn't matter." He peered at her over his shoulder. "It never did, and it never will. Now get on the damn bike."

In spite of the insane situation, Rena's body reacted to the sight of his. Zander sat astride the Harley with absolute confidence. His long, strong legs steadied the massive piece of machinery with ease, and those large hands of his, the ones that had cradled hers so gently, gripped the handlebars securely. The leather jacket, jeans, and beat-up boots only added to his tough-guy image.

What red-blooded heterosexual woman wouldn't want to climb on the back of that bike and hold on to him for several hours?

There was no denying that the man cut an imposing and enticing figure, whether he was on or off the bike. He exuded strength and control, but it was the storm beneath the calm that got Rena's motor running. And anytime his beautiful, pale-green eyes shifted into those of his dragon, it was evident that the beast still lived inside him.

Curse or no curse, Zander was a dragon.

When she didn't get on the bike, he revved the motor before flipping up the mask of his helmet. His pale, mossy-colored eyes glittered at her beneath a furrowed brow, and he jutted his thumb over his shoulder impatiently.

"Come on," he shouted over the engine. "Time to go. Unless you want to stay here and get wet."

Rena's eyebrows lifted at the sexually charged remark.

"Well, I was up for getting *all kinds* of wet earlier." She smirked, and Zander revved the engine again when she took one step closer.

"Get. On. The. Bike."

Oh yeah, he was as turned on by her as she was by him. The heat of the black-and-chrome machine washed over her jean-clad thighs as the image of a fire-breathing dragon flickered through her mind. The thought of seeing Zander shift into the beast got her heart racing, and that's when she got an idea.

A totally crazy—make that a *bat-shit crazy* idea.

"You and Zed are *identical* twins, right?"

"That's part of the problem. Yes." Zander eyed her warily. "Now let's go."

"Good to know."

If Zander's curse were lifted, then Zed's would be too, wouldn't it?

If Rena could get Zander to shift into his dragon, wouldn't the curse be broken and then his brother would be freed as well? Two birds with one stone, so to speak. A smile curved her lips as her eyes searched his, and a plan began to come together. Zander was attracted to her, that much was obvious, and if he and his brother were identical twins, why couldn't she be Zander's mate and not Zed's?

Hell, Rena wasn't looking to be anybody's *mate*, but if she were going to hook up with anyone, it would be by her choice and nobody else's. Shifter or human or fox or what-flipping-ever, Rena would retain control over her body and her life.

And her body wanted Zander's, not some guy she had never met.

The line between Zander's brows deepened as she inched nearer, but before she could respond, he turned his gaze to the highway and snapped his helmet shut.

Oh yeah. And he wanted hers just as bad.

The corners of her mouth lifted higher, and she slapped her own visor closed before climbing on behind him. Rena scooted her butt closer to his and pressed her thighs along the firm planes of his legs. She linked her arms around his narrow waist and held on tightly to him. She noted that he felt even warmer than normal.

"Are you feeling all right?" she shouted.

"Why?"

"You're hot. I mean, it feels like you have a fever or something."

"I'm fine." He revved the engine and shouted, "I don't get sick."

When his muscles tensed against hers and his back straightened, Rena closed her eyes and tuned in to his energy signature with surprising ease. His usually calm spirit was tumbling around her like a tornado, whisking and swirling in throbbing swells of power. Zander Lorens was a man in conflict. His body was telling a far different story than he likely wanted it to.

There was no mistaking what he was feeling. Lust and desire were woven throughout his energy signature, and her body warmed in response.

She couldn't do much about it right this minute, but once they got to his place, all bets were off. Rena was going to make sure that she and Zander finished what they had started back in her office.

Rena hooked her heels onto the steel pegs as she hugged him and pressed her hands against his rock-hard abs. Testing him. Pushing again, wanting to see what kind of response her touch would evoke. Her answer came when his energy pattern erupted in a surge of heat just as he hit the accelerator and tore out of the parking lot. Gravel spit up behind them, and the roar of the engine was deafening, but Rena barely paid it any mind.

As she held on to Zander and the dusty scenery whisked past them, one thought kept running through Rena's mind.

Fate could kiss her hybrid Amoveo ass.

It had been about three months since Zander had been back to his property in West Yellowstone, and he hadn't realized how much he'd missed it until he pulled up to the cabin. Of course, given the land it had been built on and the lengthy history tied to his clan, it was no wonder.

The connection he felt wasn't to the building but the earth beneath it.

Raindrops splattered onto his visor just as he shut off the engine and put the kickstand down. Rena climbed off first, the warmth and weight of her body mourned instantaneously. She arched her back in a fluid motion and stretched her arms over her head while looking around the expansive property.

"Wow!" Her breathless exclamation escaped in a sigh as she removed her helmet.

Zander dismounted the bike and tried to suppress his smile of satisfaction while he unhooked the bags. Was it weird to be pleased with how much she liked his home?

No. He shook his head, scolding himself for reading more into it than necessary. She was going to be his family, part of his clan. There was nothing wrong with feeling a sense of pride when his brother's mate expressed a fondness for his home, which was on their family land.

Rena cradled the helmet against her curvy hip with one hand and tousled her hair with the other as she turned around slowly, taking in the panoramic view. The cabin was nestled in the remote mountains and surrounded by towering trees. It was refreshing to see the breathtaking beauty of this land through her eyes. The smile on her face blinded him and made her even more luminous than ever. Her brown eyes glittered, and even as the rain fell and the dark clouds blotted out the sun, Rena shone brightly at the center of it all.

There was more to her radiance than her physical appearance. She was feisty and smart. The woman was tough too. She didn't complain once on the entire journey. Zander had met more than his share of girls in his long existence, and in his experience, most of them complained. Not Rena. She took everything in stride and rolled with the punches better than most men he had known.

Given everything he had told her, she had *still* come with him. When he got back to the hotel room last night, he had half expected to find the place empty and her on the way back to Vegas. But she hadn't run. She stayed. And that impressed him more than anything else.

"Zander?" Rena waved one hand in front of him and snapped her fingers. "Hey, are you listening to me? Do you have a key, or do you want us to stay out here and get all…wet?"

She smirked and flicked her tongue over her plump

lower lip. Zander's gaze lingered there for a moment as he recalled the sweet taste of her.

A huge clap of thunder boomed through the air and broke the spell.

"Sorry." He blinked and tossed her a set of keys. "Let yourself in. I want to put the bike in the barn."

"Barn?" The keys jingled as she caught them with one hand. "Do you have horses or cows or something? Where is it?"

"No. The terrain here is too rugged, and I'm not here often enough. Just a barn, and it's small." He nodded to the left and handed her the two bags. "More like a big shed, really. It's over there."

"Oh yeah." She slung both bags over her shoulders. "I was so impressed by the mountains and stuff, I didn't even see it. This place is really cool. Nestled in between all this natural grandeur, it's like we're the only two people on earth."

It was raining harder now. Her reddish-brown hair was clinging to her cheeks in damp tendrils, perfectly framing her face. He imagined brushing the wet strands from her skin and licking away the water that beaded nearby, down the graceful line of her neck and nuzzle the hollow of her throat...

No. Damn it. You idiot. Cut the shit.

"Go inside," he barked. "You're getting soaked. I'll take the couch. You can have the bedroom. It's a loft. Can't miss it."

Before she could even respond to him, Zander climbed back on his bike, started it up, and rode over to the small, one-story, weathered, gray barn. When he glanced back at the house through the driving rain, he

saw soft light glowing from the first floor and knew
Rena was safely tucked away inside.

In his home.

Shit.

What the hell was he doing?

Zander sighed and tilted his face to the sky, letting
the cool rain wash over him. Rena wasn't wrong when
she noted that his body temperature had risen. It had,
and it was one more aspect of his dragon that had begun
to emerge. With each layer of his clan qualities reemerging, Zander's hope for Zed's future increased.

The buzzing of his cell phone pulled him from his
thoughts. He yanked it out of his pocket as he took shelter under one of the massive pine trees near the barn. It
was raining harder now, and based on the swirling mass
of black clouds in the darkening sky, they were in for a
major storm.

The number on the screen wasn't one he recognized.
His gut clenched because he suspected it was the call he
had been simultaneously dreading and hoping for.

"Zander speaking." Zander kept his voice calm and
even, even though apprehension settled in his chest. He
hoped like hell he hadn't made a mistake reaching out
to the Amoveo ahead of time.

"Hey, this is Dante Coltari." The man's voice was
strong but held a hint of wariness. "I received a message from a mutual friend. Isadora. She said you have a
young lady with you who's...unique."

"I do."

The old witch had come through. He knew she would
be able to get him in touch with the Amoveo *and* that
she would do it discreetly.

In other words, she kept his secret for him.

The Amoveo believed the dragons were all extinct, and Zander wanted it to stay that way for the moment. They would learn the truth eventually, but it had to be at exactly the right time, or it could threaten Zed's survival.

"Thank you for calling. Isadora told me that you and your mate, who is also a hybrid, have been bringing others like her to the prince's ranch." Zander's voice was clipped and curt. He wanted to get this all done and over with as quickly as possible. "The woman with me, her name is Rena McHale. She's a hybrid from the Fox Clan. No family to speak of."

"I see." Hesitance lingered in his voice. "How do you know Isadora?"

"She's an old friend of the family."

"Right," Dante said with a snort. "Do you mind if I ask how you discovered the girl and how you know about us?"

"Yes, I do mind," he said abruptly. "I can't get into it on the phone. This is a discussion we need to have in person, with Richard and Salinda. I would ask to see the Council, but I heard it's gone the way of the dr—dinosaurs."

"Right." Dante scoffed. "Listen, man, you seem to know a lot about our people, so you must also be aware of our trouble with the Purists. How do I know you can be trusted?"

"You don't," Zander said flatly. "But you trust Isadora, and she trusts me. That should be enough. Rena needs the other Amoveo and her mate."

"Did she connect with him in the dreamrealm yet?"

"Yes." Zander left it at that and prayed Coltari

wouldn't push for more. "She's walked in the dream-realm, and she's exhibited some telepathy. Her powers are evolving quickly."

"I see," he said absently. Zander had a hunch he was writing down everything they were saying. "Any other abilities? Maybe some that would be considered unusual?"

"Like what?"

"Most hybrid Amoveo women we've come across possess powers beyond the normal clan gifts. William's wife gets psychic impressions through the photographs she takes. My mate, Kerry, can touch you and see your deepest secrets. You know, stuff like that."

"Yeah." Zander made a mental note not to shake hands with Kerry. She could blow the whole thing. "Rena is psychic, but I'll let her explain how it works."

"Has she shifted yet?"

"No, but she hasn't bonded with her mate either and—"

"True, but with hybrids, we don't know when their powers will emerge. It's been different for all of them so far."

"Can I bring her to the ranch or what?" He was losing his patience. "You can give us a history lesson later."

Silence filled the phone line, and for a minute, Zander thought Coltari had hung up.

"All right, fine. Bring her to the ranch, but no weapons. You know where it is?"

"Yeah, I know the way. We'll be there tomorrow night."

A clap of thunder shook the air as a powerful gust of wind tossed branches along the ground.

"If this storm lingers, it'll be Saturday morning. But no later."

"I meant what I said about the weapons. You'll both be checked at the gate by the guardian, Dominic, and trust me when I say he will be one pissed-off dude if you break that particular rule. If there's one clan you don't want angry with you, it's the Tiger."

"Yeah." Zander rolled his eyes at the thinly veiled threat and recalled the way Arianna would go on about their strength. "I hear they're the baddest of the badasses."

"Of the ten clans, they're among the fiercest fighters. Always have been."

Zander stilled.

"Ten?" He let his gaze drift back to the cottage and played dumb. "That's how many clans there are, right? Only ten? I thought Isadora said there used to be eleven."

"Nah, man, just the ten, and lately, that's been more than enough," Dante said with a laugh. "Unless you know something I don't?"

"We'll see you tomorrow."

Zander hit the End button and slipped the phone into his pocket.

Son of a bitch.

Dante, and presumably the other Amoveo still living, didn't think the dragons were extinct—they didn't even know about their existence in the first place. Imagine how surprised they were going to be when they found out that they had one hibernating on their property.

Chapter 11

WHEN RENA STEPPED INSIDE THE TOASTY-WARM LOG CABIN, she flipped the light switch by the door and let out a low whistle. The whole place was decked out from top to bottom like a ski chalet out of one of those ritzy travel magazines. The open floor plan on the first floor made it seem larger than it was, but somehow, it still felt cozy and safe. Directly across from the front door was a massive stone fireplace with rocks of varying shades of gray trailing all the way up to the vaulted, beamed ceiling. An overstuffed sofa, flanked by two equally cushy-looking chairs in shades of rust and brown, created a welcoming sitting area around the hearth.

On the right was a sweeping kitchen with honey-toned cabinetry and white granite countertops. A large island with barstools separated the kitchen from the open living room and would be great for entertaining—but she doubted that Zander threw many parties. Off to the left was a staircase leading to what she could only assume was the loft bedroom. When she lifted her gaze, she swore under her breath because she couldn't get over the size of the loft above. The bedroom ran the full width of the cabin and overlooked the first floor. Two other doors, both of which were closed, flanked either side of the staircase.

Rena kicked off her wet boots and hung her coat on the wall hooks to the left of the front door. She placed the bags on the bench beneath and wandered over toward the kitchen. Her curiosity was piqued when she spotted what looked like a note on the island countertop. She padded over in her sock-covered feet, grateful for the braided rugs strategically placed around the cabin. The wide-planked wood floorboards were cold and slippery, and she had a hunch she wouldn't be barefoot the entire time she was here.

She was about to pick up the note, but her hand stopped in midair, right above a bowl of fresh fruit. Rena frowned and retracted her hand, quickly folding her arms over her breasts as she surveyed the area through a more critical lens.

Everything was really clean—no dust, fresh fruit, the heat had been turned on, and there was a large stack of firewood beside the hearth. Didn't Zander say he hadn't been back here in a long time? That he was hardly ever here?

Someone else had already been here today.

Curiosity got the better of her, and she scooped up the note and quickly opened it.

Zander,

The kitchen is stocked with most of your favorites and the bed has been made. Freshly cleaned towels are in the upstairs bath. Due to the incoming storm, I had the generator refueled too. You should have all the creature comforts of home.

Much love,
Lana

Lana? Who the hell is Lana?

A flicker of jealousy flashed when Rena thought about some other woman tending to Zander's *comfort*. She ran her fingers over the smooth paper and, for a split second, thought about using her gift to take a look at this Lana chick. But when the front door clicked open, she immediately thought better of it and quickly slapped the note onto the counter.

She spun around and clasped her hands behind her back awkwardly just as Zander stepped inside. She was going to make a smart-ass remark, but the sight of him momentarily made her lose the ability to speak. Or at the very least, her mind went totally blank, because all she was capable of for that minute was soaking in the sight of him.

He was dripping wet. Water sluiced from his leather jacket, which he promptly hung up before kicking off his boots. His jeans were wet too and clung to his long, strong-looking legs.

Were the pants coming off next?

Rena swallowed hard when she let her gaze skim over his ass as he leaned over and peeled off his socks. Jeez. Even his bare feet were sexy. The dark T-shirt he wore was damp and clung to every dip and curve of muscle in his back. His ropy, well-defined arms flexed as Zander turned to face her and pushed his shaggy, wet hair off his face with both hands. His damp skin glistened in the soft, yellow light of the cabin. Zander's chiseled features seemed even more defined than before. His jaw was covered in the dark shadow of scruff, and those haunted eyes of his peered at her intently beneath dark eyebrows.

The two of them stood there for at least ten beats of her heart. Neither one said a word. Only the sound of rain pelting the roof and their breathing filled the cabin. The space that only moments ago felt open and spacious had shrunk in size the instant Zander stepped into it.

The man was like a walking flame, and it was as if all of the oxygen had been sucked from the air the instant he slipped inside. Suddenly, each breath was more labored than the last. The plan, the one she was so proud of, now seemed like a stupid idea. This man wasn't one to be toyed with.

A flicker of self-doubt niggled in the back of her mind.

What if he really didn't want her?

Maybe he really *had* only kissed her because she reminded him of Arianna?

Rena sucked in a shuddering breath as he returned her bold stare. The simmering heat in his unwavering gaze seared into hers. Warmth seeped into her chest, and her entire body shimmered beneath his inspection.

It was now or never.

Her heart raced, and her tongue flicked over her lips before she finally worked up the courage to say something.

"Your Lana," she sputtered and jutted her thumb over shoulder toward the counter. "I—I mean someone named Lana left you a note."

Rena's cheeks flamed. The hint of a smile played at Zander's lips, and he moved slowly toward her. Her befuddlement amused him? She tucked her hair behind her ears as he sidled closer and picked up the paper. Even with the barstool separating them, his towering form was close enough that his body heat, even more intense than it had been earlier, wafted over her, reminding her of the flickering flames of a fire.

She half expected steam to rise off his damp skin.

Rena leaned one elbow on the island and studied him while he read the note.

"Who's Lana?" she asked with as much nonchalant innocence as she could. "She sure is thoughtful to come over and set the place up for you."

"She's a friend."

Zander crumpled the paper and tossed it over Rena's head into the tall, white garbage can in the corner. The movement brought him even closer, and his musky, leather scent filled her head. She breathed deeply and fought the sudden lust-ridden urge for her eyes to shift.

His arm dropped to his side, and that piercing gaze flicked to hers, melting her insides bit by bit. Rena's steely resolve to seduce the big, bad dragon wavered as she gazed into the limitless depths of his haunted eyes. Swimming behind the cool facade were the lingering effects from centuries of pain and loneliness.

A kindred spirit, lost in the dark but seeking the light.

The knot in her chest, the core of her steely self-sufficient resolve, loosened. Rena knew, better than anyone, what it was like to drift through the world alone and unwanted. Zander might have been a dragon all those years ago, but he *wasn't* a monster.

He was a man deserted, cut off from both the human and the supernatural world.

Rejected by both. Belonging in neither. Just like her.

Why hadn't she seen it sooner?

"Lana lives in town," he murmured. "Keeps an eye

on the place for me, and sometimes she runs errands. Like she did today."

"Are you two *close*?" A mischievous glint flashed in his eyes, daring her to continue, and Rena was only too happy to take that challenge. "Friendly?"

"You could say that. I've known her a long time."

The gruff, gritty tone of his voice tripped over her flesh in wicked jags, and heat pooled between her legs. Rena clenched her thighs together, but the friction only exacerbated her body's reaction to his. She let her eyes drift over him boldly, wanting him to know that she was taking him in.

All of him.

"*How* long?"

Her voice was soft, in stark contrast to his, barely above a whisper, and part of her wondered if she had even spoken out loud. She swayed closer. Dangerously close. Her knee bumped the stool, and her chest was a breath away from his. She tilted her head to the side and allowed her line of sight to drift slowly across the broad expanse of his shoulders. She sighed as his throat worked when he swallowed and his Adam's apple bobbed in a movement that shouldn't have been as sexy as it was.

"Because, as we've established"—her eyes latched on to his once again—"your idea of a long time is way damn longer than anyone else's."

"Long enough," he murmured. "She's on a very short list of people I trust."

"Have trust issues, do you?"

"You could say that."

"I understand. I have a few of my own."

Rena pushed the stool out of the way with her knee, removing all physical barriers, and inched nearer until her sock-covered toes bumped his bare ones. A zing of desire whisked through her blood from even that transitory contact. Zander didn't flinch but continued to hold her bold stare with one of his own. She fought to keep her breathing steady, but when her hand brushed his, a small gasp escaped her lips as a rush of heat exploded beneath her flesh.

The infinitesimal skin-to-skin contact held the promise of so much more to come. Rena's patience was waning, and even though she wanted to dive deep, to lose herself in the sweeping rush of heated flesh against flesh, she exerted hard-won self-control. If she came on too strong, too fast, then Zander would definitely bolt. Better to slide in and slip beneath his well-fortified defenses before he even realized what was happening.

"Do you trust me, Zander?"

Rena tangled her fingers with his and sucked in a shuddering breath when Zander's human eyes shifted into the blazing orbs of his dragon. His body tensed against hers as he gently squeezed her fingers while pulling her toward him. Or was she leaning into him? Rena gasped with pleasure when her sensitive nipples raked against the lace of her bra as her breasts met the hard planes of muscle.

She allowed her own eyes to shift with a tingling snap.

"Yes," he said gruffly. "It's me I don't trust."

"Why?" Rena trailed one finger over his bare forearm, the warm skin still damp from the rain, before dipping it beneath the sleeve of his T-shirt. "Are you worried Lana will show up and find us in a *compromising* situation?"

"Lana is sixty-five years old."

"That so?" She peered at him beneath heavy lids. "Then she must know something is up with you, since we've already established that you don't age."

"Let's just say she's one of the rare humans who's familiar with the supernatural world. We were never lovers."

"Had many of those over the years?"

"A few."

Amusement flashed across his face but was swiftly smothered by unmistakable desire when Rena curled her hand around the swell of his bicep. She stopped when her fingertip drifted over a lumpy patch of flesh. The skinny line was about three inches long, and she rubbed the raised area lightly. His body wavered against hers, and his energy signature surged through the air in a rush of damp heat, reminding her of a tropical storm.

Unpredictable, intense, and wild.

To her surprise, Zander allowed her to investigate the marred flesh.

"How did you get this scar? One of your many conquests, or a jealous husband perhaps?"

She pushed the edge of his sleeve up with her thumb and stilled when she spotted two others on that arm. Rena trailed her fingers slowly along the crook of his elbow, the tiny hairs rasping deliciously beneath her fingertips, before gingerly investigating the marks on his forearm.

"I don't make a habit of bedding women who are spoken for. There's no honor in it."

"Mmm." Rena pressed her thumb against a circular scar. "What about this one?"

A pang of empathy flared as her gaze skittered from

one arm to the other. How had she not seen all of these scars before? Blinded, perhaps, by her own issues? Not anymore. Rena's hands danced gently over his bare skin, the pads of her fingers whispering along the evidence of what had obviously been a brutal, painful life.

These marks and scars were more than leftover mementos of the battles he had fought from one century to the next. Far more. Collectively, they created a road map of the unusually long lifetime he had struggled through—and suffered—alone.

"Rena…don't…"

His voice was strangled. Tight. Like he was doing his best not to sink into her touch, but of course, that only encouraged her.

"Don't what?"

The innocent tone was in stark contrast to her motives. No. There was nothing chaste or innocent about the way Zander made her feel. She was like a moth drawn to the entrancing, flickering flame. The danger was clear, and part of her knew if she ventured too close, she would be consumed.

In spite of the threat, Rena was unable—unwilling—to stop.

The heat in Zander's eyes and the hum of lust that thrummed between them was like a drum pounding in the distance, calling to her. Drawing her in with its hypnotic, erotic rhythm. Her gaze wandered over his broad shoulders, and her breath caught in her throat when she spotted a small, white scar on his jaw. The crescent-shaped area of bare flesh was free of dark beard stubble. Out of an instinct to soothe the pain, she went to touch it. Zander grabbed her hand, preventing her from stroking the age-old wound.

"Stop it."

The gruff, almost-guttural tone of his voice made her heart skip a beat, and the hungry, feral look flashing across his face did little to ease her raging hormones.

"No."

She raised her other hand, but Zander grabbed that one too and held her so that their faces were scant inches apart. Rena's fingers flexed and curled around his, wanting and needing more of him. More of his touch. Her leg drifted between Zander's, and a shuddering gasp whispered from her lips when her thigh was met with rock-hard heat.

So much for not wanting her.

"You said you wouldn't lie to me," she whispered.

"Cut it out."

"What?"

Rena arched one eyebrow and gently applied more pressure against the unmistakable evidence of his desire.

"That," he ground out.

"This?" Rena pressed her thigh against him, harder this time and in a slow, circular motion meant to incite him. "Or that?"

"I'm warning you, Rena." His energy signature raged around the room in volatile, tumultuous waves. "You have no idea what kind of game you're playing."

"Now, you see, dragon boy," she said with a sigh, "that's where you're wrong. I know *exactly* what I'm doing. I think *you're* the one who's confused. You *say* you don't want me, but your body is telling me another story altogether."

Zander released her wrists and, in a flash, cradled her face with both hands as his eyes glowed brighter. In that crimson light, she saw unmistakable desire. His desire for *her*. Rena gasped and clutched the fabric of his damp T-shirt, instinctively pulling him against her. His body hummed with tension as the hard planes of his heated, muscular torso seared along hers.

"It's true," he murmured. "My body yearns for yours."

He dragged his thumb over her lower lip, and the friction sent a wave of lust and heat directly to her core. A fission of need burned in her belly, stealing the breath from her lungs. Rena's fingers flexed and clenched as she blindly grappled for the edge of his shirt. She moaned softly as her hands settled over the hot flesh along his waist, which melded against her palms with wicked perfection.

Zander's mouth hovered barely an inch away, and their breath mingled as he held her there, his strong fingers holding her face with unexpected tenderness. It was torture—pure, unadulterated torture—to have him so close and yet so far. Rena wiggled her hips and pressed herself against him, wanting and needing him to end her torment, to offer the release she so desperately sought.

A mixture of lust and fury was carved into his features, light and shadows creating a fiercely animalistic aura. And all of it highlighted by the haunting glow of his eyes. The potent combination of danger and desire only served to fuel her craving. A shiver of anticipation rippled through Rena as the unyielding planes of his chest pushed against her breasts. With each labored breath, his ribs expanded and contracted against her in wicked jags, heightening each sensation, every one more vivid than the last.

Rena probably should have been afraid, but she

wasn't. Hell no. She had never been more turned on in her life, and it was far beyond the physical. This man or dragon or whatever label was given to him knew her better than any other creature on the planet. She didn't have to hide who she was or what she could do.

Being seen completely, with no barriers—mental, physical, or otherwise—was the most potent aphrodisiac of all.

The two of them hung there perilously, clinging to the edge of flagrant desire. Bodies humming with unfulfilled lust. Both knowing if they let go and tumbled over the precipice, into the abyss below, there would be no going back for either of them.

How could the universe want her to be with Zed but allow her to crave Zander with such merciless, wild intensity?

"Fate," he hissed. "If you understood the kind of mayhem you were toying with, you would get the hell away from me and never look back."

"I know you want me, Zander." She sucked in a deep breath, knowing full well the movement would press her breasts harder against him. Zander's nostrils flared in response. "It doesn't take a psychic to figure that out. I don't know your brother, and I don't know shit about the Amoveo or the dragons or your damned curse. And I don't care, because all I can see or feel...is *you*. And I know that you see me."

Rena raked her fingernails up both sides of his rib cage, popped up on her toes, and flicked her tongue over his lip.

"I want *you*, Zander Lorens. Not your brother. *You*." She swept her hands up his back, the muscles tensing and rippling beneath her fingers. Rena pressed a kiss to the corner of his mouth and whispered, "Right now."

Heat flashed in his eyes, and for a split second, Rena thought she had made a colossal mistake.

As a growl rumbled in Zander's chest and his lips crashed onto hers, Rena almost wept with relief. Kissing her deeply, his tongue sweeping furiously along hers, Zander groaned and tilted her head, taking total control.

Rena surrendered to him willingly. Body. Mind. Spirit. She was offering it all.

In a flurry of effort, his mouth branding her with each penetrating kiss, Rena pushed Zander's shirt up, wanting to see and feel every single inch of him. Before she could accomplish her goal, he tore his mouth away and dropped to his knees, pressing hot, wet kisses along her neck, breasts, and belly as he went. Rena bit her lower lip and tangled her fingers in his shaggy hair as he made quick work of undoing the button of her jeans.

"I want to see you."

Quivering with a yearning she didn't have a name for, Rena let out a groan of anticipation as Zander peered up at her while pulling down her zipper slowly. She gasped when his tongue, hot and hard, flicked into her belly button, and he dragged her pants and undies over her hips. She stepped out of them quickly, but before she could catch her breath, Zander ran his hands up the back of her legs and nudged them apart while brushing his lips lightly up her inner thigh.

Knowing what was surely coming next and fighting to see through the red haze of lust, Rena blindly reached for the counter's edge behind her and held on, bracing herself for the pleasure that had been chasing her since the moment Zander Lorens had roared into her life.

"I am at your mercy, Rena." His voice, gruff and gritty, whisked around her. "Do you have any idea what you have done to me? I'm haunted by you."

She shivered as each word was punctuated with sharp nibbles along the sensitive flesh of her inner thigh. Rena whimpered when he curled his hand around the crook of her right knee, dragged her leg up, and slung it over his shoulder. It was wickedly erotic and decadent to be exposed to him this way.

Open and vulnerable. Zander on his knees. Rena partially clothed and splayed out against the kitchen counter, waiting for him to feast on her.

Devour her.

She wanted to say something, to tell him about the greedy way her body craved his, but no words would come. The whisper of heat bubbling beneath the surface, a slow-burning knot of need, erupted into a full-fledged flame when Zander blew gently over her sex. A needy moan pulled from her throat, and her knees buckled at the breath-stealing sensation.

If it weren't for the counter and Zander's ironclad grip on her legs, she would have collapsed to the floor in a boneless puddle.

"Don't you understand, Rena?" he whispered against her thigh while stroking her backside with his other hand before cupping it firmly. "You'll be my undoing."

Zander's hot mouth covered her exposed heat, and Rena's world erupted. She cried out, and her head fell back as he licked and suckled her clit in slow, torturous circles. Her hips bucked, seeking out more of what he was offering, but Zander held fast, giving her no room to adjust her position.

He smacked her ass and pulled back, giving her a moment to mourn his touch.

"Don't move," he growled.

His fingers pressed deeper into her hip and thigh, and Rena watched as Zander licked her slit in one slow pass. A strangled cry of pleasure caught in her throat, and even though she wanted to urge her hips forward, she did as he asked and remained motionless.

"That's it." He pulled her lips apart gently and flicked her clit with his tongue in a swift, sharp pass. "You taste sweet and tangy, like a peach not quite ripe on the vine, but you're ready for me, aren't you? Even if only for this brief moment in time…"

Rena nodded. Every single muscle in her body was wound tight like a rubber band ready to snap, and when Zander covered her heat again, she shouted his name. Zander licked and massaged the tiny nub mercilessly, swiftly bringing her overheated body to a shattering climax with the talented lips of an experienced lover.

As wave after wave of the orgasm rippled and erupted through Rena's body, he didn't relent. Rena instinctively reached out with her mind, tangling her energy pattern with his. When the spiritual connection was made, light exploded behind her eyes, and a second even more powerful orgasm shimmered out in delicious, pulsating waves.

No!

Zander's voice shot into her head, the force of it instantaneously severing the intimate connection. Both physically and mentally. The change was jarring and, as the fog of the orgasm lifted, it was humiliating as well.

Zander abruptly released her, and when Rena's foot hit the floor with a dull thump, she held tighter to the counter to keep from falling over. Still reeling from the power of the climax and struggling to catch her breath, she shook her head, as though it might rid her of the sudden onset of embarrassment.

He stalked away. Keeping his back to her, Zander swore under his breath.

The man was still fully dressed, and she was standing there half-naked and suddenly rejected. Alone. Rena's face heated but from mortification instead of lust. She snagged her jeans off the floor and quickly pulled them on, trying to ignore the way the rough fabric rasped over her overly sensitized flesh.

Flesh he had been worshipping only moments ago.

"Wh-what is the problem?" she said between huffing breaths while buttoning her jeans. "Don't you want—"

"What I *want* is of little importance," he shouted at her over his shoulder. "I learned that lesson a long time ago. Fate is a nasty bitch, and she doesn't give a shit about anything other than fulfilling her twisted desires. Not mine and not yours. The sooner you wrap yourself around that, the better off we'll both be." He stormed to the front door and grabbed his bag.

"Hey! Hang on a minute." Rena folded her arms over her breasts and let out a laugh of disbelief. "Where do you think you're going?"

Backpack in hand, he strode to the staircase and stood there for a minute with his back to her.

"To take a shower."

She let out a huff of disbelief. One minute he was giving her the best orgasm of her life, and the next he was ditching her to go shower. Alone.

"Zander, wait—"

"The boundaries between us can't be crossed again, Rena."

"Really? Well, you probably should have thought about that before you went down on me," she replied quietly.

Zander flinched, and his shoulders squared, but he still wouldn't turn around and look at her. "I am to blame for this mess," he murmured. "I know that."

"Not entirely," she said, a shaky laugh threading her words. "I was here too, and I made no secret about what or *who* I wanted."

"Zed and I are identical twins, and you're only reacting to my genetic pattern—*not me*. You'll feel the same way about Zed."

"Bullshit."

"Sadly, it's not." He glanced over his shoulder but didn't look at her. "You have to be *his* mate. It's the only way. I'm going to take a shower."

As he disappeared up the stairs, Rena shouted, "Better make it a cold one!"

He grumbled something she couldn't quite make out before a door upstairs slammed shut. Rena let out a raspy huff of frustration and ran both hands through her hair, lacing her fingers behind her head. He wanted her. Obviously. Everything had been going in the right direction until she'd touched his energy pattern with hers.

Rena stilled.

That was it. The mental contact combined with the physical had somehow heightened their connection. Why was he so put off by that? A satisfied smile curved her lips. Zander could tell her time and again how Zed was supposed to be her mate, but she knew it was all bullshit.

Zander wanted her. She wanted him.

What the hell did fate have to do with matters of the heart or other parts of the anatomy?

Rena snagged an apple from the fruit bowl and took a juicy bite. She made a sound of appreciation and closed her eyes, losing herself in the sweet taste of it. She settled onto the stool and leaned both elbows on the counter while studying the half-eaten piece of fruit.

What was it Zander said about telepathy being an intimate form of communication between mates? She had done it once, so she should be able to do it again. And last time she hadn't even been trying to do it.

Rena spun around on the stool and swung her feet while staring at the second-floor loft of the cabin. An image of Zander, naked and wet, beneath the streams of water, flashed into her mind. His hands were pressed against the blue-and-white tile wall as the water streamed over him. Rena drew in a sharp breath as desire tugged at her from deep within her core.

Eyes closed, she sent her energy signature in search of his, and when the two ribbons of power tangled, a zap of static electricity shot beneath her skin. Rena gasped when pleasure-laden warmth seeped into her blood.

It was now or never.

And by the way, dragon boy, the only thing I want to wrap myself around is you.

A shudder of pure, unadulterated lust washed over Rena when her mind touched his. She threw one hand back and braced herself on the edge of the counter as the erotic sensation, mixed with warm flashes, ebbed and pulsed in her blood. She let out a trembling laugh of wonder and disbelief.

Stop. His voice, low and gruff, whisked into her head. *No more telepathy. Save it for my brother*.

A second later, she was cut off.

It was like a mental door had been slammed shut and all communication had been severed. Even Zander's energy pattern was nowhere to be found. An odd feeling of emptiness curled in Rena's chest. She could hear him upstairs. The shower was off, and he was still moving around in the bathroom.

Zander was here...but he wasn't.

The man had shut her out of his mind, and the rejection was oddly disconcerting. Rejecting her physical advances was something she could laugh off, but this? Getting rebuffed and ejected from his mind, cut off and left virtually alone, wounded her in a way she hadn't expected.

For a woman who was used to being on her own, Rena had never felt lonelier in her life.

Chapter 12

WHEN RENA HAD GENTLY INSPECTED THE SCARS ON HIS body, the wall inside Zander, the fortress he'd built around his heart, crumbled. How long had it been since he had let anyone get that close? It was more than the tenderness in her touch. The soft, comforting tone of her voice and the empathy woven within her energy called to him. Like a siren song filled with promises of redemption, Rena and her embrace drew him to her.

Zander had taken plenty of cold showers in his lifetime. Hell, he'd bathed in lakes, oceans, and streams that were twice as frigid as the water flowing from these pipes. But this was the only time during his lengthy life that he had done it to try and cool his eager libido. It had almost worked too, but when the wicked little vixen touched her mind to his, any control he had vanished amid the rush of lust.

When her husky voice whispered into his head, the surge of stark-naked need that accompanied it made him hard as a rock. Again. His dick twitched and throbbed almost to the point of pain. Zander pounded his fist against the wet tiles, and a growl rumbled in his chest as the overwhelming urge to claim her tore through him.

Zander had cut his mind off from hers out of self-preservation, even though it went against every single instinct he had.

When he severed the mental connection with Rena,

a leaden weight settled in his chest and spread through his soul like blood seeping from a wound that refused to heal. As the ache and longing swelled, his body responded in kind. The physical craving for her may have been sated for the moment, but the haunting loneliness wasn't.

He shut off the water with more ferocity than necessary and yanked open the glass shower door before snagging a towel off the rack. He dried himself off in swift, furious strokes, but when he caught a glimpse of his nude body in the mirror, Zander let his gaze drift over the multitude of scars. Until Rena had stopped to inspect them, he had practically forgotten they were there. Big and small, each one represented a moment from his past, battles fought and won.

His mind wandered to the feel of Rena's fingers as they danced over the damaged flesh. However, when he caught sight of a dark shadow on his left thigh, the leg that had pained him so much yesterday, Zander froze.

Anyone else might mistake the bluish-black splotch for a bruise of some kind. But Zander knew better, and dread clamped down hard and fast.

His heart began to race as he moved closer to the full-length mirror, not sure if he was seeing what he thought he was seeing. As he got nearer, his mouth went dry when he saw that the mark wasn't random or shapeless—not at all. He swore under his breath and leaned over, wanting and needing to get an unobstructed view of his leg.

With the truth creeping in like a long-lost lover with wild promises, Zander traced his finger around the dark edge of the figure-eight-like shape.

He swore in disbelief as he lifted his glowing gaze to his reflection.

It wasn't a bruise, and it sure as hell wasn't random.

If his suspicions were correct, and the universe was the merciless bitch he knew it was, then the mark on his leg was the beginning of a mate tattoo. A bitter laugh escaped his lips as he forced his eyes back to their human state and wrapped the towel around his waist. This was just one more shitty, twisted side effect of being an identical twin and only confirmed what he had believed all along—he had to get Rena to the ranch as soon as possible.

Away from him.

Far away.

Like non-touching distance.

Because all he wanted to do was touch her. Everywhere.

Zander grabbed another towel and used it to dry off his wet head, which he should probably stick back under the shower for another good, long soak.

A pounding on the bathroom door pulled him from his thoughts.

"I never figured you for a diva." The amusement in Rena's voice was clear even though it was muffled. "I need to use the bathroom, dragon boy. I have to pee."

"I'm not dressed." He looked around for his bag. "Gimme a minute."

"Don't be such a prude," she teased. "Jeez, man. Throw on a towel and go get dressed in the bedroom. Come on, I gotta go."

"Right. Sorry."

Zander grabbed his bag from the floor before yanking the door open. Rena was leaning against the wall and looked like she was about to say something but stopped in the midst of it. He stilled as her appreciative gaze drifted over his bare chest and down to the towel, which wasn't doing much to hide his reemerging desire. He quickly adjusted the bag and held it in front of him before stepping into the hallway.

"Thanks." Rena brushed past him and whispered, "I hope you didn't hog all the cold water. I could use some myself."

The bathroom door clicked closed, and Zander let out the breath he hadn't even realized he had been holding.

It was going to be a long night.

—◆◆◆—

The cool, soothing mist that was ever present in the dreamrealm drifted over Zander's bare arms as he got a handle on his surroundings. After so many years of walking the realm, it rarely took him this long to embrace the dream state. He fully expected to be in the forest with Zed. Both of them in their dragon form about to launch into battle, but this time...something was different.

Rena.

As the fog lifted, Zander cursed under his breath when Zed's hibernation cave came into focus. He was standing on the edge of the glittering pool of water, and the slow, steady pulse of Zed's heartbeat thrummed through the cave hypnotically. Encased in the towering wall of quartz on the other side of the pool was his twin brother. Curled in a fetal position with his massive wings and tail wrapped protectively around him, Zed remained trapped in hibernation.

Zander, however, was in his human form and wearing the sweatpants he had fallen asleep in. He normally slept in the nude, but given the situation with Rena, he had deemed that an unwise choice. He was so engrossed in the moment that he didn't realize right away that he and Zed weren't alone.

"What is that sound?"

Rena's voice drifted over Zander's shoulder along with her energy signature. When the distinctly feminine tendril wafted around him, he sucked in a sharp breath and wrestled for control. Eyes closed, his hands curled into fists at his side, he tried to focus on keeping his energy pattern calm. He could feel her there as she sidled in alongside him. Though they weren't in a physical plane, the effect of her presence was no less powerful.

Maybe it was even more powerful.

"It's Zed's heartbeat." His words were clipped and controlled. "He's in the dreamrealm with us but..."

Zander flicked his eyes open and glanced down at Rena, momentarily losing all capability of speech. The woman was clad in a white men's button-down shirt that skimmed over her curvy little body with mouthwatering perfection.

Holy shit.

Is that what she went to sleep in? In his bedroom— his bed—directly above the couch he had begrudgingly gone to sleep on?

How was it that something as simple as a plain white shirt could generate such a seductive look? The loose-fitting garment covered her backside, and the hem dipped to the middle of her thighs. Her legs were toned and well-defined, and her toes were painted with a bright-purple polish.

Wait a minute. Men's shirt? What man?

Irritation, mixed with a healthy dose of jealousy, fired through him. When Zander finally turned his attention to Rena's face, he was greeted with smug amusement.

"Get an eyeful?" She stepped back and extended her arms before spinning around. Rena wiggled her hips and cast a flirty glance at him over her shoulder as she popped the collar. "You should recognize the shirt—it's yours."

Relief soothed the burn of jealousy, but when she stepped toward him, he turned his attention back to Zed.

"Made yourself at home, I see."

"I suppose." Rena's voice was light with feigned innocence. "You're something of a mystery, so I did a little snooping in your bedroom. I am a PI, after all."

"Find anything?" He sighed heavily and folded his arms over his chest, trying like hell to act disinterested. "Other than my shirt?"

"Yes." She bumped her hip against him playfully before taking her place beside him again. "You have shitty taste in books and are apparently obsessed with the lives of the United States presidents. But your music, now that, I like. The Stones. The Eagles. The Doobie Brothers. All excellent. I love good old-fashioned rock 'n' roll, baby."

"Glad you approve," he said absently.

"Oh, don't be such a stick in the mud."

"Forgive me if I'm not in a playful mood, but I'm trying to figure out why you and I are here in the dream-realm with Zed. You should be with him, but I shouldn't. At least, not anymore. He saw you and recognized you as his mate the last time you were here."

"Oh, I remember." Rena snorted with derision. *"He kept growling the word* mine *over and over again, and then he tried to eat me."* She brushed one hand through her hair and let out a breathy sigh. *"And not in the good way. If your brother ever gets out of this mess, you're going to have to teach him a thing or two."*

Zander's gut clenched at the obvious reference to their inappropriate dalliance in the kitchen. He was about to remind her that had been a mistake, but the unexpected sound of movement on the ledge above captured his attention. Pebbles and dirt skittered down the wall to the right. Rena heard it too. They both turned toward the sound, and tension swirled in the air.

"What was that?" Rena hugged her arms over her breasts and dropped her voice to a whisper. *"Could someone else be here? In the dreamrealm, I mean? Because this isn't a memory like the dreams I've been in before. This is…different."*

"In theory? Yes. But that would be highly unlikely. No one else knows about you, me, and Zed, or the connection you've made. Well, except Isadora, but she would have no reason to be here."

"Who's Isadora?"

"An old friend." His gaze tripped over the ledge. *"A witch."*

"Jeez. There are witches too?"

"Among other things," he murmured.

"Hang on. Vito knows," she said simply. Rena popped up on her toes as though trying to get a better look at the ledge high above. *"Maybe it's him. He's an Amoveo, right?"*

"Victor or Vito or whatever you call him is a

broken-down old man." Disdain edged his voice, and Zander did nothing to hide it. "When an Amoveo loses their mate, their powers begin to weaken until they vanish all together. Basically, they become human. They start to age, and eventually, they die. By the look of him, the old man lost his Amoveo abilities, to say nothing of his marbles, a long time ago. I doubt he's dream walking after all this time."

Zander flicked his gaze to the rocky ledge and scanned the area, searching for the source of the disturbance, but as far as he could tell, there was nobody in the dreamrealm but the three of them.

"No one else has invaded the realm. I would sense another energy pattern." He rolled his shoulder, trying to release the tension. "I'm still not sure why the three of us are all here—together."

"Is it a problem?"

"It could be." He ran one hand over his stubble-covered chin and looked around warily. "I didn't bring us here, and since you aren't familiar with how to navigate the dreamrealm, I'm pretty sure you didn't do it. I don't think Zed could do it. Not given the state he's in. Besides, Zed and I are usually—"

"Fighting with each other." Rena finished the sentence for him. "Yeah, I know. I've been there, remember? Getting fried by you two every night for months."

"You mean the other night, when I found you, it wasn't the first time?"

"No. I wish," Rena said, laughter threading her words. "It was probably the hundredth time or thousandth. Jeez. I don't know. I lost count. The night you showed up was the first time I didn't get toasted to ashes like—"

"*Like her,*" he said solemnly.

An awkward silence hung between them as regret shimmied up his back, but he shoved it aside. A pity party wouldn't help any of them. Least of all Zed.

"*Yeah…I guess. But as we've established, I'm not her.*" She settled her hands on her hips and dipped one foot in the light-blue water. "*Whoa. This is warm. I mean, like hot-tub warm.*"

"*It's heated by the earth, an underground hot spring. The same heat source is part of what allows us to stay in hibernation. Although Zed's sleep is far longer than usual.*"

"*This is a real place, right?*" She puffed the hair off her forehead and gestured with one hand. "*I mean, I know this is a dream but—*"

"*Yes.*" Zed's heartbeat reverberated off the walls like a war drum. If Zander didn't know better, he would have said the sound was getting louder. But his brother remained motionless and buried in the wall. "*It's deep within the ground in Montana.*"

"*Wait a minute. Montana?*" Rena stilled. "*The Amoveo are in Montana too. Let me guess—*"

"*Yes,*" he finished the thought for her. "*Zed is in hibernation on the Amoveo's property.*"

"*Holy crap,*" she said with a laugh. "*I'm guessing they aren't happy about that.*"

"*They don't know about it.*" He let out a beleaguered sigh. "*Honestly, the younger Amoveo don't even know my people ever existed. This cave is deep beneath the ground, but it's still on Amoveo land. Kind of a 'screw you' from the witch, I think.*"

"*By putting him there, she made it even harder for you to get your brother out.*"

"Yup."

"Well, if you have to be trapped somewhere, this place is pretty cool." She pointed to the wall of quartz. *"Even without the hibernating dragon. This cave is wild. Exquisite, really. Look at the edges of the pool. The design is intricate. It looks almost like an artist carved it on purpose, but it was just the water, you know? Countless years of water lapping against it...tiny ripple after ripple...Let's go in!"*

She started to unbutton her shirt, but Zander grabbed her wrist, preventing her from going any further.

"Stop."

Zander swallowed against the tide of lust. Rena turned her body so they were toe-to-toe.

"What's the matter?" She peered up at him beneath a fan of dark lashes. *"It's only a dream, right?"*

"No." His impatience rose. *"It's the dreamrealm. What we do here matters and has consequences, just like in the earthly plane."*

"What kind of consequences?"

Rena inched closer. He loosened his grip on her but didn't let go, even though that was exactly what he should have done. Instead, he brushed his thumb over the warm, smooth flesh of her wrist. A list of reasons raced through his head for why they couldn't strip naked and dive into the water together. However, not one of them was loud enough to drown out or squelch the rising surge of lust.

The beast still lingered.

It was buried deep in his soul the way Zed was in the rock.

Trapped.

"You know what I think, Zander?" Rena's voice was quiet, barely above a whisper. *"I think you enjoy torturing yourself. You've been doing it for so long, I doubt you know how to do anything else."*

The truth of her words stung, and staring into those caramel-brown eyes, something inside him broke apart. Rena was like the water in the cave. Relentless. Pushing at him insistently but seductively. Each time she challenged him, she washed away another hard-earned layer of his defenses.

Rena exposed him and discovered him all at the same time.

MINE!

The gritty, animalistic voice rumbled through the cave. The force of it shook the ground. Rena almost went tumbling into the water, but Zander tugged her against his chest, holding her there, where she fit so perfectly.

"Holy shit," she whispered. She was shivering, and her energy pattern whirled around him like a tornado. *"Zander...I think your brother is waking up."*

She leaned into him and her arms folded between them, seeking shelter. Zander slid his hands down her back, telling himself he was doing it to soothe her fears, not because he simply wanted to be as close to her as possible.

"Zander!" She grabbed his chin and turned his face toward the wall. *"Zed is waking up."*

"But that's not—" Zander stopped speaking when a flicker of movement caught his attention. The cold hand of dread clamped down on his heart, because Rena was right. Zed was still encased in his hibernation cocoon

in the fetal position, but he was no longer motionless. His enormous form twitched and shifted, the way a child does inside its mother's womb.

"This is good, right?" She smiled broadly, and the beauty of it almost blinded him. "This is what you wanted. I mean, what you've been hoping for."

"Not in the dreamrealm! He can't emerge from hibernation until we get there! We need to wake up, Rena." Zander curled his hands over her shoulders and shook her, forcing her to look at him. "Right now!"

MINE! MINE! MINE!

Zed's thunderous telepathic roar ripped through their minds, and Rena threw her hands to her ears. Her eyes screwed shut as she slipped from Zander's grasp. He went to grab her, but another quake rocked the cave, and he watched helplessly as Rena tumbled into the water.

Fog rolled in, swallowing him in a cool, misty cloud. Zed's heartbeat still thundered furiously through the air. The dreamrealm loosened its hold on Zander, and for the first time in centuries, he prayed his brother would not awaken.

"Zander!"

Rena shouted his name breathlessly as she shot up in bed. Her clothing and sheets were soaked with sweat, and her heart thundered wildly against her ribs. She tried to kick off the wet, gray sheets, but they tangled around her legs as she struggled to regain her bearings. The sound of Zed's outraged roar and the suffocating sensation of being drowned still lingered. Amber light from the rising sun spilled in from the windows and burnished the swirl of bedding, assuring her she was no longer in the dreamrealm.

She was in Zander's bed.

No more cave or pissed-off dragon.

Shuddering with nerves and a healthy amount of fear, Rena was about to shout for him again when she heard Zander's heavy footsteps tromping up the stairs. This wasn't the first time she had called out for help because of a nightmare, but it was the first time someone had answered her cries.

Relief fired through her, and two seconds later, he burst through the doorway before coming to the side of the bed. Shirtless and only wearing a pair of sweatpants, his hair was tousled, and he fleetingly reminded her of a little boy with an adorable case of bedhead. Although, no little boy she knew had a ripped torso like his or one covered with a litany of scars.

"Are you all right?" he asked through heavy breaths.

The mattress dipped as his large frame settled in beside her. She squeezed her eyes shut and nodded furiously while Zander pushed strands of sweaty hair off her forehead. The tangle of fear in her chest, the one that threatened to choke her, loosened with each gentle stroke of his fingers.

"Rena?" He cupped her face gingerly, his thumb fluttering over her cheek. "Are you all right?"

"Mmhmm." Tears stung her eyes. But embarrassed laughter threaded her voice as she swiped them away. "Jeez. I'm not usually a crier Sorry, but that one scared the hell out of me."

"You have no reason to apologize." He tucked her

hair behind one ear before letting his hand drop into his lap. "You didn't do anything wrong. In fact…"

Mourning the loss of his touch more than she wanted to admit, Rena pulled her knees to her chest. She wrapped her arms around them tightly, hoping that would ease her shivering body. "What the hell happened back there?"

"Your connection with Zed is getting stronger." His mouth set in a grim line, and gruff frustration laced his words. "Everything is moving faster than I thought it would. None of the usual mating rules seem to apply. I'm not sure if it's because you're a hybrid or because Zed's cursed. Or both."

"Well, since I don't know squat about the mating process or whatever, I'll have to take your word for it." She nibbled her lower lip as she replayed the slew of information she had learned in the past forty-eight hours. "You said something about a mate tattoo, right?"

"Yes." His jaw clenched, the muscle beneath the stubble-covered flesh flickering.

Rena was tempted to touch it, but instead, she fiddled with the damp sheet tangled around her legs.

"Like the Amoveo, we find our mates in the dream-realm, and *then* we can bond in the physical plane. Once the connection has been made, the mate tattoo starts to form. The men get one on the thigh and the women, usually, have it emerge on their back."

"Wait, so a tattoo just kind of appears?"

"Each bonded pair has a mark that is unique to their mating." Zander cleared his throat as though uncomfortable discussing it. "Two dragons intertwined. But the color patterns within the tattoo are different for each couple."

"Amoveo don't get a tattoo like that?"

"Not unless they're mated to a dragon."

"I don't have one, you know. So, then, you could be wrong about me being Zed's mate." She arched one eyebrow and shifted her body. "You can check if you want."

"I don't think that would be wise." He sliced a sly glance at her and shook his head. "And like I said, nothing about your mating with Zed is normal."

Rena blanched and looked at him like he was out of his damn mind. How in the hell could he continue to think that she should be with his brother after what happened between the two of them yesterday?

"Unbelievable. You're *still* convinced that I'm supposed to be your brother's mate." She grabbed his chin and forced him to look at her. "Even after what happened in the kitchen last night?"

He said nothing at first, but there was heat in his eyes, and she warmed beneath his penetrating stare. For just a second, Rena thought he was going to kiss her. However, when he curled his hand around hers and pulled it from his face, her heart sank.

"Yes, you are," he whispered. "You have to be."

"Well, I'm sorry, but I don't buy it. And who says that's the way it has to be?"

"Rena, Zed and I are identical twins, which is unheard of for our kind. The Amoveo too. And this screwed-up situation is exactly why. When you were born, your body was preprogrammed and matched with Zed's genetic pattern, which is also mine. It's biology and fate. Plain and simple."

"So you're telling me that I'm *only* attracted to you because of fate and that I'll feel the same way about Zed."

Zander nodded curtly but said nothing.

"I don't believe you." Rena snatched her hand from his as embarrassment shimmied beneath her skin. "What about love? Or don't the big, bad dragons believe in that?"

"Love isn't a factor."

"For who?" she asked incredulously. "Because it sure as hell matters to me, thank you very much. I didn't think it ever would, but you changed all that, Zander. I *am* worthy of love...and so are you."

Zander swore under his breath and rose from the bed. Hands on his hips, he strode to the railing that overlooked the first floor of the cabin. Rena wanted to go to him. To curl her arms around his waist, press her cheek against the broad expanse of his back, and seek shelter in his strong, warm, masculine body. However, her heart skipped a beat, and her thoughts went to Zander and all he had suffered, when she saw three angry-looking slashes running from shoulder to hip.

Rena swallowed hard, recalling the battle he'd had with Zed. She couldn't begin to imagine the loss he had withstood and the years of loneliness that had followed. He wanted to help his brother, she understood that. But why did he believe his own happiness had to be sacrificed in order to achieve his goal?

The man was hell-bent on torturing himself.

"Can you answer one question for me?" Rena asked quietly. "If you and Zed are identical, then why do you believe that I'm Zed's mate and not yours? And please don't tell me how complicated it is. I'm not stupid, and if you ask me, I've been pretty damned understanding about this whole crazy mess. I deserve that much."

Rena had never believed that she'd meet a man like Zander Lorens. One who could accept all of her, the good, the bad, and the weird. Now that she had found him, the idea of losing him was unthinkable. Was the universe that cruel? Would it bring this man into her life, one she could fall in love with, only to keep him from her?

The savage irony of her situation wasn't lost on her. The raw truth seared into her heart and soul, threatening to drown her in its wake.

Zander let out a heavy sigh and leaned both hands on the railing. The muscles in his shoulders bunched as his energy signature buzzed with anger-tinged frustration. Rena rested her chin on her knees and wrestled for patience, even though all she wanted to do was go to him and kiss the scars on his back until they vanished.

"You're right. And I can't begin to tell you how badly I wish things were different."

Zander turned around slowly, and the dark, pained expression carved into his features broke her heart. He was all sharp angles and edges that looked like they were carved from stone. His ropy, muscular arms hung at his sides, but even in the relaxed setting of his bedroom, the man was a bundle of tension.

"They could be different," she whispered. Rena fought the tears that stung the back of her eyes and swallowed, even though her throat felt like sandpaper. "We can make the choice to... What if you and I—"

"I can't leave him there!" His voice boomed through the cabin, and his eyes shifted to those of his dragon. The man's voice was gritty and rife with tortured restraint. "Don't you get it? There can't be two mates for one woman, because Zed and I are identical. As far as the universe is concerned, we are one and the same."

"What if—"

"He's my brother, Rena." Quiet regret had replaced anger, and his glowing gaze flickered back to his lovely, pale-green, human eyes. "Zed is the only family I have left. He wouldn't even be in this situation if it weren't for me. I'm the one who killed Arianna—not him."

"You were both fighting. Hell, he's the one who started it. I was there, Zander. I heard the whole thing. He wasn't listening to you. He was blind with rage."

"But *I'm* the one who killed her, Rena. Me! Not him. I did it, and I'll be damned if I'm going to let my brother pay for my sins for all eternity."

"You're punishing yourself," she murmured softly. Understanding and sadness edged her words. "That's it. Isn't it? The curse isn't enough. You have to make damned sure you torture yourself for the rest of your existence."

Zander held her bold stare but said nothing. He didn't have to, because she knew she had hit the proverbial nail on the head. A pang of sorrow flared in Rena's chest, and a chill whispered over her, as though a door had been slammed shut, closing off all possibility of a future with him, and the ache inside her swelled. For a moment, Rena feared she might actually choke on the finality of it.

He tore his eyes from hers as he swore quietly and ran both hands through his shaggy hair. Rena wanted to argue with him some more, tell him what a stubborn ass he was being, but before she could say another word, he made a beeline for the bedroom door.

"The storm has passed," he said, pulling the door open.

"Has it? Still seems pretty stormy around here to me."

She arched one eyebrow, but he ignored her attempt to continue their discussion.

"We need to get on the road as soon as possible. I don't want to risk another night away, and we definitely can't walk in the dreamrealm again. We got out before Zander emerged, but I doubt we'll be that lucky next time. We have to be there in the cave with him when he wakes up. The Amoveo haven't exactly been my allies, but I need to get to Zed and help him when he wakes up. If I don't, if he were to emerge alone on their ranch... the outcome could be catastrophic."

"I bet," Rena murmured. "So they know about *me* coming to meet everyone, but they don't know about you and your brother?"

"No." He shook his head solemnly. "They don't."

"Zander..." She searched his gaze, but he looked away abruptly. The man was making a nasty habit of shutting her out and cutting her off.

"We have to leave, Rena."

"Fine," she huffed.

Rena shoved the sheets aside and hopped out of bed. Zander stilled in the doorway, his gaze rolling over her in one steady pass, lingering briefly on her bare legs. His energy signature hummed and whirled around her ferociously, reminding Rena of the way he would rev the engine of his Harley.

He could tell her a million times that he didn't want her, but it was a bald-faced lie. Words were easy to manipulate. People used them all the time to present only what they wanted the world to see. Energy signatures, on the other hand, never, ever lied. Zander's words were pushing her away, but his spirit was calling her closer.

"Help yourself to whatever's in the kitchen." He tore his gaze away as he grabbed the doorknob and started to leave. "I'll meet you outside."

When he turned his back on her, Rena grabbed the edge of the shirt she was wearing, the one she'd chosen because Zander's masculine scent still lingered in the fabric. She whipped it off over her head, leaving her completely nude in the early-morning sunlight.

"Zander?" she called. "Catch."

He turned around, and the expression of shock flicked to desire in a hot second as he caught the shirt with one hand. Rena made no move to cover herself. She stood before him boldly as her hands drifted over her breasts and then down to her belly before finally settling on the curve of her hips. To her delight, Zander's eyes shifted again. She shivered as his glowing gaze raked over her naked body, and she could practically feel his hands on her.

Rena strode toward him with slow, intentional steps, and as she slipped past him in the doorway, their bodies barely a breath apart, she paused. Her nipple brushed his bare arm, and a strangled groan rumbled in his chest. She watched his Adam's apple bob as he swallowed what she could only assume was a healthy dose of lust. Her gaze flicked down to his sweatpants, which were doing nothing to hide his growing erection.

"Thanks for the shirt," she whispered. "Looks like you need another cold shower."

Without waiting for him to respond, Rena sauntered into the bathroom and closed the door behind her. As she turned on the shower, one thought ran through her head. Before the sun went down that night, she was going to prove to Zander that nobody decided her fate except for her.

Curse or no curse.

When Rena turned around to grab the shampoo from the bag she'd left on the counter, she caught sight of her reflection, and her stomach dropped to her feet.

There, on her lower back, was a bluish-black splotch with a darker outline. She craned her neck trying to get a better look and backed up so she was as close to the mirror as possible.

Though the shape wasn't defined, the location was correct.

She could have lied to herself and acted like it was only a bruise or something. But she would only have been denying what she knew in her gut was true.

A mate tattoo.

Rena's body was betraying her, and fate was conspiring against everything her heart wanted. And her heart wanted Zander.

Chapter 13

ZANDER TIGHTENED THE STRAP OVER HIS BAGS WITH A violent tug, recalling the sight of Rena's perfectly sculpted, naked body. Sweat beaded on his forehead, and he swiped at it with the back of his hand, trying not to think about the swell of her hips or the dip of her waist. His cock twitched and throbbed against the zipper of his jeans from the memory of all that beautiful, creamy skin.

It had taken every single ounce of strength and self-control Zander possessed to *not* touch her when she'd brushed past him. When her nipple grazed his arm, all the blood rushed to his dick, leaving him light-headed. He thought he was going to pass out, but by some small miracle, he didn't. Zander kept his eyes on the wall in front of him instead of watching her disappear into the bathroom.

After that brazen move on her part, he knew there was no more screwing around. Rena may not have understood what was at stake, but Zander didn't have that excuse. He knew better than to tempt the fates and mess with the order of how things were supposed to be. Given the hell his brother had existed in all these years, Zed deserved to have a mate, and the son of a bitch was lucky as hell to find one in a woman like Rena McHale.

The sound of the cabin door closing captured his attention, and a split second later, Rena's energy signature flowed over him on the crisp October breeze. She smiled and waved as she strode toward him with an air of confidence that only heightened his attraction to her. The fallen leaves and gravel crunched beneath her boots. The clothes she wore were similar to the day before, and as she made her way to the barn, he couldn't help but note the fluidity with which she moved. Her casual beauty was breathtaking. As she got closer, it was evident she wore very little makeup, and her hair was still damp from her shower. This, of course, instantly made him think of her naked.

Wet and naked.

"There you are!"

Rena's cheerful voice shattered his dirty thoughts and brought him back to reality. Zander willed his body to cooperate, but every single one of his cells roared in protest. He squatted down next to the bike and tightened the strap over his bag, even though he knew full well the damn thing was tight enough. He had to do something other than stare at her.

"I locked up the cabin. The lights are off, and I turned the thermostat down." She held out the keys and jingled them at him. "Do you want these, or should I hang on to them?"

Zander rose to his feet slowly, the heat of her body flickering over him in subtle but unmistakable waves. He held out his hand, and she dropped the keys into his palm before plunking her bag on top of his. Rena gave him a flirty, sidelong grin as she used the extra bungee cord to secure her belongings to the bike. Her self-sufficiency was one of her most appealing qualities.

The woman was beautiful, smart, tough, and independent.

Perfect.

Shit.

He stuffed the keys into the pocket of his leather jacket and strode toward the back of the small barn, his heavy steps echoing through the sparsely occupied space. Other than a few gardening tools and a snow-blower, the place was empty. Then again, Zander didn't put the barn here to store lawn equipment. The small, gray structure, seemingly unassuming and unimportant to anyone who might stumble upon it, housed something sacred to him and his people.

"Hey, do you have an iPhone charger?"

"No. I have a flip phone."

"Dude." Rena's eyebrows lifted, and her gaze swept over him with mild disapproval. "You really are five hundred years old, aren't you?"

"What can I say?" He shrugged. "I'm not a fan of technology. If you weren't with me, I'd be camping instead of staying at motels."

"Camping? No thanks. I like plumbing. Anyway, I forgot to bring my charger, and now my phone is totally dead."

"You can use mine if you need to make a call."

"No, it's Vito." She looked away and brushed the hair from her forehead, as though suddenly uncomfortable. "It's just, well, if the people at Sunnyfarm need to get in touch with me…"

"I'm sure you can pick one up along the way."

"Yeah, okay."

She hooked her thumbs into the pockets of her jeans, and silence hung between them awkwardly for several beats of his heart.

"We should probably go then."

"We still have to do one more thing before we leave." He stopped by the back wall of the barn. "It won't take long."

"What's the matter, Zander?" Rena sighed. "Need to whack your weed before we split?"

Zander shook his head and cast a wicked smirk over his shoulder at Rena. "I hope you're not claustrophobic."

"Why?" She followed him over but moved cautiously. "What have you got back there?"

Zander squatted down and hooked his finger in the iron latch embedded in the wide-plank wood floor. Rising to his feet, he yanked the door open and coughed when he inhaled a nose full of dust and dirt. As the cloud dissipated, the steps leading into the underground chamber were revealed.

"Holy cow," Rena whispered. She moved in next to him and peered cautiously into the entry. "What the hell is down there?"

"My torture chamber," he said flatly.

"Very funny." Rena elbowed him playfully.

"The power of the dragons is rooted in the earth. It stems from the rock and fiery core from which we were born."

"Okay," she said slowly. "But why do we need to go down *there*?"

"We have to get Zed a spirit stone." Zander went down two steps before turning back to Rena. "His was destroyed when the spell was cast, and he can't emerge from hibernation without it."

Zander went down two more steps but stopped when Rena didn't immediately follow.

"Come on."

"It's pitch-black down there." She inched closer and folded her arms over her chest while peering into the dark. "Don't you need a flashlight or something?"

"No." A knowing grin bloomed, and he extended an arm, offering her his hand. "Trust me."

Rena flicked her pale-brown eyes from his hand to his face and then back again before finally wrapping her fingers around his. He tried not to notice how perfectly her hand fit into his or the warmth of her flesh as is it shimmied along his palm. But he failed. Miserably. When her eyes clapped onto his and she gave him a reassuring nod, a swell of gratitude swamped him.

Even if she wasn't meant to be his, he was grateful for the time they had shared. Letting her go was going to be the most difficult task of his five-hundred-year existence.

As they made their way down the curved stone staircase, the light from the entrance began to fade. Rena tightened her grip on his fingers as her other hand flew to his shoulder. She pressed her body against him, and her breath, a mix of coffee and mint, wafted past him in the dimly lit space. The scent conjured up images of cozy mornings and sharing coffee while snuggled in bed.

Zander shook his head. *Get a grip, man. Get a grip.*

"It's too dark, Zander." Rena's voice quivered slightly, but he could tell she was fighting her fear. "We're going to break our necks."

"No, we're not." He turned his face to the left, and when the fresh scent of her shampoo filled his head, Zander's eyes shifted with a tingling snap. Rena's smiling face, with an expression of genuine appreciation, was bathed in a soft red glow. "Use your clan vision. The Fox Clan has especially keen eyesight and hearing. Even in your human form, you should be able to access those gifts. You've been experiencing it in bits and pieces, but it'll take some practice to use them on purpose."

"If you say so."

Her tongue flicked out, moistening her lower lip as she closed her eyes. A split second later, her lids flicked open, and Zander found himself staring into the glowing, amber eyes of her clan.

"Perfect," he whispered.

"Thanks." Rena gave his hand a quick squeeze before tearing her gaze from his. "Now let's—"

She stopped speaking, and her jaw dropped as her eyes flicked down toward the landing. Zander couldn't have stopped the beaming grin on his face if he'd tried. And he didn't want to. A mixture of pride and satisfaction swirled inside him as he helped Rena discover her abilities.

"Holy shit, Zander." Her laughter bounced around them playfully. "I can see everything! I mean *everything!* Every crack and crevice. And bugs! Look! Wait—what's that?" She slapped his arm and then pointed ahead. "There's a light toward the bottom of the stairs. Go! Come on!"

She urged him to move, and he couldn't help chuckle at her eagerness. "I'm going, I'm going."

Zander took the rest of the stairs at a faster pace, with Rena moving confidently behind him. When they reached the dirt floor of the spirit cave, Zander stepped to the side so Rena would have plenty of room to explore the sacred space.

All of the walls glimmered in varying shades of red quartz. It crept up toward the ceiling and even lined the side of the stairs. Dirt and dusty, bland rock made up the floor and the stairs, but the remainder of the cave, which was about thirty feet in diameter, was comprised entirely of jagged, glittering quartz.

In the middle of it all, bathed in the soft glow of the spirit stone, was Rena. Her hands covered her mouth, and a gasp slipped between her fingers as she turned around, slowly taking it all in.

"This is amazing," she said, her hands falling away from her lips. "It reminds me of the wall that Zed is hibernating in. It's absolutely beautiful."

"Smart lady," Zander murmured. He sidled in next to her but kept some distance between them. "When we go into hibernation, our cocoon is made of our family's spirit stone. My clan is tied to quartz. According to legend, the first dragons were born of the earth eons ago. When the ground shook and volcanoes erupted as Mother Earth took shape, the first of our kind emerged from the flame and rock. We were expelled from the deepest recesses, the very heart and soul of the planet itself. The earth heals us, rejuvenates us, and, when necessary, protects us."

"The colors." Rena moved closer to one of the walls and gently ran her fingers over the lumpy surface. "These shades of red infused with gold... They are similar colors to the spikes and horns you and Zed have. And his skin was especially mesmerizing. It reminded me of a kaleidoscope. Depending on the

light or the angle, the colors shimmied and morphed.
Really beautiful."

"Yes," Zander said quietly.

"A-and you too." Rena turned to face him, and sadness edged her glowing gaze. "It was the same for you.
Identical twins…and all that."

"Also true."

"Why is it glowing?" She trailed one finger on a
protruding piece of quartz, and it glowed brighter in
response. Rena quickly dropped her hand. "That's wild!
It's like the wall is reacting to me…like it's alive."

"In some ways, it is," he murmured. "We believe
the souls of our ancestors return to the earth once their
bodies die. They come back here and join with the rest.
Their energy, the knowledge they collected during
their earthly existence, all of it resides here, ready to be
shared with the next generation."

"So…this place is kind of like dragon heaven for
your family?" she asked with a beaming smile. "Right?"

He let his gaze wander over Rena's beautiful face.
Bathed in the glow of the spirit cave, she was posi-
tively luminous. It was as if all of that inner beauty, her
strength and grace, was emboldened by the power of
this place. All he wanted was to gather her in his arms
and kiss the daylights out of her. Feel her soft, warm
body enveloped with his, and sink into her comforting
embrace. Throw caution to the wind and tell fate to go
fuck itself.

But he didn't. How could he?

"Right," he said tightly.

Zander immediately shifted his attention to the wall
on his left. He could not and would not get sucked into

her orbit when they could have no future together. He had to keep his mind sharp and his focus on the task at hand. Zander rolled his shoulder, trying to prep himself for what he knew he had to do next.

"I need your help with this part. We have to take a piece with us, but before we remove it from the cluster, it has to be imprinted with your energy signature. Zed recognized you in the dreamrealm. I'm hoping that if we mark the stone with your distinct energy, combined with the memories of our ancestors, it will help him emerge safely from hibernation. Maybe we can minimize his confusion."

He waved his hand over a piece of quartz that jutted out a bit farther than the rest. The light deep within the wall pulsed and throbbed in response to Zander's presence, and a sense of calm came over him. It was as if his mother, who was long gone from this world, had stepped behind him and put a comforting hand on his shoulder.

"I've been away too long," he said quietly.

"Why did you stay away if this place is so important to you?"

When he looked to the right, the expression of awe on Rena's face evoked a fresh pang of warmth within his chest. Sharing this with her, showing her this sacred place, made him happier than he had expected.

"Coming back here had become bittersweet. Soon, the bitter outweighed the sweet, and it sucked to be here alone. It felt hopeless. But now, sharing it with you…" His voice trailed off, and he quickly looked away from her before clearing his throat. "I mean for you and Zed. That's why we're here."

"Right," Rena said warily. "Let me ask you something.

If you guys do the dream walking stuff all the time and hibernation is part of what dragons usually do, then why are you so worried about when he'll wake up? Won't he just be psyched that you got him out of there?"

"We don't usually dream when we're in hibernation in our dragon form. The beast dominates, not the man. And Zed has been slumbering far longer than anyone I've heard of. I have a hunch it's going to take him a while to regain his human side. To be honest, the curse throws a monkey wrench into everything."

"Ah." She pressed her lips together and nodded. "That explains the way he was acting. Kind of crazy and, well, like a monster."

"We aren't monsters, Rena. We never were."

Rena tilted her head and studied him closely.

"What?" He ran one hand through his hair and tried to mask his discomfort with frustration. "Why are you looking at me like that?"

"I was just wondering what it would be like to see you change into the dragon. In real life, I mean, not just in the dream." Her voice, low and husky, rasped over him like a caress. "I bet it's one hell of a sight. Powerful. Dangerous. Seductive."

Zander's body tensed, and his throat worked as he swallowed the groan of desire. The woman uttered the secret wish he barely dared to think about, let alone say out loud. Shifting into his dragon again would be a relief, but being able to do it with Rena by his side — what would that feel like? To be able to embrace the beast but with a woman like Rena to help him tame it? Now *that* would be heaven.

Snap out of it! This is foolishness, he thought. *Pure*

*foolishness to entertain the notion. Why waste time with
a future that isn't meant to be?*

"You can block your visions if you want to?" he
asked, abruptly shifting his focus.

"Yes. Why?"

"Here," he said gruffly as he grasped her hand.
"Unless you want to be inundated with generations of
memories, I suggest you keep it locked up."

"Thanks for the tip. I think you and your brother are
all the dragon I can handle for the moment."

Zander gently placed her hand over the section he
had selected. Rena's silky smooth skin was like heated
velvet beneath his palm as he pressed it gently against
the stone. He moved in behind her, holding her hand
in place while trying not to be distracted by the feminine, flowery smell of her shampoo. Her round backside
pressed against him, and Zander shifted his stance in an
attempt to minimize their contact. He grit his teeth and
fought the rising tide of lust. Rena did little to help the
situation when she relaxed her body and let her weight
fall into him.

"Now what?" she whispered.

"Close your eyes." He dipped his head so it was next
to hers and kept his voice low. "Focus all of your attention on the stone beneath your palm." He brushed his
thumb over the dip of her wrist. "Picture your energy
signature. Imagine it's like a river, flowing around the
stone, consuming it, covering it with the essence of all
that you are. Send your indomitable strength and beauty,
all of which stems from your soul. Give him your goodness, Rena. The purity of it will help guide him home."

Rena's breathing picked up in pace, and her body

shivered against him. At the same moment, Zander sent his spirit stream to the stone. He pictured it traveling down his arm and out through his fingers before curling around the quartz like a spiritual blanket. The light behind the stone flared brightly as the connection was completed.

The images flared into his mind with shocking speed as one more of his clan gifts returned with a vengeance.

A moonlit, starry sky filled with numerous dragon silhouettes as they flew through the night, dominating the air. Streams of fire and the shrieks of their battle cries permeated his mind. His father's fallen form, bloodied and battered, with his mother weeping over him, consumed by grief. The witch. Hands raised to the sky. Winds whipping her hair around her, eyes wild as she cast the spell that doomed them all.

Zander sucked in a shuddering breath, and his eyes snapped open as the memories evaporated.

A muffled cracking sound of the stone being released from the wall bounced around the cave. Zander tightened his grip over Rena's hand as he pulled loose the sacred piece of quartz with an unsteady hand.

"Are you okay?" she asked, her voice gentle and soothing. "You're shaking."

It took a moment for Zander to find his voice. "Did you see that?" he asked on a gruff whisper. "The memories?"

"No. I protected myself, like you asked me to." She turned her face toward his, and her body melted against his perfectly. "Why? What did you see?"

Part of him –hell, most of him— wanted to share it with her, to tell her that his powers were slowly but surely coming back, but that would be selfish. He had to keep her focused on Zed. When his brother woke up, Rena would be confused enough as her body responded to Zed. It was up to Zander to minimize that confusion as much as he could.

With Rena still sheltered against him and with her arm cradled in his, Zander gently turned their hands over. The glittering spirit stone was nestled in Rena's palm, and a soft red light emanated from the center. Rena's fingers closed over the precious piece of quartz, and she turned her face toward his. Her mouth, those full lips, scant inches from his.

How easy it would be to dip his head lower and...

"Nothing." He cleared his throat. "It's not important."

"Is that it?" Her husky whisper curled around him seductively. "Are we done?"

An ache bloomed in Zander's chest as her question hung in the hauntingly quiet space of the spirit cave. Standing there, surrounded by the sacred, ancient ground, all Zander could think about was the mark on his thigh and how badly he wanted it to be completed. But once Zed woke up and saw Rena, Zander knew the mark would begin to fade.

He would step aside, but how desperately he wanted her. All of her.

"Yes," Zander murmured, his lips brushing the edge of her ear. "We're done."

Without another word, he released her and strode to the staircase. He didn't look back. He couldn't. He knew if he did, the expression on her face would be as heart-broken as the pain he sensed in her energy signature.

Making his way to the surface, he expected Rena to say something or to challenge him, as she had a habit of doing. She seemed to delight in it, in fact, but none came. They climbed onto the bike and took off down the driveway without either one saying a word, and her silence nagged at him.

Bullshit. It tore at his soul to know he was hurting her. Arianna's father was right.

Zander was a selfish son of a bitch. He wanted Rena all to himself. He wanted nothing more than to turn the bike around, go back inside his cabin, and spend the entire winter showing her just how much he desired her.

But he didn't.

With miles of highway ahead of them, Zander prayed he would be able to walk away from her once his brother was safe. His one consolation in this whole damn mess was Zed. Zander knew that even if he didn't have the strength to let Rena go, he could count on his brother to do the one act Zander hadn't been able to complete in five centuries.

Zed would kill him.

Chapter 14

"I NEED TO FILL THE TANK. GO ON AND GRAB YOURSELF something to drink or eat, if you want." Zander handed her a twenty-dollar bill and glanced at his watch. "We have about two hours to go, so hit the restroom if you need it. I want to get to the ranch well before sundown, and I don't plan on stopping again."

"Okay. Do you want anything?"

Rena took the money, and her heart skipped a beat when Zander's bare fingertips grazed hers. He hadn't spoken much since they left the cabin, and he was avoiding looking her in the eyes again.

"No."

He turned his back on her to deal with the gas pump, continuing the cold-shoulder routine he'd started that morning after they left the cave. He had been curt and distant ever since they got the spirit stone for Zed. Each averted gaze and monosyllabic answer to her attempts at conversation was like a stab in the heart. He was doing his best to distance himself from her and doing a damn fine job of it.

"Suit yourself," she said wearily.

Without looking back, she made her way inside the small convenience store and was immediately hit with a cloud of cigarette smoke. An older woman with warm, hazel eyes smiled at her after taking a big drag off her Marlboro Light. Bleach-blond curls quivered around her lined face, a face that had probably once been beautiful but was now weathered from years of smoking.

"Afternoon." Her voice was raspy. "You two look like you been on the road awhile."

"Yes, ma'am." Rena slid the twenty over. "He's going to fill the tank, and this should cover it."

"Sure, sure."

"Do you have any cell phone chargers?" Rena looked around, and hope dwindled. "It's for an iPhone."

"Nope. Sorry, darlin'. I ain't got nothin' like that here." The woman blew out a cloud of smoke and held out her hand. "My name's Viola. What's yours?"

"Oh." Rena blinked in surprise but accepted the woman's greeting over the dingy countertop. "Hi. I'm Rena. It's nice to meet you."

"You too." She adjusted her round, soft-looking form on the gray metal stool and peered out the window at Zander. "That's a fine-lookin' man out there."

"Yeah." Rena's cheeks heated, and she turned toward the shelves behind her. "He's something, all right."

"Where you two headed?"

"A friend's ranch a little farther upstate." Rena's gaze lingered on the snacks without really seeing them. "Another two hours or so and we should be there."

"You two been datin' long?"

"Um…we aren't dating." Rena gave her a tight smile. "Just traveling companions."

Yeah right, she thought. *You are so full of it, Rena. Lie to yourself and the nice lady.*

"Sorry," Viola said with a hacking cough. "Don't mean to be nosy, but it's been so damn slow today, I feel like I'm goin' crazy. My dang television is busted, so I can't even watch my programs."

"It's okay."

"It can get kinda lonely in here sometimes." She crushed her cigarette out in the overflowing ashtray and kept talking while Rena looked around. "I live in the little apartment in the back there. The only thing my no-good late husband ever did was leave me this place. I ain't got no family or nothin' and, well, I guess I count on my customers to keep me company. Never was good at what you'd call long-term relationships. But I like it most of the time, bein' by m'self, I mean."

An awkward silence fell between them when the woman stopped rambling, and Rena instantly felt the urge to continue the conversation.

"So, I guess you don't have any kids?"

"I did but not no more."

Rena's heart sank, and she spun around, horrified at having brought up a subject that was probably painful.

"Oh no! I feel like a jackass," she sputtered. "I'm so sorry."

To her surprise, Viola didn't look upset. A faint smile played at her lips, and she held up one hand, stopping the rest of her fumbling attempt at an apology.

"Don't go feelin' bad. She ain't dead or nothin'." She reached under the counter and pulled out a single scuffed, white baby shoe. The older woman held it up between her thumb and forefinger, a broader smile covering her wrinkled face. "At least, I don't think she is. I gave her up for adoption a few months after she was born. I tried to keep her, but I couldn't manage. I was only sixteen and dead broke. I wanted her to have a better life than what I could give her. I'm better by m'self anyhow. But a pretty, young girl like you probably don't understand that."

"Viola," Rena murmured. "You'd be surprised."

"Guess I would." She coughed loudly. "Life is full of surprises, ain't it? Never can tell what's gonna happen."

"Girl," Rena said with a laugh, "amen to that."

Silence followed again as Viola turned the small shoe over in her hand, a whisper of sadness covering her face.

"Um, do you mind if I ask how old she would be now?" Rena swallowed hard. She knew it was ridiculous to think for one second that this woman could be her birth mother, but crazier shit had been happening, so why not that?

"Bethany, that's what I called her, she'll be forty-two next week."

"Oh." The ball of nerves in Rena's stomach loosened a little. Nope. Not her. "You really were a baby yourself, then. Weren't you?"

"Yup. Sorry." Viola sniffed and swiped at her eyes before shoving the baby shoe back under the counter. "Not sure why I told ya all that stuff."

"It's okay." Rena gave her a reassuring smile. "I have one of those faces. People feel compelled to tell me stuff. Do you ever think about finding her? I never knew my birth parents either, and, well, lately…I've been curious."

Understatement of the century.

"Records were lost years ago, and I figure it's probably for the best." She waved one hand around. "Ain't like I got anythin' to offer her other than this old place."

"You love her," Rena said quietly. "I'd say that's something."

"Well, ain't neither here nor there." Viola grabbed another cigarette. "I won't bother you anymore. Let me know if you need help findin' stuff. Sorry for all my blabberin' on."

With the older woman's phlegmy cough ricocheting behind her, Rena perused the sparsely populated refrigerated case in the dusty gas station, but nothing jumped out at her. She wasn't really hungry or thirsty. Hell, her stomach had been in nervous knots since they'd left West Yellowstone, and eating was the last item on her to-do list. Her gaze landed on a bottle of red cherry cola, and her lips lifted at the corners. The bright color reminded her of the quartz cave, but her smile faltered when she recalled the way Zander had gone from hot to cold in a nanosecond.

One minute they were nestled up to each other, bodies and spirit streams merging as intimately as they could without being naked, and the next he was high-tailing it out of there like she had rabies. Contrary to his big, bad plan, Rena had no intention of hooking up with Zed, and she was running out of patience with Zander's martyr routine. Once they got to the ranch, she would check out the Amoveo and help him wake up Zed.

But if the dragon twins kept up with the whole you-have-to-mate-with-Zed crap, she was going to get the hell out of there.

Old Viola had the right idea about being alone, and until recently, Rena had been of the same mind-set. Being on her own was how it had always been, for the most part, and how it probably should be. And how it could be again.

After all, her life in Las Vegas would be waiting for her when she got back.

Her chest clenched, and a pang of sadness flared at the idea of leaving Zander. It was silly. She had known the man for only a few days, and now she couldn't imagine her life without him. Which was kind of insane for a woman who prided herself on being on her own.

A flicker of movement reflected in the glass door, and Rena looked behind her, expecting to see Zander, but it wasn't him. A shady-looking guy wearing a ratty, brown hoodie and dirty, baggy blue jeans was at the counter of the dingy little store. He had his back to her and was shifting his weight back and forth nervously. Every alarm bell in Rena's head went off, and a tickle of fear shimmied beneath her skin.

The dude was up to no good.

Rena moved slowly toward the front of the store, between two rows of shelves stocked with various snacks. She glanced out the front window for some sign of Zander, who had gone to the restroom, or another customer, but the place was deserted. This little gas station was in the middle of Bumblefuck, Nowhere.

She wished like hell that she'd kept the handgun on her instead of in her bag, where it wasn't doing her or the older woman at the register a damn bit of good. Moving cautiously, Rena caught Viola's frightened gaze. Her hazel eyes, filled with fear, jumped from the man to Rena, widening in a plea for help or maybe a warning. Rena didn't have time to figure that part out, because a split second later, she realized she'd made a grave error.

The guy spun around and pointed his gun at her, confirming her suspicions about how unhinged he was.

"Don't move, lady!"

Rena held her hands up and stopped short. He looked like a meth head or druggie of one kind or another. The guy was totally strung out and shaky, which meant his gun could go off with one wrong move. She had seen plenty of drug addicts during her days on the street, and this poor bastard was an all-too-familiar sight. Her heart thundered in her chest, but she fought to keep her breathing normal. Staying calm was her best bet.

Keep the guy talking.

"I'm not going to try and stop you," Rena said evenly. "You're the one with the gun."

"That's right." He grinned, showing her a mouthful of blackened, rotted teeth. He had a wicked case of meth mouth. "Get over here, where I can see both of ya."

The guy jerked the gun toward the counter, and Rena complied. She glanced outside again. What the hell was taking Zander so long?

"Empty the register." His voice was edged with anger and desperation. "Do it now."

"Please…" Viola's shaking, frightened voice filled the little store. "Don't shoot me. Take the money. Take whatever you want. I ain't got much."

"Shut up." He pointed the gun and grew more agitated by the second. "Move faster, you old bitch."

"I'm sorry," she whimpered.

"It's okay, Viola," Rena murmured. "He's going to get his money, and then he'll leave."

"Shut the fuck up!" He swung the gun toward Rena again. "Or I'll shoot you in the face."

Viola whimpered and stuffed the money from the register into a plastic bag with trembling hands. When she leaned forward to give it to the guy, she knocked over a small gum display, sending the packages clattering onto the floor.

"H-here." She shoved the bag across the dirty laminate counter and stepped back with her hands in the air. Mascara smudges mixed with tears streamed down her cheeks. "That's all of it. Everythin' in the register."

"Bullshit!" He pounded a fist on the counter. "Where's the safe?"

"Th-there's no safe," she whimpered. "I swear I'm tellin' you the truth. You gotta believe me."

The guy cocked the gun, and the murky, deranged energy tumbling from him was beginning to make Rena sick to her stomach.

"Yeah," he spat, "well, I ain't no mind reader, so I don't gotta believe shit."

Mind reader? Duh! Rena almost rolled her eyes at her stupidity. She may not have had her gun, but she wasn't powerless.

Zander! Rena instinctively touched her mind to his. *There's a guy in here holding up the store. He's got a gun and—*

Before she could finish the thought, Zander appeared in the doorway. With the sun's glare behind him, his tall, broad-shouldered figure filled the space like an avenging angel—although the glowing, bloodred gaze of his dragon didn't look all that angelic.

It all happened in a split second.

Poor Viola got one look at Zander, and her face twisted in a mask of shock right before she fainted, falling to the floor in a heap.

"What the hell?" The guy spun toward Zander.

"Look out," Rena shouted. "He's got a gun!"

Moving like some kind of ninja warrior in a blur of inhuman speed, Zander dove forward, grabbed the gun, and twisted the guy's wrist behind his back. As he pulled him into a choke hold, the druggie's face bloomed from red to almost purple. He gasped for air and struggled against Zander's far larger frame. The last image Rena saw before gunfire rang out was Zander's furious expression over the guy's shoulder as both men dropped to the floor.

Rena's hands covered her mouth during the agonizing seconds of silence that followed. Their feet stuck out past the row of shelving, and at first, neither man moved. Her heart thundered in her chest as she inched closer and sought out Zander's energy signature with her own. She let out a strangled cry of relief when she felt the slow, steady pulse of his energy merge with hers.

White-hot fear burned in Rena's chest when the druggie suddenly scrambled off Zander and ran out the door without looking back. Rena raced over and dropped down to her knees. Zander was on his back and blood seeped from a wound in his stomach, creating a gruesome stain on his shirt.

"Oh my God," Rena said in a strangled voice.

She pushed aside the bloody garment and stifled a gurgle of horror when she caught sight of the wound. Instinctively, she pressed both hands on it in a futile attempt to slow the bleeding. Zander's eyes fluttered open and he groaned as he tried to sit up. Rena pressed a hand on his shoulder and pushed him back down.

"Don't move!" Her voice shook even though she was

doing her best to remain calm. "We have to stop the bleeding. Shit. You need an ambulance, Zander."

"No, I don't," he said through gritted teeth. Each word was made with concerted effort and clearly caused him pain. "Go outside. Get two handfuls of dirt—not the dusty shit in the lot. Earthy and damp. As much as you can."

"What are you talking about?" Her fear was replaced by frustration. "How is a bunch of dirt going to help you? You need a damn doctor."

"Just do it," he barked. A coughing fit wracked his body, and the veins in his neck bulged as he fought another wave of pain. "Fuck me, that hurts. Go, Rena. Now!"

"Okay, okay," she whispered. Rena rose to her feet on shaky legs, her hands covered in Zander's blood. "I'll be back. Just hang on."

She ran outside and scanned the pavement as she turned the corner of the cinder-block building. Tears blurred her vision, and panic swelled as she stumbled on a crack in the tiny parking lot before making a beeline for the trees. Rena dropped to her knees on the ground covered with pine needles and started to dig. Dirt clung to her sticky, bloodstained hands. She barely felt the brisk fall wind as she clawed away the dried surface before reaching the rich, moist soil beneath. The scent, fresh and earthy, filled her nostrils, instantly putting her at ease. Her panic ebbed as she scooped up two heaping handfuls of the fragrant dirt and ran back into the store.

Rena dropped to her knees beside Zander and fleetingly noted the woman was still passed out behind the counter.

"Now what?" She held her handfuls of dirt over him and laughed nervously when some sprinkled out of her shaking hands. "Shit, sorry."

"You're doing fine. I'm going to live. Immortal, remember?" He tried to smile, but it looked more like a grimace. The guy was bleeding to death, and he was worried about keeping her at ease. "Press as much of it as you can into the wound."

"You want me to put dirt *in* there? Don't doctors try to sterilize wounds on most people?"

"Yeah, but I'm not most people, am I?"

"You definitely aren't," she murmured.

"Hurry, please. Getting shot is bad enough, but passing out would be really humiliating."

He winced and reached into the pocket of his leather jacket. The effort was obviously painful, and Rena felt stupid for asking questions when she should have been helping him. She was usually good at keeping a level head, but blood and guts weren't in her wheelhouse. Her stomach lurched, and she focused on not puking all over him.

Rena puffed her hair off her forehead and threw a prayer to the universe as she did what Zander requested. She gingerly patted it down and smoothed the heap of bloody dirt like she was creating some kind of macabre sand castle. Laughing nervously, she sat back on her heels and wiped her sweaty brow with the back of her hands.

Hands that looked like she had just buried a body.

"Okay, now what?"

"Check on the woman," he said between clenched teeth.

His face was twisted in a mask of pain as he placed the spirit stone on top of the dirt-covered wound. His fingers shook, and the stone tumbled down, but Rena caught it.

"Her name is Viola, and she's still passed out." Rena carefully put the piece of quartz back onto the dirt. "You, however, are a mess. Literally and figuratively. Okay, it's where you put it. What now?"

"Stand back," he bit out between clenched teeth.

Rena pushed herself to her feet and put some space between her and Zander. Just enough to make him happy but still close enough to help him if he needed her. He told her that his people were connected to the earth, but this wasn't at all what she had expected.

Zander let his head fall back to the floor as he settled both hands over the stone. Before she could ask anything else, a bright light emanated from beneath Zander's hands. Rena was mesmerized by it. A low, pulsing sound began to strum though Zander's energy signature and surrounded her in thick, strobing waves. As the light grew brighter in strength, so did the throbbing sound, but the mound of dirt started to shrink. Rena watched in pure fascination as, a moment later, the light flashed so brightly, she had to shut her eyes against it.

When she opened them again, Zander was already rising to his feet.

"What the hell?" Rena gaped at him as he brushed dirt from the bloody hole in his shirt.

"Good as new," he said wearily.

Zander went to zip up his leather jacket, probably to hide the bloody shirt, but Rena ran over and grabbed his hands. She pushed them aside before tugging up the offending garment. Rena swore under her breath. The wound was gone, but Zander had a fresh scar in its place. It was dirty and bloodstained but seemingly healed.

"Holy crap," she whispered. "That is absolutely

incredible! Is that how you've been able to survive all these years?"

"Not exactly," Zander said, his voice tight and curt. "I can't die because of the curse, but being able to do *that* made it tolerable. The earth, combined with the power of the spirit stone, heals me a hell of a lot faster than it would without it. But I still feel pain."

"How horrible," she said through quivering lips. "It's like you've been killed over and over. Your body heals just so you can get hurt again. That's totally messed up."

Tears stung her eyes, and her throat tightened with a tide of sadness and sympathy. This man had endured centuries of loneliness and the kind of pain that only existed in Rena's nightmares. She wished that the witch who did this to him was still alive so she could kick the bitch's ass.

"It's called a curse for a reason," he said humorlessly. His pale-green eyes clapped onto hers, and his voice dipped to barely a whisper. "Vito wanted me to suffer. He got his wish in spades."

"Vito," she murmured. Rena stilled as the truth of his words sank in. "He's the one who hired the witch… Jesus, Zander. I—I'm sorry. I…"

Rena ran her fingertips lightly over the puckered scar, which was already fading to a pale pink from an angry red. Zander's stomach muscles flexed as Rena carefully inspected the healing flesh. The smell of dirt, blood, and his naturally male scent filled her head, making her dizzy. All she wanted to do was gather him in her arms and kiss every single scar on his skin. She lifted the shirt higher, exposing more of Zander's torso, and she sucked in a sharp breath when she saw several other scars.

"Oh my God," she whispered. Rena ran her thumb over a jagged mark that looked like it had been there for years. He tensed but didn't pull away. "What in the hell have you been through? Every time I look at you, I discover more scars."

Zander's strong fingers curled around her wrists as he gently pushed her hands away before zipping up his jacket, covering the bloodstained shirt. Rena's eyes met his, and empathy swelled. Pain lingered there, and it wasn't purely physical. The man may have more bodily scars than she could count, but the emotional trauma was surely no less damaging.

Perhaps worse.

"Nothing I haven't deserved," he murmured. He grabbed a pack of wet wipes from the shelf and handed them to her. "Here."

Rena took what he offered and began to clean her hands off while she fought the urge to argue with him. Before she could say anything, the sound of movement behind her caught their attention. She had practically forgotten the other woman was there. Viola had finally woken up, and the expression of confusion on her face was almost comical.

"Little girl, can someone please tell me what the devil is going on?"

Viola's fingers clutched the counter as she peered warily above the edge, glancing from Zander to Rena. As she rose to her feet, the older lady grabbed her cigarettes and quickly lit one with shaking fingers. She brought it to her lips and took a long drag before settling her ample backside onto the metal stool.

Rena's brain scrambled as she glanced down at the

bloody, dirty smears on the floor. How the hell were they going to explain this mess? Zander beat her to it.

"You fainted," Zander said calmly. "And I guess I scared the guy off when I came in. He ran out of here and didn't look back. I'm sure he's crossed the state line by now. I doubt you'll have any more trouble with him. It was nothing. Really."

The woman looked from Zander to the mess on the floor and raised her eyebrows.

"I bet he did." She sucked another long drag from her cigarette. The end burned bright orange. "Looks like you scared more than the snot out of him. That's a lot of blood for a lot of nothin'."

"Maybe we should call the police," Rena said, uncertainty soaking her voice. "I mean…"

"No," she said slowly. "I don't think they'd buy one iota of my story. Do you?"

Rena opened her mouth to protest, but Zander clasped her hand in his and squeezed it gently.

"No, ma'am." He threw a hundred-dollar bill on the counter before pulling Rena toward the door. "Thank you, and sorry for the mess."

"You sure you're okay, mister?" She pointed to the floor. "Looks like you got hurt somethin' awful."

"I'm fine. Just a nosebleed."

Her penciled-on eyebrows lifted. "That so?"

"Yes, ma'am. We'll be getting out of your way now."

That's it? Rena touched his mind with hers and fleetingly noted how easy and right it felt. *We're just going to leave?*

It's for the best. He smiled at Viola as he responded to Rena with a clipped, curt tone. *There's no video surveillance in this place. We should get out of here while we can.*

No video? Rena flicked a quick look around. Zander was right. No cameras. She hadn't even thought of that. *Good. Then I need to do something before we go.*

"Hang on." Rena yanked her hand free from Zander's and went to the counter with Viola's gaze pinned to her. She ignored Zander's frustrated sigh. "You aren't crazy, Viola, and I am sorry for the mess. But before we go, I'd like to do something for you, if you don't mind."

"Depends." She blew out a stream of smoke and pointed her cigarette at Zander. "It involve your friend over there?"

"No, ma'am."

"Your eyes gonna start glowin' funny too?"

"No." Rena extended her arm onto the counter and turned her palm up. "It's about you and your baby girl. Can you give me her shoe?"

"Rena," Zander said in a warning tone. "This isn't a good—"

"It's fine, Zander. Why don't you wait for me outside?"

Zander grumbled something with discontent as the door of the store swung shut behind him. Rena didn't take her eyes off Viola.

"I can help you find her."

"How?"

"Remember how I said that people tell me stuff?"

"Mmhmm."

"Well, sometimes," she said with a smile, "their stuff tells me stuff. I can't make any promises, but I might be able to tell you more about what happened to your daughter."

The worn and scuffed white leather baby shoe felt cool against Rena's sweaty palm. The old-fashioned footwear, similar to ones she had seen in black-and-white photos or bronzed for posterity, was remarkably tiny and seemingly innocuous, with no story to tell.

Seeing visions was a gift and a curse. But today, if she could find this woman's long-lost daughter, it would definitely be a gift. Within seconds, subtle waves of heat shimmied and pulsed, tickling her fingers with static electricity before permeating her skin and seeping into her blood. The familiar buzz rushed up her arm with the fingerprint-like energy ribbon all humans left in their wake. While not as strong or thick as Zander's, it was still clear and distinct.

Rena's eyes fluttered closed, and she focused on keeping her breathing steady. Be calm. Focus. She had done this, searched for the lost, countless times before, but the rush of power that came with it never failed to surprise her. Until she had met Zander, Rena didn't know why she had this ability or how the hell she was able to do what she did—but she was grateful for it.

Hell, she was grateful for Zander. He had given her answers to questions that had shadowed her her entire life, and now Rena could do the same for Viola. Rena's lips lifted at the corners, and excitement bubbled. For the first time, she realized just how lucky she was.

Her power really was a gift.

The buzzing sound, one only Rena could hear, grew louder, and then the images flickered to life in her mind's eye. Rena pushed harder, needing to put herself in the memory, so she could see it all. A bright light flashed, and though she expected pain, none came. She sucked in a sharp breath, and when she opened her eyes, Rena was no longer standing in the small store—she was inside the vision.

But for the first time, Rena wasn't seeing the past... she was witnessing the present.

A young girl, about ten or eleven years old, with dusty, light-blond curls and dark-brown eyes, sat on the steps of a small home. A woman, probably in her forties, who looked a lot like Viola and the child, stood on the porch behind the girl. She was holding open the screen door and smiling broadly. Rena couldn't make out what they were saying as their voices drifted through misty air. Though Rena could see them, they were unaware of her presence.

But then again, she wasn't really there. She was a voyeur of sorts.

It was like stepping inside a family movie. Rena clutched the baby shoe tighter as she looked around, seeking any information that would help identify where the woman and child were. Rena moved closer to them when she spotted a pile of mail and newspaper on the steps next to the girl. She inched nearer as the stomach-rumbling aroma of an apple pie baking wafted through the air, and she read the address on the top envelope.

Kristin Ricker, 534 Bowdoin Road, Kansas City, Missouri.

"Gotcha," Rena whispered.

Having found what she needed, Rena stepped back and closed her eyes, shifting her focus back to the little gas station.

A split second later, a throbbing ache welled in her chest, stealing the breath from her lungs. She opened her palm and let the baby shoe fall from her grasp, breaking the connection. With a gasp, Rena stepped away from the counter and, to her surprise, was met with the steely, strong warmth of Zander's embrace.

Her body hummed from the energy of the vision connection, and her heart thundered against her rib cage as she fought to regain her composure. He curled his arms around her waist and held her tightly, but that only made her quiver on the inside.

"I—I thought you left," she said shakily.

"You all right?" he asked quietly, ignoring her comment. "For a second, I thought you were going to faint."

"I'll be fine. That transition was kind of abrupt. That's all."

He loosened his hold on her but didn't let her go. Rena turned her head slightly to the right and sucked in a deep breath, one meant to clear her mind. However, Zander's earthy scent, with a hint of leather, did little to help.

"Let me go," she whispered.

He didn't. In fact, it felt like he had tightened his grip on her instead.

"D-did it work?" Viola sputtered. She settled onto the stool again. "Did you see something? Is my girl alive? You were spaced out. Your man looked awful worried about you."

"He's not my man." Rena slipped out of his embrace. She shot him the side eye. "Not at all. I'm hooking up with his *brother* in a couple of days. Right, Zander?"

Rena could swear she saw him flinch, and his energy signature flickered, but he said nothing. Good. She hoped that hurt him. Maybe it would do him good to get a dose of his own medicine.

Even though she didn't mean a word of it.

"Right," he growled. "I'll meet you outside. We have to go."

"Okay." Viola hoisted herself off the stool and came around the counter. "You see somethin', girl?"

"Yes," Rena said as she ran both hands through her hair, attempting to soothe her rattled nerves. "I think you have a granddaughter too."

"A granddaughter?" Viola let out a short laugh. "That's like a Shake 'n Bake family."

"Seems like it." Rena let out a slow breath. "Your daughter looks good. Real good. It's like one of Norman Rockwell's paintings over there, complete with fresh baked apple pie."

"Norman who?"

"Never mind," Rena said with a smile. "Bottom line: she has long blond hair, like yours, but her eyes are a darker brown. The girl, her daughter I think, looks like she's about ten or eleven. Not quite a teenager but not a little kid either."

"Yes." Viola nodded, her eyes filling with tears. "My baby's eyes were dark, and she had blond hair like me."

"And she seems happy."

"Where is she?" Viola's voice shook, and she swiped at her cheeks. "Could you see where she's at?"

"Kansas City, Missouri."

"I ain't never been to Missouri."

"Well, now you have an excuse to visit."

Rena snagged a pen from the counter and the receipt pad. She quickly scrawled the name and address onto the paper and handed it to Viola, who accepted the information with quaking fingers.

"Her name is Kristin now. You can do an Internet search to confirm that name and address."

"Thank you so much," Viola whispered.

She gathered Rena up in a clumsy hug. Rena's gut instinct was to shrink from the display of affection because she wasn't all that comfortable touching other people. But she didn't. Instead, she patted Viola on the back, albeit kind of awkwardly, and said, "You're welcome, and good luck."

Once she was outside, Rena looked over her shoulder at the small store. The woman had flipped the red-and-white sign over to CLOSED. She couldn't blame the woman for closing up shop. She'd had a hell of a day.

"Everything okay?" Zander's deep voice pulled her from her thoughts.

"That was different," Rena said quietly.

"Which part?"

"All of it." She gave him a small smile. "You getting shot and healing with dirt wasn't exactly my typical afternoon. The vision was weird too though. Usually I'm in the past, inside a memory. But this time, I was in the present."

"Your powers are evolving, but you shouldn't have done that," Zander scolded. "What if she tells someone? You have to learn to be more careful with your gifts."

Zander handed her the helmet and climbed onto his bike. He was obviously annoyed, but Rena didn't care. She was feeling far too content about having helped Viola.

"What's she gonna say?" She put her helmet on. "'I saw a guy's eyes turn glowing red, and he bled on the floor. There was a robber, but then there wasn't. A psychic woman told me where to find my long-lost daughter.' Be serious, Zander. She won't say anything. All she's worried about now is getting connected with her family, and good for her."

"We should've left right way, Rena." He started the bike and revved the engine but didn't seem to feel any better. "And you shouldn't have taken a chance like that. It was foolish."

"She had already seen your eyes shift, Zander, not to mention the blood from the wound you magically healed." Rena rolled her eyes. "Give me a break."

"That would have been easy for her to explain away. People see what they want to see, Rena, no matter what the truth might be."

"I guess you're right," Rena said quietly.

Like him, she thought. If anyone knew about lying to themselves, it was him.

"I wanted to help her, and I'm not sorry I did."

His glittering, pale-green eyes peered at her beneath a dark, furrowed brow, studying her with something she couldn't quiet identify. Anger? Pity? Frustration? Before she could zero in on it, he slapped his visor down and jutted his thumb over his shoulder to the seat behind him.

"Get on!"

"Right," Rena shouted over the roar of the engine. "I wouldn't want to be late for my arranged marriage to your *brother*! Heaven forbid we keep the universe waiting."

Zander revved the motor and kept his eyes straight ahead, pretending he didn't hear her. But she knew damn well he had soaked in every word. Rena climbed on behind Zander, and she couldn't help but linger on his comment.

People see what they want to see.

The stubborn man knew what he was talking about, didn't he? Zander didn't want to see Rena as his mate. All he could do was picture her as the woman who belonged to his brother, and all she could see was *him*.

Chapter 15

Two hours later, they had reached the gate of the Amoveo ranch, and Zander's stomach was in knots. He wanted to hit the gas and drive right on by, taking Rena with him. But he didn't. Instead, he pulled up to the massive iron-trimmed, wood gate at the end of the driveway, which was, as he suspected it would be, closed. It was connected to what looked like miles of fencing around their expansive property. No houses or structures were visible from the road, but a few horses grazed nearby. Grassy fields of green and brown flowed into a sea of towering trees, and snow-capped mountains loomed large in the background.

Zander had to admit that the Amoveo had maintained one hell of a beautiful property, and given the number of years that had passed, it was doubly impressive that they had managed to hang on to it.

"What are you waiting for?" Rena shouted, her grip around his waist tightening. "Don't drag this out, man. Just hit the buzzer. I want to get the introductions over with. You know, rip off the Band-Aid."

Zander braced his feet on the ground and steadied the bike with the ease of experience. He scanned the area, a sense of dread nagging at him.

"I should text Coltari and tell him we're here."

He pulled his cell phone out of his pocket, but before he could text a word, Rena tapped his shoulder and tightened her grip on him. A gust of chilly October wind whisked around them along with Rena's energy signature, which buzzed with tension.

Look. Her voice touched his mind on a shaky whisper. *In the tall grass, to the left. I-Is that what I think it is?*

Zander sensed the other energy signature in the air at almost the same time as Rena brought it to his attention. He scanned the grasses and within seconds spotted exactly what Rena was referring to.

The guardian, a massive beast with glowing, golden-amber eyes, was barely visible; his striped coat blended into the landscape as it was meant to do.

I see him, Zander responded coolly. *And he sees us.*

Shit. It irked him that the guardian got the jump on him, even if only for a moment or two. Of course, if Zander had been in full possession of his abilities, that never would have happened.

He slipped his phone back into his pocket and curled his fingers around the handlebars of his bike as the beast stalked closer. They could bug out of there if they had to. It was unlikely that the prince's guardian would attack them, but he wasn't taking any chances with Rena's safety. Coltari had mentioned this Dominic guy was a hothead, but then again, that was typical for his clan.

Holy shit, Rena's voice whispered into his mind on a shaky whisper, and Zander had to brace himself against the intimate, erotic sensations that came with it. *It's a freaking tiger. In Montana. Why aren't the horses wigging out?*

They know him, and he's not some random tiger. His name is Dominic. He's a member of the Tiger Clan and the prince's guardian. Zander kept his voice calm and sent her waves of reassuring energy while trying to keep his own reactions under control. *Remember, Rena, the Amoveo weren't fond of my people. So for now, keep my situation under wraps. Okay? Don't bring up the Dragon Clan or Zed. As far as Dominic is concerned, our only reason for being here is to connect you with your people. I'm just a delivery boy.*

Yeah, she said sarcastically. *And I'm just a regular girl. They're gonna know something is up with you. Your energy signature is much stronger than a human's.*

Not if I said I had witch's blood in my veins.

Are you sure they're gonna buy that?

They better, Zander scoffed. *They'll swallow that a hell of a lot easier than the truth.*

I feel better knowing my gun is in my bag.

No, it isn't. He knew she was going to be pissed. *No weapons allowed. I stashed it behind that old gas station right before—*

You had no right to do that!

You're not going to need it here, and besides, I didn't have a choice.

You know what? Rena's voice wavered. *I'm getting real tired of that excuse.*

Zander didn't respond but kept his sights on the guardian.

The beast moved slowly through the grasses, prowling and stalking them the way a tiger would in the wild. Zander's lips lifted at the corners as he flipped up the visor of his helmet and waved at the guardian. He kept his mind closed to everyone except Rena, wanting to avoid telepathy with the Amoveo. As far as they were concerned, he was just one of the select humans who knew about the secretive supernatural world.

Zander could feel Dominic's attempts to telepath with him. The mental nudges were strong, but he was able to block the guardian from his mind. The tiger's ears flattened, and a low growl rumbled in the air as Zander suppressed a satisfied grin. He suspected that Dominic sensed his energy pattern was stronger than a normal human, but that could be easily enough explained away with his cover story.

Use your telepathy, Rena. Zander curled his fingers around the handlebars again, and the muscles in his shoulders bunched. He revved the engine. *Show this big bastard that you're part of the family.*

Fine. But you're not off the hook about the gun situation.

I wouldn't expect to be.

"Good, because you're not," she said out loud, adjusting her position on the bike. "Here goes nothing."

A subtle buzzing in her energy signature told him she was telepathing with the guardian. A split second later, his suspicions were confirmed when the beast shifted into a man. Rena's body tensed against his, and her arms tightened around his waist like a vise.

Holy crap, she whispered. *That was weird. You weren't messing with me. They really are shapeshifters.*

No, Rena. A laugh threaded his words. *I wasn't messing with you.*

Don't ask me to do telepathy with them anymore. Her fingertips pressed into his stomach in a subtle but seductive movement. *I don't like it…unless it's with you. I mean, I don't even know that guy, and I just let him in my head. It's too intimate or something.*

Zander nodded his understanding but didn't answer her. He was afraid the tone in his voice would betray him. It gave him great pleasure to know she only wanted to telepath with him, but his joy faded swiftly when he thought of Zed.

After you connect with Zed, he said flatly, *you'll want to shut me out too.*

Whatever. Rena sighed wearily.

Dominic was as impressive in his human form as he was in his Tiger Clan form. He was a hulking, muscled brute, as tall as Zander but bulkier. His short, military-cut, jet-black hair and sharp, dark eyes gave the impression he wasn't one to screw with, and the jagged scar that ran down one side of his face sealed the deal. He looked as formidable as any Amoveo warrior Zander had known back in the day. Clad in black-and-gray military fatigues, combat boots, and a black T-shirt, he approached the gate. Zander spotted a massive dagger holstered to his waist with a brown leather sheath. No gun. But that wasn't surprising. With his speed, strength, and likely military training, he would have little need for it.

"Welcome." His steady, intense stare was pinned to Zander as he opened the gate. "We've been expecting you. Follow the driveway up to the main house. Dante and Kerry will be there to meet you both. Don't stray from the driveway. You go from here to there. End of story."

"Not a problem," Zander replied coolly.

He slapped his face mask down and nodded curtly at Dominic, who held the gate open for them. As they pulled up the driveway, the horses whinnied loudly and galloped away from the sound of the motorcycle.

That's rich. Rena's nervous laughter peppered her voice. *Those horses don't freak out about a tiger, but the roar of a Harley gives them fits.*

Welcome to Wonderland, Zander said humorlessly. *You are officially going down the rabbit hole.*

Zander glanced in his rearview mirror. Dominic had already closed the gate and was striding into the grass with his fierce stare locked on them. His form shimmered, and in an instant, he was once again in his tiger and stalking them through the grass. The beast in Zander, the one that had been silenced for so many years, stirred in response and made him long for the freedom and power of his dragon.

He slowed the Harley as they traveled up the long driveway and entered a section that felt like they were in a tunnel of trees. Zander kept his senses alert, but when they reached the crest of the hill, the world opened up, and the full spectacle of the Amoveo ranch came into view.

He pulled the bike to a halt and took a moment to survey the impressive Amoveo homestead. The property stretched out as far as the eye could see. Acres upon acres of fields ran into the wooded, mountainous terrain. To the right was a massive colonial-style home. The sprawling, white clapboard structure with black shutters harkened to a time gone by. Alongside it to the right was a long red-and-white barn that obviously served as a horse stable. Sections of the field were cornered off with white board fences, and at least ten other horses—Arabians if he wasn't mistaken—grazed lazily on the grass.

The driveway forked in front of them. It dipped to the

right, toward the barn and the house, and to the left, he saw at least three cabins, smaller versions of the main house, but if Zander had to guess, he would say there were others. Isadora had said this place was more of a compound or commune than a ranch. At the center of it all was a long, cylindrical-shaped structure that most people would assume was a heated barn, but Zander knew better. That seemingly innocuous building hid the sacred meeting hall of the Amoveo Council.

"Oh my gosh," Rena said. "It's absolutely beautiful, Zander."

Before he could agree with her, two people stepped out of the main house and made their way down the stairs of the wraparound porch. A man and woman held hands and waved at Zander and Rena with big friendly smiles. Zander knew immediately they were Amoveo. Even from this distance, their distinctly strong energy patterns gave them away.

"It's game time," he said over his shoulder. "Are you ready?"

"Do I have a choice?" she asked with a curt laugh. "Let's do it."

Zander drove slowly down the hill, his heart thundering in his chest with anticipation and apprehension. He wasn't afraid of the Amoveo, not by a long shot. But now that he was there, on the property, with his brother's freedom within reach, Zander realized how close he was to the end of the journey.

If all went well, he and his brother would finally be free. Zander would have everything he had dreamed of.

Everything except Rena.

Bringing the Harley to a halt, Zander kicked the stand

down and shut off the engine. He expected Rena to climb off the bike, but she didn't. Her arms remained curled around his waist, and her energy signature hummed with a hint of fear and excitement. He pulled off his helmet and hooked it onto the handlebars before settling his hands over hers, pressing them gently against his stomach.

"You can do this," he murmured. "You're not alone, okay?"

"Don't go anywhere." Rena loosened her grip a little and whispered, "I mean it, Zander. Like, *do not* leave me alone with any of them. At all."

The man and woman, who were obviously mates, gave each other a knowing look as they approached Rena and Zander. Coltari was in the Fox Clan, like Rena, and they were known to have excellent hearing. Since he was a pureblood mated Amoveo, his powers would be at full capacity. The chances were better than average the man had heard exactly what Rena said.

"Hi!" The woman, a statuesque, raven-haired beauty with alabaster skin and a lush, curvy figure, gave them both a big smile. Zander couldn't put his finger on it, but he knew her from somewhere. "I'm Kerry, and this is my mate, Dante. You must be Rena and Zander."

"Hey! I know you." Excitement laced Rena's voice as she scrambled from the bike and took off her helmet. "You're Kerry Smithson. Gosh, you're even prettier in person, and I definitely had no idea you were, you know…"

Before Zander could ask what Rena was talking about, she hooked her helmet onto the back of the bike and slapped his arm, gesturing toward the couple.

"Sorry," he said with a wave. "Hi."

"I can't believe you didn't tell me that we would be

meeting a supermodel today," Rena said with a wide grin. "Kerry was one of the first plus-size models to make it big. Oh wait, you like curve model better, right? I mean, that's the correct term."

"I'm semiretired now, but either works for me." Kerry put her hand out to Rena. "Kerry Smithson Coltari, part-time model, full-time wiseass, and Amoveo hybrid from the Panther Clan."

"Rena McHale," she said, shaking Kerry's hand. "Private investigator and, supposedly, part of the Fox Clan. But so far no fur or fangs."

Zander's gaze flicked to Kerry as her energy pattern began to hum. What was it Dante had said about his mate? She could see a person's secrets with one touch?

"Shifting is usually the last of the gifts to emerge," Dante interjected.

Dante shook Rena's hand. As with all Amoveo men, he was well over six feet tall with a muscular build and would be considered handsome by most. Zander's eyes flicked to Rena's delicate hand, which was engulfed in the shifter's far larger one, and jealousy swelled briefly. Zander shoved it aside. After all, he damn well had to get used to another man touching her.

Like his brother, for example.

Shit.

"Welcome to the family, Rena." Dante smiled broadly as he released Rena's hand. "I'm Fox Clan as well."

"Yeah, but she's got that extra something special," Kerry said in a casual, matter-of-fact tone. "You're psychic, aren't you?"

"I am," Rena said with a nervous laugh. "How did you know?"

"Takes one to know one." Kerry winked. "I peeked in your head a little when I shook your hand. Skin-to-skin contact gives me some inside info. But I promise I only took a small peek. Just enough to make sure you're the real deal. And you are. All of the hybrids have an extra gift or two. We think it's because the human parent was psychic in some way."

"Oh, cool. Well, I have no idea who my parents are or were. I was in foster care all my life, and when I was fourteen, I took off on my own." Rena sliced a glance at Zander and hooked her thumbs in the back pockets of her jeans. "I can see other people's memories when I touch objects but no shapeshifting yet."

"Once you find your mate, the rest of it will fall into place." Kerry gave her mate a loving smile. "Trust me."

"Right, that's what I hear."

"And you are?" Kerry tilted her head and gave Zander a narrowed gaze. "Not entirely human. Because I don't have to touch you to know that you aren't just a regular guy."

Shit. She could tell something was up with him, which meant Zander's time was running out. He had to speak to the prince before everything blew up in his face.

"He's a witch," Rena blurted out. "Or part witch."

"Really?" Kerry's dark eyebrows lifted as she looked from Rena to Zander. "That's…interesting. You're a warlock?"

"He's *part* witch." Rena shot him a look. "Right?"

"Zander." He nodded curtly, not confirming or denying the claim. "Good to meet you both."

He dismounted the Harley on the opposite side, keeping the bike between him and their hosts. Zander didn't miss the knowing glance exchanged between Kerry and her mate.

"Welcome to the ranch." Dante stepped closer to the bike and extended his hand to Zander. Not wanting to be completely rude, Zander quickly accepted the offering. "I'm Dante Coltari. You and I spoke on the phone."

"We did."

"You didn't mention your heritage."

"I didn't think it was important," Zander said casually. "I don't practice magic. Never learned. In spite of how often Isadora tried to teach me."

"That's unusual." Kerry was giving him a look that told him she wasn't buying one bit of his story. "Most people can't wait to embrace their supernatural gifts."

"Well, I'm not most people."

"You can say that again," Rena muttered.

"There's more to your story." Kerry wagged a finger at him. "And I'll figure it all out sooner or later."

Zander gave Kerry a tight smile and nodded at her but didn't offer to shake her hand. He was surprised when she didn't press the issue. The woman was perceptive in more ways than one.

"Kerry and I have been seeking out the other hybrids and, when possible, bringing them here to the ranch. It's private and safe, the perfect place for you and others like you to explore your gifts without fear of discovery."

"I feel like I've been through the spin cycle." Rena folded her arms over her breasts and shrugged. "Zander found me a few days ago, but it feels like years. I'm getting answers to some of my questions, but then I just get more questions."

"Girl, we so have to talk." Kerry laughed. "Tatiana wants to meet you too, and she has her own war stories to share."

"She's a hybrid too?"

"Oh yeah. There are four other hybrids who live here on the ranch, but they aren't mated yet, and actually, they aren't even here at the moment. They're at Malcolm and Samantha's place at the beach. Two of them are from the Eagle Clan, like Malcolm, so he's showing them how to master their flight skills."

"Malcolm and Samantha?"

"Sorry." Kerry laughed. "Sam is my bestie. She's a hybrid from the Wolf Clan, and her hubby is a pureblood from the Eagle Clan. They live in Rhode Island with their daughter. They're doing some training with the newbies out at their place for a month or two. If you stay on long enough, you'll meet all of 'em. For now, Tati will be your best resource because, like me, she's already been down the road you're traveling."

"I hope you don't need me to remember all that, because my head is seriously spinning."

"Don't scare her off, princess." Dante pressed a kiss to the top of her head and wrapped his arm around her waist. "Why don't you let Rena get settled in before you inundate the poor woman?"

"Oh, fine," Kerry huffed with feigned irritation. "We have plenty of time to give you all the gory details."

Ironically, for the first time in centuries, time was something Zander didn't have.

"I need to speak with Richard," Zander interjected. "As soon as possible."

"Why?" Kerry arched one dark eyebrow, her lips

lifting at the corners. "Your job was to bring Rena to us, and you did. And why would *you* need to see the prince?"

"It's...personal," Zander said warily.

"I'm sorry, but the prince isn't here," Dante replied. "He and Salinda, his mate, are at the annual summit in Geneva with the other supernatural leaders. You really don't have to worry about Rena's transition. We've never had any trouble with the new arrivals, and at this point, introducing a hybrid to our world has become commonplace. Richard doesn't get involved with the process anymore." He held up one hand and quickly added, "He'll want to meet you, of course, but he doesn't handle the transitions. Kerry and I do all of that with help from some of the others."

Zander's jaw clenched, and irritation shimmied up his back, the muscles in his neck and shoulders bunching with the rising tension. He fought the instinctive urge for his eyes to shift and struggled to keep his energy pattern smooth. The prince was the only one he would even consider speaking to about Zed, and now that wasn't even an option.

He had no idea how much he could trust Dante, and he wasn't willing to risk Zed's safety, or Rena's, by taking any chances. If he didn't come up with a new plan, his brother could be lost forever.

"Dante's right." Kerry dropped her voice to barely above a whisper and kept her dark-brown eyes pinned to Zander. She slipped out of her mate's embrace and moved closer to the bike as she pushed her long ebony hair off her shoulder. Zander didn't move. She was trying to get close enough to touch him. "In fact, you can leave, Zander. There's no reason for you to stay, is there?"

"No!" Rena stepped to her left, directly in front of Kerry, effectively blocking Zander. "I'm not staying here without Zander. I trust him with my life, and based on the ginormous tiger I saw back at the gate, I don't feel that *safe*. If he leaves, I go with him. That's the deal. Take it or leave it."

Tense silence hovered over the group, and Zander feared they had made a grave mistake by coming here. Maybe he should have taken his chances and snuck into the cave in the dead of night, but after getting a load of the guardian, that definitely wouldn't have ended well. His presence, foreign and unwelcome, would have been immediately detected and hunted down.

On the other hand, now that he was here on the property, sneaking into the cave was a much more feasible plan. Nobody would question his presence. Attempting to wake Zed without bringing the Amoveo into the loop was a gamble. It was still risky but not as uncertain as trusting the Amoveo. If he shared Zed's location and they weren't as charitable as he hoped, his brother would be completely vulnerable to attack.

Nope. He flicked his gaze from Kerry to Dante. He would wait until they were all asleep and then make his move. He would have to handle Zed on his own.

"I'll stay on, if you don't mind," Zander said evenly.

"Fine." A smile bloomed on Kerry's face. "The guest cabin is big enough for both of you, and we want you to be comfortable here, Rena. If you want Zander to stay, then he can stay."

"Really?" Rena glanced over her shoulder at Zander and then back to Dante and Kerry. "That's it?"

"Yeah, girl." Kerry stepped back, and Dante slipped

his arm around her waist again. "That's it. You're not a prisoner here. You're a guest and welcome to stay as long as you want."

"My mate is absolutely right, and don't worry about the big brute at the gate," Dante said with a warm smile. "That's Dominic, and his job is to protect you and everyone else here on the ranch. He's on your side. We all are."

"Dominic looks scary, but Tati will be the first to tell you, he's actually a giant pussycat."

"Don't let Dom hear you say that," Dante scoffed.

"Eh." Kerry waved him off. "You Amoveo men love to growl and beat your chests, but deep down, you're all a bunch of softies."

Zander stilled when Dante kissed Kerry on the lips, lingering just long enough to make him uncomfortable. He flicked his gaze to Rena, and his heart somersaulted in his chest. What he wouldn't give to have that kind of comfort level and partnership with her.

"All right." Kerry clapped her hands and rubbed them together vigorously. "Let's get you two settled at the cabin, and then I'm sure you'll want to get washed up before we give you the grand tour of the property."

"Sounds good," Rena said politely. "Thank you."

"We'll grab the golf cart, and you guys can follow us," Dante added. "The guest cabin is the last one on the right, about a quarter mile down that way."

Zander nodded to his hosts and climbed back onto the bike while they went toward the barn where two white-and-green golf carts were parked. As Rena climbed on behind him, Zander let his gaze drift over the mountain looming large behind the main house. He started the engine and cast one last glance at the mountain that entombed his brother.

This is it. Rena's voice rushed into his mind like a cool breeze on a hot day, soothing and offering relief, and all Zander wanted to do was sink into it. Lose himself in her beauty and strength. *Thank you, Zander. I'm nervous and kind of freaking out about all of this, but thanks for finding me.*

Before he could utter a response, Rena's lips brushed against his ear. The gentleness of the kiss threatened his resolve, but Zander held fast. He gripped the handlebars tightly and revved the engine as the golf cart with their hosts drove past.

A growl rumbled in his chest as he pointed the bike down the hill and took off, dirt and gravel spitting up behind his wheels. Rage and jealousy surged, because by the time the sun set tomorrow night, her kisses and kindness would no longer be given to him.

For the first time in five hundred years, Zander truly longed for death.

"This is the guest cabin?" Rena asked as she looked around the luxurious open space of the bright, airy cottage. "It's beautiful."

To the left was a sparkling kitchen with white cabinets and stainless steel appliances. At the center was a generous living area with soft, cushy-looking couches and chairs, all gathered around a stone-and-brick fireplace. Off to the right was a small sitting area with a lovely bay window. It was the perfect nook for morning coffee or a lazy Sunday afternoon with a newspaper crossword. The whole space was awash in varying shades of blues and grays, giving the house a warm, welcoming feel.

Everything about the house radiated casual elegance, including Kerry. Rena tugged her jacket around her and smiled at her new friend. The woman was wearing a plaid shirt, jeans, brown boots, and a down vest, but she still looked like she was ready for a cover shoot. Rena, on the other hand, felt like a frumpy, dirty mess after so many hours on the road. Were all of the Amoveo as beautiful as Kerry was?

If so, Rena was sure she was going to stick out like a sore thumb. She had earned plenty of money over the past few years, but she didn't spend it unless she absolutely had to. After living with nothing for as long as she did, she preferred the fat, stable bank balance to luxury items.

"You could fit my entire apartment in about half of this room," Rena said with an awkward shrug. "I'm definitely not in Vegas anymore."

"The kitchen is stocked, but if there's something you really want, let me know and I can have it delivered from town."

"I'm sure it's fine," Rena said quickly. "It's more than fine. Thank you."

"Check this out." Kerry grabbed her by the hand and dragged her to the sliding glass doors that led out to a spacious cedar deck. "Nothing beats the view, and it's even better from upstairs in the master bedroom."

"Wow," Rena breathed. "You aren't kidding. I bet the sunset is absolutely breathtaking. I can see mountains in Vegas, but somehow, it's not the same."

Lush mountains surrounded the property and provided

a spectacular view from every angle. This sure as hell beat the world outside her windows in Las Vegas, which was mostly cement and blinking neon with a ridge of the mountains in the distance. Rena turned around to ask Zander what he thought, but the man was nowhere to be seen.

Son of a bitch. So much for not leaving her alone.

"Where's Zander?"

Rena was about to head back into the living room, but Kerry hooked her arm in Rena's and pulled her back to the slider.

"He's outside." Kerry tapped the glass of the door. "And by the looks of it, he's putting up a tent."

"What the hell?"

Rena tugged the slider and stepped onto the deck, the cool, crisp Montana air briefly stealing her breath. Sure enough, Zander was in the backyard, standing next to a brown, dome-shaped tent while Dante looked on.

"What are you doing?" Rena leaned both hands on the railing. "Did you not see this gorgeous house? Why are you putting up that damn tent?"

"Because I'm going to sleep in it," he said flatly.

She gaped at him, and her cheeks heated. After everything they had been through, he would rather sleep in a stupid tent than under the same roof with her. Well, if that wasn't insulting, then what was?

"You can't be serious. It's been rolled up in a bag on the back of your bike for ages. It probably stinks."

"Nope." Zander stuck his head inside the tent briefly. "Smells fine to me."

"You'll freeze out here."

"Cold doesn't bother me."

"Oh really?" Rena narrowed her eyes at him. *Care to tell our hosts why the cold doesn't bother you?*

"I'm hot-blooded," he said with a shrug.

Rena let out a huff of frustration and folded her arms over her breasts. The man was infuriating and had an answer for everything. Unfortunately, none of them was the response she was looking for.

"You know," Dante added, "it's not a bad idea, sleeping under the stars…kind of romantic. What do you say, princess?"

"Don't go getting any ideas, Tarzan," Kerry said with a curt laugh. "You've been my mate long enough to know that I'm not a fan of the outdoorsy stuff. The human side of me really loves plumbing and electricity, but if you boys want to sleep in a tent together, knock yourselves out."

"I couldn't have said it better myself," Rena muttered. "Ooohh. I hope he gets pneumonia."

She spun around on her heels and stormed back inside the guesthouse with Kerry close behind. Fine. He could sleep out there, and she would stay in here. Distance was probably good for them, but even as the thought whisked into her mind, she knew it was a lie.

"Why are men so annoying?" Rena threw her hands in the air. "I mean, seriously. I could spend a hundred years with that guy, and I still wouldn't get how his brain works."

"That's an age-old question of the universe. We want to know why they're annoyingly stubborn, and they want to know why we overanalyze everything."

"Oh." Rena's shoulders sagged. "I'm doing that, aren't I?"

"Yup. But don't sweat it. This is all part of the process," she said with a wink.

Rena was about to ask what process she was referring to, but Kerry had other plans.

"Grab your bag, girl." Kerry lounged by the banister. "I'll show you the rest of the place, and then we'll give you two a tour of the property."

Rena shouldered her duffel bag and followed Kerry upstairs. She could have continued the conversation, but then she would have risked spilling all kinds of beans. Besides, Rena wasn't great at making friends, and while she instantly liked Kerry, Rena was wary about saying too much.

There were two bedrooms and one bathroom, all of them decorated similarly to the first floor. Rena let out a whistle as she tossed her bag onto the king-size canopy bed. An entire wall of windows opposite the bed showed off the grandeur of the landscape around them. Rena strolled over and let out a sigh, which started out awed and rolled into a growl of frustration because she also had a great view of Zander and his stupid tent.

"He's your mate, you know," Kerry said with a chuckle as she lay on the large bed. She put her hands behind her head and crossed her ankles. "I saw it when I shook your hand."

Rena spun around and stared at the woman, her mouth opening and closing like a fish out of water before finally regaining the ability to speak.

"How could you know that?"

"It's a gift," she said with a dramatic sigh. "Most of the time."

"Yeah, I know what you mean, but I'm afraid you're wrong—at least that's what *Zander* would tell you."

"I'm never wrong." Kerry folded her hands in her lap and quickly added, "Not with my visions, I mean. I saw you with him—he's your mate. You guys even end up getting matching tattoos. You'll get one on your back, and he gets one on his thigh. They're pretty cool too—a pair of intertwined dragons."

"Dragons?"

The word slipped from her lips on a shaky whisper as her mind went to the early sign of the mate tattoo on her back. Was Kerry right about Zander, or was she seeing his identical twin, Zed? The urge to press Kerry for clarification was strong, but her need to keep Zander's secret overpowered everything else.

"Yeah. I mean, I would've expected a fox tattoo, you know? For the Fox Clan." Her brow furrowed as she sat up and swung her feet over the bed. "That's the only image in the vision that I didn't understand. I mean, you guys being mates makes total sense. You're obviously crazy attracted to each other, even though you're both fighting it."

"Am I that transparent?" Rena sat on the edge of the bed next to her new friend. "I am so out of my element. I have no game, as they say, at least when it comes to men. I don't know what my problem is. I have never, and I mean *never*, been this screwed up over a guy. It's like he knows exactly what buttons to push. One minute I want to punch him the nose, and the next…"

"It's not just you, babe. That guy has it for you bad." She jutted her thumb toward the window. "Did you see the monster emerge when you shook Dante's hand?"

"M-monster?" Rena swallowed hard.

Holy crap. Had Kerry seen Zander's eyes shift in the vision?

"Yeah." Kerry laughed. "You know? The jealousy monster. The dude was totes jealous. For a second, I thought he was going to punch Dante in the throat."

"Oh." Rena breathed with relief. "Right. That monster." She paused for a moment and asked, "Zander was jealous?"

"Oh yeah. I didn't need to touch him to pick up that vibe."

Rena flopped back onto the bed and let out a groan of frustration. "Then why the hell does he keep shutting me down, and why is the big jerk insisting on sleeping out in that smelly tent?"

You know why, she thought to herself. *Because he thinks you should be with his brother. But you can't tell her any of this, now can you?*

"Now *that* I don't know, but I'm betting, deep down, *you* know the answer to that question. This whole fated-mate business is trickier than I would have thought. I can relate. I fought it in the beginning too."

"You did? But you and Dante seem totally perfect together."

"Oh yeah, we are now, but at first, I wanted to push him as far away as I could. And besides, Zander isn't Amoveo, so I guess I can understand how he'd have a really tough time wrapping his head around the whole mate deal. After all, he might have some witch's blood in him, but he's *not* a shifter."

"Right," Rena said quickly. "He's definitely not Amoveo."

She sat up and gave Kerry an awkward smile, because she wanted nothing more than to change the subject. There was no way to talk about this topic honestly without bringing up Zed or the curse or the Dragon Clan.

Great. Screwed again.

"Can we take a tour of the property now?"

"Sure, but I thought you said you wanted to change first. I know you've been on the road awhile."

"Nope." Rena shook her head before rising to her feet. "If I do that, it will be too tempting to crawl into bed and pull the covers over my head. It's better if I keep moving. Besides, I have too many questions for you, and sleep will probably be next to impossible."

Not to mention unsafe. If Rena ended up in the dreamrealm, then there was a good chance she would disturb Zed. The notion of a pissed-off dragon descending onto this ranch was enough to make her nauseous. She had seen the kind of destruction the dragons were capable of in the dreams, and she couldn't imagine it would be any safer in real life.

"You're sure you don't want to rest for a while?"

"Positive."

"I gotcha." Kerry slapped Rena's knee playfully. "And don't stress out about Zander. He'll come around. After all, the universe has paired the two of you together, and if there's one fact I've learned from this crazy, supernatural world, there's no escaping fate. You can fight it. You can question it. Hell, girl, you can even tell it to take a flying leap…but you cannot escape it."

Rena followed Kerry into the hall and downstairs to find Zander and Dante waiting for them on the front porch. When Zander's pale-green eyes clapped on to hers, she couldn't help but smile, and to her surprise, he gave her a small smile in return. He put her at ease. In spite of the craziness, simply seeing him made the knot of tension in her gut loosen, letting her breathe that much easier.

Every single ounce of Rena's soul, every fiber in her body, told her that this man was supposed to be part of her future.

Not his brother. *Him.*

But if Kerry was right and fate was inescapable, then what Rena wanted would be of little consequence.

"Oh, by the way," Kerry said, as she sashayed down the porch steps, "Dante and I are hosting a dinner party tonight in honor of your arrival. If Salinda were here, she would host it at the main house, but since she's not, you'll have to settle for our place."

"My girl makes the best desserts." Dante hooked his arm around her waist and kissed her cheek quickly. "Who would ever have thought a princess like her would love baking?"

"Watch it, Tarzan." Kerry elbowed him playfully before linking her hand in his. "Keep it up, and you'll be eating takeout for a week."

"What time?" Zander interjected none too delicately.

"Around seven," Kerry said casually. "But we're flexible."

"Seven is fine." Rena shot Zander a look and touched his mind. *You're being rude.* "Thank you, Kerry."

I didn't come here for dinner parties. I came to get my brother and introduce you to the Amoveo. That's it.

Really? What about delivering me to Zed so I can be his concubine? Rena shot back. *You forgot that part.*

Rena knew she was being hard on Zander. Bitchy even. But she had to do something to make him understand her position. Pushing her away wouldn't get her closer to being with Zed. All it did was hurt her, and that was the piece of information Zander didn't seem to comprehend.

"You bet." Kerry looked from Rena to Zander, and her eyes narrowed almost imperceptibly. "You'll get to meet William too. Dom will be there with Tati, and you'll see what I mean about him being a big pussycat."

"They're looking forward to meeting *both* of you," Dante said with a pointed look to Zander. "After all, you're the one who found Rena."

"Yes!" Kerry's voice surged with excitement. "We can't wait to hear all about how you stumbled across each other. But save it for dinner. I wouldn't want the others to miss out on what I'm sure is an interesting story. For now, let's start with a tour of the property."

Zander's mouth set in a grim line. He nodded as though he was in agreement, but Rena knew better. As they followed Kerry and Dante along the driveway, she touched her mind to his, wanting and needing the intimate contact. She had to admit, communicating with him that way had begun to put her at ease.

What are we going to tell them?

I'll think of something.

How about the truth? You know what they say, the truth shall set you free...or something like that.

When Zander didn't respond, Rena shifted her focus to Kerry and climbed into the backseat of the golf cart. Zander slipped in next to her, and when his leg accidentally bumped hers, the man instantly moved away.

Her heart sank as he adjusted his position, keeping his body as far from hers as the seat would allow. The thing between them, whatever it was or might have been, was over.

The dalliances they shared had been seemingly erased, and he was acting like none of it had ever happened. The man behaved as though he could barely stand the sight of her. Tears stung the back of her eyes, but she willed them away. She had never cried over a man before, and she sure as hell wasn't going to start now.

Chapter 16

THE GROUP OF AMOVEO SITTING AT THE RUSTIC, WOOD DINING table in Kerry and Dante's house were surprisingly normal people. Kerry and Dante were at either end of the table. When Rena and Zander arrived for dinner, she was relieved when Kerry told her to sit on her left. Rena had never been to a dinner party before, and even though she had been nervous, her fears were unfounded. Most of the evening's conversations revolved around how each of the couples had gotten together.

Rena noted that all of their pairings began with a shared dream…just like her and Zander.

And Zed.

Damn it.

Rena scooped up the last bite of the delectable vanilla cake with lemon and raspberry filling, doing her best to not think about her screwed-up situation. She glanced to her left and fleetingly noticed that Zander had barely touched his dessert. In fact, the guy had hardly eaten any of the sumptuous meal that had been prepared for them by their hosts.

At the moment, he was staring at Dominic with nothing less than a stone-cold glare, but to his credit, the guardian wasn't taking the bait. He was sitting directly across from Rena. Kerry had been right about him—the man looked far less ferocious with his mate, Tati, by his side. William, a cool customer with long blond hair and a piercing, dark stare, was seated on the other side of Zander.

If anyone had happened upon their casual dinner party, they would never have suspected that most of the people at the table could shapeshift into animals simply by thinking about it. They were all at ease with each other and had done a damn fine job of putting Rena at ease as well, if not Zander.

Getting his brother safely out of hibernation was probably the only development that would improve his broody mood. But Rena was determined not to let him spoil this moment for her, because she couldn't recall a time in her life when she had ever felt at home anywhere. Looking around the table at the smiling, welcoming faces of her new friends, Rena finally understood what other people meant when they talked about feeling at home.

"Rena?" Kerry's concerned tone pulled Rena from her own thoughts. "Are you okay? You look like something's bothering you."

Silence fell over the group, and all eyes turned to Rena. Being the center of attention was never something she enjoyed, and she instantly became self-conscious. Rena sat up straighter and smoothed the skirt she wore. Jeans hadn't seemed like an appropriate choice for a dinner party with their hosts. Luckily, she had packed one black skirt that paired nicely with her favorite red cowl-neck sweater and her black leather boots.

"Oh, no," Rena said quickly. "Actually, I was just thinking how nice this is and..." She let out a short laugh and quickly added, "Never mind. It's silly."

"I'm sure it's not," Tati interjected. She was a

hybrid from the Wolf Clan, and her warm eyes, which always seemed to be smiling, crinkled at the corners. "Remember, we've all been down the road you're traveling. I doubt you'd say anything that could shock us."

Zander grunted something that was almost a chuckle and tossed his napkin onto his mostly full plate. Rena gave him the side eye before smiling at Tatiana. She may not have had tons of experience attending dinner parties, but she knew Zander's behavior was rude.

"Right." Rena knew that wasn't entirely true but appreciated Tati's efforts. Though her desire to make Rena feel comfortable wasn't all that surprising, considering she was the Amoveo's resident healer. "I want to thank all of you. I've never had a home, not a real one, anyway. And to be honest, I've felt more comfortable here over these past few hours, with all of you, than I have anywhere else in my entire life."

Zander's energy pattern ticked up a notch as he sat back in his chair. Rena sliced a glance at him and almost laughed out loud, because he seemed annoyed or insulted about what she had said. The irony was that *he* was the main reason she had begun to feel at ease, but the stubborn man couldn't see it. If it weren't for him, she would still be living only part of her life, not all of it.

"And I suppose that I have Zander to thank for that," Rena added. "He's the one who...filled in the blank spots and showed me what I am, what and who I've always been."

"Hear, hear." Dante raised his wineglass. "I think a toast is in order."

Everyone gathered their wineglasses, including Zander, but he didn't look too happy about it. His shaggy, dark hair drifted over his eyes as usual, and he seemed to be avoiding eye contact with everyone—including her. He obviously didn't like being the center of attention any more than Rena did.

"To Zander and Rena." Dante lifted his glass toward the two of them. "The newest members of our growing community. And for me, personally, it's nice to have another member of the Fox Clan here on the ranch. So thank you, Zander, for bringing Rena home."

Zander nodded curtly as everyone clinked glasses but, as usual, said nothing. Jeez. The man had practically become a mute since they'd arrived, and it was starting to grate on her. When they had walked over to the cottage earlier, Rena tried to talk to him about what they were going to say in regard to how he found her. All he said was, *I'll handle it*. And when she asked him about how he planned on dealing with Zed's situation, he just shrugged.

Infuriating!

His grunting, monosyllabic routine was back in full force and driving her to the brink, testing what little patience she had left.

Damn it. Rena had to keep the focus on something other than him.

"William, your mate, Layla, is a hybrid too, right?" Rena asked after a healthy sip of her Cabernet. "Cheetah Clan?"

"She is," he responded coolly. "She sends her apologies but is delayed on an assignment. Layla's a photojournalist, and this trip is taking longer than anticipated. No one is more unamused by her absence than I am."

"What about you?" Rena shifted her attention to Tatiana. "I know you're a doctor, but are you psychic too?"

"Not exactly." Tati lifted one shoulder. "I can telepath with animals, and I use our visualization abilities to help me when I'm treating a patient—animal, human, or Amoveo. I was a veterinarian BD."

"BD?" Rena had zero idea what that meant. "What does that stand for?"

"Before Dominic," she said, smiling before taking a sip of her wine.

Laughter erupted from the group, and Rena found herself laughing right along with them. Even Dom, who spent most of his time scowling, cracked a smile when his mate pressed a sweet kiss to his scarred cheek.

"So the ladies are hybrid, but the guys are..."

"Pureblood," William chimed in. "I am a member of the Falcon Clan—Gyrfalcon to be more specific. All of the hybrids we have found, so far, have been female."

The guy was one cool customer. It kind of made sense to Rena that a man who could shift into a bird would be somewhat aloof. But every time he spoke of Layla, his demeanor softened.

If there was a single quality all of the Amoveo men had in common, it was the unwavering adoration of their mates. Pure, unadulterated love flowed freely between them, and Rena would have been lying if she hadn't admitted to a pang of jealousy.

What would it feel like to have someone love her so completely and openly? No hidden agendas. No fear of discovery. Pure and simple love. The notion would have seemed outlandish only a week ago, and now, it was within reach. The universe was dangling it in front of her in the form of the brooding hunk of man next to her. How could she possibly make him see what she did?

He was supposed to be her mate. Not his brother. Him.

"I've come to loathe that term, however," William added. "The Purists have turned *pureblood* into a dirty word."

"Kerry was telling me that these Purists don't like the fact that humans have been able to mate with your kind. The war started because they were trying to hunt down the hybrids?" Rena quickly added, "Us, I mean."

Her face heated with a little embarrassment. This wasn't an *us and them* scenario. For the first time ever, she was part of a group. Maybe even a family. She flicked her gaze to Zander. Her heart somersaulted in her chest. He was all the family she needed or wanted. She genuinely appreciated the kindness of the Amoveo, but none of it would matter if Zander weren't there with her.

"Regretfully, that is true." William was formal and stiff but not void of emotion. Sadness edged his voice. "This rift was unprecedented among our kind, and only recently have we been able to regroup. Part of that process has been finding the other hybrids and bringing them to the safety of the ranch. In fact, we are hoping to reinstate a new council when Richard and Salinda return from the summit. It will be the final step in reuniting our race."

"The last four years have been rough," Dante added.

"What happened to them?" Rena asked. "The Purists, I mean."

"Their leader, Artimus, was killed." Dominic's deep baritone rumbled through the room in such a way that

Rena thought he might actually turn into a tiger right at the table. "Most of the Amoveo who followed Artimus only stayed with him because they feared him. After he was killed, all but a few returned to their clans, but some..."

"The war got bloody on both sides," Tati added. She covered Dominic's hand with her own. "Dom's sister was killed."

"I'm so sorry," Rena whispered.

Dom nodded, his expression grim and pained. Rena wasn't sure how long ago he had lost his sister, but it obviously still hurt like hell for him to talk about it.

"It's taken these past few years to try and heal a lot of wounds, physical and otherwise." Tati jutted a thumb toward Kerry. "She and Dante have found almost all of the others like us, and we've worked really hard to show everybody that hybrids aren't the boogeymen. Nobody is trying to breed the Amoveo into extinction, which was the nonsense Artimus was spouting."

"I don't get it." Rena shook her head and looked from Dante to Kerry. "If your mates are predestined, then how could these Purist Amoveo argue with the universe if humans had become part of the equation? I thought there wasn't a choice when it came to mates."

"A common misconception," William said quietly.

"Our bodies may be programmed to be attracted to each other," Tati said, "but we have the freedom to choose whether or not to follow through and commit to it."

"Fear," Zander interjected. His tone was cold and detached, and the room fell silent as all eyes turned to the one person who'd barely spoken all night long.

"Humans. Witches. Vampires. Amoveo. Whatever. All creatures fear what they don't understand."

Rena swallowed the lump that had suddenly developed in her throat. She knew what Zander was referring to even if they didn't. All these years later, and he was still furious with the way the Amoveo of his time had treated the dragons. Rena took a huge swig of her wine and wished someone would change the subject.

Everyone nodded solemnly in agreement, and an awkward silence fell over the group.

Kerry was the one to get the conversation going again.

"So, how did you two meet?"

"Well…uh…Zander," Rena began, "you've been quiet tonight. How about if you tell the story?"

"Not much to tell," he said casually. "It was an accident, really. I was in Vegas for a little downtime, and I ran into Rena on the Strip. When I picked up her energy, I knew right away what she was. I called Isadora, and here we are."

"I don't believe in accidents," Kerry murmured.

"Believe what you want." He shrugged. "That's the story."

"No dreams?" Kerry asked before taking a sip of her wine. "Witches can walk in the dreamrealm."

"Nope. No dreams. Sorry."

"That's a surprise."

"Yeah." Zander grunted. "Well, life's full of 'em."

Another painfully awkward silence fell over the group, and Rena wanted to crawl under the table from embarrassment. She couldn't believe how rude Zander was being. However, Tati saved the conversation by changing the subject, and Rena could've kissed her.

"Layla was a foster kid too."

"Really?" Rena said. "But I thought you two were sisters."

"Well, officially, we're adopted siblings. Layla came to live with us at our family farm in Maryland when we were all about twelve years old. Blood has little to do with loving someone. Although, my twin brother, Raife, is pretty awesome too."

"You're a twin?" Zander asked quietly.

"Yup."

"So am I," Dante said. "My sister, Marianna, favors the Bear Clan, however."

"It's not that uncommon." Tati gave him a big smile and ran her hands through her brown hair. "We're all fraternal twins, obviously. Raife lives in Maryland with his mate, Sylvia. She's human, by the way. Psychic but human."

"Have any of the Amoveo ever had *identical* twins?"

Rena tried to be nonchalant about her question, but she feared her energy signature would give her away. Based on her nerves, it was probably fluttering around the room like a bird frantically looking for an open window.

"No." Dante shook his head as William and Dominic agreed. "No way."

"Oh man," Kerry said with a roll of her eyes. "That would be a clusterfuck of epic proportions."

"I can imagine," Rena murmured.

"Dealing with the Purists was bad enough." Tati held up two hands and let out a curt laugh. "I can't fathom the kind of jealousy and fighting that would happen if two Amoveo men thought they were mated to the same woman."

"Or two Amoveo women, for that matter." Dante laughed. "I'm with Tati. The Purists were bad enough."

"Yeah," Zander said flatly. "You guys seem pretty above it all. The Amoveo would *never* persecute anyone who was different from them. You're all so civilized."

A stunned silence fell over the group as Dominic and Dante exchanged a concerned look.

"Perhaps you should explain your meaning," William said in a deadly quiet tone. "That sounded like an insult."

Rena placed her hand on Zander's leg and squeezed, praying he would keep his big mouth shut. "He didn't mean—"

"Just saying." Zander shrugged and sat back in his chair like he owned the place. "You had some harsh words for the Purists earlier."

"They tried to kill our mates," Dominic bit out.

"Right," Zander scoffed. "The Purists were bigots, a bunch of assholes who hated what they didn't understand—anyone who was different. Believe me, man. I get it. That's a story older than time itself."

"We don't tolerate bigots," William said flatly. "Do you have a problem with that?"

"Forget it, man," Zander said on a heavy sigh. "It doesn't matter anymore."

Zander, Rena whispered into his mind. *Why are you picking a fight with them?*

I can't sit with these hypocrites for one more minute. You're punishing these people for crimes committed by their ancestors. It's ridiculous.

"It's getting late," Zander said abruptly. He pushed his chair back and stood up. "Thanks for dinner, but we should be going."

He turned his fierce, pale-green eyes to her, and they glittered at her between strands of dark hair. Rena tried to touch his mind to hers, but he shut her out, which flipped her switch from embarrassment to anger. After all of the stuff they had been through, he was shutting her out?

"Come on, Rena."

"No." Her jaw set, and she folded her hands in her lap. "I'm not ready to leave."

"Fine." He glanced at Kerry and nodded. "Thanks for the meal and the hospitality. I'll be leaving tomorrow morning. Rena is settled, and I think it's best if I bug out sooner rather than later. Good night."

"What do you mean you're leaving in the morning?" Rena called after him. He stopped but didn't turn around. Zander's broad-shouldered frame filled the doorway that led out to the porch. "I—I thought..."

What about your brother and the curse? Tomorrow night is the deadline.

Not your problem anymore. I'll get Zed out on my own. The hibernation chamber is damaged, and I no longer have the luxury of time. I'll get him out and off the property before they even know he's there. We'll be out of here at sunrise.

You're crazy!

"Don't worry about it, Rena. Good night."

"Zander!"

He stormed out of the house, the front door slamming behind him, leaving her alone, embarrassed, and furious. These people had welcomed the two of them here with open arms, and from the moment she and Zander had arrived, he had been acting like a big jerk.

"Oh," Kerry said with surprise. "Um, okay."

"I'm so sorry," Rena whispered.

She fought her rising temper as she stood from her chair. She almost laughed out loud when all three men rose as she did. People rarely treated her with such reverence, and she wasn't even sure how to handle it.

"Please, sit down. You've all been nothing but hospitable, and for reasons I can't go into, the big chip on Zander's shoulder isn't because of the five of you."

"It's okay." Dante sat in his chair again and gave Kerry a knowing smile. "We all understand how difficult the mating process can be."

"You mean…all of you know that we're…" She melted back into her chair. Rena wasn't sure if she was relieved or concerned. She couldn't very well go into details, now could she?

"I didn't tell them." Kerry made a cross sign over her heart. "I swear! They all figured it out on their own. All I did was confirm their suspicions. But like I told you earlier, the attraction between you guys is totes obvious."

"Attraction?" Rena laughed out loud. "I thought that was a clear case of annoyed irritation."

"And sexual frustration," Dante interjected.

"Amen," Dominic muttered. "I can attest to that."

"Oh, it wasn't that bad." Tati elbowed him playfully. "Speak for yourself, Doc."

"You should go talk to him," Tatiana said with one of her warm, comforting smiles. "Seriously, get out of here, woman. Nothing is going to get settled until you and that brooding fella get your shit straight."

"Hear, hear." Kerry raised her glass and added, "Plus, if you do decide to bond with Zander, your powers will really blossom."

"She can telepath," Dominic said flatly. He turned his dark eyes to her. "But you've kept your mind closed to us since I spoke to you at the gate."

"Yeah, sorry, but it's too personal or something. I'm not comfortable with it."

"Understood." Dominic nodded curtly but didn't seem annoyed. "Some Amoveo only want to communicate that way with their mates, unless it's an emergency."

"Have you shifted yet?" William asked with his typical bluntness. "I would think not."

"Uh...no."

"None of us did at first either," Tatiana added. "It didn't happen until we were well on our way to committing to the mate bond."

"How does that happen?" Rena asked. "The whole bonding thing?"

"I'll tell you later." Kerry winked.

"Oh." Rena's cheeks flamed. It obviously had to do with sex. "Right."

"Yeah," Kerry said slowly. "You don't know much about your birth parents, do you?"

"No." Rena shook her head briskly. "I don't know *anything* about them. I was literally dropped on the doorstep of a police station. At least, that was the story I was told, but who the hell knows?"

"So no clue about your Amoveo heritage?" Kerry's brows raised, and she gave Rena a skeptical look. "You have absolutely zero connection to *any* Amoveo."

"Well...not exactly."

Rena folded her arms over her breasts, unsure about how much she should say. Why had Zander left her here alone to try and navigate this situation by herself?

"There is a man…"

"Ha!" Kerry clapped her hands. "I knew it. The old guy, the one I saw when I touched you yesterday. He's Vasallus."

"Huh?" Rena was feeling dumber by the second.

"When an Amoveo's mate dies, the one left behind will begin to age, lose their powers, and basically become human," Dante clarified. "We refer to those Amoveo as part of the Vasallus family. They usually choose to stay connected with our world."

"But this guy obviously didn't," Kerry said quietly. Her brow furrowed. "What can you tell us about him?"

"His name is Vito." She took a deep breath, deciding exactly how to word her response. "He's from the Fox Clan, but I didn't even know what he was until Zander found me. Anyway, Vito's wife and daughter died a long time ago. I was a street kid in Vegas. Vito took me in and trained me how to be a PI. He brought me into his business. He took care of me, and now I'm taking care of him."

"Why wouldn't he tell you who and what you are?" Dominic's deep voice was filled with suspicion. "That makes no sense. He would have to know you're a hybrid Amoveo. Your energy signature gives you away. Vasallus lose their powers, but they can always detect energy patterns, especially another Amoveo."

"To protect her?" Kerry hypothesized. "He must've known about the Purists."

"Possibly," William added.

"I don't know." Rena held up both hands as if in surrender. "Believe me, I'm as baffled by all of this as you are."

"Where is he?" William sniffed. "We should speak with him."

"It won't do you any good." A swell of sadness rose up as she thought of how confused Vito was when she'd left him at Sunnyfarm. Had it only been a few days ago? It felt like a lifetime. "Vito has dementia, like full-on memory loss. He doesn't even remember who I am half the time. He gets me confused with his late daughter a lot."

"I'll speak to the prince," Dante said quietly. "He may know who this man is or, at the very least, have heard about the loss he suffered."

Rena bit her lower lip and looked at her fingers tangled in her lap. Should she tell them his real name? If she did that, would the prince figure out who Zander was? She didn't want to lie to her new friends, but she also didn't want to risk Zed or Zander's safety.

"Well, I think it all happened a really, really long time ago. I'm sure the prince wouldn't know him."

The others exchanged knowing looks.

"What?" Rena glanced at Kerry. "Am I missing something?"

"Richard and Salinda are over three hundred years old." Kerry patted Rena's hand and gave it a quick squeeze. "And they don't look a day over thirty-five."

"Another bonus of bonding with your mate," Tati said. "You'll hardly age."

"That's a perk." Rena's brows lifted, and she let out an awkward laugh. "No Botox needed."

"If this Vito person is from the Fox Clan, then I would propose that Rena is somehow related to him." William turned his ebony eyes to her, studying Rena intently, which unnerved her. "Perhaps you're a niece or cousin of some kind."

Rena rested her elbows on the table and put her head in her hands, letting out a long, slow breath. All of this would have been a hell of a lot easier to digest if Zander had stayed there to back her up, but he was probably sulking in his tent, thinking up ten different ways to introduce her to his brother.

"You okay?" Kerry rubbed her shoulder. "I know this is a lot to take in."

"Yeah." She lifted her head and gave Kerry a weak smile. "I'm just tired, and if you all don't mind, I think I'm going to excuse myself and call it a night."

"It's all good, girl." Kerry leaned over and pulled Rena into a warm hug. "Take it one step at a time, and don't fight it. The universe has a way of working everything out, even if it's not what you were expecting."

"Thanks," Rena whispered.

Chapter 17

RENA SAID HER GOOD-BYES TO THE OTHERS AFTER PROMISING to join them all for a ride at the stables in the morning.

Once she was outside, the cool Montana air filled her lungs. It was far colder here than it had been back in Vegas, and the winds had picked up. The moonlight had been blotted out behind a bank of clouds, and based on the smell in the air, a storm was coming. A smile curved her lips. Zander had been right about her senses getting sharper.

Rena stopped for a second and closed her eyes. She tilted her nose to the sky and noted each of the scents she could identify. Hay. Horses. Earth. Cake from the party. A gust of wind rushed over her, and with it came Zander's distinctly male scent, that mix of leather and musk. Rena shivered and wrapped her arms tighter around her before hurrying along the dirt road. Her senses weren't the only part of her that was on overload. Rena's heart was teetering on the edge of a cliff, and falling over into the abyss seemed all too possible.

When she rounded the bend, she was surprised to see the lights on inside their guesthouse. Her brow furrowed. She had turned them all off before she left, which meant Zander must be in there. Then, as if on cue, the son of a gun touched his mind to hers.

If you're done chatting with your new buddies, we need to talk. His voice, deep and gruff, whisked into her mind suddenly and caused her to trip over her own feet. *Now, Rena.*

She regained her balance, and anger shimmied up her back, the intense surge of emotion causing her eyes to shift with a tingling snap. Rena stormed up the steps of the cottage and tore the door open before stomping inside. Zander was standing at the sliding glass door to the deck with his back to her, but he spun around as the door slammed shut.

"You've got balls, mister."

"Excuse me?" He pushed his hair off his forehead before settling his hands on his hips. She noticed he was barefoot and wearing only a T-shirt and jeans. The man sure had made himself comfortable. "What's the problem?"

"I trusted you," she seethed. Her anger dissipated and gave way for the hurt beneath it, like sand spilling through an hourglass. "And you *left me* there. They started asking me questions about Vito and my heritage. You promised you wouldn't leave me alone, and then you ditched me at dinner. And now you're saying that you're leaving in the morning. You're just gonna split? That's it? Poof. You're gone?"

"If you would—"

"You don't want to be my mate or whatever you want to call it, fine! But at the very least, I thought you were my *friend*."

Rena closed the distance between them, each step punctuating her burgeoning frustration with him and the entire damned situation. The whole time, Zander remained silent, but his eyes had shifted, and the crimson orbs gleamed at her fiercely. His tall, muscular body loomed over her, but he didn't make a move toward or away from her.

"I thought I could count on you," she whispered shakily. "Boy, was I wrong."

"Rena—"

"No, Zander!" She poked him in the chest with one finger. "You don't get to say anything to me right now. Do you have any idea how hard it was for me to let you into my life, let alone into my heart? I've spent almost my entire existence protecting myself, not letting people in, and keeping everyone at arm's length. And then you came along and turned my entire world upside down."

"Hang on—"

"No! You left me alone after promising me you wouldn't, and *then* you have the nerve to bark orders at me, summoning me over here like I work for you. I don't want to listen to you right now. I'm too pissed. I know you want to talk about your brother and me mating with him or getting him out of hibernation. But you know what? I don't want to hear it. I'm going upstairs, and I'm going to take a shower."

"We need to talk," he growled.

"Too bad. You'll have to wait. My back is killing me from riding on your damned motorcycle, and I need a good soak. Not only that, but I want to pretend for five minutes that my life hasn't gotten completely out of control. I want to delude myself and act like I haven't *fallen in love* with a man who is hell-bent on ditching me and giving me to his twin brother like I'm some kind of hand-me-down bicycle."

She turned away with every intention of running upstairs, because the last thing she wanted to do was cry in front of him like some stupid, pathetic, lovelorn girl. Rena wanted to drown her tears in a steaming-hot shower, but Zander's massive hand curled around her bicep, preventing her from going anywhere.

"Rena," he whispered. "Please wait."

Humiliation tinged with heartbreaking loss flooded her, because she could swear she detected pity in his voice. Rejection was bad enough, but pity? Oh, hell no. She would not let him feel sorry for her.

"No! Don't you dare look at me like you feel sorry for me."

"It's not you I feel sorry for," he ground out.

"Good. Because I'll get over you," she shot back. "It's not even you that I'm pissed at. I'm disgusted with myself, because I did what I *swore* I would never do." Rena yanked her arm free and shoved at his chest with both hands. "My life was just *fine* until you came barreling into it. I knew how to do that, you know? I knew how to be alone. I was an expert at standing on my own two feet and not needing anyone else. But now...do you have any idea what loving you has done to me?"

She sucked in a shuddering breath and, regardless of how hard she willed them to stop, the tears fell anyway, her body once again betraying her heart. Through the blur of tears, Rena's gaze met Zander's, and she braced herself for the rejection she knew was inevitable.

He didn't love her. Or he wouldn't. But did it matter?

Either way, he was not meant to be hers.

Unable and unwilling to see that look of abject pity on his face, Rena shoved past him and yanked the sliding glass door open before running outside. Blind with tears, she ran from the deck and out into the fields behind the house. She ran faster than she ever had in her life, and in the distance, she heard him calling her name, but Rena didn't look back.

Thunder rumbled overhead, and lightning streaked across the sky, briefly illuminating the mountain ahead. Rain began to fall and pelted her face as the wind whipped over her, mixing with her salty tears. Everything Rena had learned over the past few days raced through her head.

Zander. Vito. The dragons. Arianna.

Amoveo.

And finally, in her mind's eye, she pictured a fox. Its eyes burned bright, glowing in the dark, calling to her like a lighthouse guiding home ships lost in the fog.

Power surged through her body as the winds picked up, whisking around her, and static electricity crackled over her skin. Lightning flashed as Rena pumped her arms and legs before leaping over a fallen log blocking her path to nowhere. Her body stretched, and her muscles tingled as she soared through the air, but when she landed on the other side…it was on four legs. Not two.

Rena skidded to a halt in the tall, wet grasses that flicked her in the face, suddenly and acutely aware that her center of gravity was far lower than it had been before. She regained her footing and rose to her full height. The grass, which moments ago had been at her knees, was now just below her chin. Her heart hammered in her chest, and her blood rushed in her ears like a river. When she went to lift her hand, she found herself staring at a small paw. Dark-red fur trimmed in brown covered her everywhere she could see. Driving sheets of rain poured down, and when she glanced behind her, she discovered a long, furry, white-tipped tail.

Holy shit.

Somehow, Rena had shifted into her fox, but she had absolutely no idea how she had done it. She sat down on her haunches, and her ears pricked up when she detected a familiar voice in the breeze.

"Rena!" Zander's voice cut through the night and rose above the sounds of the storm. "Rena! Are you all right?"

Reacting on instinct and still somewhat stunned by her sudden and unexpected transformation, Rena reached out and touched her mind to Zander's. Relief flooded her when their thoughts mingled with effortless familiarity.

I'm okay but…I'm furry.

A clap of thunder rattled the air, and Rena hopped up onto the log in an effort to have a better look at her surroundings. With her sharp night vision, it didn't take her long to spot Zander, but even without the heightened sense, she would have seen the eyes of his dragon. He cut a towering, formidable silhouette, and when the lightning cracked across the sky, illuminating him from head to toe, the sight of him stole Rena's breath.

The man was beautiful.

Wild. Dark. Dangerous.

His thick, muscular arms hung at his sides, and wet, shaggy hair clung to the sharp angles of his square jaw and high cheekbones as the wind whipped around him. The T-shirt he wore was completely soaked, a second skin showing off the dips and curves of his muscular torso. He strode slowly toward her, every inch of him taut and primed, as though ready to leap into action at a moment's notice.

When he got within a foot of the fallen log she was standing on, lightning shot across the sky behind him in jagged, angry streaks. Rena held her breath as Zander crouched down, getting almost eye to eye with her. He folded his hands in front of him, his forearms resting on his thighs, and studied her with unnerving intensity.

Well…say something.

She sat on her haunches, her long tail curling around her out of instinct. Her wet fur clung to her in odd, unfamiliar ways, and she couldn't help but recall bad hair days as a human. She'd be willing to bet this looked way worse.

Zander? I must look like a drowned rat.

"No," he whispered. "You're beautiful."

Thanks. Rena held her head high, hoping to maintain some kind of dignity. *But do you have any idea how I can turn back into myself?*

"You are still you, Rena." His lips lifted at the corners, and he tapped her snout. "Just a different side of you."

A smaller and more vulnerable me… Now how do I change back?

"Close your eyes and picture your human form," he murmured as he rose to his feet and took a step back.

That's it? She cocked her head to one side. *Are you sure?*

"Yes. It's not something you forget how to do."

Like riding a bike?

"Exactly," he said with a soft laugh. "Oh, and make sure to picture what you were wearing, your clothing. Otherwise—"

You mean if I don't, I'll be naked? Her eyes widened.

Zander said nothing but nodded curtly in response.

Great. Going from furry to nude would be one hell of a switch up, so she immediately thought of the outfit she had been wearing at dinner. Rena had her doubts that this would work, but since she had little choice other than to take his advice, she did as he instructed. Her eyes fluttered closed, and she concentrated on the image she had seen in the mirror tonight before leaving for the dinner. The wind and rain whisked over her furred body, but she kept that picture in her mind. Within seconds, the prickly, static-electricity sensation surged, and light flashed behind her eyes as her body erupted back into her human state.

One moment, she was sitting on the log. The next, she was all arms and legs, flailing in the air like a fish out of water. Rena would have fallen off the log and onto her ass if Zander hadn't been there to catch her. His arms, like bands of steel, curled around her as he dropped to his knees and caught her midflail. As her head cleared and her center of gravity returned to normal, Rena became acutely aware of Zander's body securely cradling hers.

Howling wind and rain raged around them as the soundtrack of thunder roared in time with wild streaks of lightning. Her heartbeat pounded against her rib cage, and Zander's chest rose and fell alongside hers. It made her feel better to know she wasn't the only one out of breath and that she had some kind of effect on him too. His glowing gaze, like two rubies shining in the night, wandered over her face lovingly.

Cherished, she thought. *This must be what it feels like to be cherished by another person.*

Zander embraced her firmly, but beneath the

unyielding strength, she sensed tenderness, and the combination of the two was almost more than Rena could bear. Ever since she could remember, she had railed against the storm of her life. Fighting. Clawing and scratching her way to survival. She often wondered, on those nights she was on the street, alone and cold, what it would be like to feel completely safe.

Now, staring into Zander's glowing gaze, with his arms wrapped around her, Rena finally knew.

Tears stung her eyes as the swell of emotion collided with the physical sensations, and for a brief moment, Rena thought she could drown in it. She became acutely aware of each spot where his heated flesh met hers. One of her arms was draped around his neck, and before she even realized what she was doing, her fingers were threading through the damp strands of his hair. Her other arm was curled between them, and she had gathered the wet fabric of his T-shirt in her fist.

"Nice catch," she whispered shakily.

"Thanks." The word came out in a shuddered rasp, and his arms tightened around her almost imperceptibly. "You're a quick learner."

"I'm still annoyed with you, you know."

Rena licked the cool raindrops from her lips, and his gaze lingered on her mouth. The heated look in his eyes sent a shock directly to her core. All she could think of was having his lips on hers.

"Won't be the last time, I'm sure."

"Why?" She trailed her fingertips over his scalp, delighting in the feel of his wet hair as it slipped through her fingers. "Plan on having a lot of fights with your sister-in-law?"

"No," he growled.

Rena's breath rushed from her lungs on a gasp as he swung her body like she weighed nothing at all and laid her out beneath him on the thick blanket of wet grass. In a blink, he was over her, his arms on either side of her head, caging her in, and the hard, heavy length of his body settled between her legs, as though that was exactly where he belonged.

Always.

"No." It was a whisper this time. His voice was gruff and hesitant as the lightning lit up the ebony sky behind him, but he was taut, firm, and hot above her. He pinned her to the ground with body, mind, and spirit. Rena couldn't have moved even if she had wanted to.

And she definitely didn't want to.

The sharp angles of his jaw and the glow of his eyes created a ferocious expression, but when another shot of lightning flashed, it lit up the tenderness that lurked beneath. In that instant, with a single rush of power from nature or the fates or her own heart, Rena saw Zander's true face.

He was a ferocious protector with gentleness at his core.

A man hiding a beast.

Rena wondered fleetingly whether the beast contained more gentleness than the man. Perhaps when his dragon was banished, buried deep beneath the surface, it dragged some of Zander's tenderness down with it.

How else could *the man* have survived all these years? Alone.

She lifted one hand from his chest, where both of her palms had landed, and cupped his cheek with quaking fingers. The scruff of his unshaven jaw rasped against her flesh in wicked little streaks. His eyes fluttered closed as he leaned into her touch before pressing a kiss to the inside of her hand.

"No to what, Zander?" she said on a shuddering breath. Rena tangled both hands in his hair, her fingers curling around the wet strands. Wanting nothing more than to pull him closer. To feel him everywhere. "Please...tell me."

"No to the fates," he said. "He can't have you, Rena."

Zander tilted his hips and pressed the hard length of himself against her heated core. Rena opened her legs, giving him better access, and sighed a wave of pleasure, and need curled in her gut.

"From the moment I saw you, I've wanted you for myself. I'm a selfish bastard. Because..."

Zander pushed himself off her and knelt between her legs. For a split second, Rena thought he was going to put the brakes on again, but her fears were dispelled when he tore his wet shirt off over his head and tossed it aside. His bare chest was slick with rain and glistened in the flashes of the storm. Rivulets of water trailed a path over the dips and valleys of his muscles, catching in the dark line of hair that disappeared under the waist of his jeans. With her enhanced vision, she could see every scar, each one a chapter within his lengthy life story. Rena ran her fingertips along the ripples of his stomach muscles, which contracted and flexed beneath her touch.

He bowed his head and let her explore the damaged flesh. His hands curled into fists and rested on his thighs. Their combined energy patterns mingled and danced around them in the air, the tempest between them matching the storm from Mother Nature gust for gust, flash for flash. There would be no more hiding, no more pretending that the attraction they felt was simply some kind of biological side effect.

Every single ounce of Rena's soul cried out for his, and with each labored breath, Zander's spirit called to hers. Shaking with a potent combination of desire and apprehension, Rena sat up and shifted onto her knees facing him. She settled her hands on his shoulders before sliding her fingers along the hard line of his collarbone until finally grasping his face, forcing him to look at her.

"Tell me," she murmured, her thumb rasping along his temple. "Please, Zander. Don't leave me out here alone."

"I know what I'm supposed to do, what is expected of me. I know you don't need me, Rena, but I sure as hell need you. Tonight and every night for the rest of your life. The rest of mine." His gravelly voice skittered over her seductively in the dark. "I understand what the universe is telling me to do. I should walk away. Let fate take its course for you and Zed. But I can't do it. I'm a *son of a bitch*, Rena McHale. And if you had any sense at all, woman, you would do what I can't—and leave. Right now. Go back inside that cottage. Lock the damn doors, and tell me to go straight to hell. Because if you don't, if you stay here, I am going to take you and make you mine. My brother and the fates can be damned, and so can I. Because all I want, for whatever meager existence I may have left, is *you*."

Pain edged his eyes, and desperation mixed with desire laced his words. His body shook as if he was doing his best to restrain himself—restrain the beast. To hold back all of his desire so that he could give his brother even a fraction of the life that Zander had already lived.

That was when Rena knew what she had to do.

She dropped her hands from his face, and Zander winced visibly, as though the loss of contact pained him. He lowered his gaze and squeezed his eyes shut, his shoulders heaving with a heavy breath. A smile curved Rena's lips as she grasped the edge of her sweater and pulled it over her head before throwing it aside, leaving her in a black, lacy bra and skirt.

Without a word, Rena gathered his hands in hers and placed them over her breasts. A growl rumbled in his chest, and his head snapped up as his glowing gaze latched on to hers.

"I'm yours," Rena whispered. "My body. My soul. All of it. *I* choose *you*, Zander Lorens."

Like a flash of lightning, he was on her. A force of nature. Wild and powerful. Zander's mouth crashed onto hers. His tongue demanded entrance, and Rena opened to him, her arms linking around his neck, pulling him close. Her breasts crushed against his chest as his experienced fingers unclasped her bra and quickly pulled the lacy fabric from her damp, heated skin. Never once did he break the kiss, and Rena sighed into his mouth as he laid her out beneath him once again.

His mouth blazed a trail from her lips to her throat as he divested her of the rest of her clothing, leaving her naked and wet, with the storm raging around them. Rena shivered with anticipation as he moved down her body, pressing kisses along her rib cage and her belly. She tangled her hands in his slick, shaggy hair as he settled between her legs and hooked his arms beneath her thighs, anchoring her to the ground.

"I want to taste you," he whispered. Zander licked rainwater from her belly button, before moving lower. "All of you."

Rena cried out when he covered her sex with his mouth, his tongue flicking over her clit in one slow, purposeful pass. She tried to move her hips, to urge him on, but he held her still, keeping her a willing prisoner. He licked and suckled. Slowly at first, and with each wicked pass, Rena thought she would go mad with need. The orgasm coiled deep in her belly, and she lifted her head, wanting to watch him feast on her. It was erotic and wanton to see Zander touch her this intimately. Rena had had plenty of sex in her life, but being with Zander seemed like so much more.

She gasped when his glowing gaze met hers as his tongue slipped deep inside her and their minds tangled intimately.

You're mine, Rena. The guttural growl of his words skittered inside her head as he continued licking and suckling her sensitive flesh. *Every part of you…is mine.*

The intense combination of their mental connection and the physical was almost more than she could bear. Rena cried out as a wave of pleasure slammed through her body. Her back arched, and one of his hands cupped her breast as they jutted toward the sky, as though begging him to claim them. The orgasm began to bloom, rippling deep inside and spreading out beneath her skin like flames, threatening to consume everything in its path, bathing and baptizing her as his.

But Rena was greedy for more.

Not yet. Breathless and close to the edge, Rena tangled her fingers in Zander's hair and whispered into his mind. *I want you inside me when I come.*

A guttural groan erupted as he pushed himself to his knees. Rena sat up and barely noticed the rain that continued to fall as she undid the button of his jeans. She pushed his hands away when he attempted to help her and grinned at him.

"My turn." She smacked him on the leg playfully. "Stand up."

Zander's face was a mask of desire and concentration as he rose to his feet.

Rena shifted onto her knees and swiftly released the heavy length of him from the strict, confining denim. His cock sprang free, and a fresh rush of heat flared between her legs as she took in the gorgeous sight of him. She tugged his jeans down past his hips, just far enough to give her access to what she wanted.

She curled one hand around the base before licking her way along the hot stalk of flesh. He gathered her hair in his fist as she covered him with her mouth and took him deep. Zander groaned when Rena ran her tongue over the smooth head before taking more of him in. She alternately worked him with her mouth and her hands, wanting to give him the same explosive pleasure that he had given her. His hips began to pump faster as she picked up the pace, and just when she thought he was reaching his limit, Zander grabbed her upper arms and pulled her to her feet.

He released her, and to her surprise, her quivering legs kept her upright as he swiftly rid himself of his jeans and kicked them aside. The thunder rumbled as

Zander pulled her back into his arms. His rough, heated palms grazed over her ass and over her back and shoulders before settling over her biceps. She sighed as the hot length of his erection pressed against her belly, and the ache between her legs swelled to an insistent, throbbing need.

"No more playing," he murmured. His fingertips dug deeper into her flesh as the hard plane of his thigh slipped between her legs and pressed against the swollen heat of her sex. "I want you, Rena McHale. As my mate. Tonight and every night from now on." His words were edged with gruff desperation, and the broken look in his eyes made the last of the walls around her heart crumble. "Will you have me?"

Yes. Rena pressed her hands to his cheeks and touched his mind with hers on a whisper. *I'm yours, Zander.*

He kissed her deeply as they dropped to their knees, the soft, wet grass serving as their marriage bed. Clinging to him, Rena let her head fall back as he blazed his lips down her throat. Her hands, greedy for more, traveled over his back, and she ran her fingers along the trio of long scars, fleetingly recalling where they had come from.

Rena pulled back and took in the beautiful imperfections of the man that was Zander Lorens. When the lightning flashed, Rena caught sight of a shadow on Zander's leg—but it wasn't a shadow at all. Her heart swelled with relief and gratitude. It was the mate tattoo. And that's when she knew what she needed to do. Without a word, she turned around and dropped to all fours before slicing a seductive look at him over her shoulder.

He was kneeling behind her, his glowing gaze pinned

to her lower back as his large hands gripped her hips firmly. Rena shuddered as the hungry look in his eyes grew when he spotted the mate tattoo.

"You bear the mark," he murmured reverently.

Rena shuddered as he trailed his fingers lightly over the tattoo, which had materialized only a day ago but had obviously been there forever, waiting beneath the surface.

Waiting for him to bring it to life—bring *her* to life.

"You see?" Rena said, her voice shaking with unfulfilled desire. "I belong to you, Zander. Not Zed. Not the universe or the fates...you."

Mine, his voice roared in her mind as he speared inside her with one powerful thrust. Rena shouted his name and pressed her hips back, wanting to take him deeper—needing him to touch her deep inside, where no one else had ever been. As he thrust into her time and again, sliding in and stretching her, Rena hung on to the grass, arching her back. She spread her knees, opening herself up, taking everything he had to give and, at the same time, giving him all she possessed.

As the orgasm began to crest and Zander's pace picked up, Rena whimpered with pleasure, and he whispered into her mind, *Te semper et in perpetuum amabo. Adiuro me tibi. Largior. Gloria.*

With one final pass, Zander shuddered as his own orgasm erupted in time with hers, and he buried himself to the hilt on a groan.

Rena's body shook as he slumped over her, and they both collapsed onto the ground before rolling over onto their sides. With Zander still buried deep inside her, Rena reached around and curled her hand over the mark on his thigh. A groan rumbled in his chest as he linked his arms around her waist, holding her tightly against him even as he slipped from her body.

"And you belong to me," Rena whispered. She turned her face toward his as he nuzzled her ear. "Always."

As they lay together, bodies intertwined, Rena realized the rain had stopped, and the moon, luminous and full, was fighting to break free of the clouds. Mother Nature had finally stopped raging at the world around her. The blissful silence gave Rena hope. Perhaps the tempest that her life had become would finally be calmed as well.

Chapter 18

ZANDER MADE LOVE TO RENA TWICE MORE WHEN THEY GOT back inside the cottage, and if he'd had his way, they would have continued on until sunrise. But time waits for no one, and Zander's time was running out.

To say nothing of Zed's.

It hadn't taken long for Rena to drift off to sleep, and even though he wanted nothing more than to join her, Zander knew it was now or never. He glanced at the moon and, based on the position, was fully aware of the little darkness he had remaining.

He pressed a kiss to her soft cheek, which elicited a sleepy mumble, but to his relief, she didn't wake up. Moving carefully, not wanting to disturb her, Zander slipped from the toasty cocoon of sheets and blankets, which were heated by Rena's luscious, curvy body. When he rose from the bed and moved silently to the door, he glanced back at her one more time.

Moonlight bathed every inch of her lovely form in its silvery glow. She was on her belly, and her dark hair was splayed out on the pillow like a halo. The sheet was draped precariously over her beautiful bottom, leaving the graceful arch of her torso exposed. His gaze drifted down to the mate tattoo that was now fully formed along the base of her back. His lips lifted at the corners, and his hand went instinctively to the matching mark on his thigh.

Two dragons intertwined in a loving embrace. The colors, varying shades of scarlet and amber, had begun to emerge as well. Zander knew if he survived the night, the tattoo on his leg would fill in with exactly the same hues as the one on Rena's back. They had made love, and he had said the dragon's sacred mating rite.

If he succeeded in his quest, his bond with Rena would be unshakable, and his brother would be free.

But that was a gigantic if.

Zander slipped outside silently, noting the significant drop in temperature as he made his way to his tent. The Montana wilderness hummed around him, various creatures of the night buzzing and scurrying while paying him no mind. Before stepping into his tent, he closed his eyes and searched for the Amoveo's energy signatures. If Dominic or any of the other Amoveo warriors were lurking nearby, he would pick up on it immediately. Of course, that would be a complication he simply did not need or want.

To his relief, he found none other than the steady thrum of Rena's energy signature as she lay sleeping upstairs. Zander dressed quickly and grabbed Zed's spirit stone along with his own. If there was any hope of his plan working, Zander would need the power of both pieces of quartz in order to free his brother. He slipped the stones in the pocket of his jeans before stepping out of the tent and casting one last glance to the bedroom window.

Convinced she was still safely asleep, Zander took off across the field and toward the mountain. He ran swiftly and silently through the tall grasses without looking behind him. There was no turning back now.

With the prince away and the younger Amoveo totally unaware of the dragons, Zander knew he had no other choice. He had to try and awaken Zed on his own, but the timing had to be exactly right. If he could get into the cave and use the crack in the hibernation cocoon to his advantage, the energy in the spirit stone *might* be enough to bring him out of it, finishing what Rena's presence in the dreamrealm had started.

When Zander reached the tree line, he finally stopped for a moment to catch his breath and be absolutely certain nobody was nearby. The lights of the main house twinkled in the distance, and one or two glimmers flickered from the cottages, but all was quiet. Not even the ten or so horses in the barn had stirred or been alerted by his presence. Zander pulled his cell phone from his back pocket and checked the time.

Sunrise was in thirty-four minutes to be precise—in this situation, every moment counted.

He had to wait until just before sunrise to awaken Zed. If the beast remained in control and his brother was unable to hear him, then at least the sun would force Zed to shift back into his human state.

In theory.

He climbed the rocky hill and followed the path, the one he still knew by heart. It may have been five centuries since Zander had set foot on this land, but he remembered it like it was yesterday. When he reached the rock formation embedded in the face of the mountain, he recognized the flower-shaped protrusion immediately, but panic set in when he saw the entrance to the cave had been covered by at least one rock slide over the years.

Zander dropped to his knees and pressed his hands to the ground.

The image of Zed encased behind the cracked wall of quartz flared into his mind. *His brother's body twitched frantically, and the crack began to grow*.

They were out of time.

He started pulling away the rock and dirt, all the while praying the entrance wasn't entirely caved in. Grunting with effort, Zander pushed aside one of the larger rocks, and when the dust cleared, a rush of relief swelled when he saw a narrow but clear path into the cave far below.

He was about to make his way inside when the ground rumbled beneath his feet. Zander stumbled backward as rock fell, covering the entrance again. The shaking continued, and he braced himself against the trunk of a nearby pine tree. His heart thundered in his chest because he had a dreadful suspicion what was causing it.

The shaking stopped as abruptly as it had begun.

Perhaps it was only a normal tremor in the earth or maybe—

The ground trembled again, harder this time, and with it came an all-too-familiar and bone-rattling roar. The sound was muffled at first, but as the shaking grew stronger, so did the battle cry of his brother. Zander swore and backed down the hill, immediately turning his attention to the ranch in the distance.

He had to warn them. Rena and the others could shelter in the council meeting hall.

Before he had gone ten feet, a sickening crack shattered the silent Montana night as the ground opened up. Zander spun around and watched in horror as a long fissure erupted down the mountainside, opening the earth like a zipper. The force of the quake tossed him to the dirt, and Zander rolled to the right, narrowly avoiding tumbling into the gaping crack. He scrambled to his feet again, and as the shaking continued, he fought to maintain his footing.

Everything stopped, and the world fell eerily silent. It was as if all the forest creatures were acutely aware of what was coming next. Zander's breath came in heavy, labored gasps as he scanned the unearthly quiet of the mountain. There was no sound. It was as if the earth itself was holding its breath.

Zander's heart skipped a beat when he spotted an eerie, cherry-red glow emanating from the crack toward the top of the steep, rocky incline. He held his breath and forced himself to stay calm, but even as that thought raced through his head, Zander knew it wouldn't matter. He glanced to the sky. It had brightened slightly, but there was still far too much darkness left for his liking.

A snuffling sound, similar to that of a bull getting ready to charge at a matador, rushed through the air. Rock and dirt fell away along the sloping mountainside as the snuffling rumbled again, like an otherworldly warning. Zander turned his attention back to the crack in the face of the mountain, and a swirl of conflicting emotions fired through him.

For the first time in five centuries, Zander found himself staring into the glowing, furious gaze of his brother. But it wasn't really Zed, was it?

It was the dragon.

And it was *pissed*.

Rena's voice, shaking and scared, whisked into his mind. *Zander!*

Get Kerry and the others to the council's meeting chamber. Right now, Rena! It's the only place you'll be safe.

But—

His gut reaction was to continue embracing the intimate connection, but he knew that could only put her in more danger. Now more than ever, he had to protect her. She would be no match for Zed given the state he was in, and neither would the other Amoveo. He shut his mind to her and kept his attention on his brother.

If the curse was truly being broken, then Zander would be able to fight fire with fire, and for the first time in his miserable existence, the beast might save the man.

The fog of the dreamrealm rolled around Rena in lazy, billowy clouds, and for the first time, Rena wasn't afraid—not even a little bit, because she knew Zander would be there waiting for her.

"Zander?" Her voice sounded funny in this space and echoed around her like a ball bouncing wildly in a rubber room. "Are you here?"

The fog lifted, and Rena found herself in Zed's hibernation cave, but Zander was nowhere to be seen. Zed was still buried in the wall of quartz. Unlike the last time she was there, he didn't look like he was moving. But there was a crack running up and down the length of the quartz wall, and that gave her pause.

Her sense of safety began to ebb away. What would happen if Zed started to wake up and Zander hadn't gotten there yet? Wearing only the bedsheet, which was wrapped around her like a towel, Rena grew acutely aware of her nakedness and exactly how vulnerable she was in here.

She arched one eyebrow and glanced down at her state of undress.

"Well, this is what I wore to bed, sort of," she mumbled under breath. "Zander? Seriously, where are you? If you're trying to teach me something, can you just come out here and tell me what it is? I'm starting to freak out a little."

"He's not here." The voice, while it wasn't Zander's, was familiar, but she sure as hell didn't expect to hear it in the dreamrealm.

"Vito?" A smile covered her face as she looked around the rocky cave, but the man was nowhere to be seen. Rena focused her efforts and sought out his energy signature. Sure enough, within seconds, she detected his energy pattern, the one with the funny hum of static. "I know you're here, and I know that you're Amoveo. It's okay. Zander told me everything—about me and you and him and…Arianna."

"Did he now?" Her friend's voice bounced around the cave, leaving her unable to pinpoint his location. "You mean he's learned something after all these years? Like how to tell the truth, for example? Too bad he and his bastard brother couldn't tell my daughter the truth. They led her on and allowed her to believe—"

A chill rushed over Rena and raised all the hairs on her bare arms. There was something about the tone of his voice that made her uneasy. Ugliness laced his words, and Rena wished like hell that Zander would hurry up and get there. He had fallen asleep next to her, hadn't he?

"That's not true, Vito." She kept her voice calm and even, not wanting to upset him but at the same time needing to set him straight. *"Arianna played them against each other."*

"She was only a child," he shouted. *"Too young to understand what kind of danger she was in or the power she was toying with."*

"Where are you, Vito?" Rena pleaded. *"Please come out where I can see you. I'm new to the dreamrealm stuff, and I don't really know what I'm doing. Come on, you're scaring me."*

Silence hung in the cave like a lead blanket, and Rena turned around, frantically searching for him. A sense of foreboding crawled over her skin, and she swiped at her neck, as though a bug lingered there.

"I'm right here, girl."

When Rena spun back around, she almost laughed out loud with relief. Vito was standing on the other side of the pool, directly in front of Zed's hibernation chamber. He looked like he had when she'd first met him almost ten years ago, and this was the first coherent conversation they'd had in a long time. He stood tall and proud. His thick shock of white hair was neatly coiffed, and he was wearing one of his blue suits that he had always liked so much. But it was his eyes that stood out the most. They were glowing amber...just like hers did.

They were the eyes of his clan.

"Wow, you look great." Laughter mixed with tears and threaded her words. *"And you sound great too! I've missed you, Vito."*

Rena started to walk around the narrow edge of the pool, but he held up one hand and shook his head abruptly.

"No. Stay there, Rena."

"What?" Her brow furrowed, and she tugged the sheet tighter around her. "Why? I don't understand."

"I know." He was fiddling with the large, gold ring he always wore on his right hand. The one that had once belonged to Zander's family. "I'm sorry, but this was the only way."

"What are you talking about?" Confusion fired through her. "How are you even here? I mean, you sound great, but when I saw you a couple days ago… you know…the dementia. I though Zander said that you lost all of your powers?"

"Walking in the dreamrealm is all I have left of my Amoveo gifts. This is the only place I feel at home anymore." He lowered his gaze to the ring and pulled it from his finger before holding it up. "In the earthly plane, I've been lost. Confused. But when I saw him again, with you, the ring woke me up. It brought me back so I could finish what had been started."

"Vito?" Rena's voice shook, and she inched around the edge of the pool. "That ring, it belongs to Zander's family, doesn't it?"

"It did once." He nodded solemnly, and tears fell. "I took it after the dragon slayer killed their father. This is when they're most vulnerable, you know. When they emerge from hibernation and at sunrise, of course. Their transition isn't as easy as it is for our people. They're limited to the night. That's how the dragon slayers were able to destroy them. Once they knew where the lairs were, the rest was easy enough."

"Vito…what's going on?" A sense of foreboding shimmied up her spine.

"The witch told me that I could use this if the boy found a way to lift the curse before—"

"The five-hundred-year mark," Rena whispered. *"It's tomorrow."*

"I never really believed I would need it. All I had to do was live long enough to make sure the curse was never broken and that they were never freed. How could I let them go unpunished after what they did to her? They have to pay, Rena. You must understand that."

His face, etched with deep lines of bitterness, pain, and regret, was bathed in the eerie reddish glow from Zed's cocoon. Rena's vision blurred, and her heart broke for the only family she had ever really known.

"But they have paid, Vito." Rena let out a curt laugh. *"Believe me. Zander is covered in scars from more injuries than I could count, and Zed has been completely tortured. Hell, Zander is worried that even if Zed does wake up from hibernation, his brain might be totally fried or something. Trust me. Your curse worked. These two men—not boys, by the way, men— have been paying for the consequences of their foolish, impulsive behavior for the past five hundred years. Come on, Vito. Isn't that enough?"*

Vito shook his head, and it was obvious to Rena that he hadn't heard a word of what she said. Or maybe he had but it didn't matter to him. All he seemed to care about was finishing off Zander and Zed.

"But then, I saw you, Rena, and I knew that it would happen all over again. You looked so much like her, like my Arianna. You aren't her, of course, but so like she was." He sniffled and swiped at his eyes but kept his gaze locked on the ring between his fingers. *"You*

were of the Fox Clan too, and I knew that if I had found you…so would he. He would be drawn to you, like he was to her."

"I'm not Arianna, Vito. Zander knows that." Dread curled in Rena's chest as her heart broke. *"Is that why you took me in? Because you wanted to use me to lure Zander here? You were just using me this whole time?"*

"No!" His rage-filled shout ricocheted around the cave, and his eyes blazed orange. *"I wanted to protect you. From him and his selfish, savage nature. I knew if he came for you, it would be your undoing. He will destroy you, just like he did Arianna. He took her from me. But I can stop it. I can stop it all."*

He turned his now-human eyes to hers and whispered, *"I'm sorry."*

Before Rena could ask him what he was talking about, Vito turned around and slammed the ring into the crack of Zed's hibernation cave. A brilliant blood-red light flushed, and Rena had to shield her eyes from the power of it. She cried out when the earth began to shake, making her stumble backward. With the cave rumbling around her, Rena grasped the edge of a nearby rock for balance and forced herself to look toward the light.

A scream, one she barely recognized as her own, tore from her lips.

Vito lay motionless. His vacant, lifeless gaze stared out from beneath a pile of stone. She wanted to go to him, but movement above him captured her attention as the earth began to tremble with more force. Rena's breath came in sharp gasps as she slowly trailed her gaze up the jagged fissure in the quartz wall.

The dragon twitched and writhed, like a butterfly

trying to emerge from its cocoon, and with one final rumble, the beast's tail unfurled, sending a wave of quartz and dirt into the pool of water. Rena shielded her face from bits of flying debris. When she turned her gaze back to the beast, it had stopped moving. She held her breath for several beats of her heart. With the sound of her own blood rushing in her ears, Rena waited, uncertain of what to do next.

But when the eyes of the dragon opened and zeroed in on her, Rena backed away slowly and repeated one thing over and over again:

"Wake up! Wake up! Wake up!"

Rena hadn't learned much about the dreamrealm, but she knew enough to know that if Zed had awakened here, everything was about to blow up on the earthly plane. The Amoveo were going to find out just how real the Dragon Clan was.

Rena shot out of bed and tumbled to the floor with an undignified thud. When the cottage started to shake, she thought she might still be in the dreamrealm, but after a few seconds, she regained her bearings. She rose to her feet on unsteady legs and immediately realized that Zander was nowhere to be seen.

Zander! Answer me, you big jerk!

Get Kerry and the others to the council's meeting chamber. His curt, gravelly voice cut into her mind forcefully. *Right now, Rena! It's the only place you'll be safe.*

But—

Like a door being slammed shut, Rena was cut off from Zander's mind.

"You son of a bitch," she whispered.

He said he had a new plan but never got around to telling her what it was. Perfect. The quake finally stopped, and Rena quickly dragged on her jeans, boots, and a sweater from the duffel bag. She knew what she had to do, and when another rumble rippled through the earth, Rena had zero questions in her mind about what was causing it.

She had to warn the others.

She raced downstairs, and without thinking about the consequences, she focused on Kerry and reached out to her with her mind.

Kerry! Rena's voice sounded shakier than she would have liked. *We have a problem.*

No shit. Kerry's blunt response was no surprise, given what Rena knew of her already. *We're in the field behind your cottage.*

A modicum of relief fanned through Rena's chest, but she didn't respond, because she still wasn't sure how she was going to explain all of this. Rena tugged open the slider and raced outside to find five sets of glowing eyes staring at her from the waning darkness.

Rena stopped on the deck and took stock of the bizarre menagerie. By her count, there was a massive tiger, a fox—one that was much larger than she was in her clan form—a hulking wolf, a sleek black panther, and standing on the railing was an enormous bird of prey with glowing, dark eyes that conjured images of the moon.

"Holy shit," Rena said with a rushing breath. "Where's the ark?"

Now is really not the time for jokes. William's clipped tone shot into Rena's mind, and the falcon screeched as it fluffed its feathers. *Where is your mate?*

The earth shook again, and Dominic let out a bone-rattling roar in response.

There's something wrong. His voice, more of a growl, touched their collective minds. *We've never had earthquakes here, and is anybody else picking up the strange spike of energy in the mountains?*

"It's Zander and his twin brother, Zed," Rena blurted out. "They're dragons, okay? Cursed dragons, and one of them is all kinds of screwed up."

That explains the tattoos I saw, Kerry chimed in. *But what about—*

This is crazy. Dante snorted. *There's no Dragon Clan.*

That is not entirely accurate, William began. *There was, but we believed they were extinct.*

You knew about this? Dominic leaped through the grass and roared at William. The tiger's eyes blazed with fury, and he lifted his lip, showing a mouthful of razor-sharp teeth. *I thought you and the prince told us all of the Council's secrets.*

Why would it matter? William ruffled his feathers again, and his sharp gaze flicked to Dominic. *We believed they were extinct.*

The earth shook again.

Not so fucking extinct now, are they? Dominic snarled.

"The Council chamber," Rena interjected. "Zander said you would be able to find shelter there."

We're not leaving the ranch exposed, and we sure as hell can't let a damned dragon get near the human population. Dante's voice, calm but firm, joined the conversation. *But Kerry should take you and Tatiana to the chamber.*

"No offense," Rena said with a curt laugh, "but you

guys don't stand a chance. Trust me. I've seen Zed up close in the dreamrealm. He'll eat you for a midnight snack."

You all need to calm down. William's aloof tone was more than a little irritating. *If memory serves, the dragons were limited with their shifting ability. Once the sun rises, he will be forced into his human form, and at that point, you can dispatch him easily, Dominic.*

"He's right about the sun. Listen, we don't have time to debate this, and nobody is getting *dispatched*." Rena trotted down the steps and pointed to the mountain. "That rumbling you feel is Zed breaking out of his hibernation cocoon. He'll be in his dragon form, and he's completely confused from being stuck in the dreamrealm like that for five centuries. And since the sun isn't going to be up for a little while, we are about to have a serious problem."

How the hell are we supposed to fight a dragon? Kerry asked, her lithe, sleek, black-furred body practically invisible in the dark, but those yellow eyes of hers were tough to miss. *I never got that chapter in the Amoveo training manual.*

"I guess we'll learn by doing," Rena murmured. "I'm going to help Zander, but maybe you guys should go to the chamber."

As the others all started speaking at once, Rena closed her eyes and pictured her clan form. Within seconds, static electricity crackled over her skin in a prickling blanket as her body shifted. She dropped to all fours and shook her furry self, trying to acclimate as quickly as possible.

Stay or go. Rena touched her mind to the group and glanced over her shoulder at them. *Zander's my mate.*

I have to help him, but I can't ask the rest of you to put yourselves in danger.

Another massive quake shook the ground, and William took off into the air. Rena's heart sank because she assumed they wouldn't be coming with her.

She couldn't have been more wrong.

I'll do a sweep of the mountain. William's voice, proud and sure, came through loud and clear as he soared high above. *And provide recon from the air.*

When Rena went to look for the others, they were no longer behind her but flanked her on either side.

Roger that, Dominic's growly, gritty voice chimed in. *Watch your six.*

That's military speak for watch your back, Tatiana added.

Well, since the dragons can breathe fire, Rena said shakily, *keep an eye on your sevens, eights, and nines too.*

If we have to, we'll use the distract-and-confuse technique. It works really well on a toddler temper tantrum. Kerry sidled in next to Rena, her yellow cat eyes glowing brightly in the night. *Dragons are big, but we're fast. We can use visualization to confuse the shit out of him. The old disappearing-and-reappearing act will come in handy tonight.*

I have no idea what that is, but we can use all the help we can get.

With her friends surrounding her, Rena actually believed they might stand a chance in a fight against Zed. Maybe their sheer presence and numbers would distract him, and they could keep him at bay until the sun rose. It was a long shot but the only one the group seemed to have. They all made their way toward the mountain, but when the ground shuddered even stronger this time, Rena's hope began to dwindle. They moved faster, running through the tall grasses toward the frightening source of the unnatural quakes.

Hold. Dominic's deep voice stopped them all in their tracks. *I see a light where there shouldn't be one. Up to the left side of the mountain face—ten o'clock.*

Everyone stilled, and Rena's heart beat in rapid-fire pulses as her gaze skittered over to the eerie glow he was referring to. Before she could confirm to the others what it was they were looking at, the side of the mountain exploded in a deafening eruption of rock, dirt, and trees. They all ducked as the debris rained down on them, but it was the massive shadow blotting out the moon that sent terror directly to Rena's core.

The beast was loose.

Okay, that is a big damn dragon. Kerry's quivering voice whisked into Rena's mind. *What the hell are we going to do?*

Fall back, Dominic growled. *Now! Tatiana, Kerry, Rena. All of you, now!*

He's right, Dante interjected.

What we need, Kerry said with a sidelong glance to Rena, *is another dragon.*

My thoughts exactly, Rena murmured. *Zander, where the hell are you?*

As Zed bore down on them, swooping through the sky like the angel of death, eyes blazing like flames, Rena did the one thing she knew might save them and the exact opposite of what Dominic wanted. She leaped ahead of the others and raced toward the fallen trees and rocks while fighting to connect with the mind of the man who might still reside within the beast.

Zed! Rena scrambled on top of a pile of rocks and struggled to connect with his energy signature, so similar to Zander's and yet so strikingly different. *I'm here. I'm the one you're looking for.*

The beast spun in the air and shrieked, immediately changing directions as its furious gaze scanned the ground below. Its wings pumped, the sound reminiscent of a jet engine, as it hovered in the air, searching.

Searching for her.

Zander? Rena reached out, hoping and praying that he was still alive. *Please tell me you're okay.*

When Zed pinned his gleaming eyes to hers and a low growl ricocheted through the air, Rena's heart skipped a beat.

Oh shit.

MINE! The growl of the beast roared in Rena's head as it flapped its enormous, leathery wings and nose-dived in her direction. *MINE. MINE. MINE.*

But before Zed reached her, another shadow erupted from the trees to her right, and Rena watched in horror as the deadly history between the brothers began to repeat itself.

Chapter 19

WHEN ZED HAD EXPLODED OUT OF THE SIDE OF THE mountain, rock had fallen on top of Zander, almost knocking him unconscious. He pushed himself to his knees and pressed a hand to the gash on his forehead in an attempt to stop the blood from dripping into his eyes. Through the haze, he saw Zed hovering above the earth. The sight of his wings spread wide and his tail held out proudly behind him was both terrifying and exhilarating.

His brother was free from hibernation. Now all Zander had to do was keep the rest of them alive until sunrise. The sky was brightening, and pale purple edged the horizon, night slowly but surely giving way to day.

Just a few more minutes…

Dizzy and nauseous, Zander blinked and fought to clear his blurred vision, but it was the sound of Rena's voice that snapped him out of it.

Zander? Her voice was shaky and thick with fear. *Please tell me you're okay.*

Zander would not and could not allow history to repeat itself.

He scanned the wreckage below and, within seconds, spotted Rena. She was in her clan form, standing on top of a pile of rocks, and he was taken aback by her regal stature. She was Amoveo through and through. How could he ever have doubted her ability to embrace what she was?

A wild screech seared the air, snapping Zander from his thoughts, but it was the sight of Zed, spearing through the air toward Rena, that awoke the beast within.

Rena's red-furred body looked impossibly small compared to the hulking form of his brother as he bulleted toward her with single-minded focus.

Zander's protective instincts swelled as rage and fear collided to create a powerful surge of energy. His eyes shifted harshly, and a growl rumbled in his chest as he ran toward Rena with the image of his dragon squarely in his mind's eye. His body hummed and buzzed almost to the point of pain as the shift began to take hold. Searing licks of electrical current, akin to flashes of lightning, discharged beneath his flesh as the formidable power of his dragon erupted from the deep.

With a rage-filled scream, Zander leaped from the earth, and with every ounce of strength, he willed the change into being. In a blinding blaze of light, his human body vanished, and the dragon emerged.

Out of practice with the size and power of his heavy, winged body, Zander tumbled through the air and slammed into Zed, sending both of them to the ground in a heap. Dirt and rock flew toward the sky as their enormous bodies tangled across the earth, leaving a wide swath of destruction in their wake.

Zander whipped his tail as he opened his wings wide, quickly pinning his brother beneath him, but Zed's strength matched his own. Zander opened his mouth and roared, breathing a wicked stream of fire into the air while fighting to keep his feet on Zed's wings.

He had to keep him out of the air.

Zed! he screamed, striving to push through the jumbled, tangled mess of his brother's mind. *That is not Arianna. You've been in hibernation—*

Zed responded with a fire-breathing roar, which Zander narrowly missed by ducking to the right. It was also the opening Zed needed to leverage his body weight and throw Zander off before flipping around and landing on his feet. Zander countered, and the brothers faced off, slowly circling each other.

Zander flicked his gaze to the left when he spotted movement in the field behind his brother. Dominic and the other Amoveo were in their clan forms and watching from the tall grasses, their eyes glowing brightly between the blades. His heart sank, because Rena was nowhere in sight. Zander returned his gaze to his brother and lifted his spike-covered tail, wanting it ready to strike but praying he wouldn't have to.

Liar! Zed roared and popped his wings wide. His clawed hands flexed and curled, the sharp tips flashing as he shifted his weight restlessly. Zander knew all too well what kind of damage those claws could inflict. He had three slashes across his back to prove it. *She's mine. She doesn't love you.*

The sky grew brighter, and if Zander was right, he only had to hold out a few minutes longer.

I know! Zander shouted vehemently. *She was toying with us, Brother. Using us. Arianna was not my mate. Or yours. Please, try to remember what happened… We were cursed by the witch. After the others were killed by the slayers. Damn it, I know you're in there somewhere! Zed, that is not Arianna!*

No! Zed shook his head and snuffled loudly, but his

horned brow furrowed as he zeroed in on Zander once again. *Liar!*

Rage. Jealousy. Frustration. Confusion. And it was all directed at Zander.

Zed! Rena's voice, strong and confident, shot into their joined minds. *He's telling you the truth!*

They both snapped their heads toward the sound of her voice and the lovely, almost-musical energy signature of Rena McHale. Still in her clan form, she stood on a massive boulder, the brisk fall wind making her dark-red fur flutter. Her glowing amber eyes were wide and fixed on Zed. To her credit, she didn't run or flinch but instead held her ground.

Please listen to me. Her tone was sweet and almost melodic as she sat on her haunches, her thick tail curling around her, giving her an air of serenity amid the chaos. *Zander is telling you the truth. Arianna is long gone. You've been in hibernation for five hundred years. Fighting. Surviving. Night after night. But you're free now…both of you.*

With a shimmery blast of static, Rena shifted into her human form, and Zed let out a roar of dissent as he made a move toward her. Zander wasted no time and body slammed his brother out of the way before carefully scooping Rena up in one clawed hand and taking to the sky.

Hang on! He pumped his wings and kept his sights on the horizon. *The sun is coming up. Just a few minutes more…*

Holy crap, she shrieked, her voice touching his mind sharply. *Don't you dare drop me, Zander Lorens.*

He swooped over the trees and headed for the top of

the mountain, fully expecting Zed to take pursuit, but the sound of snarls and growls below captured his attention. Zander held Rena safely against his chest and spun in midair, pumping his wings while using his tail for balance, so they hovered safely above the ground.

Zed was being attacked by the others from every direction, and the sun was beginning to rise. William was dive-bombing Zed's face while Dominic had attached himself to the base of the tail. Snarling and growling, Dom was holding on like a rodeo rider trying to stay on a bull. The others surrounded him and took turns charging Zed before vanishing in thin air and reappearing on the opposite side.

Son of a bitch, Zander whispered. *I don't believe it.*

"Distract and confuse!" Rena shouted. "Just like Kerry said."

Yellow and gold sunlight crested along the horizon, and a spasm shot through Zander's body.

The sun is coming up... It's working, Zander murmured and glanced at the horizon as a cramp wracked his body. *On both of us. Shit. Hang on, Rena.*

Another muscle spasm rippled up his back, and Zander faltered in midair before quickly dipping into a dive. As the sun crept higher and the horizon brightened, Zander could feel his dragon slipping away. When his massive, clawed feet hit the ground, he set Rena down as gently as possible but stumbled backward as the power ebbed. His vision blurred, and his body weakened as the shift took hold. With quivering limbs and sweat covering his flesh, he collapsed onto the damp earth in his human form and glanced past Rena just in time to see his brother's body erupt in a blinding flash of light.

Exhausted and sweating, Zander tried to push his shaking body off the ground, but it was no use. As the darkness closed in, the last image he saw was Rena's worried face, and in spite of his situation, a smile curved his lips.

Zed was free. Rena was safe. He could die a happy man.

~~~

Zed and Zander were both out cold. The twin brothers who were identical in almost every way were both back in their human forms, but neither man moved. Zed, however, was completely nude until Dante took off his shirt and covered him.

"Perhaps they're dying?" William asked curtly. He stood between the two men and looked from one to the other. "Their energy patterns are faint."

"No!" Rena was kneeling next to Zander and held his hand in hers as she brushed his shaggy hair off his forehead. His shirt was torn away and bloodied, revealing the many scars on his chest. "But I don't know why they aren't waking up."

"They look so much alike, it's spooky," Kerry whispered. "The only differences are the scars on Zander. Jeez. By the look of him, he's been through hell."

"I know." Rena glanced over her shoulder at the others. "I'm sorry that I kept the truth from you. Zander said the history between the Amoveo and Dragon Clan isn't exactly happy."

"Ah, don't worry about it." Kerry shrugged. "You're not the first Amoveo who wanted to protect her mate. Trust me."

"We could have avoided a lot of this drama if we had

known about the dragons to begin with, *William*." Dante shot him a pointed glance. "You should have told us. We could have prepared for something like this."

"It's a moot point now," William said coolly. "We have a more pressing matter at hand."

"It wouldn't have mattered," Rena murmured. "Vito, the man I was telling you about, hired a witch to curse them because his daughter was killed when they were fighting over her. Zed was trapped in hibernation, and Zander was stuck in his human form."

"To live with what they had done," Kerry murmured. "Man. That's one tough curse."

"So that's what all that stuff was about at dinner last night." Dante settled his hands on his hips, his expression grim. "No wonder he had a chip on his shoulder."

"Your boy Zander is one tough cookie though," Tatiana murmured. She squatted down next to him and inspected the marks on his torso. She ran one finger over the circular scar from the gunshot in the convenience store. "This one looks pretty fresh."

"It is. He was shot." Rena sniffled. "Right before we got here, but he used—" Her heart thudded in her chest when she realized what they needed. "Oh my God! The spirit stones. That's it."

Rena started rummaging through Zander's pants pockets, and she almost wept with relief when her fingers curled around the two lumpy pieces of quartz. She pulled them out and kissed them both.

"What's with the rocks?" Kerry asked.

"They're spirit stones, red quartz from his family's sacred land. All of the families in the Dragon Clans have a particular stone that's of significance. Zander used it to heal the gunshot wound, and if I'm right, then we should be able to use them to wake them up. Dominic, Dante, get Zed and bring him over here, on this side of me."

She gestured to her right and looked at the stones in her palms as the two men laid Zed out next to her. Rena took the stones and placed them in the hands of the brothers before clasping her own on top, sealing the bond.

"Here goes nothing."

She closed her eyes and sent her energy signature in search of theirs. Within seconds, the connections were made, and a violent surge of power shot from the stones as Rena was inundated with a swirling mass of images.

Dragons of all colors and sizes were perched on top of a jagged mountain range at sunset. Wings spread wide and eyes blazing, the army of creatures roared to the sky before launching into the darkness. Amid the flurry of memories that flashed through her mind, Rena spotted Zed and Zander. Young men. Brothers by blood. Friends by choice. Until Arianna slipped between them and shoved the men apart.

"Time to make some new memories," Rena murmured. She turned her attention to Arianna and willed the ghost of her vision away. "I think we've seen enough of you."

With a gust of wind, Arianna's form swirled before vanishing in the mist, and the forlorn expression on Zed's face almost broke Rena's heart.

"It's okay, Zed." She took Zander and Zed by their hands, picturing the spirit stones within, and smiled at

each of them. Rena whispered, "You're free. It's time to come home."

The vision faded, and Rena fought the tide of dizziness as she released Zander's and Zed's hands, removing the stones. She rubbed at her eyes furiously as she looked from one man to the other.

Zander sat up with a groan and pressed his hand to the wound on his forehead as Rena tackled him with a hug. She flung her arms around his neck and let out an undignified sob of relief. He tangled his hands in her hair and pressed his mouth to her throat.

"Thank you," he murmured. Zander pulled back and cradled her face in his hands. "I love you, Rena McHale."

Rena sniffled and rested her forehead against his, reveling in the feel of him.

"Uh...hello?"

Zander and Rena spun around to find Zed staring at them with a puzzled expression. His eyes shifted and glowed brightly as he rose to his feet while warily studying the Amoveo, who had effectively surrounded him. Zed held the shirt around his waist, covering his nakedness. She couldn't blame the guy for feeling vulnerable. It was a sensation she had become familiar with since opening her heart.

"Zander?" His voice was raspy and raw, but was that a surprise? He hadn't spoken in centuries. "What happened?"

"You don't remember anything?" Zander asked as he and Rena stood to face his brother. "None of it?"

"Do you know who I am?" Rena asked warily.

"No." The line between his eyes deepened. "I've never seen you before."

"Good." Rena nodded and gave him a big smile. "I'm Rena, Zander's mate."

"Uh...hello."

"You really don't remember what happened before you went into hibernation?" Zander asked, his arm curled around Rena protectively as he pulled her against him. "Arianna? The witch? Hibernating for five hundred years?"

"What? Five hundred years? No." Zed shook his head slowly. "The last thing I recall is Arianna asking to meet me in the woods." His brow furrowed. "And fighting with you...but I—I can't remember why exactly. It's all foggy."

"Here," Rena murmured. She took Zed's hand in hers and gave him the spirit stone. "You're going to be okay, Zed." She looked up at Zander and handed him his. "You both are."

And for the first time in her life, she knew she would be too.

"Are you sure you want to leave?" Tatiana asked, her worried dark eyes lingering on Zed. The healer was not fond of it when her patients ignored her advice. "It's only been a few weeks. Maybe you should stay here a while longer. You know, get used to this millennium a little more?"

"She's right, Zed." Rena hated to see him leave when he had only just arrived. "Why don't you come back to Zander's cabin with us? It's your place too. Family land and all that."

"No." He shook his head curtly and adjusted the pack

on his back. "You've all been very kind, but…I need space. Besides, the earth has told me all I need to know."

"Right." Dante nodded. "That's an interesting gift your clan has, but you should still stick around for a while."

"I get it," Kerry said with a smile. She pulled Zander into a big hug that he accepted reluctantly. "The dude was buried underground for hundreds of years. If anyone needs some space, it's him."

Dante and the other Amoveo said their good-byes, which left only Zander and Rena at the end of the ranch's driveway with Zed. The sun was setting, and the glow of the horizon cast a fiery light over the land. The sight of it reminded Rena of the army of dragons she had seen in the last vision.

"You gonna walk?" Rena asked with a wink. "Or fly?"

"Walking sounds good to me." Zed gave her an awkward smile and shrugged. "I've seen enough of my dragon for a while. Besides, there's not enough cloud cover tonight. The humans would see me, and I wouldn't want to wind up on the YouTube."

"It's just YouTube." Rena laughed. "Not *the* YouTube, but I can't say that I blame you."

"Right." He shrugged awkwardly. "I obviously have more catching up to do."

"Are you sure we can't convince you to stay?"

Zander's voice was gruff and edged with genuine sadness. Rena held him a little tighter. She knew how hard it was for Zander to let his brother go. He'd spent centuries working tirelessly to free him only to lose him again.

"Another week, maybe?" Rena asked gently.

"Richard has said we can stay as long as we like. The

Amoveo of this time are not the same as the ones we knew. They've…evolved."

"That seems to be true, but I don't belong here, Zander, and neither do you." Zed's mouth set in a tight line, and he turned his gaze to the darkening sky. "You and I don't belong in this time. There's no place for us. We're the last of an extinct race."

"We are," Zander agreed solemnly. He linked his hand with Rena's, obviously needing comfort or reassurance. "But you don't have to be alone, Zed. Wandering the earth by yourself is overrated. Trust me."

Zed looked down the empty road. Rena sensed a heavy sadness in him, a far cry from the angry, confused creature she had evaded in the dreamrealm. He had been out of control. Blind with fury. Mindlessly lashing out at everyone and everything. It didn't surprise her in the least that he wanted nothing to do with his dragon.

"What happened to the others?" Zed zipped up his coat and stuffed his hands back in the pockets of his jeans. "Are you sure they're *all* gone?"

"Slayers ambushed and murdered what was left of our people." Zander sighed heavily. "After we were cursed, I took off. I couldn't stay knowing that what we had done had contributed to the annihilation of our kind."

"What about Gunn and his group? They usually avoided the troubles with the clans and kept to themselves."

"Who's Gunn?" Rena asked.

"He was the leader of a small cluster of dragons who lived farther south, what you know as Oklahoma. There were about twelve of them. I assumed they fell victim to slayers like the others. I never saw or heard from them again."

"Maybe it's better that way," Zed murmured. Stoic and detached, he turned to Zander and extended his hand. "Farewell, Brother."

Zander looked from Zed's hand to his face and back again before pulling him into a tight embrace. Zed peered over Zander's shoulder at Rena, and if she didn't know better, she'd have sworn he was smiling. He slapped Zander's back briefly before he let him go.

"Don't be a stranger." Rena pressed a quick kiss to his check.

Zander and Rena stood together at the end of the driveway and watched Zed until he disappeared down the road. Hand in hand, they strolled silently up the driveway toward the houses.

"You okay?" she asked quietly.

"Yeah," he said with a heavy sigh. "For the first time in a long time, I'm not indestructible anymore, and believe it or not, that's a relief."

"You ready to get out of here?" She bumped his hip with hers. "I love this place. It's beautiful, and the Amoveo have been cool, but I left a whole life behind in Vegas. I have some superannoyed clients who want their cases solved. Patricia has been playing secretary for me, and Vito…"

Rena's voice trailed off. She didn't want to start crying again. After all, Zander's brother, who he just got back after eons, had left. She should be supporting him, but there he was, looking out for her feelings.

"Any word about his condition?" Zander stopped walking when they reached the crest of the hill, the ranch sprawling out below. He took both of her hands in his and kissed her forehead, the sweet gesture keeping the tears at bay and reminding her exactly why she loved him.

"No change," she said in a shaky breath. "Still in a coma."

"I'm sorry." Zander pulled her into a tight hug. "I know you loved him."

"Like you love Zed." Rena lifted one shoulder and looked up at the purple-hazed sky, the stars just beginning to make an appearance. "In spite of everything, you fought for him. Night after night. No matter what he said to you or what he did, you didn't give up."

"Neither did you," he whispered.

Rena shook her head and laughed before pressing her forehead to his chest. Zander's arms tightened around her, and he kissed the top of her head and murmured, "What?"

"You've shown me all kinds of magic, right?"

"Right," he said slowly.

"Telepathy."

Rena looked up at him and settled her hands on his waist, her fingers slipping beneath the fabric to the warm flesh beneath. She would never tire of the feel of him. The way his body fit perfectly with hers in every possible way. Each curve. Angle. Every breath and beat of her heart was in time with his.

Two hearts beating.

One love found.

"Mmhmm." Zander palmed her ass.

"Shapeshifting." She popped up on her tiptoes and pressed a kiss to his throat.

"Mmm." He slid his hands beneath her shirt and wrapped them around her waist, his fingers digging into her skin tantalizingly. "That's a big one."

"But you know what was the best magic of all?" She pulled back, and her eyes shifted as they clapped on to his glowing gaze.

"What?" he rasped as he cupped her face with both hands and waggled his eyebrows at her. "The hot sex?"

"No." She poked him in the belly as they both dissolved into laughter. "The best magic was making me fall head over heels, hopelessly and perfectly, in love with you. You're a good man, Zander Lorens…and one badass dragon. Now, how about if you give me a ride and take back the skies? After all, they aren't meant for man, are they?"

He gathered her in his arms and kissed her deeply, reminding her once again that she was cherished.

Truly, madly, deeply cherished.

And loved.

Zander broke the kiss and smacked her on her butt playfully before stepping back, giving him ample distance to shift. Rena's heart raced with anticipation as she slowly walked backward with her gaze pinned to him. He stretched his arms wide and tilted his face toward the sky. A rush of electricity buzzed in the air, the power of it stealing Rena's breath. With a blinding flash of light, Zander's body erupted into the towering and graceful dragon she had come to know and love.

Tall and proud, standing on thick hind legs, he stretched his wings wide. Rena let out an awe-filled gasp as the moonlight flashed over his glistening, scaled skin, a kaleidoscope of reds and golds dancing to life. The horns above his eyes gleamed in the silvery evening light, as did the deep scarlet spikes along his tail, which he curled around him like a cat. Zander dropped his clawed hands to the ground and lowered his head in deference to her. His pointed ears lay flat against his skull, and his eyes fluttered closed.

Rena moved in, needing to slide her hands over his soft, smooth skin.

Your chariot awaits, my lady. He lowered his wings and flattened them just enough so she could use them to climb onto his back.

"I'm always surprised by how soft you are," she whispered. "And warm. I thought your skin would feel rough or scaly, but it's not... It's like velvet. See? You're all kinds of magical, dragon boy."

Rena grabbed hold of one of the spikes on his back and stepped onto the edge of his wing. Zander lifted her gently, giving her just enough help so she could swing her leg over. She straddled his neck and sat between two of his spikes, which created a makeshift saddle, as though that spot had always been meant for her. She leaned forward and curled her fingers around two of the smaller spikes along his neck.

"How about it?" she whispered. "Are you ready to take back the sky?"

If I have you, Rena, I'm ready for anything. Zander snuffled and rose onto his hind legs, his wings tucked in and his muscular body tensed beneath her. *Hold on! Get ready for more magic.*

Rena shrieked with delight as Zander launched into the sky and the brisk November wind whisked over them. As they soared low above the Amoveo property, Rena closed her eyes and reveled in the feel of her energy signature as it melded seamlessly with his.

Rena and Zander were finally *free*.

There were no more secrets. No more fighting for survival.

Rena didn't question who she was or wonder about her worth.

She finally knew what it meant to be loved.

To be cherished. Completely and without reservation.

Loved by a man with the heart of a beast.

"SAMANTHA," HE WHISPERED IN HIS DARK SILKY VOICE. *Sam's skin tingled deliciously with just one word from him. A smile played at her lips as she waited for him to call her again. Her silent prayer was answered as he murmured her name. "Samantha." That same delightful rush washed over her like the warm waves that rippled by her feet. She stretched languidly on the sandy beach, and her eyes fluttered open. She was home.*

She sat up and glanced at the familiar seashore of her childhood home. Sam knew it was only a dream. It had become a familiar one. The ocean glowed with un-natural shades of blue as if it was lit from beneath. The sky swirled with clouds of lilac and lavender. She stood up and relished the way the soft, pebble-free sand felt on her bare feet. A gentle breeze blew Sam's golden hair off her naked shoulders, and her long white nightgown fluttered lightly over her legs.

She closed her eyes and breathed in the salty air. He was near. She could feel it. Her blood hummed, and the air around her thickened. She'd come so close to seeing him many times, but she always woke up just before she found him.

Not this time.

This time she would stay on the beach and call him to her. It was her dream after all, and she was getting tired of coming up empty-handed. Eyes closed, she tilted her face to the watercolor sky and waited. Her heartbeat thundered in her ears in perfect time with the pounding waves.

"Samantha," he whispered into her ear. She stilled, and her mouth went dry. He was standing right behind her. How the hell did he get there? Where did he come from? Why couldn't he stand right in front of her where she could actually see him? This was supposed to be her dream, her fantasy. Jeez. Can you say intimacy issues?

Sam jumped slightly and sucked in a sharp breath as large hands gently cupped her shoulders. She should open her eyes. She wanted to open her eyes, but the onslaught of sensations to her body and mind had her on overload. Samantha shuddered as he brushed his fingers lightly down her arms leaving bright trails of fire in their wake. He tangled his fingers in hers and pulled her back gently. Sam swallowed hard as his long muscular body pressed up against hers. He was tall, really tall. She sighed. If he looked half as good as he felt, she was in big trouble.

"It would seem that you've finally found me," he murmured into her ear.

Sam nodded, unable to find her voice amid the rush

of his. She licked her dry lips and mustered up some courage. It was a dream after all. Nothing to be afraid of. She could always wake up. But that's what she was afraid of.

"Why don't you ever let me see you?" she said in a much huskier tone than she'd intended. She pressed her body harder against his and relished the way his fingers felt entwined with hers.

He nuzzled her hair away from her neck and placed a warm kiss on the edge of her ear. "Come home," he whispered. His tantalizing voice washed over her and he seemed to surround her completely. Body. Mind. Soul. Every single inch of her lit up like the Fourth of July.

"Please," she said in a rush of air. Sam wrapped his arms around her waist and relished the feel of him. It was like being cradled in cashmere covered steel. Leaning into him, she rubbed her head gently against his arm. He moaned softly and held her tighter. The muscles in his chest rippled behind her, and his bicep flexed deliciously against her cheek. "I need to see you."

Eyes still closed, she turned in his arms as he said softly "Samantha."

Sam tumbled out of bed and landed on the floor with a thud. Breathing heavily and lying amid her tangled bedclothes, Sam stared at the bland white ceiling of her soon-to-be former apartment.

"Talk about a buzz kill," she said to the empty room. "Typical. I can't even get good sex in my dreams." She puffed the hair from her face and pushed herself up to a sitting position. Sam grabbed her cell phone off the nightstand and swore softly when she saw the time. She was going to be late. Crap.

—∽∿∽—

The steamy August air swamped Samantha the moment she stepped foot onto the cracked New York City sidewalk. On any other day the stifling summer streets of Manhattan would drive her crazy—but not today. Sam smiled. Today was her last day of work. No more horrid tourists with even more horrid tipping skills. No more nights spent fending off her married and truly unfortunate looking boss. No more waitressing at T.G.I. Friday's in Times Square. Thank God!

Sam let out a large sigh, a mixture of exhaustion and relief, and slipped her aviators on with a cursory glance up to the towering buildings. She squirmed slightly as sweat began to bead on her brow and trickle down her back. Adjusting the heavy backpack, she wove her way through the pedestrian-riddled city and nestled the small iPhone earbuds snuggly into her ears. She hit shuffle on the slim iPod. A familiar tune filled her head; she couldn't help but walk to the beat as she wove her way through the minefield of tourists. Samantha mumbled the occasional "*pardon me, excuse me*" as she navigated the slow-moving gawkers in Times Square. Why did they feel the need to stop and look at every skyscraper? This was another part of living and working in New York City she definitely would *not* miss.

Sam trotted down the steps into the subway station and pushed her sunglasses up onto her sweaty head. She swiped her card in the turnstile and slid through the narrow gateway toward the platform. Stealing cursory glances at the various subway-goers, her attention was captured by a young woman who was clearly fresh out of college. She reminded her of herself—about ten years ago. Sam smiled and shook her head as the train screeched its way up to the platform. The hot air blast that accompanied it actually provided momentary relief from her sweaty state. She pushed her way into the crowded train with the rest of the subway rats, and her gaze wandered back to the young coed. She sat almost expectantly on the seat across from her, as if her lifelong dream may come leaping to life right in front of her at any moment.

Sam vaguely remembered that feeling. She had moved to the city right after college graduation. The moment she had that BFA in hand she packed it all up and moved to the Big Apple. As a young artist with age-old dreams, the city seemed the only logical place to go. It held the promise of excitement and glamour, a far cry from the sleepy seaside town she grew up in. Clearly promises were made to be broken. The young girl glanced up and caught Sam's eye. She delivered a quick, shy smile before looking away. Sam couldn't blame her. No woman in her right mind would maintain eye contact with a total stranger on a city subway.

The train shuddered to a stop in Grand Central Station, and Sam made a speedy escape into the muggy, bustling crowd as she switched trains for SoHo. She had one more loose end to tie up before she could officially leave NYC.

Gunther's Gallery.

Sam exited at the Spring Street station and hustled along the narrow side streets, grateful that the pedestrian traffic wasn't quite as crazy here as it was in midtown. She turned onto Thompson Street, and the small, but sweet gallery came into view. Sam smiled, and her heart gave an odd little squeeze, knowing that this was really *it*.

She opened the heavy black lacquered door with an audible grunt and stumbled into the refreshingly cool gallery. The heat made the wood swell every summer, and a body slam was commonplace to open the damn door. She was instantly greeted by a shrieking Gunther.

"Kitten," he squealed and pulled her into a vigorous hug, which was immediately followed by a kiss on both cheeks. "You're late…" He released her with a playful shove. "I can't believe you're leaving me here all alone in this big bad city." He stuck out his lower lip in a dramatic pout, crossed his delicate arms across his chest, and stamped his foot.

Sam chuckled and dropped her backpack onto the black leather bench by the door. "Oh, please." She rolled her eyes. "You've got Milton to keep you company. He is the gardener to your flower, isn't he," she teased.

"Bitch." Gunther stuck his pierced tongue out at her, turned on his heels, and huffed back to the reception desk. "You're just jealous because my boyfriend is cuter than that douche you're dating."

Sam held up both hands in protest. "Excuse me, douche I *was* dating. I broke up with him like a month ago." Sam leaned onto the reception desk with her elbows and placed her chin in her hands. "We can't all be gorgeous and in high demand like you Gunther," she said, batting her eyelashes dramatically.

Gunther patted her on the head. "That's true, kitten."

He sighed and brushed a stray lock of hair off her face. "Maybe if you gave yourself as much attention as you gave to your artwork, you'd find a hottie too."

Sam glared at him through narrowed eyes. "Now who's being a bitch? Besides, my experience with Roger is just the latest example of how bad my taste in men is." She let out a sound of defeat. "I give up."

"Sounds to me like someone needs to get laid," he said with haughty confidence.

Sam slapped his cheek playfully. "Gunther, not all of us think with our libidos. You know me well enough by now to understand that a man has to get me here," she said pointing to her heart, "before he can get me here." She punctuated by grabbing both of her breasts.

"Honey, you just haven't met the right man. Trust me, the right guy will get you here, there, and everywhere," he said with a flourish.

Sam laughed and shook her head doubtfully. "I don't think so, honey, at least not for me. I'll take a good book and a hot bath over sex any day."

"Clearly, you've never had good sex." He sighed and made a tsking sound.

Sam opened her mouth to protest but stopped before she said anything because the cold hard truth was that he was absolutely right.

Sam pushed herself away from the desk and turned her back on him. Worried he'd see right through her, she pretended to admire the artwork that currently occupied the tiny gallery.

Sam stopped dead in her tracks at the sight of various brown paper-wrapped pieces leaning against the back wall. Her throat tightened, and tears pricked at the back of her eyes. She stuffed her hands into the pockets of her khaki pants in an effort to get control over her conflicting emotions.

"Hey, you don't have to leave you know." Gunther's gentle tone matched the comforting arm he wrapped around her.

Sam laid her head on his shoulder and sniffled. "Well, no one can say I didn't at least give it a shot." She lifted her head up and planted a kiss on his ridiculously smooth cheek. "You gave me lots of shots. Thanks, Gunther."

Gunther snapped his fingers. "Honey, my family owns this building in which I live and work. If I can't occasionally share these luxuries with my friends then what the hell good is it? Am I right? Yes," he said, confidently answering his own question. "I am."

He smacked her on the butt as she walked away from him toward the back of the gallery.

Sam smiled and wiped at her eyes. "I'm going to miss you." She took a deep breath, hoping to steady herself. She ran her fingers along the smooth brown paper and took a mental count. One was missing, and she could tell by the sizes that it was her favorite one.

"Gunther," she said in a slightly panic-laced voice. "Where's my mother's portrait?" *Woman and the Wolf.* It was her favorite and most personal piece. The woman and the wolf stood side by side looking out over a stormy ocean. Her mother's hand lay gently upon the massive head of an enormous gray wolf, long golden hair blowing in the breeze. Although a storm and the ocean raged around them, both the woman and the wolf exuded serenity amid chaos.

Smiling broadly, he clapped his hands. "I was wondering how long it was going to take you to notice that piece was missing."

Sam tilted her head and gave him a confused smile. "Well, don't keep me in suspense. Where is it?"

"I sold it," he said proudly.

"Sold it? When?"

"This morning," he said with obvious satisfaction. "As soon as I opened, this guy came in and bought it. Boy, oh boy, what a hottie too." He fanned himself dramatically.

Sam shook her head. "I don't get it? If you had the pieces all wrapped up, how did he even see it?"

"Well, I know it's your favorite, but it's mine too. I was really, really hoping you'd let me keep it here. It would've been like having you with me all the time. So I had it hung behind the gallery desk." He gave her a self-satisfied smile and brushed past her to the front desk.

Sam stared after him with a dumbfounded look on her face.

He glanced over his shoulder at her. "Kitten, you look like you're catching flies."

Embarrassed by her obvious shock, Sam snapped her mouth shut.

"Here's your check," he said holding an envelope out to her. "Minus my commission, of course."

Sam took the envelope from him. She rubbed the paper between her fingers. She should've been happy, thrilled in fact, but it was sad too. That portrait had been the most personal piece she'd ever created, and it tugged at her heart to know she'd never see it again.

"I really did adore it, but I do have one question though. Why the wolf?" He placed his hands on his slim hips. "I mean, I get that it's your mother and the beach where you grew up and all of that," he said quickly. "But why the wolf? You don't see a lot of wolves at the seashore."

"No," she said absentmindedly. "You don't." She'd always had an affinity for animals, wolves in particular. They had haunted her dreams for years, but when she moved to the city the dreams had stopped—at least until recently. "I dreamed about them a lot as a child. They were never scary though. The wolf was always protective. I don't know." She sighed. "Like a talisman or something."

"Talisman? Sounds hot!" He wiggled his eyebrows at her.

Sam gave him a slap on the arm. "No, you horn-dog, it wasn't like that. They were comforting and peaceful." Her thoughts went back to her painting and she could practically hear the waves. "Just like the ocean," she murmured. "Wild and free, but somehow comforting at the same time."

The phone rang, interrupting their conversation, and Gunther rushed over to answer it. As he chattered away with one of his buyers, her thoughts wandered to the evening of her thirtieth birthday. It was a memorable day simply for the milestone it was, but it was more. That night, for the first time in over ten years, she dreamed of the wolf.

Only this time, she *was* the wolf.

Gunther hung up and let out a loud exasperated sigh. ate dealing with new buyers. They always call up k such stupid questions. *When are you open?*" He ed with a grimace. "I mean honestly. What in gay hell? Haven't they heard of the Internet? We have a website for a reason people!"

His rant pulled her from her memories. "Thanks for everything, Gunther," she said with a small smile. "I'll give you a call in a couple of days about where to send the others."

"That's another thing. I think we should keep these for a while. If we hang them up here, there's a chance they'll sell. Sitting in Nonie's garage… ain't nobody gonna buy 'em. Now come over here, and give me a hug." He pulled her into his arms and planted a big wet kiss on her cheek. "You take care of yourself, kitten. Don't forget to come home and visit Milton and me once in a while."

"That's just it," she said quietly. "This city was never home for me." Her thoughts went back to the portrait. "Tomorrow I'm going home."

—⁓—

Malcolm stood stone still on the balcony of his family home. He overlooked the predawn ocean, which stretched endlessly before him. As he breathed in the cool, salty air, he closed his eyes and willed himself to relax. His hands gripped the railing, turning his knuckles white. He was beyond edgy, full of anticipation for the days ahead. He had waited years for her to arrive, and tomorrow she would finally be here. He shoved himself away from the railing and paced back and forth, mirroring the beast caged within. She would be here in just a few more hours.

Malcolm Drew was the last in his family's branch of the Eagle Clan. His family was one of ten animal clans among the Amoveo, a powerful, ancient race of magical shapeshifters. Malcolm was a Golden Eagle, and more than anything he wanted to keep his clan's bloodline running, but he could only do that with his mate. Without her, he was doomed to a painful, solitary existence, and eventually death. Malcolm had heard stories about those who went unmated. He shuddered at the images those nightmarish tales conjured up.

Finding female company was not a problem. He'd had many women before, but they were merely a momentary amusement that left him unsatisfied and lonely. Like all Amoveo, his uncommonly large eyes were his most striking feature. The women he dallied with always seemed to comment on them. His were an unusually light brown, and in the right light gleamed yellow. He never worried himself too much with his appearance. He considered clothing an annoying necessity and barely ran a brush through his long, shaggy hair.

He felt anxious, not just for her arrival, but for her safety. For generations his people had been hunted by the Caedo family, a fanatical group of humans who had discovered their existence. They had not lost anyone to a hunter in many years, but the threat always loomed. He shook his head in frustration and stood with his arms crossed tightly over his chest. So many obstacles lay before them.

His thoughts wandered to his parents. The story of their courtship and mating had been the stuff made of legends. Growing up he'd observed their obvious love for one another with intense curiosity. Given that mates among their people were predestined he often wondered if the love grew over time, or was it a lightning bolt, an instantaneous connection? They claimed that the bonding was immediate, but secretly he had always doubted it. He scoffed audibly at the very idea of it with no one but the gulls to hear him. He'd encountered several females, both human and Amoveo, but he never came close to feeling anything that resembled love. Lust? Sure. Love? Not a chance.

However, that all changed in a flash the second he found Samantha. His body warmed at the mere memory of that moment, and he closed his eyes in an effort to recapture it. Last night's connection in the dream realm had helped solidify their bond even further. However, his brow furrowed, and tension rippled up his back as one intruding thought returned. What if she refused him? His eyes snapped open, and he let out a low growl at the one thought that nagged at him relentlessly. Malcolm had heard that occasionally, a female would refuse the match. He shook his head at the futility of refusing. Why refuse what was imbedded in their souls? His skin suddenly felt two sizes too small as that question continued to beg at the back of his mind. His human form had become a prison from which he abruptly required release. He needed to fly. He stretched his arms wide, tilted his face to the twilight sky, and visualized his eagle form. Silently, he uttered the ancient word "verto" and shifted.

Instantly, he soared high over the crashing sea. He loved the feel of the salt air along his feathered body. His binocular vision spotted schools of fish as they moved through the waters below. The cool, early morning air caressed him and carried him along. His mind, body, and spirit relaxed. His tense muscles loosened to some extent. Malcolm closed his bright yellow eyes and reveled in the freedom and simplicity of the moment. He extended his wings to almost the brink of pain and rode the current with practiced ease. The image of his mate slipped into his mind and warmed his heart.

All too soon, he was torn from his revelry as an enormous muscle spasm tore through his feathered body. He wobbled midflight and struggled for control as his energy began to slip away. His body shuddered, and he knew the shift was coming. He struggled to maintain his clan form and immediately turned back toward his house. Malcolm strained against the shift and flapped his leaden wings with every ounce of energy he had. In a blinding flash of pain and frustration, Malcolm shifted just before he got to the deck of his home. He gritted his teeth, and in a flailing mass of arms and legs, he landed with an audible thud on the wooden planks. He lay there for a moment in a heap. Nice, he thought, very dignified.

Breathing heavily with sweat trickling down his spine, he stood and straightened out his clothing, thinking how nice it would be to have all of his abilities back. At full strength, he could shift smoothly and easily. He had recently passed his thirty-second birthday and was losing strength by the day. There was only one thing that could help him rejuvenate—being with his mate. Samantha. He had known who she was for many years. He'd dreamed of her since his adolescence. Under normal mating circumstances, she would've dreamed of him as well. The mate connection was always made in the dream plane first. If she had been a typical Amoveo female, she would've been looking for him as well. She would've recognized him the instant their dreams connected. His mate, however, was anything but ordinary.

Samantha was a hybrid and the first of her kind. Her mother had been a human. Her father had been the last of the Gray Wolf Clan, and they had been almost completely exterminated. Now that he was gone, she was the last. The most difficult part was that she didn't know it.

———

After a record long good-bye with Gunther, Sam hopped the "4" train and picked up the "R," which took her right into her Park Slope neighborhood. Well, according to her it was Park Slope, but there were many people who would've debated her on that. Once she moved to Brooklyn, Sam learned that the neighborhood lines were up for discussion. Where Sam lived was known by locals as anything from Park Slope to South Slope or Sunset Park or Windsor Terrace. In other words, it depended on which realtor you spoke to, but Sam didn't care. She loved the neighborhood and would miss it — but not enough to stay.

She took her time walking back to her apartment on Prospect Avenue. After all, this was the last time she'd be doing it. Tomorrow she was going home. Back to Nonie and the beach.

Home.

The very idea of it made her smile. Sam fished the keys out of the side pocket of her pack, lost in her own reverie. As a result she didn't see what was waiting for her on the building steps. Startled, she found herself face-to-face with what was quickly becoming the biggest mistake of her life.

"I've been waiting here for a God damned hour!" Roger's contemptuous tone brought her to a screeching halt. "Where the hell have you been?"

Roger Van Dousen, a trust fund baby who never grew up, was the ex-boyfriend from hell. They had only dated for about a month and had been broken up for about as long, but apparently Roger didn't get that memo.

He seemed like quite the catch at first. Wealthy, educated, polite, and handsome. However, his true nature became glaringly clear after just a few short weeks. Roger was a controlling, self-indulgent asshole with an overblown sense of entitlement. He should be the poster child for how-not-to-raise-your-child-if-you-have-lots-of-money. Essentially, he was a forty-year-old toddler.

His face, almost purple with anger, was covered in sweat. His perfectly coiffed salt and pepper hair was slicked back against his head. Sweat had seeped through his starched shirt, and his hands were stuffed into the pockets of his dark suit pants. She had heard the expression *seething with anger* but had never actually witnessed it until just this moment.

Sam removed the earbuds of her iPhone and looked him up and down through narrow eyes.

"Well, Roger. I'm really sorry to hear that," she said in the most calm and condescending tone she could muster. "I'm not quite sure how you can be upset about waiting for me since I didn't even know you were coming over. Besides, we broke up over a month ago."

He made a loud scoffing noise and crossed his arms over his chest. "Oh really? What about our conversation last night? I told you I was coming to see you and that this breaking up nonsense had to stop."

Sam cocked her head slightly and rolled her eyes. "What the hell are you talking about? Our conversation consisted of me hanging up on you after telling you — for the one hundredth time — that I never want to see you again."

He loomed over her and moved down one step closer in a clear effort to intimidate her. He blocked her path up to the door of her building, and his face, quivering lips and all, was just inches from hers. She couldn't believe that she'd ever been remotely attracted to him. Oh, he was handsome. No one would argue with that. The guy looked like he just stepped out of a Tommy Hilfiger ad. Perfect clothes, strong jawline, suntanned, and well-manicured from head to toe. However, his short fuse and sense of entitlement had quickly made him the most unattractive man she'd ever met.

Sam wanted nothing more than to back away and put some physical space between them. Her heart was beating a mile a minute, and the sweat trickling down her back was no longer from the heat. She stood her ground. He'd never hit her, but Sam suspected it was only a matter of time before he did. If people really could smell fear, she probably stunk to high heaven.

Sam didn't take her big blue eyes off of his. She swallowed hard before she spoke and prayed her voice wouldn't quiver and betray her growing fear. He was a bully, plain and simple. The worst thing she could do would be to let him know that he scared her. Like all bullies, fear only fanned the flames of his perceived power.

"Get out of my way, Roger," she said in a low and surprisingly deadly tone. "You and I are over, and if you don't stop harassing me, I'm going to file a restraining order."

Mustering up her last shred of courage, Sam attempted to shoulder past him to her door. Before she could get by and make an escape into her building, he grabbed her arm and yanked her against him. His fingers dug mercilessly into her bicep, and his alcohol-stained breath blew hotly on her cheek. Sam winced away from him.

"Don't you dare try and walk away from me," he seethed. "You think you can get a restraining order against me? A Van Dousen? My family is hooked into everything in this city."

She glanced around, frantically hoping to spot someone, anyone, who might be walking by but only the occasional car sped past. Her predicament going completely unnoticed was a cold, hard reality of this city. Another thing she would not be missing.

He shook her again, hard enough to make her teeth rattle. "Look at me when I'm speaking to you. I know that you plan on moving back home."

Her shocked eyes darted back to his face, and he grinned.

"You can't hack it here in the city, so you're going to move back home with your old Grandma? You've failed here in New York. No one wanted your art. Your ridiculous attempts at showing in the galleries failed miserably."

The truth of his words stung. She had failed to make it as a real artist. The critics had said her work lacked imagination and soul. *Too realistic and not enough heart*—that was the quote that haunted her. But it was from her heart, and that's what hurt so much. Having her work criticized like that was too much, more than she could stand. How could she paint things that were so personal, so intimately a part of her, but no one else could see it? She could paint a picture with the same precision as a digital camera, but who the hell wanted a painting of something that they could get from a photograph? Tears of humiliation and failure stung the back of her eyes. She blinked them back, refusing to allow this son of a bitch to see her cry.

"You're pathetic. You know that? Do you really think you'll do better than *me*?" His incredulous tone matched the look of disgust twisted into his features. "You're just a waitress." Sam cringed. He said the word *waitress* as if it were something filthy he'd just stepped in. "You're not an artist. You serve people. You're 'the help.'" He laughed cruelly and continued his tirade. "In fact, you should be down on your fucking hands and knees, thanking your lucky stars that I picked you. You could be with me in a penthouse overlooking Central Park, but you choose to stay here." He nodded his head toward her building. He spun her violently and grabbed her with both hands. "We're not over unless I say we're over. I decide. Not you," he screamed. "*Not you!*"

Pain flashed hotly up her arms and into her shoulders as his fingers dug deeper into her. Sam fought to keep the tears at bay. Her face burned with a potent combination of fear, embarrassment, and anger. However, the fear that he might actually hit her was overtaken by raw anger. How dare he treat her this way? She wasn't a piece of meat or something he could just order out of a catalog. He didn't own her, and she didn't owe this rat bastard anything. This selfish bully represented every sleazy art dealer, salesman, and bar patron she had been forced to endure over the last eight years.

No more.

Her existence was hers and no one else's. Her life, her successes, and her failures were all hers. She belonged to nobody but herself.

"You would rather stay in this hovel or go live with some pathetic old woman than be with me?"

Nonie? This bastard had the audacity to call her grandmother pathetic? The moment he dragged Nonie into his venomous tirade, something dormant inside of her sparked to life.

A low rumbling noise seemed to come out of nowhere and surround them. Samantha's eyes tingled, and the rumbling grew louder. The sound vibrated through her chest and radiated throughout the rest of her body. Somewhere in the back of her mind she rationalized that a subway must be going by at a most opportune moment.

Okay. One point for NYC.

"Don't you dare talk about my grandmother that way," she ground out. Her voice sounded so odd, almost like a growl. If she didn't feel her lips moving, she wouldn't even believe that she was the one speaking. "Now, you take your filthy hands off of me."

Roger's eyes grew as big as saucers, and his face went ashen. He snatched his hands back from her arm as if she'd burned him. He shook his head furiously and mumbled something she couldn't quite make out. She watched with smug satisfaction as he half ran, half stumbled down the steps away from her. The rumbling subsided as Roger disappeared around the corner.

"And don't come back," she shouted victoriously in

a voice she actually recognized. Sam did a little happy dance as she slipped the key into the door of her soon-to-be former building. Time to throw out the rest of the trash.

———∿∿∿———

Roger didn't stop running until he reached the limo. He threw the door open and dove inside, slamming it shut quickly and locking it behind him. He opened the small refrigerator, grabbed the bottle of single malt Scotch, and proceeded to swig directly from the bottle.

His driver, Rudolph, who didn't even have time to get out and open the door for him, braced himself for the tongue lashing that was sure to come next.

"I'm so sorry, sir. It won't ever happen again, Mr. Van Dousen." He sat perfectly still, braced for impact. However, no temper tantrum came. Rudolph glanced into the rearview reluctantly. "Will your girlfriend be joining us, sir?" He hated to ask anything about this artist chick because it always seemed to send him over the edge.

"Her eyes," he hissed. "Her eyes. You should've seen her eyes." Roger leaned forward and pointed at Rudolph with the bottle of Scotch still firmly in his grip. He rocked back and forth and continued mumbling to himself.

Rudolph cleared his throat to stifle the laugh that began to bubble up. If it came out within earshot of his employer, it would lead directly to the unemployment line.

"Yes sir, Mr. Van Dousen. I'll just give you some privacy for the ride home, sir."

He hit the button for the privacy divider and held back on his laughter until it closed with an audible thump. The Golden Boy had finally lost it.

About the Author

Sara Humphreys is an award-winning author of paranormal and contemporary romance. The third book in the Amoveo Legend series, *Untamed*, won two PRISM awards, for Dark Paranormal and Best of the Best. The first two novels from her Dead in the City series have been nominated for the National Readers' Choice Award. Sara is also a professional actress. Some of her television credits include *A&E Biography*, *Guiding Light*, *Another World*, *As the World Turns*, and *Rescue Me*.

She loves writing hot heroes and heroines with moxie, but above all, Sara adores a satisfying happily ever after. She lives in New York with Mr. H., their four amazing sons, and two adorable pups. When she's not writing or hanging out with the men in her life, she can be found working out with Shaun T in her living room or chatting with readers on Facebook.

For a full list of Sara's books and reading order, please visit her website, www.novelromance.net.